Not a Bird Will Sing

Audrey Howard

CORONET BOOKS
Hodder and Stoughton

First published in Great Britain in 1998
by Hodder and Stoughton
A division of Hodder Headline PLC
First published in paperback in 1998
by Hodder and Stoughton
A Coronet Paperback

10 9 8 7 6

British Library Cataloguing in Publication Data

Howard, Audrey
Not a Bird Will Sing
1. English fiction – 20th century
I. Title
823.9′14 [F]

ISBN 0 340 66613 7

Typeset by Hewer Text Composition Services, Edinburgh
Printed and bound in Great Britain by
Mackays of Chatham PLC, Chatham, Kent

Hodder and Stoughton
A division of Hodder Headline PLC
338 Euston Road
London NW1 3BH

Not a Bird Will Sing

'We're not old enough yet, *annsachd*,' he whispered, 'but I'll come back. D'ye believe me?'

'Promise.'

'Aye, I promise. Will ye wait?'

'Yes.'

He said something else then, a long sentence in what she took to be Gaelic and though she could not understand the words she was woman enough, even at twelve, to recognise what was in him, and herself.

They both smiled . . .

More Coronet paperbacks by Audrey Howard

The Mallow Years
Shining Threads
A Day Will Come
All the Dear Faces
There Is No Parting
Echo of Another Time
The Woman from Browhead
The Silence of Strangers
A World of Difference
Promises Lost
The Shadowed Hills
Strand of Dreams
Tomorrow's Memories

About the Author

Audrey Howard was born in Liverpool in 1929 and it is from that once-great seaport that many of the ideas for her books come. Before she began to write she had a variety of jobs, among them hairdresser, model, shop assistant, cleaner and civil servant. In 1981, out of work and living in Australia, she wrote the first of her nineteen published novels. She was fifty-two. Her fourth novel, *The Juniper Bush*, won the Boots Romantic Novel of the Year Award in 1988. She now lives in her childhood home, St Anne's on Sea, Lancashire.

When we two are parted all the world is grey,
Hope and joy and comfort, go with you away
Away, alas, with you away.
Not a flower will blossom, not a bird will sing,
Lacking that sweet summer you alone can bring
You, alas, alone can bring . . .

Part I

Part I

1

The child first came to Eliza Goodall's notice when Eliza walked down from the farm one wet day in search of her best "layer", a pretty but contrary brown hen usually to be seen strutting and scratching round the farmyard. Now and again the stupid bird had a fancy to deposit her daily egg in the cleared ditch on the field side of the hedge which bordered Primrose Bank. If the hen hadn't been such a good little layer Eliza would have said to the devil with her, letting the dratted thing come home when she felt like it but Eliza had grown quite fond of the independent little madam and had even given her a name: Clucky. Not very original, she smiled to herself, and she hadn't let on to Tom, of course, but that's the sound the hen made. Not "cluck-cluck-cluck" like the other hens but "cluckee-cluckee-cluckee", with the emphasis on the "eee".

That was what Eliza was calling, softly, of course, in case there was anyone about, as she trudged down through the rain-sodden field alongside Primrose Bank, peering from time to time beneath the dripping hedge.

It was May. Eliza would remember the month and the year precisely since they had just heard that an attack had been made on the queen's person by the nephew of the crack-brained enthusiast, Feargus O'Connell, whose family were known to be feeble-minded. The attacker was demanding the release of Fenian prisoners, it was said, thrusting an old flintlock in Her Majesty's face. What was the world coming to when not even their dear queen, who would be fifty-six years old this month, was safe from madmen, her Tom had said to Eliza only this morning.

The child, no more than eight or nine by the size of her, was swearing, using language even men about the farm would hesitate to use and when Eliza parted the newly burgeoning hawthorn hedge and squinted curiously through it, she could see why. It was raining, a slanted, heavy rain which drove directly into the front of the cottages, running down the stone walls in a torrent which then made its way to the lowest point which was, with the passage of many feet, the rough path which led to each doorway. From there it ran with a gleeful chuckle under the ill-fitting door and into the living-room of each cottage, all of which had their doors shut except one.

"Bugger it . . . bugger it . . . bugger it . . ." the child at the open door was shouting into the downpour as she dashed a broom made from twigs time and time again into the river of rainwater which gurgled over the step and on to her bare feet. She was herself soaked through, her ragged skirt and bodice sticking to her like a second skin. Her long, matted hair was plastered to her small skull, hanging to her waist where it ended in twisting ringlets, and rainwater ran across her face and into her eyes which blinked furiously. Where it had run it left tracks in the grime.

"Hell and damnation", and "bugger it" were two of the mildest epithets which fell from her childish lips as she continued her resolute but unsuccessful attempt to hold back the force of water which was just as resolute in its determination to get in.

"I think you're beaten," Eliza called through the gap in the hedge. "I should wait until the rain stops, then you can mop it up."

"I'll not be bloody beaten," the child snarled, apparently undismayed by the disembodied voice, shocking Eliza even more, not with the words but with the venom, the bitter hatred with which they were spoken. It was as though she bore a deep grudge against the elements that were doing their best to inundate her home while she, like Canute, was equally resolved to hold them back.

Eliza said so, amusement in her voice. "I know you're doing your best, child, but can't you see you're fighting a losing battle? Canute gave up in the end, you know."

There was a gate a few yards further on and, lifting the latch, Eliza let herself through it, sinking at once into the evil-smelling mud which lay on the track. She was hindered for an anxious moment or two by the glutinous sludge which seemed ready to suck the very boots from her feet, but pulling each one in turn from the mire with a squelch which sounded disgusting, she managed to stagger towards the child.

"Well, 'appen 'ooever 'e is don't give a tinker's toss about sittin' wi' 'is feet in a puddle o' mucky water burr I do. I've just scrubbed that . . ." – here using a word that made Eliza blanch – "floor, an' gorrit dry an' all which is bloody 'ard goin' at best o' times. Then this lot started" – pausing to glare up into the greyness of the low and drooping clouds – "an' I might just as well've sarron me bum an' twiddled me bloody thumbs fer all't good it did."

Suddenly, as though accepting the sense of what Eliza said, the child sighed resignedly and stopped plying her broom. She looked up. Her eyes were the palest blue grey, so pale they were almost transparent, as though they were windows through which might be seen what was in her mind. Round each iris was a line the colour of charcoal. They were quite the most extraordinary eyes Eliza had ever seen, enormous in the girl's thin face. The lashes surrounding them were long, dark, fine, curling in a fan almost to her delicately arched eyebrows. She scratched busily in her armpit, hunching her shoulders as though to ease the wet fabric of her bodice from her back and Eliza had an urgent desire to step back since she had no wish to carry away some creature the child obviously harboured.

The child's eyes widened. "Oh . . ." she said, recognising who Eliza was as she bobbed a hasty curtsey. Eliza found herself with nothing to say, which was ridiculous for as the wife of the man who owned these tumbledown, quite terrible cottages, she had the right to say whatever came into her head, but the child was so unusual, not only in her looks but in her manner, Eliza could do nothing but stare.

" 'Oo's Canute, anyroad?" the child said at last. "Does 'e live round 'ere?"

Released from her strange abstraction, Eliza smiled. "He was a King of England a long time ago. He sat on the seashore as the tide rose and commanded the waves to come no nearer. They took no notice, of course."

The child considered this gravely, scratching again, this time the nape of her neck.

"What's seashore?" she asked with great interest.

Eliza blinked, not only surprised by the question but blinded by the downpour which was getting heavier.

"Well, it's where the land meets the sea."

"An' what's waves?"

"That's the sea itself as it strikes the shore."

"An' what does tide do?"

"It goes in and out."

"Where to?"

Eliza laughed out loud and shook her head, scattering raindrops from the brim of her old bonnet. The child, one hand on the door latch, the other still clinging to her broom, looked taken aback, then, with a sound which was infectious, began to laugh too. A throaty laugh unusual in one so young, a joyful laugh, though what this poverty-stricken girl had to be joyful about was beyond Eliza's understanding. It was obvious she was not at all sure what they were laughing at either, but her merriment, the bright enquiring expression on her face, astonished and delighted Eliza.

But how to explain to this child who had evidently never seen the sea, the shore, or possibly anything that was not within a hundred yards of her squalid home, what they were? It was like trying to describe colours to a man who had always been blind. Eliza had been a school teacher in the small country town of Prescot before her marriage to Tom Goodall. Not in all her years in the chalky, chilly schoolroom, gritting her teeth as she did her best to instil the alphabet and a sum or two into the apathetic children whose parents sent them there, had she come across one who cared a fig for learning. None had shown more than a half-hearted interest in what she had tried to teach them. They knew, as she did, that the moment an opportunity arose of earning wages they would be withdrawn by their parents from the class. That they were there simply because there was no work available. When it was they would be put to odds and ends of farm labouring or the girls to taking the place of a mother in the care of their younger brothers and sisters. It was a precarious business bringing up a family, usually ten or twelve children, and an education, no matter how badly it was desired, came a poor second to the simple need of survival. The foundation stone of a new ragged school in West Derby had just been laid but the question of how many pupils were to attend seemed to be one to which there were only vague answers.

"Well, I'm getting soaked out here so perhaps I'd better be . . ." Eliza began but at once the child stepped back with an odd gesture of hospitality, indicating that Eliza should come inside.

"Yer'll 'ave ter tekk them boots off, though," she said sternly. "I've just scrubbed this bloody floor. Not that it'll be clean fer long, like, not when they all gerr 'ome. Pa does 'is best but me brothers're sods an' our Rose an' Iris an' Marigold's not much better. I tell 'em if they'd soddin' floor ter scrub 'appen they'd tekk more care. I've me work cut out, I can tell yer, wi' ten of 'em traipsin' mud all over me flags."

"Ten? Oh dear."

"Aye, wi' me mam an' pa an' me it mekks eleven of us. Pa, our Arthur an' Douglas're clearin' them ditches fer Mr Goodall up by Park Moss terday an' our Eustace – 'e's five, or is it six? – Mr Goodall's purrim ter't gate in top field, openin' an' shuttin' it, like, which mekks it 'andy fer them what wants ter get through wi't waggons. Me sisters're 'elpin' out wi't sowin' o't mangold-wurzels so yer can imagine state of 'em when they gerrome. Wi' a bit o' luck 'appen they'll've thought ter tekk off their boots. Mind, we've a rain butt at back." This was said with such pride she might have been boasting of a fine carriage and six matched horses. "Wi' all't rain we get it's not often it's empty."

"No, I can imagine."

Eliza felt the strangest emotion flood through her and knew it for what it was. Enchantment! She was enchanted, fascinated, charmed by this comical scrap of a creature, this child, so practical, so natural in her manner, so accepting of her place in life and yet with a resolution to make it as good as she could get it. She had met no one like her, not as a school teacher nor later as the wife of a small but well-to-do farmer who employed dozens of the casual labourers and their children from these cottages.

"Come in then if yer comin'," the comical scrap said.

Leaning on the door frame, pulling off her sturdy boots and dropping them on to the step, Eliza stepped down in her stockinged feet on to the unevenly tiled floor. It was wet and slippery. The dampness inside the cottage made it seem cold and yet there was a fire burning on the raised bricks of the hearth. Smoke from the chimney billowed out into the room as a gust of rain howled down it, but beyond waving her hand in front of her face and coughing drily, the child appeared not to notice it. Perhaps in her childish wisdom she knew what her family's resources were and they did not allow for the mending of a smoky chimney.

In the fire itself was a pan of something simmering, probably a small square of bacon and a few vegetables which, with plenty of filling potatoes, was a staple of the poor. A table with uncertain legs stood in the centre of the room, about which were four broken wooden chairs and several upturned boxes. There was an ancient dresser leaning against one wall on which were displayed an assortment of chipped pots and pans. Amazingly, for such items were not usually to be found in the possession of a family such as this one, on either side of the fire were two of the most dilapidated armchairs Eliza had ever seen and she wondered where they had come from. The stuffing had all but gone in both of them and so had the original colour, whatever it had been overlaid with what looked like decades of grime. The room was bare and depressing, despite the golden crackle of the fire, with nothing in it that was was not essential to living except for a large jar on the cracked windowsill in which a bunch of wildflowers had been carefully arranged. A mass of bluebells, already wilting, mixed with the yellow of ragwort and the deep, reddish pink of valerian. Eliza was certain it was the child who had put them there.

Suddenly the girl became shy as though at the realisation of sharing her kitchen with the wife of the man who not only employed her family but all the families who occupied the cottages on Primrose Bank. She stood, one bare foot on top of the other, her eyes cast down, her hands twisting in her skirt. Eliza waited before speaking, hoping to give her a moment to regain the astounding confidence she had previously shown but the child did not speak.

"What's your name?" Eliza asked encouragingly.

"Poppy. Poppy Appleton." Still the lowered gaze.

"And do you have no work to go to, Poppy?" It was unusual, unless there were younger children to be cared for, to find a child of working age at home.

Poppy lifted her head, her pale face strained with what seemed to be a problem of enormous proportions.

"I did 'ave. I can do all sorts, me. I 'elped wi't 'arvest last back end. I can do weedin', pickin' stones, spreadin' dung fer't ploughin' in, tater plantin', all sorts. I were put ter scarin' rooks from't corn what were just sown when I were a nipper. I done gleanin', that's pickin' over't stubble fer ears o' wheat," she explained kindly, "an' I've gathered apples fer't cider mill. All sorts," she declared stoutly. She shrugged. The heavy work, the long hours entailed in the jobs she had just described appeared not to disconcert her. If Eliza was honest, since she had always known children did this kind of work, it had not concerned *her* up to now. Most of those who worked for her husband, earning a few coppers a week, were graceless creatures, slow-witted and scarcely more intelligent than the cows they herded at milking time. Now, when it came to this child and what she was forced to do because of her family's circumstances, it suddenly seemed a scandal and a sin.

"Me mam were in't family way," Poppy was saying. "Badly she were. One of us 'ad ter stop at 'ome fer a day or two. Me mam reckons I'm only one what's not cack-handed round't kitchen so it were me."

"I see. I hope your mother is recovered."

"Oh aye, she's back on 'er pins now. She's up far field transplantin' cabbages terday. She'll be soaked through an' all. I'm ter go termorrer."

"And . . . the baby?"

"Oh, babby died."

"I'm so sorry."

"She'll 'ave another," she said with the wisdom of experience. Babies were easy to get in her world.

There seemed nothing further to add to this careless indifference in the matter of birth and death, the cycle of reproduction which was inflicted on most women in this child's social group. Women were either pregnant or just recovering from childbirth with scarcely a month or two between these two states, accepting it as a fact of life. It was their husbands' only pleasure, that fumbling, grunting act in the dark of the night, the only one which cost them nothing and who were their wives to deny them, not unless they wanted a black eye and a thick ear. They would probably suffer both and still get put in the family way so best say nowt and let him get on with it.

Poppy's face glowed suddenly as some thought struck her.

"I could mekk yer a cup o' tea if yer like," she said as

though she was well used to entertaining visitors such as this one. "While yer wait, like. Rain might go off in a bit."

"Well, if you're sure it won't deprive your family."

"What's that mean?" this remarkable child asked suspiciously, turning back from the hearth where she had been just about to reach for the brown earthenware teapot on the shelf above it.

"It's . . ." Eliza had the extraordinary notion that it might be an affront to Poppy's pride if she told her the truth. Tea was not easily come by at eightpence and a farthing a pound on a farm labourer's wage which was between ten and fifteen shillings a week. The tea leaves, if they were available at all, were used several times so that the last brew was scarcely more than hot water.

"I would love a cup of tea, Poppy," she began, "but . . ."

"But what was it yer said – deprive?" It was apparent that Poppy was reluctant to let it pass. She was frowning as though at something she did not expect to like.

Eliza sighed. "Deprive. It means to take something which the person giving it . . . can ill afford to give."

Still Poppy looked puzzled. This woman who she knew as Farmer Goodall's wife had the queerest way of speaking, not just the words she used, which Poppy didn't always understand, but the way she strung them together. Still, it hardly mattered, did it, since she was not likely to have much to do with her, was she?

As if deciding it was too hard to make head or tail of what Mrs Goodall was saying so she might as well ignore it, she whipped back to the hearth and carefully measured from the tin beside the pot a scant half-teaspoon of tea. With neat, careful movements, none of them wasted, she poured the hot water into the teapot, put on the cracked lid, then set it on the hearth to mash beside the bricks which held the coal.

"Won't be burra minnit," she said comfortingly, moving across the flooded floor, her bare feet swishing in the inch or so of water that lay there. From the dresser shelf she took down two teacups, neither one matching the other, and two saucers which were again of a different pattern. They were all scrupulously clean, if a bit knocked about.

"Yer'd best get that coat off," she went on in her practical manner. "I'll 'ang it on't back o' chair while it dries."

The child might have been the adult and the adult the child. Eliza did as she was told. Seated in the rotting armchair, her feet lifted out of the water and placed on an equally rotting footstool, she sipped the weak tea. There was a splash of milk in it but no sugar and it was without doubt the worst cup of tea she had ever tasted.

Tom Goodall was a prosperous farmer who owned a fair bit of mixed farming land to the south of Old Swan and Knotty Ash and three miles east of Liverpool. The Liverpool to Manchester railway lay across Tom Goodall's land. It had opened for traffic over forty years ago when Tom's grandfather, a canny North Countryman, had been alive and it was said he had made a pretty penny out of the transaction with the railway company. This had enabled him to purchase old Ned Grimshaw's farm, once known as Jordan's Farm, before Ned had married Alice Jordan. Ned had bought an inn on Prescot Lane which he had called the Grimshaw Arms and it was still owned by the same family today.

Tom's father and then Tom himself were of the same stripe as old Seth Goodall so that whenever a bit of land adjoining Long Reach Farm came on the market it had been snapped up and added to the Goodall acreage.

The row of tied cottages, one of which housed the

Appletons, belonged to Tom Goodall and in them, six in all, lived Tom's casual labourers, those who had no particular trade but could turn their hands to most manual jobs about the farm: hedging, ditching, draining, haymaking, filling dung carts, cleaning out yards and cowsheds and dragging over the land in readiness for sowing root crops.

The employed men who had a proper trade, the head cowman, carters, men who ploughed and sowed the fields, stockmen who cared for Tom Goodall's valuable herd, married men, most of them, lived in well-built, well-maintained, *permanent* cottages which were clustered about the farmhouse itself. These dwellings had slated roofs, whitewashed walls, inside and out, diamond-paned windows and each was set in a plot of land, perhaps a quarter of an acre, where a pig might be kept for fattening, and chickens, and where vegetables for their own consumption were grown. The cottages had three bedrooms, a parlour and a back kitchen, a privy to each family, and the occupants were expected to keep themselves and their cottages to the standard Tom demanded. They considered themselves to be, and were, a cut above the rough labouring class to which the Appletons belonged. They and their forebears had worked Goodall land as long as the Goodalls themselves and they were sober, hard-working, church-going, dependable men and women, proud of their labour and the neat cottage to which it entitled them.

Not so those who lived in Primrose Bank, which, as though old Ned Grimshaw's ancestors had done it deliberately, tongue in cheek, could not have been less appropriately named. There was not a primrose, nor indeed a flower of any sort within sight. The cottages stood in a meandering row well out of sight of the farmhouse, the track itself seldom less than six inches deep in mud through which Tom Goodall's herd plodded and, to Poppy's perpetual annoyance, across which they spread their droppings. The front door, opening as it did directly on to the track, was often splattered with their mess and the stench was enough to put you off your grub, Poppy complained, and she was a country lass used to country smells!

Primrose Bank had been thrown up before the coming of the railway when Ned Grimshaw's father-in-law, who had been known for a tight-fisted old bugger, had no brass to spare for the comfort, nor even the health of his farm labourers. They had been built without foundations on to bare earth, cramped, two-storeyed affairs with a downstairs living-room no more than twelve feet by twelve feet and a tiny back scullery. Upstairs there were two bedrooms, into the smallest of which led the ladder that was the only means of getting up there. There was no ceiling. The bedrooms were directly under the eaves through which the rain often seeped and in which lived an assortment of animal and bird life. The windows were so constructed that they could not be opened and in hot weather the inside of the cottage was unbearably stuffy.

There was a narrow passage between each cottage leading from the track up to the back where the privies, two of them to be shared by six families, were placed. There was no drainage and sometimes matter from the privies escaped, finding its way between the buildings and on to the front track. The passing of sanitary legislation over thirty years ago had not affected the folk who lived in Primrose Bank! All the water had to be fetched from the public pump down the track so washing of persons or clothing was not considered a priority by the residents, with perhaps the exception of Poppy Appleton.

Tom Goodall was a hard man but he was fair, a man

who prided himself on his decency to his workforce, but the labourers, those who rented living accommodation in Primrose Bank, had proved to be as unconcerned with the state of their own welfare and comfort as pigs in a sty. They would sit with their boots in the rain puddles which collected on their floors until the leather mouldered, he complained to Eliza, like animals who know no better. Should a roof fall in or a door part from its hinges he had it seen to, for after all it was his property, but for the most part he simply left them to it. As long as they paid their rent on time and performed the tasks he set them with the diligence he demanded then he let them live in their own squalor if that was how they liked it. Besides, they were of a transient nature, inclined to move on a whim, or if they thought they could do better elsewhere, hiring themselves and their families out to farmers in other parts of the county at the Michaelmas hiring fairs with no thought for the future. They would pile their goods and chattels on to a handcart and simply move on; another family would be hired, move in and the cycle would be continued.

Reuben Appleton's cottage was an exception as far as cleanliness was concerned and that was due to his youngest daughter who might have been born with a bloody scrubbing brush in her hand, he was fond of saying to his slatternly wife. Whenever their Poppy was not working in the fields she was at it in the cottage, always on her knees, a coarse sacking apron wrapped about her diminutive figure – she had begun her activities at an early age – her abundant hair neatly tucked away in a kerchief. She would remove her stout hobnailed boots and her woollen stockings and go about barefoot, begging the others to do the same and save "her" clean floor but they rarely took any notice of her. Martha and Reuben, both good-natured and feckless, who often asked one another where their Poppy got her pernickety ways from, would sometimes give in to her. Anything for a quiet life, they would sigh, but Poppy's brothers and sisters thought she was a bloody nuisance, and told her so. They weren't walking about on no cold, damp flags with nowt on their feet, they declared and if she didn't give over and let them alone they'd land her a clout that'd rattle her teeth.

Eliza sipped her tea and listened to the hiss and splatter of the rain falling down the chimney and hitting the glowing embers of the fire, and the slow drip of water coming from somewhere above her. It plopped rhythmically into something, probably a bucket, but Poppy seemed not to notice or was so used to it she did not hear it. She sat quietly in the depth of the chair on the other side of the fire, her bare feet tucked under her, drinking her tea with evident enjoyment. Mostly she just gazed into the heart of the small fire, only once getting up to stir whatever was in the pan. She had a quality of stillness about her, giving the appearance of drawing in on herself as though her surroundings, despite the evidence of her hard work, were something from which she felt the need to escape. The place could not be said to shine or sparkle, for there was nothing in it from which a light might reflect. No brass or copper, no ornaments of any kind, no glassware or mirror, but every surface was scrubbed clean. Across the floor the rainwater, in which flotsam of some kind floated, continued to eddy from beneath the ill-fitting door.

And yet despite her quietness, that feeling of pause in her active domestic pursuits, she had an air of suppressed humour, a brightness of spirit which shone from her luminous eyes whenever she glanced up at Eliza. Nothing was going to beat Poppy Appleton, her vivid, bird-like expression seemed to be saying. It was as though inside her was a bubble of joy, a light of hope, contained for the moment with the need for seriousness, for assiduity to the work on hand but which, when the moment allowed, would escape and transform her into a lark, soaring high above the earth in great cartwheels of exuberance. She was a child who had known nothing but drudgery, poverty, neglect and probably hunger. Many of the labourers on the farm found their way on pay day to the Grimshaw Arms where their wages were poured down their throats, creating empty bellies for their children. There was nothing anybody could do about it, Tom said, for it was not his place to say how they were to spend their money, was it? He only gave them work and paid them for it and his responsibility ended there.

This home, though as clean as this scrap of a girl could get it, was a poor home. The rest of the family, apparently ten of them, were out working in Tom Goodall's fields, and tomorrow Poppy would make the eleventh. She could not be spared to sit idly at home, or even spend her days keeping it clean for the others.

The words were out of Eliza's mouth before she had time to wonder how they had got there in the first place.

"How old are you, Poppy?"

"Eleven in August, ma'am."

"Then how would you like to come and work for me?"

2

At first she did exactly what she had done in her own home. She took a bucket of water, the water hot from the boiler, a scrubbing brush and some common soda and got down on her knees to scrub. The only difference was that when she had the floor exactly to her liking there was no one to come traipsing muck and manure all over the immaculate surface she had just achieved. Her clean floor stayed clean and the gratification she knew was enormous. She was urged to keep the place spotless. She was applauded for keeping the place spotless and it gave her a sort of dizzying joy to hear Dilys tell Mrs Goodall that in all her years as a dairymaid she'd never had as good a little skivvy as Poppy Appleton. Poppy was not offended to be described as a skivvy even though a skivvy was the lowest form of life in the ranks of domestic servants. To Poppy Appleton, who thought paradise to be a place where every surface would be clean enough to eat your dinner off, being a skivvy was a bloody sight higher and better and more satisfying than working in the fields in mud up to your arse-hole!

She had been quite overwhelmed by the splendour of Mrs Goodall's dairy which had seemed to the child who lived with ten others in a room twelve feet by twelve feet to be as big as a church. Mrs Goodall had been a school teacher, Dilys told her when she got to know her better and realised that a bit of a chat did not stop the new girl from working. Mrs Goodall had taken the fancy, when she and Farmer Goodall had married and she had been compelled to give up teaching, to set up what she described as a "model" dairy. Don't ask her what it meant exactly, Dilys added, but there was not another like it in the whole of the county. There had always been a dairy at Long Reach Farm, of course, as there was on every mixed or dairy farm. Before the coming of the railway, all the milk that came from the Goodall herd that could not be sold in the immediate neighbourhood had to be turned quickly into butter or cheese. The task, naturally, had fallen to the women of the family. Previous Mrs Goodalls had made butter and cheese, taking them with their eggs and poultry to St John's Market in Liverpool and Eliza kept up the tradition though not in such great quantities.

Once a week on a Saturday the cart was got out and driven to the market loaded up with cheeses and butter and eggs and trussed fowls. Mrs Goodall drove it, dressed in her respectable and plain grey serge skirt and jacket with a white cotton blouse beneath it. She wore the same outfit winter and summer, the only difference being that in the winter she threw over it a long, waterproof Ulster cloak with a good woollen lining, for it was cold behind a stall. Sturdy black boots and a close-fitting black bonnet which covered her greying hair completed the outfit. She had never been a fashionable woman, nor a pretty one and she had often wondered what Tom Goodall had seen in her, for she was almost twenty-five when they married and he had been a handsome, well-set-up and thriving farmer. They had raised two sons, born within a year of one another, and buried several other babies, including two girls, in the family plot in St Anne's Church. She sometimes thought privately that the reason she had taken such a fancy for Poppy Appleton was because of the loss of her daughters. Well, not a fancy exactly but the child was so promising – she could think of no other word to describe her – so diligent, so eager to learn and so wasted in the environment in which Eliza had found her she could not in all conscience leave her there, could she? Or so she told herself. She was not sure what would come of putting her in the dairy but the child's family were so slapdash and uncaring and would constantly drag her back down with them if Poppy wasn't removed from their influence. Eliza was immensely proud of her dairy and it seemed to be the only place for Poppy since the child was so concerned with cleanliness. At the first opportunity she meant to bring up the matter of Poppy's living in at the farm, which would ease her away from the pressure of her good-natured but slatternly family.

Eliza's dairy was totally self-sufficient. It was sited next to the farmhouse on the north-facing wall where it kept cool in the summer. It had four large, airy rooms, all in use since Dilys and Eliza and Nelly, who was a bit slow-thinking but a hard worker, produced a great deal of cheese; the fourth room, which had been built on at Eliza's insistence, was needed not only for its making but for the storing of it while it matured. There was a plentiful supply of hot water, since every cheese mould and ladle, every milk churn and strainer, every pail and even the wooden yokes which were used to carry in the pails of milk from the milking shed had to be scrubbed and scoured at least once a day. The hot water came from the boiler which stood beside the sink and pump in the corner of the butter making room. All the floors were slightly sloped to allow for drainage. The walls were tiled with pretty Dutch tiles of blue and white and round them were rows of stone shelves on which the dairy utensils stood.

The whole building, which was dazzling with whitewash on the outside, had to be kept scrupulously clean. Pails and crocks were deep scoured with great attention to cow hairs, for if Mrs Goodall should find one in any part of the process it would be woe betide Dilys Williams who had been Mrs Goodall's head dairymaid for ten years.

Dilys, though married, was childless and therefore able to continue her dairy work. She was as plump and brown as Eliza's favourite hen and just as fussy. She even walked like Clucky, her head bobbing forward with every step so that her voluminous mob cap swayed backwards and forwards as she moved. She was an excellent dairymaid, accurate, careful and quick, very particular, but she was afflicted with what were known as "dairymaid's legs" which came from standing hour after hour, day after day on the cold flagged floor of the dairy. They were hideously swollen and knotted beneath the fullness of her skirt, but only her husband knew what pain she suffered, since she did not want to lose this good, well-paid job of hers and under such a kindly mistress, not until she and Evan had enough saved for a little cottage of their own when they retired.

It was in the sale of fresh milk that Eliza Goodall had realised the potential for profit and if it had occurred to her she might have come to the right conclusion as to why Tom had taken her as his wife. He was a good farmer but he was not clever though he recognised someone who was. She had a good "business" head, a head for figures and the knowledge of where lay the means of making money. Since the railways had opened up the city markets, dealers based near convenient stations had snapped up local milk supplies, one of which had been the surplus from Long

Reach Farm, making Tom Goodall a splendid return. All in all he often told himself privately, Eliza had proved a sound investment and a good breeder, since she had given him his two sons who would take over the farm when he was six feet under.

As a reward he allowed his wife, to keep the "butter money", the "egg money" and anything else she might make from her chickens and geese. He would have been surprised if he had known how much that amounted to and where it was invested.

That first day in the dairy at Long Reach Farm Poppy had worked harder than she had ever worked before, even in the fields at haymaking. Dilys, who had not yet become aware of the sterling qualities the new girl possessed, had set into her at once since she could not for the life of her see why Mrs Goodall had employed her in the first place. She and Nelly, with Mrs Goodall to help and keep an eye on things, had managed very well without her. This big-eyed, thin-faced and skinny waif from Primrose Bank, which was known for its unwholesome condition, did not look at all promising, she decided, and must be put to the test at once.

"Now them's cream settin' dishes over there, see," she said crisply, indicating a long row of the prettiest bowls Poppy had ever seen, a creamy white on the inside and a warm tawny colour on the outside. Each had a large lip. They stood on a table so clean it looked as though it had been bleached. "An' them's milk basins beside them. Understand, do you?"

"Aye," said Poppy. She had put on her "best" skirt and bodice since what was good enough for gleaning and stone-picking would not do in Mrs Goodall's model dairy. She was swamped by an enormous white cotton apron and a frilled cap evidently made for someone with a much bigger head than hers. It completely covered her hair, sitting on her eyebrows and the tops of her ears, without which it would have slipped over her face. On her feet were a pair of "pattens" which consisted of nothing more than light soles of wood fastened across the arch of the foot with thongs. Mrs Goodall liked them – this was a phrase she was to hear a dozen times a day – Mrs Goodall liked them, for not only did they keep the bare foot from the flagged floor but they were easy to keep clean. These were put on at the door of the dairy, leaving your everyday sturdy hobnailed boots at the entrance, Mrs Goodall had told Poppy before placing her in Dilys's efficient but inclined to be officious hands.

"Well, me an' Nelly scoured the lot of 'em last night afore we left ready fer today, didn't we, Nelly?"

Nelly, similarly attired to Poppy, nodded vigorously, knocking her cap over her eyes so that for a moment she was blinded. Nobody smiled. Nelly pushed the frill of the cap back up to its normal position just above the bridge of her nose. She peered from beneath it like a small animal from its burrow, her head slightly tipped back in order to be able to see, which gave her a haughty air that couldn't have been further from the truth, Poppy was to learn. No one was more good-natured than Nelly Pickles. She was willing to give, and generously, not only of what she knew but what she was. She bore no grudges, not even when later it became apparent that ten-year-old Poppy Appleton was to take precedence over fifteen-year-old Nelly Pickles who had come from the workhouse to work for Mrs Goodall three years ago. She was no oil painting, even she knew that. Her face was bumpy and a kind of dough colour and her eyes were as green and small as gooseberries. Her hair was a harsh gingery red and it was doubtful she would ever catch the eye of any chap, but her wide, smiling mouth told Poppy she had a kind heart and would always be willing, in these first confused days, to give the new girl a shove in the right direction.

"Rightio," Dilys continued. "They 'ave ter be done every day, mind," nodding at the dishes. "They're for skimmin' the cream off the milk, see."

"Aye." Poppy refrained from nodding her head after seeing what had happened to Nelly.

"Now them other dishes over there're made of sycamore 'cos it don't affect the taste o't milk, see."

Dilys came from Wales and ended almost every sentence with "see".

"Now, when the cream's risen, an' not before, mind, it's lifted off wi' a skimmer and then the milk's poured inter that churn over there, see."

Poppy turned obediently to the brightly polished churn and nodded carefully.

"Think yer could manage that, then?"

Poppy nodded again briefly, wary of her cap.

"Rightio, me an' Nelly'll watch you. Make sure yer know what yer doin'."

It seemed she knew exactly what she was doing and, remembering how long it had taken Nelly to get the hang of things, Dilys was jubilant at the new girl's progress that day though she was careful not to say so at once. Best see how she shaped first.

Poppy continued to "shape", scrubbing for hours at a time, only being allowed to do a "proper" job when Dilys deemed it the right moment, which was when Poppy had proved to Dilys she could do it. Butter churning was one. The barrel churn had to be turned end over end until the butter "came". When that happened the churn was "worked" to remove the excess buttermilk. Once, in the days before it became a model dairy, this was done by the cool hands of the dairymaid, if she could be trusted to get them clean first, but Mrs Goodall, to whom hygiene was a god, had installed butter presses and butter beaters so that her goods were virtually untouched by human hand. No complaint of "bad" stomach had ever been made about her produce.

At the end of the first week Dilys had begun to wish that she had kept Nelly to the scrubbing and put the new girl full time on the butter and cheese making. She was quick and neat in her movements, obsessively clean and was so keen to learn she could do the whole process, apart from the butter shells and patterns, which Nelly still needed a guiding hand with at times, as though she had been at it for years. She had even learned, without apparent effort, the art of milking. They changed into print aprons for this job and, it must be admitted, Nelly was good at it.

"There's yer stool an' yer ter start there wi' Gracie. Don't mix the buckets 'cos we 'ave ter know 'ow much each cow gives. Just pull on them titties, that's it, an' squirt it inter't bucket. Tekk yer time fer't cows don't like no rush. Press yer 'ead inter Gracie's flank, it's comfier that way an' give us a shout if yer need owt."

They began their day early, just before five o'clock. Mrs Goodall had given instructions that Poppy was to come to the back kitchen door before reporting to Dilys where she felt some surprise and a thrill of satisfaction when an enormous bacon sandwich was thrust into her hand by a woman who was a stranger to her.

"Get that in yer, Mrs Goodall ses, and there's a cup o' tea ter go with it."

Poppy had never, in all her life, drunk such a glorious cup of tea, hot and sweet and just the thing to wash down her bacon sandwich. It would set her up for the day, she thought exultantly as she hurried in the wake of Mrs Goodall towards the dairy, since she had eaten nothing but a bowl of half-cooked gruel over the glimmer of a fire at Primrose Bank. She was further amazed when, at ten o'clock, another mug of tea was sent over to the dairy accompanied by a plate of delicious meat pies and some freshly baked bread. Her little stomach strained over the unaccustomed food and her heart rejoiced as she belched happily into her scrubbing bucket.

Later in the day they received more milk for churning from Evan, who, beside being the head cowman was Dilys's husband. A stocky little Welshman, he was, who had more affinity with the cows he and his lad, Tommy, helped to milk than with human creatures. He was without much in the way of conversation beyond "come by 'ere, girl" to whoever his eye fell on as he delivered the fresh, still-warm pails of milk to the dairy. The "come by 'ere" was a sort of general order from Evan meaning, on this particular occasion, "Here's the milk, come and get it."

"This is Poppy," Dilys said to him tartly, since there had been no time for introductions in the milking shed earlier in the day. Her attitude then seemed to say that she didn't know what on earth she was going to do with this little scrap of a thing Mrs Goodall had foisted on her. She didn't look as though she could lift one of the miniature tin churns of milk with the gleaming brass fittings which were for the household's consumption, let alone a full-sized churn. A quart the small churn held and wouldn't the child be struggling to carry even that? her raised eyebrows asked him.

Evan merely grunted but Poppy thought she saw the suggestion of a wink from one of his dark brown eyes. A true Celt was Evan, dark of hair and skin and eyes, with a fine singing voice which was reserved for his cows.

"Now then, look you, girl, Nelly'll fetch me that hair sieve an' I'll show you how ter sieve the milk and get it inter them milk basins," was the next task Poppy was allowed to try.

"Rightio, Mrs Williams." Nelly darted away like a butterfly skimming across still water, quick and light on her feet. Slow of thought she might be but give her an order she understood and it was done cheerfully and quickly almost before the words were out of Dilys's mouth.

"Now then, girl, when it's sieved the milk'll be left in the basins, see, for twenty-four hours," Dilys told Poppy, daring her to say she didn't understand, "then it'll be skimmed just like I showed yer this morning."

Poppy understood perfectly, risking a careful nod of her ballooning cap, and so it continued.

Dilys was to wonder time and again how any child as slight as Poppy Appleton could possibly get through as much work as she did. Nelly was a good worker, a steady worker and gave no cheek but she would never make a decent butter shell, or get the hang of stamping the weighed oblongs of butter with Mrs Goodall's stamp.

It seemed next to no time before Poppy Appleton was doing every job that was to be done in a dairy. Twice a week they churned except when it was hot when it was done every day. It was the first job of the day, after milking, of course, taking about twenty minutes to half an hour, each of them using a churn. A good steady motion, Dilys told Poppy, neither too quick nor too slow or the cream would heave and swell from too much air being forced into it. At this time of the year when the cows were in the meadows eating their natural food the colour of the butter was just right, a sort of delicate cream, but in the winter when they were stall-fed the butter was almost white and had proved unpopular at the market. A good trick was to scrape a carrot into a clean piece of linen cloth, dip it in water and squeeze it into the cream. It brought it up a treat, Dilys told the fascinated child.

Fascinated! That didn't say the half of it. Dilys had never had a pupil with such an inquisitive mind, she told Mrs Goodall. It was questions, questions, questions all the time, some of which Dilys found difficult to answer, like why the butter came! It just did. Where did the curds come from? Why did the cream rise to the top of the milk? Poppy had a voracious appetite for knowledge, Dilys confided to her mistress, and was proving to be a proper little helper. Not that Nelly wasn't, or anything like that, but Poppy had a *flair*, if Mrs Goodall didn't think that was too foolish a word, for learning, for picking up and hanging on to what Dilys told her. She didn't need telling twice.

Poppy loved the work and she loved the dairy. It was like working in heaven or what she would like heaven to be if she ever got there. The exacting demand for cleanliness satisfied something in her that had been stifled by her years of living in the muck and muddle her own family not only tolerated but actually seemed to relish. Every morning as she took off her boots, slipped on her pattens and stepped from the yard into the cool order and immaculacy of the dairy she felt a sudden lift of her heart and the shaping of her mouth into a contented smile. Each room had two windows tightly netted against flies and dust, and the floor, which she had scrubbed last thing yesterday, would shine like a many patterned jewel in the early morning light. On the spotless shelves were the neatly arranged tools of the business. Wooden buckets with brightly polished brass bands, churns, setting bowls, cream bowls and jugs. There was not a soiled cloth or a dirty utensil in the place and the fresh smell of cleanliness was a soothing balm to her who had just come from the shambles of her own overcrowded and festering home.

She became almost speechless with wonder when she tried to describe to her mam and pa exactly what she did each day. Her pa would wink at Mam. "What did I tell yer, Martha?" he would grin, "Give kid a scrubbin' brush an' bucket an' she's medd up. I don't know where she gets it, damned if I do," glancing with total unconcern about the cluttered, squalid room where already Poppy's absence was beginning to show. She did her best when she got back from the dairy, attempting to clean up the mess created by her family that day, but she had been up since four thirty and after fourteen hours of hard, manual labour, felt only like falling on to the palliasse beside Rose, Lily, Iris and Marigold and sinking into the depths of sleep. Pots and pans cluttered the table top, still congealed with yesterday's meal. A pair of muddy boots stood in the centre and sprawled across them was next door's cat. Arthur snored and farted in the best chair with his bare and filthy feet on the stool where a short while ago Eliza Goodall's feet had rested. Lily and Marigold, only half dressed with their unbrushed hair hanging limply about their pale faces, fought over the last bit of apple pie which had been left over from the Goodalls' meal the night before and which Mrs Goodall had told Poppy to take home for her mother. She would need a bit of extra feeding up, she had said kindly, since giving birth was very debilitating. "Debilitating?" Well, it means to take away your strength, she had explained patiently. Eliza kept forgetting Poppy's passion for knowing the exact meaning of every new word she heard!

Rose Appleton was out, courting a hedger from the next farm which Martha Appleton prayed would not end with their Rose in the family way. That was what had happened to her sixteen years ago when she herself was the same age as their Rose. Sixteen and Reuben nineteen and now would you look at them living, eleven of them, in a place barely big enough for a family of four. It could have been worse. There had been a child between Poppy and Herbert, another between Herbert and Eustace and another two since then. At the time she had been sad at the loss of her babies, poor little souls, but she supposed it had turned out for the best in the end.

Iris Appleton lolled, elbows in the mess on the table, her bottom on an upturned box, squinting at the fashion pictures in a tattered magazine, salvaged from some rubbish pile. Herbert and Eustace could be heard from the track at the front of the cottage, screaming with delight as they and hordes of other children chased a rat into the fields. Only Douglas, who was twelve, was missing and only the Good Lord knew where he'd got to. He'd end up on the *Lahore* one of these days, would Douglas. He was for ever roaming about the countryside with the tide of human flotsam which spilled out into and from the maze of narrow streets about Liverpool. The *Lahore* was a sturdy old wooden-wall vessel which, at the end of its glory days, had been transformed into a training ship for awkward and recalcitrant boys. A floating reformatory anchored in the river a third of a mile from the shore which accommodated three hundred boys and if their Douglas was not curbed it would be three hundred and one!

Poppy began to grow and fill out and as summer drifted by and autumn crept closer she was six inches taller and nearly a stone heavier than she had been when she had begun work in Mrs Goodall's dairy, thanks to the abundant and nourishing food Mrs Goodall provided. Since her best clothes no longer fitted her Mrs Goodall had rooted out an elderly grey flannel skirt she herself had once worn and being a thrifty woman had not thrown away. There was a bodice to match and with a stitch or two here and there the garments were pulled into a vague semblance of fitting the child. The hem had been shortened and the outfit, giving room for further growth, would last her through the winter, Mrs Goodall told her practically. There was a petticoat, snowy white and edged at the hem with a bit of frayed lace and even a "chemise", as Mrs Goodall called it, to go under the bodice.

But the most exciting event to Poppy was the wearing of the much mended but clean pair of drawers Mrs Goodall said she must put on since to be without was not decent. Poppy did not know this, never having seen a pair, let alone worn them and indeed had not even been aware that such a garment existed, but if Mrs Goodall said it was so that was good enough for her. Besides, Mrs Goodall told the enthralled child, it would be decidedly warmer in the dairy in the winter.

Poppy was enchanted. Poppy had one ambition in life and that was to be exactly like Mrs Goodall who, it seemed to her, was the epitome of what a lady should be and if she patterned herself on her mistress she felt she couldn't go far wrong.

Poppy would never forget the first time she had entered the kitchen of Long Reach Farm. It was on the first day of working there and at twelve o'clock precisely she had been surprised when Dilys put down the butter beaters she was using and announced that it was time for some grub. Grub? What did she mean? Poppy had wondered, though of course she knew what grub was. Nothing had prepared her for the reality of it.

The door from the yard into the farm kitchen was round the corner on the west-facing wall of the farmhouse. She had hovered there for a moment at five o'clock that morning when she had been handed the tea and bacon sandwich but she had been so nervous she had been blind to everything but the food and the appearance of Mrs Goodall who had come to take her "across", she had said.

Now its full glory was revealed to her. If Dilys had been drawing her up to the altar of St Anne's Church, Poppy could not have been more overwhelmed, her eyes enormous in her pinched face as she blundered over the doorstep. She kept bumping into things as she stared about her: the table, one of the benches, Mr Goodall's beautifully carved and polished Windsor chair, Mr Goodall himself who grunted in surprise, and even Cook as she whisked from the oven to the table with a bubbling pan of thick, mouth-watering vegetable soup.

"Watch where you're going, girl," she scolded.

Poppy had to be taken by the hand and led to her seat on the bench next to Evan and Tommy, who was a bachelor and therefore fed at the Goodall table. She nibbled on what was put before her, as timorous as a mouse who cannot believe that the cheese it is eating is not about to be snatched from its plate. She felt like an intruder in the richness of a prince's palace, her dumbfounded expression seemed to say. She had never seen anything like it. Clocks and cutlery, shining plates and finely embroidered napkins. Pictures of cows and pheasants and Mrs Goodall's two handsome sons who acted as though the swirl of activity about them was no concern of theirs. They had talked of milk yields and silage and other matters of a farming nature to their father and had spared, in their youthful manliness, not a glance for Poppy Appleton.

There were three maidservants and a woman whose sole task it was to scrub the kitchen floor, the pantry and scullery, the stone-flagged passageways, the back step and anywhere else Cook decided was in need of a good "going-over". She was, possibly, the only other person on the farm who did more scrubbing than Poppy Appleton.

The kitchen was an enormous room with an enormous table in its centre and several smaller ones against its walls, all made from yellow-white sycamore, which had stood up to generations of pounding, chopping and scouring, of baking and mincing and kneading, of rolling and grinding.

From the ceiling hung smoked hams, bunches of onions, nets of mushrooms and dried herbs. There were pots and pans of every size and kind, iron and copper, hanging from the walls which were whitewashed every six months. The temperature of the room was always high and the climate intensely busy, blasted by fires and ovens, for everything that was eaten, not only by her own menfolk, but by the servants who ate sitting beside them, was produced in Eliza Goodall's kitchen or her dairy.

The farmhouse was old. It had been old before Tom Goodall's grandfather had bought it from Ned Grimshaw, but alongside the huge, open fire, over which a leg of pork was being spit-roasted in readiness for the Goodalls' evening meal, was a huge enclosed range, the very latest in modern cooking, cleaned out and blackleaded each day by the scullery maid. It was known as a kitchener. It had on one side a large, ventilated oven and on the other a fire, or roaster. The hotplate above was where dishes were kept at a good temperature and as an added concession to modernity it contained a back boiler made of wrought iron with a brass tap and a steam pipe. Tremendously expensive, of course, at twenty-three pounds ten shillings but worth every penny in Eliza Goodall's opinion and Tom could well afford it.

Two kitchen dressers of gigantic proportions were crammed with matched tea services and dinner services in a sturdy blue willow pattern which Poppy thought were the most exquisite things she had seen, even better than the setting bowls in the dairy. There were cream jugs and sugar bowls, meat platters, vegetable dishes and soup tureens, all gleaming and set on the shelves in an orderly fashion and Poppy wondered what they were all used for.

Evan and Tommy were working their silent way through a second bowl of soup, dipping in huge hunks of bread then lifting them, dripping, to their mouths. Evan, because Dilys was a dairymaid and therefore not at home in their cottage to cook him his midday meal, was allowed to eat with the other servants. Married men normally went home or, if they were working a way out from the farmhouse, took their "noon-piece" with them, usually a hunk of cold bacon or cheese, and bread. This, of course, was not always the way on a farm but Eliza, who knew human nature and had her own opinions on the way work should be done, had persuaded Tom that well-fed servants were contented servants and would work better because of it. She was proved right.

She usually was. Look at Poppy Appleton!

3

It was at dinner-time one day in early September that Mrs Goodall dropped her bombshell. Her voice from the end of the table where she always sat, though not loud, cut through the hubbub of conversation and everyone in the kitchen stopped speaking and turned to look at her.

"I'd like a word with you, Poppy."

Cook, as though she expected something of further import to be said, carefully put down the tray of scones she had just removed from the oven, placing it on the hotplate above. May, the scullery maid, being the youngest at fourteen and last to be taken on, was on her feet removing dirty plates from the table and replacing them with clean ones and she almost let one slip through her fingers. A small smile lifted the corner of her rosy mouth as though the thought of what she hoped was to come did not displease her. Her seniors, Aggie and Clara, had just tucked into cold lamb and salad with new potatoes and were seated with the rest of the servants and when everyone was served it would be May's turn to sit down and eat.

Turning from Mrs Goodall, the two older women looked at one another, then at Dilys who surely would know what this was all about but Dilys looked as mystified as they. The menfolk, master and servants, did not show a great deal of concern since, whatever it turned out to be, this was surely women's doings! They continued to tuck into the apple pie and thick whipped cream just come from the dairy, spooning it in to their mouths with the application of men fuelling a boiler.

Mrs Goodall was dressed in her usual plain and simple fashion which, though it had none of the frills and furbelows gloated over by the fashion-conscious ladies, suited her rather forbidding style. The bustle was currently in vogue, the skirt flattened in front and bunched out behind over a crinolette. In addition to the frills and flounces there might be ribbon bands, ruching, braid, fringes, tassels, feathers, lace and broderie anglaise. Seventy to eighty yards of trimming could be employed on a skirt alone but Eliza favoured none of these, keeping to an untrimmed but well-made grey serge with a touch of immaculate white at the throat and wrists.

She was a homely woman but she had a good complexion and a kindly expression which lit her ordinary blue eyes to a warmth that spoke of humour. Her hair was thick and curling, going grey now at forty-five but inclined to spring about her head if not kept well restrained within a small white cap called a breakfast cap, with streamers of ribbons down her back.

The cap bobbed an inch or two as she spoke.

"I will see you in the parlour, Poppy, if you please," she continued as she stood up, her voice inclined to sharpness and at once, as she finished speaking, every head and every pair of eyes, speculating on what this could mean, turned back to look at Poppy. What had the child done? was written on every face but surely it couldn't be that bad. She was well known for being a grand little worker, you'd only to hear Dilys going on about her to know that. And not just in the dairy, neither. Let her see one of the maids beating a rug or hanging out the washing and if Poppy Appleton had a minute to spare she'd be giving a hand, and as friendly as a puppy with it. She'd even offered to help Tommy drive the cows back to the pasture and her scarcely higher than the beasts' rump. Aye, a sunny little maid and a firm favourite with them all and it'd be a rare shame if she was in trouble over something. Happen it was summat to do with that draggle-tailed family of hers; why Mr Goodall kept them on was a mystery to them all. Surely there were more deserving families who would be glad of work and a cottage to go with it. A family who would not allow it to fall into the dreadful state of dirt and disrepair the Appletons had. The child did her best. Had they not seen her carrying buckets of water from the pump at the end of the track and her no bigger than six pennorth o' copper. All them big lads and not one offering to carry a bit of water for her. She had an afternoon off once a week like they all did but she seemed to spend it doing nothing but cleaning up after that good-for-nothing lot who, it seemed to them, it was inconceivable could be related to Poppy.

Would you just look at her now, sitting there in her spotless white apron, her cap the same, and if it was too big for her had she not had the gumption – which couldn't be said about Nelly who had got into a habit of for ever pushing the thing up – to put a stitch or two in it to contrive a better fit.

Her face, which had been rosy and shining with good health and happiness and the scrubbing she had given it before dinner under the tap in the butter-making room, had turned a transparent white. Her hands, the nails neatly cut and as clean as she could get them, trembled for a moment in her lap but she held her head up for all that as she nodded at Mrs Goodall.

Poppy could feel the sudden draining away of her strength,

a feeling so strange it seemed to leave a great hollow space inside her with nothing to fill it. Her arms and legs felt leaden and she was sure when she stood up, if she could stand up that is, she would be unable to move. Her mistress sounded so annoyed and though Poppy could think of nothing she had done, or failed to do, that would warrant a summons to Mrs Goodall's parlour where the more serious misdemeanours of the servants were dealt with, she must have made some dreadful mistake. Why else was Mrs Goodall, and in front of the others too, marching her off there?

Oh, please God, please God, don't let me lose this splendid job, she prayed to a deity she knew very little about. The Appletons weren't church-goers or even believers in the benefit of prayer but she'd heard of Him and knew that He was the one most folk turned to if they wanted something. Perhaps He would listen to Poppy Appleton because honestly if Mrs Goodall turned her out she didn't think she could bear it. To go back to the fields, the mud, the smells, the bare, filthy feet, the bare, ragged dress, and the loss of her drawers. If anything signified the going up in the world of Poppy Appleton it was the wearing of drawers! To have nothing to look forward to as she looked forward every morning to that almost holy moment when she changed her boots for her pattens and stepped over the threshold into the dairy.

"Can you manage without Poppy for ten minutes, Dilys?" her mistress asked the dairymaid coolly, as though Dilys were at fault as well and Dilys could only mumble that she could. The occasion was so singular, for misdemeanours were uncommon in the well-run household, that as Poppy trailed despondently at Mrs Goodall's heels every pair of eyes followed them, even those of Tom Goodall.

He and his sons exchanged glances and shrugged then resumed their meal, indicating to Cook that they'd have those scones now, and a pot of fresh butter. Servants and their problems were nothing to do with them, their attitude said, at least those who did not work outside.

"Come in and sit down, Poppy," Mrs Goodall said as they entered the parlour, waving to a chair in front of the large desk which stood not quite in the centre of the room. It was neatly stacked with piles of papers and books, none of which meant anything to Poppy since she couldn't read. There were two mullioned windows, one overlooking what was known as the side yard, the other giving a view of the garden at the front of the farmhouse, which they all knew was a source of great pride to Mrs Goodall. It had two gravelled paths leading from the front door in a perfect circle to the white wooden gate and in the centre of the circle was a statue of a fish standing on its tail in a fountain of water that came from its mouth.

It astonished and delighted all those who saw it for the first time, for a fish on its tail was the last thing you expected to see in a farmhouse garden. Even the garden was unusual but then Eliza Goodall was an unusual woman, let it be said. The story was that when Eliza married Tom Goodall she had begged her father, who had been a doctor, if she might bring the fish from the well-tended garden that had surrounded her home in Prescot to her new home at Long Reach Farm. Her father had granted her wish and had died soon after. It was said that Mrs Goodall loved that fish since it was a token of the fondness that had existed between her and her father; and if the man whose job it was to see to her garden allowed the slightest trace of verdigris to form on it he was in for a tongue-lashing. A bit like a cow hair, Dilys was fond of saying!

The water in the little pool that formed about the statue of the fish was clear and sparkling in the September sunshine that fell on the garden from morning till night and the sound of it was pleasantly soothing, drifting through the half-opened window. The flowerbeds that encircled the paths were an eruption of colour as snapdragons and sweetbriar, sweet william and peonies, pinks and Canterbury bells and spears of hollyhock vied with one another in catching the eye of the beholder.

The parlour itself was plainly a room for working in with nothing of the usual feminine clutter one associated with a room of this sort. There was a large fireplace of stone, on the hearth of which stood an enormous arrangement of freshly picked roses in a copper bowl, the only concession to a woman's occupancy of the room. There were several closed cupboards and a bookcase with every shelf crammed with books. There was a shabby sofa under the window which looked out on the garden with some cushions thrown on it, and several spindle-backed chairs with rush seats stood against the wall under the yard window. Some large object was set in one corner of the room with a fancy shawl thrown over it, a piece of furniture of some sort, Poppy supposed, though what it could be was a mystery to her.

Mrs Goodall arranged herself neatly behind the desk in a chair matching those against the wall, evidently a set of six. Poppy sat in the sixth. Mrs Goodall reached for a pile of already neatly arranged papers and began to shuffle them, standing them on end and tapping them until she had them to her liking, then replaced them where she had found them. She did the same with another pile while Poppy watched her apprehensively then, as though taking a plunge into unknown waters, her mistress squared her shoulders. She continued to look down at her hands which now rested on the desk top. She took a deep breath as though what she was about to say was of great seriousness and could not be rushed. Poppy's heart sank and she felt a great desire to burst into tears. She couldn't bear this, really she couldn't and if Mrs Goodall didn't get on with it she'd jump up and run from the room. She must have done something so bloody dreadful her mistress found it hard even to speak of it and the worst thing was she had no idea what it could be. If she'd been late for work, or broken a setting dish, or spoiled the butter she could perhaps understand Mrs Goodall's air of gravity but as far as she knew she'd done nothing wrong. Bloody hell, Dilys would be the first to tell her if she had.

But suddenly Mrs Goodall raised her white-capped head and smiled and Poppy thought it was the loveliest smile she had ever seen. The sun came out and flooded her heart and she wanted to dance and sing and turn cartwheels but instead she smiled back tentatively. Mrs Goodall would hardly sack her, would she, not with that lovely shining look of . . . what was it? Poppy didn't know; she only knew she liked it. It seemed to suggest that something wonderful was about to happen and when it did, when Mrs Goodall told her what it was, Poppy wanted to cry again which was bloody daft but made a queer sort of sense.

"I think, that is if you agree," Mrs Goodall told her, talking to her as if she were an adult with a mind of her own and not a child just gone eleven years old, "that it might be better all round if you were to live in at the farm, Poppy. It's for you to decide, of course, since you may not want to leave your family. I would not dream of making you but if you do decide to come you can still visit them whenever you have a spare moment. Every day if you wish as long as it does not interfere with your work. I know it will be a wrench to leave your mother but she is only at the end of the track and very accessible." Her smile deepened. "That means she is within reach, child. Now I shall come and talk to your mother and father before you make any decision but I thought with the winter coming on with the dark mornings and evenings, it seems only sensible, and safer, if you were to come at once. I would be glad if you could avoid that walk in the dark. You're growing up now, you know."

She leaned back in her chair, resting her straight spine against the wood. She was calm, controlled as she always was but an older, more experienced person than Poppy might have seen the hidden excitement in her.

What difference did growing up make? Poppy remembered thinking, her mind fizzing with the joy of what Mrs Goodall was saying. She was not afraid of the dark, nor that anyone would interfere with Poppy Appleton. Her pa might be shiftless, concerned only with his weekly wage and how far it would stretch in the Grimshaw Arms but he and her brothers would pulverise any man who laid a hand on one of their own.

Still, if Mrs Goodall wanted to believe there was danger on the path down from the farm to Primrose Bank then who was she to argue, especially if it meant she could live in at this grand place. "And there's another thing, Poppy," Mrs Goodall went on, unconcerned, it seemed, by Poppy's mesmerised silence. "It came to me recently" – *Recently!* She'd thought of nothing else since the child had started work in the dairy – "how . . . handy it would be if someone in the dairy could read and write. Besides myself, of course. Dilys is a good, steady worker and I could not manage without her, which I shall make plain to her when the time comes but she is too old now to learn new tricks." She raised her eyebrows and grimaced, drawing Poppy into a small conspiracy. "You must not tell her I said so, naturally. We would not want to hurt her feelings. But you do see how advantageous this would be to us both, don't you?"

Oh yes, oh bloody hell, yes! She had never before heard the word Mrs Goodall had just used but she knew its exact meaning. She could sense it in the way Mrs Goodall was acting. She was unable to say so, of course. She could not speak at all she was so overwhelmed with it and to think she had come into this room expecting at the least a telling-off, at worst the sack. Instead she was to leave Primrose Bank which would, no matter what Mrs Goodall thought, be no hardship at all, move into the farmhouse where, if the kitchen and this room were anything to go by, would be a bloody sight better than anything she had known up to now.

Not a hint of what was going on inside her head showed in her impassive expression and in that first moment Eliza Goodall felt a prick of disappointment. She had expected a great outpouring of jubilation, excitement, wonder, gratitude, perhaps tears, but Poppy sat like a stone on her chair, her face as white as the petals on the roses in the hearth, and just as silken smooth, though in it her eyes blazed as brilliantly as the stars in a winter dark sky. And at last Eliza understood.

Poppy's heart fluttered in her chest. She wanted so desperately to say to this wonderful woman who had already given her so much that she would never let her down. That she would give thanks to her to the end of her days for what was being offered to her. How many girls like Poppy Appleton, with Poppy Appleton's background and upbringing, if you could call what her mam and pa had done for her an upbringing, had the chance to learn a proper trade, a well-paid trade that could be done anywhere in the land. Not that she had any intention of leaving to find out, ever! And on top of that she was to learn to read and write and perhaps one day, when Dilys was too old, Mrs Goodall might consider her, Poppy Appleton, for head dairymaid.

It was heady stuff. It took the breath from her lungs,

the speech from her lips, the capacity for movement from her limbs. Dammit to hell, why couldn't she open her gob and tell Mrs Goodall how she felt? But something vice-like had her in its grip making her speechless and she could do nothing but stare, her enormous eyes locked with those of her mistress.

Mrs Goodall seemed to understand, which didn't surprise her. She had always understood how it was with Poppy Appleton. She leaned forward again, placing her forearms on the table and clasping her hands together loosely.

She smiled. "I see you approve, Poppy," she said softly, gladly, Poppy thought. "But first we must speak to your parents," though Eliza Goodall laboured under no delusion that Reuben and Martha Appleton might object to the removal of one of their tribe from the overcrowded cottage. They'd miss the work the child did or perhaps, on the other hand, being a careless and slovenly lot, they would merely adapt themselves to living once more in the filth and clutter Poppy kept at bay. She'd have to make sure the child did not dash over there whenever she had a moment and scrub the place down, which would be just like her. Eliza Goodall had plans for Poppy, beyond even teaching her to read and write, and it didn't include playing skivvy to ten – was it ten? – good-for-nothing Appletons.

She felt the warmth and excited anticipation flow through her and it was all she could do not to stand up and move round the desk, to kneel before Poppy, take her hands between her own and tell her not to be afraid. She'd come to no harm under Eliza Goodall's wing, just the opposite. She meant to make something special of this young girl who, apart from her bonny looks which Eliza had never had, reminded her of herself at the same age. She'd had a love of learning, encouraged by her father. A need for order, a yearning for more than she had and if she'd been a man would have done well in the world of business. Her own sons saw her as no more than Mother, fond of her but with no interest in what interested her. Perhaps if her baby daughters had lived it would have filled some empty space within her, given her a vessel into which she could have poured the strength and purpose in herself. A repository for the skills she herself had, not just in making a success of her dairy but her love of music, her talent at the piano, her passion for books and interest in art. Think of taking her to the Walker Art Gallery, the library, the museum, the theatre . . . Oh, Lord, all the places her husband and sons had no interest in, indeed thought of as "unmanly".

To this child for whom she had felt a fascination from that first moment in the rain last May, she could give it all. All the stored-up knowledge that nobody else wanted. The business acumen which had proved itself and which was a source of quiet pride to her. Just look at how adaptable the child was, over the last few months exceeding all Eliza's expectations which had formed in the cottage in Primrose Bank when she had been offered a cup of tea by a barefoot ragamuffin who had acted the gracious hostess as though born to it. And she had proved as good as Dilys in the dairy with her proficiency, her diligence, her quickness, her deft and graceful care, her bright intelligence and spirit.

It filled Eliza Goodall with a bubbling joy and she wanted it to begin at once.

"Would you like me to show you the room you're to have, Poppy? That's if you decide to come. We have four attic rooms. Cook has one, Aggie and Clara another and May and Nelly the third." She paused for a moment, a frown wrinkling the bridge of her nose as though at some distant troubling thought, then it cleared. She stood up briskly and smoothed her skirt. "You would have your lessons here with me at the end of the day but I thought it might be best if you were to have the fourth room to yourself. You might need to study or perhaps read one of the books I shall introduce you to so you see . . ." She left the sentence unfinished but there was still that feeling of something troubling her, as though at the back of her mind she was convincing herself that everything was going to work out for the best. She knew she was favouring this young girl and she was well aware that there might be resentment among the others, none of whom could read or write, that at eleven years old the new dairymaid was to learn both, and to have her own room to boot, while Aggie and Clara, who had been with her for years, were still to share. They had made no objection before, despite the spare bedroom, since they got on well, as did May and Nelly, mainly because Nelly was so even-tempered it was hard for May to fall out with her.

But this! She hadn't even discussed it with Tom and yet, would he care? As long as he had three good meals a day, a warm bed at night and no squabbling among the female servants he would make no objection, surely?

Poppy watched her, noting the play of expressions on Mrs Goodall's face and her intuitive mind knew at once what was troubling her. What were the others to think, the kitchen servants, the housemaids, and the two who were her friends in the dairy, but she couldn't turn it down because of that, could she? She couldn't allow a chance like this to slip through her fingers just in case it offended someone, could she? She was only eleven and small for her age but she'd fight the lot of them for this and if they didn't like it then they could bloody lump it.

But first things first. Mrs Goodall had spoken of going down to Primrose Bank to see her mam and pa and somehow she must get there before her mistress and make sure the place was as presentable as she could get it. It had not been too bad this morning when she left since she had done a bit of "bottoming" last night, shifting their Iris and Arthur, grumbling as she did it, from place to place, glad that her pa was at the pub, Rose out sparking with Alfie Hargreaves and the rest sitting on their backsides in the late evening sunshine. All except their Douglas, of course, and only the devil knew where he'd got to. Herbert and Eustace were up the field with the Glover kids and it had been a good opportunity to get a bit done. But what would it look like now, or rather this evening after a day of her family's orderless activities had put it back to the state it was in every night when she got home?

She stood up and, in an action that mirrored her mistress whose every move she admired beyond measure, smoothed down her dark grey skirt, then, now that ordinary, everyday things were occupying her mind and not the magical, fairytale wonder of what was to come, she became brisk and businesslike.

"I'd best get back ter't dairy, ma'am," she said, moving towards the door. "Dilys'll wonder where I am."

"Dilys knows you're with me, child. I'm sure she could spare you for a few more minutes. I thought . . . well, I'd like you to have a peep at your room. I put in . . . one or two things you might like."

Poppy turned towards her and her face, which had lost that white, shocked look of being knocked sideways by something she could not understand, was rosy again, rosy and soft and curiously unchildlike. Her life had made her unchildlike. She had, from an early age, made up her mind that she would not succumb to the slatternly ways of her mother and sisters and it had been a hard, uphill, wearying, *ageing* experience, but she had not wavered. She was an unusual child but she was just that, a child, and suddenly with this last promise of something special it all became too much for her. It bore her on to the tears she had not shed for years. Not since Frankie Glover had knocked her down with his hard, twelve-year-old fist and split her lip open. She wouldn't have cried then but she had been only five years old and the sudden awareness that no one really cared, not even her mam, had distressed her more than the pain of the split lip.

Now she shed the tears of a child who is overcome to the point where she is no longer able to bottle it up. She bent her head until her chin was on her chest, sobbing as though her heart were broken, her slender body shaking, her shoulders heaving, her nose running.

Eliza started forward. "Poppy, child, what is it? Has something . . . ?"

"Nay . . . please, ma'am . . . I can't . . . I just can't stand any more. It's all so . . . lovely." Her voice shook with the force of her emotion. "Nowt like this 'as ever 'appened ter me an' I'm . . . I'm just . . . bowled over, like. I must go . . . eeh, I'm that sorry an' after all yer've said. I'll see yer at 'ome . . . later and then p'raps termorrer when . . ."

Whirling about, she grasped the door latch, lifting it clumsily, and before Eliza could say another word of comfort or reassurance to tell her she fully understood, she ran from the room.

That evening the Appleton family were vastly put out when their Poppy – and should they feel surprise at it? they asked one another – had them moving their bums from here to there and back again, crying shrilly that Mrs Goodall was to call and would Arthur shift himself and put on his boots. Mrs Goodall didn't want to look at, or sniff for that matter, his filthy feet, she told him and did her mam think she could comb her hair in honour of their visitor.

"Me 'air? What's up wi' me 'air?" Martha, who had had a hard day helping with the harvest, wanted to know and what in all that was holy was Mrs Goodall coming to see them about? Surely she could have summoned whoever it was she wanted to speak to, to her back door for a word, and honestly all she wanted to do was put her bum down in the armchair and her swollen feet on the stool until it was time to climb the ladder for bed. It was too bad, really it was, and them all worn out with a day's work and what did she want with them? she asked Poppy over and over again plaintively.

Poppy couldn't or wouldn't say.

You could have knocked her down with a duck's feather, Martha was to say again and again, stunned with shock when she learned what Mrs Goodall wanted from them. First to Reuben and then to any one of her children who would listen to her. Her older daughters didn't know what all the bloody fuss was about, they said, and were astounded when their Poppy rounded on them, telling them off for saying "bloody", a word which had been frequently on her own lips up to now. Anyway, catch them wanting to live up at the farm with that old school teacher, they added. Worse than being in gaol and as for learning to read and write, what bloody good would that do their Poppy? She'd still be nowt but a skivvy in a dairy. Still, there'd be one less to share the palliasse so something good had come out of it.

But despite her heart-searching, Martha was impressed with what was to happen to one of her own. Unlike her daughters she had the illiterate woman's awe for the written word and the thought that their Poppy was to be initiated into its mysteries was a marvel and yet, at the same time, a worry to her. Mrs Goodall told her that Poppy was quite unique – that meant different, she explained – and for some reason she and Poppy had exchanged a knowing smile which excluded everyone else, even her who was Poppy's mam. And of course they knew their Poppy was different. She always had been, right from a babby, with all her madness about being clean, as opposed to mucky which didn't bother the rest of them a bit. As long as they'd a full belly, which they had for the most part even if at times it was only taters when Reuben spent too long at the Grimshaw Arms, that was all that mattered.

Still, she'd be sorry to lose her, she told Reuben that night in the grubby depths of their bed, which was to become a great deal grubbier without the ministrations of her youngest daughter. It was all very well for Mrs Goodall, who had only those two lads of hers, to talk about the advantages – that means good things, with another smile at Poppy – that this would bring her but Poppy was Martha's little lass and there'd been something . . . funny in Mrs Goodall's face whenever she glanced at Poppy and Martha's mother's heart had not cared for it. Martha Appleton was not familiar with the word possessive so funny was the best she could come up with. She was not prepared to admit that she was jealous of the obvious regard Poppy felt for Mrs Goodall, nor a sadness that she and Reuben couldn't provide for the child what Mrs Goodall was to provide. On the other hand she did wonder whether they were letting the lass get above herself with all this learning that was to be stuffed in her head. What did Reuben think?

Reuben snored gently in reply and on the other side of the curtain which divided the room Poppy heard her mother sigh. She was sorry to leave Mam and Pa and wished it could be different but it wasn't. She knew her mam was anxious about her and the loss her wage might mean to the family but she'd make it plain, when she got her mam on her own, that she'd still put it in her hand every pay day. Not for the others, she'd make that clear, but for her mam.

No, you had to grab the chances when they came at you in this life and that's what she meant to do. Starting tomorrow! Tomorrow she was to take whatever belonged to her, though what that could be in this poor house she couldn't imagine, and carry them up to the farmhouse. She would be shown her room, the room in which, for the first time in her life, she was to sleep alone, and from then on, what wonders were to be unfolded for Poppy Appleton's eyes to behold?

Pushing their Iris away and removing her knee from the small of her back she turned over and in the thick and foul-smelling atmosphere of unwashed bodies Poppy fell over the edge of anticipation and into a child's deep and dreamless sleep.

4

It *did* cause trouble and the first intimation of it came from Tom Goodall. He demanded to know if his wife was off her head or something, to have thought up such a bloody daft scheme. Teach one to read and they'd all want to be at it, sitting about with their noses in a book from morning till night with no work done and then where would they be?

"Don't be silly, Tom," Eliza said mildly. "Not one of them is capable of learning. If they're not too old like Aggie and Clara and Dilys, they're not bright enough. Can you imagine May or Nelly with a book in their hands? They've had no education despite it being available to them, though the day will come when it will be compulsory, I'm sure of that. The 1870 Education Act," she went on with that air of knowing everything, which irritated Tom, "says that a school must be placed within the reach of every English child in the land but until those schools are built it doesn't do them much good, does it?"

"No, I suppose not," Tom grunted impatiently, running his hand over his thinning hair which had once been thick and dark. He was a well-set-up, contented man, was Tom Goodall but he had the firm chin and the tightly satisfied lips of a man who is contented because he generally got his own way. But he was out of his depth here. His sons had both gone to the local grammar school and had received sufficient education, at least in his opinion, to equip them for their future as farmers. Eliza had wanted more for them but as neither of the lads had showed any interest nor ambition for the fine university she had envisaged for them, it had come to nothing. As long as they could read a farming manual and add up a column of figures, what more was required of them? Tom had argued and that had been that.

He didn't agree with her over the question of education for the masses either but he was wary of getting into an argument over something that he knew nothing about. She was passionate about learning, was Eliza, and she was clever and if she said compulsory schooling was coming then come it would. It was just that this fancy she had to take up the Appleton girl, who came from the worst family on his farm – and like others before him he wondered why he kept them on – might it not create more trouble than it was worth? Eliza had explained to him how helpful it would be to have one of her girls able to read and add up, and he supposed he could see her point but he did wish she'd consulted him first. Tom Goodall liked to think that his word was law in this his own domain and it was perhaps more the way she had gone about it than the actual deed that annoyed him. She'd no right without asking him high-handedly to remove the child from her parents and fetch her to live at the farmhouse. And supposing, when she had learned what Eliza was to teach her, she started to lord it over the others, he asked her, thinking herself better than them? What then? And having a bedroom to herself would only cause resentment and ill-feeling among the other servants, particularly the two older ones who surely should be given the chance of having the same. No, it wouldn't work. Why, they'd have that woman who spent her days on her knees with a scrub bucket, the one he frequently fell over in the passage, demanding an education next, he muttered, but he was running out of steam by then, not really caring enough to argue further. He'd had his say and let Eliza know that the child was allowed to stay only on his say-so.

Gradually he forgot she had not always been there at his table three times a day. Besides, she was a taking little thing, comical as a clown in her enormous cap, all big eyes and as mim as a mouse just as he liked females to be, answering only when spoken to, and that politely. She was a dainty eater too, making none of the rootling, slurping noises young Nelly made and was scrubbed so clean her childish skin glowed. It was obvious she thought herself to be the luckiest lass this side of the Mersey. Tom liked that. Though it was not he who had brought her here it was his benevolence that had allowed it and he found he enjoyed the shining look of gratitude she cast in his direction. She would slip into her place on the bench that stood beside the table just before five in the morning, nodding shyly at him then, her eyes cast down, would plough through a great bowl of porridge followed by eggs, bacon, fried bread, mushrooms, eating as much as himself and his two sons, he swore, growing before his very eyes, stoking herself up for the first half of the morning before elevenses were taken round to the dairy.

The same at dinner-time when she would appear with the other dairymaids, eating her head off and, he noticed, more at ease with them there. Inclined to chatter and laugh, not too much or he'd have given her a stern look. He liked to eat in a bit of peace and if the servants became too frisky he soon let them know it didn't please him.

Poppy's new life was a revelation to her. The first thing Mrs Goodall insisted upon was a bath. She was not even sure she knew exactly what that was, only that it had something to do with water which she didn't mind since she hated dirt. She was to take one of these mysterious things every week, she was told, winter and summer. All the other maids did so, even Nelly who had never mentioned a word of it to her which was peculiar to say the least. Nelly's life was so uneventful Poppy would have thought the weekly stripping off and immersing herself in a tub of hot water was something Nelly would have had a lot to say about.

She nearly died of embarrassment the first time.

"Off with those duds, child," Mrs Goodall said briskly, eyeing Poppy as if she were a chicken she was thinking of plucking in readiness for the oven. Poppy's mouth fell open then shut again, lips compressed primly at the thought of standing in front of another human being without a shred of clothing to keep her decent, but Mrs Goodall was becoming impatient.

"Come along, Poppy, all of them, yes, even your drawers and then get into the tub. The water's just nice. There's the soap and a wash cloth and don't be long because there is only the one tub and the others are waiting their turn."

Poppy left her cap on. Well, with her hair being so long and thick, when she sat down in the water, as Mrs Goodall was implying she should, it would come up to her chest and her hair would get wet.

Mrs Goodall laughed out loud then reached to whip off her cap and her hair fell about her. She was glad because she felt so exposed with not a stitch on her. She'd never in her life taken all her clothes off and certainly never immersed her whole body in water. A good wash to her was to scrub at every bit of flesh that was visible including her neck and ears, her hands and arms to her shoulders and her feet and legs up to her knees. But the rest of her was covered up so it couldn't really get dirty, could it?

She was as surprised as her mistress when, standing nervously on the rug on which the tin tub had been set before being filled, she saw the distinct line of demarcation where the "good washes" she had had, particularly since last May when she began working for Mrs Goodall, came to an end. The rest of her was a sort of dull grey with creases and lines where the dirt had become ingrained. Awful it had looked and she felt deeply ashamed of it. She had seen it before, of course, when Mrs Goodall had tricked her out in her new clothes when she began work in the dairy but she'd been alone when she changed into them and her body's familiarity had caused her not to notice it.

Mrs Goodall was plainly shocked.

"I see we have our work cut out here, Poppy," she said gravely, "so I'd best give you a hand. And your hair, well, I think it should be cut shorter, don't you? Has it never known the scissors?"

Poppy frowned. She couldn't remember ever having seen such a thing as scissors in the place which, until this morning, had been her home.

"No, ma'am," she whispered, shivering, not knowing whether the cutting of hair was painful but expecting the worst.

She couldn't really describe how she felt when it was all over and when she tried to tell May, whose turn it was next, the scullery maid told her to "shurrup an' look lively since I want ter get to me bed even if Miss Clever Clogs don't." Poppy didn't care. She felt as though she'd shed pounds and pounds in weight and she was convinced if she didn't keep a good hold on a chair back or a door knob she'd float right up to the ceiling, bobbing there like a balloon. Having her hair cut hadn't hurt at all, thank goodness – trying out one of her new, more refined expressions – and when it was done, the hair washed and dried, her brown curls had sprung about her head in a riot of sweet-smelling abundance, reminding her of one of the flowers in Mrs Goodall's garden, soft and thick and lovely to touch. It fell over her forehead to her eyebrows and covered her ears and the back of her neck but when she tried her cap on again she felt just the same as always which was good since she didn't want them all staring.

Mrs Goodall had handed her two clean white nightgowns, telling her what they were since Poppy had looked perplexed, not having the slightest idea what their purpose might be. She said she was to wear one in bed tonight and the second one was for next week after she'd had her bath. The first one could then be washed. The same with her two sets of new underclothes, she explained. Yes, her underclothes were her drawers and bodice, she continued patiently, and when her hair was completely dry Poppy was to turn out the lamp as she had shown her, climb into bed and go to sleep.

May and Nelly were to bathe next so the tub was removed to their room. Mrs Goodall said goodnight, the door was closed and for the first time in her just over eleven years Poppy Appleton was alone in a room of her own. It was nearly dark out but the oil lamp which Mrs Goodall had left her formed a golden circle about the small attic room, flickering ever so slightly in a stray draught from the open window. It spilled over the top of the pine chest of drawers – the drawers empty but for her clean nightdress and underclothes – turning the wood to a shade of pale polished saffron. There was a drawn-thread runner on it, white but tinted to lemon by the lamplight. On the runner stood a bowl of flowers, of what sort Poppy didn't know and she was not aware that Eliza Goodall had picked and arranged them herself. The iron bedstead was covered in a white cotton bedspread, easy to wash, Poppy's practical mind thought. The ceiling sloped and beneath the tiny dormer window was a washstand supporting a large, rose-painted water jug and basin. Behind the door were a table and chair, the chair tucked beneath the table, and on the table were half a dozen books, some leather-bound. At the window, hanging from a brass pole, were white curtains to match the whitewashed walls.

Standing beside the lamp on the chest of drawers was a pretty, tilting mirror set in a pine frame to match the rest of the furniture. Poppy approached it cautiously for the first time, staring in astonishment at her own reflection. Her skin was the colour of honey in the light from the lamp and her eyes, wide and intense with nerves, looked like enormous pools of grey-blue iced water in the flush of her face.

But it was the sight of her hair that amazed her more than anything else. It was dry now and it bounced and swirled about her head, the colour of it gold shot and silken. Was that Poppy Appleton in there? Was that how she looked? Were her eyes blue or grey, and how had she failed to notice, since after all she had seen it hanging down to her waist before it was cut, the vibrant, curling softness of her hair? It must be the washing that did it, she decided, and the shortness of it, but she didn't know what her mam would say when she saw the state of it. Perhaps she could keep her cap on when she went to Primrose Bank, she thought distractedly.

Sighing, unexpectedly homesick for her mam and pa, who had never been anything other than heedlessly kind to her, she turned away from the mirror, bending down to smooth the hooked rug on which her bare feet rested. It was made from many colours and materials and was quite beautiful to her child's eyes, like the flags which lined the dairy floor. Everything in the room was beautiful and she couldn't think why she suddenly felt so bloody lonely. There, she'd said the "bloody" word, just in her head, of course, but Mrs Goodall said it wasn't nice to swear and she really was doing her best not to. It was hard at times when something came to trouble, annoy or perplex her but she was doing her best to cure herself of the habit. Other words, too, that Mrs Goodall didn't like though she didn't really understand why, but there, if Mrs Goodall said it was wrong then that was good enough for Poppy Appleton.

Her eye fell on the books which were placed in a row on the table, prevented from falling over at each end by two heavy objects shaped like fat animals of some sort. At least they had snouts and eyes and ears so she supposed they were animals, though not from these parts she decided.

She moved hesitantly across the small room, her shadow moving with her, floating and wavering on the wall and ceiling, a blurred blackness against the golden orange glow of the lamplight.

The books smelled lovely. She hadn't known that books could smell lovely but then she knew nothing about such things, did she? She bent her head until her nose was an inch from the end one, breathing in the curious aroma of it, then, greatly daring, she put her finger on it. She let it rest there for a moment and when nothing dreadful happened drew the book slowly and gently from its place in the row. Holding it with both hands for fear of dropping it, she placed it flat on the table. Again she waited. It lay there, the first book she had ever touched in her life, then, drawing in an apprehensive breath, her eyes widening, she opened it.

The first thing she saw was a cat! Yes, a bloody cat –

forgetting her vow – sitting on a mat something like the one beside the bed, licking its paw and seeming to smile as though it had just dipped it into a saucer of cream. A cat! Right there in front of her and as real as the one in the barn on the far side of the yard.

Tentatively she touched it, running an awed finger across its tawny-coloured fur and was surprised to find it cold and flat. She turned another page and there, running after what looked like the ball Glover's lot had once found, was a cheerful black and white dog. There were all kinds of funny marks on the pages, none she could recognise, but the pictures were grand, cows and sheep and horses and hens and pigs and indeed everything that she herself had seen a hundred times about the farm. It was a miracle, really it was, to see living things captured and put on the pages of a book. Now and again she'd had a glance in the tattered papers their Iris salvaged from somewhere or other. They'd had pictures of ladies and gentlemen in them but such strange and incomprehensible creatures they were, Poppy had found she could not identify or believe in them, not like the dog and the cat and the horse in the book. The colours were splendid too, and they appeared so real it was quite amazing.

But her feet were cold and it was shadowed in this corner of the room. She glanced about her furtively as though there might be someone watching, someone who would be horrified if they could see what she was up to then, holding her breath, she picked up the book, tiptoed across the rug and climbed gingerly into the bed. Infinitely precious, the book was held away from her, as carefully and meticulously as she might hold a crystal bowl which could shatter at the slightest touch.

Leaning back on the pillow, the light from the lamp falling

across its pages, she studied each one in turn, her face serious and intent, her eyes wide with wonder. Through the half-open window an owl quavered in the spinney but the other night creatures were silent as though they must not disturb the enchantment of the child.

Later, as she made her own way to bed and seeing the line of light beneath the child's door, Eliza opened it softly and peeped inside. Her face melted into a euphoric smile. It had happened as she had hoped it would. Moving quietly so as not to disturb her she took the book from Poppy's sleeping hand and turned out the lamp, her heart filled with something she did not as yet recognise.

Poppy could understand and read every letter in the *Picture Alphabet Book* by the end of October, the very book that had taken her on her own first journey into the joy of learning. Six weeks was the target set by Eliza Goodall when she realised that Poppy was that exceptional being, a true scholar. Well, perhaps not a scholar in the academic sense of the word, she told Tom in the privacy of their bedroom, but what she could only describe as a "learner". Someone who absorbed knowledge as easily and as eagerly as she ate the good food Cook put in front of her and the pints of fresh milk Eliza encouraged her to drink, her being such a skinny little thing.

"It'll come to nowt," Tom grumbled, climbing into bed and yawning. "You'll see, it'll lose its novelty before the month's out. Not that it matters. She'll never make more than a good dairymaid."

"You're wrong, Tom. She's an original is Poppy." Eliza finished plaiting her thick greying hair then reached to turn out the lamp.

"Rubbish," said her husband, turning his back on her as she climbed into bed, falling at once into the deep

sleep of a man who works hard and long and is entitled to it.

It had begun on her second night at Long Reach Farm.

She had been considerably startled when, at the sharp
knock on her door, she awoke that first morning, the knock
and the crowing of the cock right outside her window
bringing her up out of her nest of warm blankets like a
small animal leaping from its burrow. She had slept well,
not waking once in the night. She had been worried that
she might wake up and, finding herself alone, be lonely, or
even afraid without the sighing, snoring, shifting presence
of her family about her. It had not happened but when she
opened her eyes the shock and wonder of finding herself
where she was had been intimidating and at the same time
filled her with excited anticipation.

First she relieved herself in the chamber pot which matched
the jug and basin and which was cunningly hidden beneath
the washstand, marvelling at its beauty. Then, even though
she'd had the bath the night before, she gave herself a
thorough all-over wash in the cold water she found in
the jug. There was the lovely smelling soap in the dish, a
wash cloth beside it, and a soft towel hanging over the rail
at the side of the washstand; having enjoyed the feeling of
light-headed freedom from dirt the night before she thought
she'd try it again. She couldn't bear to think of those dreadful
tide marks she had carried before the bath and, besides, she
was putting on brand-new, never-before-worn – by anybody
– *underclothes*.

Her day with Dilys and Nelly was exactly as it had been
every day since she had begun work in the dairy, apart from
Dilys's good-natured enquiry into her first experience of
sleeping in a room and a bed of her own. And of course there

was the lovely comforting feel of the enormous breakfast she had started out with. Trying not to think of the slabs of cold porridge her family would be eating, that is if anyone had remembered to make it the night before, she had eaten everything Cook had put in front of her, unaware of Mr Goodall's amused eye on her, or of May's resentful chucking of her full plate down before her.

"There's lucky you are, child," Dilys said in that funny Welsh way she had, "to be chosen by Mrs Goodall for this grand learning, but we've work to do by 'ere."

Mrs Goodall was to be off to the market the next day so Poppy and Dilys made butter shells while Nelly weighed and stamped neat half-pounds and pounds of butter, using the special set of scales kept in the butter room for the purpose. Mrs Goodall's stamp had been especially carved for her with an oblong medallion on it, in the centre of which were the letters EG. Wreathing round the medallion were entwined rosebuds, perfect in every detail. It looked quite wonderful when the stamp was used correctly and Nelly, after three years of practice, was a dab hand at it.

Poppy and Dilys stood side by side before the scrubbed stone slab, both with a pair of "patters". Taking up a piece of butter about the size of a pigeon's egg and with a couple of deft twists of the wrist, they produced a little shell of butter, curved and crinkled, closed and pointed at one end, open like a petal at the other. They were as perfect as any shell picked up at a wave's edge. Twenty-four to a pound and very popular with the midddle-class hostess who liked something a bit special to put before her dinner guests.

Nelly, having finished the weighing and stamping, began to scrub where she had worked then went to fetch the big, wicker butter baskets, a pile of ready-cut oblongs of paper and a neatly folded heap of snowy butter muslin.

"Go an' tell mistress we're ready by 'ere, lass," Dilys instructed her and when Mrs Goodall appeared, bringing her order book with her, the four of them began to pack pounds, half-pounds and shells of butter into the basket in accordance with the orders in the book, those that Mrs Goodall's customers had given her last market day.

There were eggs, brown and white, graded into sizes, washed and polished by Poppy, counted out and arranged in muslin-covered baskets. Scrubbed wooden trays were carefully filled with plucked and dressed carcasses of fowls, each one holding half a dozen, all of which would be packed into the cart, then a neat tarpaulin cover drawn over the lot. Mrs Goodall liked to be at the market by seven thirty so all must be done by nightfall so that she could make an early start.

It was as night fell and the evening meal was over that Mrs Goodall stood up and indicated to Poppy that she was to do the same and follow her.

"And you can remove your cap now, Poppy," she said over her shoulder as she made for the door to the passage. "There is no need to wear it when you are in the house."

There was total silence as those about the table assimilated this astonishing remark, waiting to see Poppy Appleton remove her ballooning cap. They'd all heard of the bath and the cutting of her hair, even Mr Goodall and his sons, though it had gone in one ear and out of the other where they were concerned. None of them had ever seen her capless, not even Dilys and Nelly, apart from that first day when Mrs Goodall had issued her with one. All the maidservants had long hair, like Mrs Goodall herself, either scraped back into a tight bun, or tidily crammed into the confines of a mob cap. Neat and clean they must be but it seemed the child's hair had been so long and tangled Mrs Goodall had had no option but to hack it off.

The silence went on and on as Poppy, giving the impression she was going to the block, dragged off her cap and pushed a small hand through her hair, her face crimson but resolute in its defiance. It was not her fault she looked such a guy, was it? her expression appealed, and if one of them, especially that May who had resented her ever since it was revealed she was to learn her letters, said a word Poppy didn't care for, then . . . Well, she didn't know what she'd do, for this job and this chance meant everything to her and she could hardly cause a ruckus at the table, could she?

Her glossy hair leaped from under her hand and about her small head with a merry will of its own, falling at once into a riot of shining brown curls about her face and ears. Her eyes were enormous, smudged with thick brown lashes, a soft blue-grey that was like velvet in her peach-bloomed, honey-tinted face. She lifted her pointed chin and set her full, creamy pink lips, glaring about as though daring anyone to laugh.

"Bloody hell," said young Master Johnny, the spoon carrying his second helping of Cook's baked batter pudding with stewed plums to his lips, tilting and dripping its contents on to his shirt.

"That'll be enough of that, lad, if you please," his father admonished, but he, like the rest of them, was struck dumb by the change in the little lass. A child she was, no more than ten or eleven but by God she looked right comely without that ridiculous cap Eliza insisted all the maidservants wear. Perhaps that was why. With young men in the house perhaps any attractions the females might have needed quenching and those bloody caps certainly did the trick!

"Well, tha' look raight grand, chuck," Cook, who came

from Yorkshire, said kindly. "I never knew tha' was so bonny." She chuckled richly, "An' I'd shut me gob if I were thi', May Jebson, lest the flies gerrin."

In a sudden glow of pleasure, since it seemed she didn't look too bad with her hair cut off, Poppy followed her mistress from the room and into the parlour, conscious of the open-mouthed stares which went with her.

"Sit down at the table, Poppy," Mrs Goodall told her, and though outwardly she was calm, inside Poppy trembled in trepidation. She was not afraid of Mrs Goodall, far from it, for she, like the rest of the servants, recognised a kindly mistress when she had one. It was fear of letting her down, of being unable to do what Mrs Goodall wanted her to do. Of being stupid and clumsy so that Mrs Goodall would despise her, abandon her and where would her grand chance be then? Not here, at Long Reach Farm where she was so happy. Dairymaids were ten a penny, she had learned that, but a dairymaid who knew her letters was something special.

She sat down, straightened her shoulders and set her soft mouth firmly. She lifted her eyes from the large sheet of paper set before her on which there were dozens of queer shapes and looked at Mrs Goodall with steadfast attention.

Eliza cleared her throat and picked up a ruler with a strangely trembling hand. Her own heart was going ten to the dozen but like Poppy her apprehension did not show in the smooth calm of her face.

"Now then, Poppy, you see before you a sheet of paper on which I have inscribed the twenty-six letters of the alphabet. You must learn these letters in order that you may read and write. Without them you are nothing. I will say each one to you and you will repeat it after me."

Twenty-six times the quiet voice of the teacher fell into the silence, pointing at each letter with the ruler as she did so and twenty-six times the pupil's voice repeated the sound, faint and timorous.

"But it is not the A or the B or the C that are important, Poppy, but their sounds," Eliza continued, looking down at the glossy curls and the fragile neck of the child as she bent over the paper. She would have liked to put a reassuring hand on her head but she knew it would only distract them both, though for different reasons.

Phonetically she repeated the sound each letter made and, totally bewildered, Poppy repeated them dully. She had been told these funny little marks were one thing and sounded like thus and now Mrs Goodall was telling her that the first thing she'd said wasn't right and the second thing was, so how the bloody hell – forgetting in her confusion her promise not to swear even to herself – was she to make sense of it?

Then Mrs Goodall got the book out. The familiar book with the smiling cat and the running dog and the horse that was pulling a plough. Within half an hour she had hit upon the connection between the picture of an eye and the letter I. She had never seen a peacock in her life but the sound as she repeated, "P is for Peacock," after Mrs Goodall made perfect sense and when Mrs Goodall pointed out that P was for Poppy as well, she was enchanted.

"What else can you think of beginning with P, Poppy? That is the P there. Can you recognise it?" pointing with the little stick she held in her hand to the book in front of Poppy.

Poppy studied it to get it firmly in her mind before she answered.

"Yes," she said positively.

"Well then, what else begins with P? On the farm, say?"

Poppy considered it, mentally going through the animals

that lived at Long Reach Farm, frowning in deep concentration as she said to herself, "P . . . P . . . P," then it came to her in a blaze of excitement.

"Pig."

"Very good. Anything else?"

Poppy racked her brains, then, as light shone even more brightly into the dark corners of her unused mind, she turned exultantly to her teacher, bouncing, like the child she was, up and down in her chair.

"Plough," she beamed.

"Excellent, excellent, clever girl." Mrs Goodall smiled down at her. "And have you noticed anything else about your own name? Your name is Poppy and begins with P but what else does your name have in it? See, I'll print it out for you and then you shall tell me."

It came to her after much wrinkling of her brow and hunching of her shoulders. There were five little "marks" that made up her name, she could see that. She had learned to count to ten, having ten fingers, from Dilys. The first one was a P. But hold on, she said out loud to her fascinated teacher, there were two more Ps in the middle of it. She turned up a face burning with the fervour of one who has just discovered the Holy Grail.

"Good, very good, I'm pleased with you and your progress in such a short time but we must stop now. Yes, I know you're interested and want to go on and so do I but it's getting late. I want you in bed each night by eight but if you like you may take the alphabet book back to your room to study it. See if you can find any more letters you recognise. Only for half an hour, mind, then you must go to sleep. I'll look in and make sure you've turned off your light."

It began that night, the strong bond that was to grow between the woman and the child. It had been unbalanced until then and was to continue to be so for a long time, as it is between generations, the child holding the woman in awe, admiring her, imitating her mannerisms and speech, wanting to be exactly like her. The woman, though she was not consciously aware of it, had cast the child in the role her own daughter would have had, a parent-child relationship that made no allowance for Poppy Appleton's independent nature and upbringing.

One day they would be equals but for now they were both completely satisfied with no thought of where this evening was to lead.

5

May said that if Miss Clever Clogs didn't give over rattling on about "A is for Apple," and "B is for Bat," that "one and one is two and two and two is four," she'd land her one. Who did she think she was, anyroad, showing off, butting into every conversation with her everlasting boasting and criticising those who were above her? Who the heck cared that "the cat sat on the mat," and anyway, if that's what all this reading lark was about, she was glad she'd not bothered with it, just as though Mrs Goodall had given her the chance and she'd turned it down.

"Well, I like that," Poppy answered furiously, for the one thing she was most careful to avoid was exactly what May accused her of. Mrs Goodall had impressed upon her most vigorously that on no account was she to flaunt her new-found skills in front of the other servants. Most of them would not begrudge it to her and would probably be interested to hear of her progress but there were others who would not, naming no names, and so Poppy was to keep it to herself, unless asked, of course.

May was jealous, Poppy knew that, violently jealous and would make trouble for her if she could. "Miss Clever Clogs" was the only insult she could get away with, at least in front of the others but if she caught Poppy on her own she called her every disparaging name she could lay her tongue to, knowing Poppy wouldn't tell on her. One day, she would whisper, just wait, one day you'll come a cropper and I'll be there to see it.

"Sticks and stones may break my bones, May Jebson, but words will never hurt me," Poppy would fling back at her, which was something she'd read in a book and it certainly flummoxed May who could make neither head nor tail of what it meant. When it came to a war of words Poppy, as well as being able to read, had a quicker mind than May which often left the scullery maid with her mouth hanging open in confusion. She'd never got over "the kid" being given a room of her own when May had to share with daft Nelly and whenever Mrs Goodall was absent she wouldn't leave it alone, picking at it like a scab on a grazed knee, never allowing it to heal until Cook turned on her and told her that would do.

"What's it like?" Nelly had begged to know on the day after the first lesson. "Did it 'urt much?"

" 'Urt?" Poppy was bewildered. "Why should it 'urt?"

"Well, all them funny squiggles like them in Mrs Goodall's book bein' forced inter yer 'ead. I shoulda thought it'd 'urt like mad fer them ter gerrinside."

Nelly had come from the Female Orphan Asylum in Myrtle Street and though some effort had been made to teach the inmates to read and write, Nelly had not been an apt pupil. She was big and strong. She had been at the asylum since someone had handed her in like a poorly wrapped parcel as an infant, but she had been well fed and cared for. She was of a cheerful disposition with no resentment at the life fate had handed out to her. She'd clean and scrub, do the laundry, iron and indeed anything of a domestic nature but put a book in her hand and she turned to stone. Still, what she did learn was enough to qualify her for the job of dairymaid and Eliza Goodall had never regretted bringing her to Long Reach Farm when she was twelve years old.

"They tried wi' me at Myrtle Street an' by 'eck it didn't 'alf 'urt me 'ead. They 'ad ter stop else I think I'd a' died," she said simply.

"Well, it don't 'urt me," Poppy answered, somewhat scornful of Nelly's disclosure, "an' it wouldn't a' killed yer, yer daft 'apporth. I know it's 'ard sometimes," thinking back to her struggle with the letter X which, no matter how furiously she tried she just could not find a "stands for" word. There were several and Mrs Goodall had told them to her but they were not words she had ever come across, nor knew the meaning of so Mrs Goodall had said to forget it for now. Not that she meant to, of course. Having come this far she didn't mean to let any daft old letter get the better of her.

By Christmas she could read, haltingly to be sure and sometimes without any sense of what she had said, but she knew all the words of the nursery rhymes in the nursery rhyme book and soon Mrs Goodall was going to start her on a proper story book, one called *The Water-Babies* which she was looking forward to immensely. It was all very well repeating,

> Blow, wind, blow, and go, mill, go,
> That the miller may grind his corn,

but it wasn't very interesting, was it? But before *The Water-Babies* she must practise her writing which Mrs Goodall had just started her on. Now that she knew the letters – they were not called marks, her mistress had told her, but letters – by shape and sound, and how they formed into words, she must now put them on to paper.

Again she was faced with a large sheet of paper, blank, this time except for her name printed across the top, dazzlingly white in the light from the lamp. Beside it was an inkpot made of cut glass with a pretty silver lid that lifted off. Lying next to the inkpot was a pen with a steel nib.

"Now, hold the pen so and dip it carefully into the ink, Poppy," Mrs Goodall told her, showing her how, "Not too deeply or it will blot and not too shallowly or it will run dry in the middle of a letter. Carry the loaded nib gently across to the paper and then I want you to write your name, copying what I have done."

She had to dip the nib into the ink for every letter and each time it started on its dangerous journey from the inkpot to the paper her heart beat so fast and so hard she felt as though it would jolt her hand, but when she had finished, setting every letter on the line Mrs Goodall had drawn for her, there stood her name. Poppy Appleton. Capital letters for the start of each one, small letters for all the rest. It was a bit wobbly here and there but Mrs Goodall said that with practice she'd soon get over that. She was flushed with triumph and wanted to run out to the kitchen and show Cook and Nelly, Aggie and Clara what she had done but she knew, even if Mrs Goodall let her, May would spoil it for her, sniffing and sneering and asking what good it would do her. Her family was nothing and she was nothing and the hours Miss Clever Clogs spent learning would be a complete waste of time.

By spring she was writing proper sentences, as she had learned to call them, filling pages and pages with all the things that happened on the farm, for Mrs Goodall said she must learn "composition" and the best way was to write about things she knew. She could do her "add ups" and "take aways" and her "times tables" right up to twelve twelves are a hundred and forty-four and Mrs Goodall was already entrusting her to read out to Dilys and Nelly the orders to be made up for Saturday's market.

A year. A year since she had begun work in the dairy and even she knew she had altered, not only in her appearance, which was trim and clean and not unpleasing, for Mr Goodall's approving eye told her so when it fell on her at meal times, but in her manners, in her speech, in the way she thought. She would not be twelve until August but she felt herself to be grown up, a responsible and hardworking member of the Goodall household, trusted by her mistress.

Every week on her afternoon off she went down to Primrose Bank to see her mam, loaded with all the good things Cook, whose favourite Poppy was, and Mrs Goodall, who was her role model in life, insisted on giving her. Her mam had had two more pregnancies since Poppy left, both ending in miscarriages and somehow it seemed to have taken the stuffing out of her. Not that she had much after seventeen years of marriage to Reuben and the child-bearing that resulted, but even the little spark she had kept burning inside her thin, worn-out body had fizzled out with the last. She was thirty-three years old, or perhaps thirty-four, she couldn't remember. Folk like them took no count of birthdays but she looked like an old woman, her body distorted after so many pregnancies it was hard to tell if she was carrying a child or not. Her face had become grey and sunken and her eyes were apathetic, not even lighting up at the sight of the rich steak and kidney pudding, the apple dumplings, the remains of a fruit cake, the packet of tea and the dozen eggs Mrs Goodall had packed in the basket for her.

"She'll need building up, Poppy," Mrs Goodall had said

kindly, after her last miscarriage, knowing how Martha Appleton must miss this good child of hers. The rest were nothing, no good, not even the four remaining girls doing a hand's turn to make their mother's life easier. Martha had not worked since March and her wages were missed and had it not been for the hampers of food Eliza sent over, which Tom knew nothing about, naturally, would have fared ill. And Eliza knew Poppy set to each week and did her best to clean up the cottage, not for *their* sake, but for her mother's, though it was doubtful her mother cared. Eliza hadn't the heart to stop her since she knew Poppy was fond of her mother and was perhaps a little bit guilty about what she saw as her own grand position in life. Poppy Appleton was only a dairymaid but it was grand indeed compared with Martha Appleton's wretched existence.

Poppy felt like skipping as she crossed the side yard to the gate. Happiness quivered in her, moving her heart joyfully in her chest, little ripples that extended to every part of her body so that even her toes seemed to tingle with it.

It all dissipated like sunshine behind a cloud as she opened the door of the cottage and stepped inside.

"Lily's buggered off an' our Douglas's bin arrested," was her mother's first cry on that bonny day at the end of May.

Poppy had enjoyed the stroll down from the farm, through the meadow which was already carpeted with the soft pink of clover, the dashing yellow of buttercups and the bright azure blue of speedwell. A cuckoo was calling, the sound of it borne on a breath of jasmine-scented air from Mrs Goodall's garden. The track down from the meadow to Primrose Bank was a dazzling tunnel of white, the hedges bowed under the heavy fragrance of hawthorn blossom. The ditches on either side of the track frothed with celandine and lady's smock and the dust of the track puffed under her feet as she walked, golden in the spring sunshine. There had been no rain for a week and the land was dry and soft with none of the cold damp and misted misery of a year ago.

A few fields away, just beyond the boundary of Long Reach Farm, ewes called plaintively to lambs who leaped and butted one another in a frenzy of play and, nearer home, cows lowed and Evan's voice rose in a rich, vibrant baritone. He loved to sing to "his" cows, did Evan, though Dilys told him he was daft, see. Evan believed that the black and white Fresians, introduced from Holland in the last twenty years, gave even more milk when he sang to them. The best milkers in the world, they were. Only last year Buttercup – there was always a Buttercup in a dairy herd – gave over two thousand gallons of milk, but still a chorus of "Men of Harlech" never went amiss.

The singing, the lowing of the cattle were all part and parcel of Poppy's lovely new life and she knew she wouldn't change it for all the tea in China. She was going somewhere, not just down the track to see her mam, but beyond today, or even tomorrow and when she got there, when she arrived, she would know it. It was all wrapped up in her books. She had finished *The Water-Babies* and was halfway through *Alice's Adventures in Wonderland* and when she had read that Mrs Goodall said she thought it was time to start her on something a bit more grown up. Mrs Goodall said many things, a lot of which Poppy didn't understand yet, but she would one day, when her education was complete. She'd know as much as Mrs Goodall and surely that would entitle her to the position of head dairymaid, when Dilys was gone, of course.

Her mind, so far reaching in the world of her books, took her no further than the dairy since her knowledge of the world itself went no further than the farm gate beyond which she had never been.

Her mother's words brought her back to reality with a nasty bump and at once the dream scattered, dashed away not only by her mother's whining voice but by the familiar miasma of accumulated filth and growing fungus hanging about the room which got worse with every visit. Had it always been like this, she wondered desperately, doing her best not to breathe it in, and if so how had she borne it, or was it that a year of order and attention to the eradication of dirt had undermined her strong stomach, making her want to gag and turn away blindly to the fresh air outside?

She could smell unwashed bodies, the eye-stinging stench of urine, last night's meal which must have consisted of burned, boiled potatoes and half-rotten eggs, the noxious breath of decayed teeth and what seemed to be the offensive stink of the rags her mother had used since her last miscarriage and which were neither changed nor washed regularly. There was something badly wrong with her mam, still to be bleeding after all these weeks and perhaps if Poppy could get up her courage she might ask Dilys, or even Mrs Goodall for her advice. With the country-bred girl's understanding of birth, whether it be animal or human, particularly a girl brought up in a big family, she was aware that blood came with being born but she could not remember her mother being like this before. Poppy had been around for five or six of her mam's confinements and she seemed to think her mother was up and about, as recovered as she ever could be, days after the birth. Maybe Dilys or Mrs Goodall would be able to tell her what to do, for not only did her mam look bad she stank like a rotting carcase.

"Oh, Poppy, lass, 'tis grand ter see yer," her mother wailed, "but yer've come to an 'ouse o' sorrow, that's fer sure. See, give yer mam a kiss then mekk me a cuppa tea an' I'll tell yer all about it. Fire's gone out, sorry, lass. Them lazy buggers left me wi'out a birra kindlin' an' 'ow the 'ell am I ter lay bloody thing wi'out kindlin', I ask yer? Aah, lass, what're we ter do? What's ter become of us wi'our Lily gone fer a whore an' Douglas 'auled away by't scuffers . . ."

"Yer what?" Poppy stared open-mouthed in horror at her mother. "What yer on about? A whore . . . scuffers?"

"Wharr I said, a whore, fer yer can call it nowt else an' 'ow I'm ter 'old me 'ead up I don't know," just as though Martha Appleton and her family were respected pillars of the community.

"Mam, Mam, give over an' calm down. It's no good workin' yerself inter a state over it. I'm 'ere now so sit back an' put yer feet up on't stool. No, don't say another word until I've medd us a cuppa tea."

"Eeh, it's all right fer you up in that grand place, Poppy Appleton, wi' nowt ter worry yer," her mother continued wildly, running her coarse and dirty hands across the equally coarse and dirty sacking apron she had on. Poppy wondered why. Not to work in that was for sure. "Yer don't know yer bloody born wi' nowt ter do all day but mekk a birra butter an' cheese. Yer want ter be down 'ere wi' all this soddin' lot under yer feet, always wantin' summat ter eat an' messin' up me place just when I gerrit decent."

Poppy looked about her. Her mam's "decent place" was knee-deep in rubbish, discarded clothing and other bits of rags. The remains of several meals were on the table with a scattering of food-encrusted pans. There were two unskinned rabbits hanging from a hook in the ceiling which had evidently been there some time by the smell. Flies were everywhere and other scurrying things on the walls and floors which made Poppy's skin crawl and she wondered despairingly how one family could get a place into such a festering eyesore in the short space of a week. That was how long it was since she had got out a bucket, filled it from the water butt – empty today – and, applying the strong soap they used in the dairy and which she had brought with her, given the place a couple of hours of deep scouring.

She lit the fire first while her mother babbled on and on about Douglas and somebody called Conn who was leading him astray, though from what Poppy knew of her brother he wouldn't take much leading. She trekked down to the pump with the bucket, nodding politely at several of the other occupants of the row of cottages who lolled idly in the doorways of their homes. She wondered why they were not all out in the fields, stone-picking or rook-scaring or hoeing the newly planted potatoes but she had enough on her mind without considering them.

" 'Ow's yer mam, Poppy?" the women asked, knowing of Martha Appleton's troubles, since they were similarly affected on a regular basis, but doing nothing to help her, it seemed.

"Nicely, ta," she answered, though she knew it wasn't true.

The fire was whispering on the hearth and with a good cup of strong, heartening tea in her hand, Martha pulled herself round a bit, glad of an ear into which she could pour her troubles since none of the others cared. God, it was lovely to have their Poppy at home and with the part of her that not only missed her good girl but begrudged Mrs Goodall's stealing of her, she speculated on the chances of fetching her back home again. She needed someone to look after her and it was a sovereign to a farthing that none of the others would volunteer. She just couldn't seem to get herself right after this one and with Poppy back at Primrose Bank, keeping the cottage clean and cooking them a bit of decent grub, Martha'd be on her feet in no time.

"Now start from't beginnin', Mam," Poppy told her, wondering if she dared sip from the chipped cup which she had just soaked in boiling water. God only knew what was in them cracks!

It seemed that Douglas had been running around with a gang of lads from the dark and crowded cellars in the tenements which lined Brooks' Alley. Bad lads who lived on their wits, stealing whatever they could wherever they could, breaking into houses and taking stuff that they sold to men this Conn knew in the underworld of Liverpool. They were not violent. They did not attack folk which was likely why they'd been let off with a light sentence. Three months on the *Lahore*, the magistrate had given them, since none of them were above thirteen and some of them only nippers. Did Poppy know that thousands of homeless and neglected children, barefoot and with nothing on their backs but a few rags, haunted the alleys of the city, sleeping rough in doorways and always hungry? By God, it made her thankful for the good home they'd got, didn't Poppy agree?

The reformatory schools, three alone in Liverpool, two for boys who apparently were naughtier than their female counterparts, and one for girls, had been opened, which gave the courts authority to send anyone under the age of sixteen to one of them at the end of any prison sentence of at least fourteen days' duration. They could expect hard labour, hard fare, a hard bed and discipline so strict it should deter the most ambitious offender, it was said.

The training ship *Lahore* was another project resolved upon by the gentlemen of the city to help in the reformation of its young citizens. Beside the advantage of being anchored in the river, which was a strong deterrent to escapees, it had the added severity of a naval type of control, discipline and training which many of the lads needed.

The *Lahore* was ready for business in January 1856, a floating reformatory to which boys under the age of sixteen were sent in the hope of redemption and it must be said that in a great many cases it had succeeded. It was boasted that letters came from all over the world where men who had once been inmates were now respected members of the community in whichever country they had settled.

Lads sentenced to a spell on the *Lahore* had to be strong and able-bodied. They had to be able to withstand the severe punishments that were handed down for the smallest misdemeanour. Solitary confinement on a diet of bread and water was one. Flogging was another. It was known that several boys had drowned in a bid for freedom, others swept out to sea in a stolen rowboat, but fortunately Martha knew none of this as she moaned out her story to her daughter.

" 'Ave yer seen 'im?" Poppy asked, surreptitiously placing her untouched cup of tea on the table.

"Don't be bloody daft, girl," her mother spluttered, reaching for another piece of the fruit cake Cook had sent over. " 'Ow's me or yer pa ter get down ter't Assizes? I'm not well enough an' yer pa's workin'. Mind," taking comfort from the thought, "I reckon it'll do our Douglas a birra good. 'E's too big fer yer pa ter tekk strap to 'im, burra wallopin' now an' then won't 'urt 'im."

Poppy shook her head doubtfully and her glossy curls bounced.

" 'Oo's this . . . what did yer say 'is name were?" she asked.

"Conn, our Douglas called 'im but don't ask me any more about 'im 'cos I don't know. I sor 'im once waitin' by th'end o't track fer Douglas, leanin' on't wall, 'e were, as though 'e'd nowt else ter do but lounge about all day, smilin' an' noddin' 'is 'ead at me like I were a bloody lady an' 'im a gent come ter call."

Martha paused and her mouth twitched in a half-smile as though at the memory of something which pleased her. "Good-lookin' lad, big an' all, wi' the brightest red 'air I ever seen in me life. Anyroad, 'e'll not be loungin' about now fer a bit an' neither will our Douglas."

"But whorr 'ad they done, 'im an' our Douglas?"

"Nay, pinchin' stuff, I shouldn't wonder an' God knows whorr else. Douglas were always a wild one."

"Aye, I know." Poppy sighed, though to tell the truth their Douglas's predicament had been brought on by himself and she could not find it in her heart to be sympathetic about it. Same with this Conn, whoever he was. Deserved it, they both did and it was nowt to do with her.

For politeness sake she asked, "But what's this about our Lily?" Lily was only sixteen and had always had an eye for the lads, Poppy knew that. She had heard her pa take to her sister times, telling her she'd end up on the streets if she didn't watch her step and it seemed he was right. She'd heard, though she hadn't told her mam at the time since again she felt it was nowt to do with her, that their Lily'd lift her skirt – she couldn't drop her drawers because, like Poppy up to a year ago, she never wore any – to any man for a tanner. Put her on a street corner and she could make a couple of bob in an hour, she'd heard her say to their Marigold, which wasn't bad considering her pa, depending on the time of the year, only earned twelve to fifteen shillings a week.

"She left last Monday. 'Ad a row wi' 'er pa an' buggered off." Martha was feeling much better now. The fire, the tea, the company and the cake, the whole of which had disappeared, had cheered her up no end. Poppy had put her bloody clouts, which had piled up disgustingly this week, in to steep, promising to slip over with some fresh ones begged from Cook later in the evening if she could. Feeling warm and comfortable for the first time in a week, in fact since Poppy had last called, Martha sighed contentedly. She always felt a vast improvement in herself when her good girl was with her and if she didn't pick up soon she was going to broach the subject to Mrs Goodall of having their Poppy back to live at home. Not to give up her job, of course, but to come home each night to see to her mam. There was more room now with their Lily gone and Rose getting married next month which left only three girls to the bed, including Poppy, where before there had been five.

"What they row about?" Poppy asked, not caring one way or the other really. She had no particular affection for any of her sisters, who were a no-good, slovenly and idle lot in her opinion, and if Lily wanted to earn her living and probably an early death on the streets of Liverpool then that was her lookout.

"Oh, usual," Martha answered philosophically. "Strollin' outer't barn, she were, wi' that Tommy . . ."

"What, Tommy the cowman?" Poppy stared in horrified indignation. Tommy was an old man, at least thirty, a bachelor who had a snug room above the cowshed. Poppy liked Tommy, at least she had up to now, for he always had a smile or a wink for her or a bunch of poppies, seeing that was her name, he said, knowing she liked them in her bedroom. Well, she wouldn't speak to him again, the dirty old devil, she thought, messing about with a girl young enough to be his daughter.

"Aye, 'e's a bloody man, in't 'e, wi' a cock same as any other." Ignoring the shocked expression on her daughter's face she went on, "An' what do men like ter do wi' their cocks, our Poppy, but stick 'em in anythin' what moves."

It was said with some bitterness and not a little irony for Reuben Appleton, who had reduced her to what she was now with *his*, wasn't much bothered at the moment. Even he couldn't stomach the state of her just now.

"Will yer give the place a birrof a tidy before yer go, queen?" she asked her daughter ingratiatingly. "Only yer can see 'ow I am an' t' others aren't bothered."

"I can see that, Mam," Poppy sighed. She had brought *Alice's Adventures in Wonderland* with her, convinced her mam would be as enchanted as she was with the March Hare and the Dormouse at the tea party and that with a bit of luck she might read a chapter or two to her. Take her out of herself, out of the cottage and the pitiable life she led there and into a fantasy world of make-believe. It would do her good and it would be a chance to show off her own new skills to her mam who surely must be proud of her, and a bit of practice always came in handy. Sometimes Nelly slipped into Poppy's room at night and Poppy would read out loud to her of all the wonderful things the characters got up to. Nelly was bewitched by it all and fulsome in her praise and admiration of Poppy's cleverness. It would be lovely to hear the same praise and admiration from her mam. The book lay in the bottom of the basket in which she had brought the food but instead of the book she took out one of her engulfing sacking aprons. It was spotlessly clean, which you wouldn't be able to say about it in an hour's time.

All the female servants had been given a length of pretty sprigged cotton to be made up into a summer dress in a style of their choice and Poppy's was folded up in her drawer at home, which was what she now called the farm. It was the first dress she had ever had which had been worn by no one but herself and every night she took it out and stroked it wordlessly, her heart too full to allow her even to form thoughts in her head. With Mrs Goodall's help she had picked a style, simple and charming, at least that was what Mrs Goodall called it, and the sewing woman Mrs Goodall employed had made it up for her and for them all. It was quite, quite the most beautiful thing she had ever owned and no power on earth would make her wear it in this cottage. The colour was a shade of pale corn with sprigs of golden primroses printed on it and around the waist was a narrow golden velvet sash tied at the back in a bow. Nelly had chosen green, to match her eyes, she said, and May a vivid pink since May was fond of bright colours, but Poppy liked hers the best and could not wait to wear it at the June Fair which was coming to Old Swan next week. Aggie, whose old mother lived over that way and whom she visited on her day off, had told them that already preparations for the fair, which took place in Tom Goodall's big field – lying fallow this year – were under way. Stalls were being erected, swingboats and roundabouts put up and a helter-skelter which was four times higher than the farmhouse. The field stood just in front of the Grimshaw Arms.

It was also the start of the cricketing season so the team, of which Johnny and Richard Goodall were members, was to take on that from the Liverpool Union Crown Glassworks, the first match of the year. The team had been got up by Captain Adam Cooper of Coopers Edge and it was his wife, who had once been Sally Grimshaw, who owned the Grimshaw Arms. It was a mixed team, socially, made up of any young man who was handy with a cricket bat. It included farm boys, ditchers, labouring lads and several sprigs of the gentry, one of whom was Captain Cooper's eighteen-year-old son, Dominic. The Goodall boys came somewhere in between the two.

There would be a dance in the evening held in the large marquee erected in the next field and Mrs Goodall had given

the maidservants permission to take Saturday afternoon off
to go to the fair or to watch the cricket match, whichever
they preferred and then to attend the dance in the marquee.
It went without saying that none of them was to set foot in
the Grimshaw Arms. There would be a piper and a fiddler to
play the folk dances, the Dashing White Sergeant, Sir Roger
de Coverley, the Lancers, the polkas, the valetas, and though
Poppy was too young to join in she would wear her new
dress and with Mrs Goodall and Dilys would sit and watch
the fun.

Today she wore the neat but unbecoming skirt and bodice
Mrs Goodall had cut down for her last year when she began
work in the dairy and which was a better fit now she had
grown. It was the outfit in which she worked on the farm
and with her apron covering her from neck to ankle she
began the daunting task of bringing some kind of order to
the squalid cottage in Primrose Bank.

"Oh, you 'ere," their Rose said ungraciously as she slammed
into the kitchen, her boots scattering clods of dry earth from
the potato field where she had been digging all day, her
attitude implying that Poppy was nothing but an interfering
busybody who should keep her nose out of what didn't
concern her.

"An' a bloody good job an' all," Poppy snapped back.
"Don't it ever occur to yer ter give place a lick over now
an' again? Like a bloody pig sty, it is," completely forgetting
her new-found refinement in her fury as she began with
maddened vigour to brush the dirt this way and that as
though not sure what to do with it. "An' mind them bloody
boots. I've just done this floor an' now yer've tracked muck
all over it again. Couldn't yer 'ave tekken yer boots off
at door?"

"No, I bloody couldn't. Anyroad, what's it ter do wi' you?

Yer don't live 'ere no more, stuck up little cow wi' yer airs an' graces. Ever since yer went up ter't farm yer've bin t' same. Not good enough for yer now, we're not. Anyroad, what this place is like don't concern me. I'll be outer 'ere next month, thank Christ, when me an' Alfie's wed."

"Yer could still clean up a bit, couldn't yer?" Poppy stuck out her chin and brandished the twig broom as though about to clout her sister with it. "An' me mam . . . well, me mam could do wi' a wash an' all . . ."

" 'Ere, listen you, I'll get me a wash when I bloody well feel like it," her mother shrieked. "I don't need me own daughter, a kid o' ten . . ."

"Eleven."

"All right, eleven, ter tell me I could do wi' a wash."

"Yer could; yer all could. I don't know why I bloody bother."

"Neither do we, do we, Mam?" Rose screeched, her sister's good fortune evidently rankling even now. Rose would have liked a nice clean job in a dairy, or even in Mrs Goodall's kitchen but she had not been offered it and it had not occurred to her to wonder why.

Martha Appleton suddenly drew back from the brink, for this youngest daughter of hers who was red-faced and tight-lipped in an effort not to burst into incensed tears, or at least land their Rose one, which wouldn't be wise since Rose was seventeen and a big girl, was worth ten of any of them. Besides which, if she was to fall out with her she would miss the grand food Mrs Goodall sent over each week. On top of that she still had the fancy to demand the return of her lass to her own home and bugger Mrs Goodall, but for now it might be wise to smooth things over. As Rose said, she'd be gone next month so best keep her trap shut until then.

"Now then, our Rose, the lass is right. Place is a

mess but she'll soon purrit right, won't yer, queen. See, pass me that tea yer left. I know it's cold burr I don't like waste an' I'll 'ave wharrever's left in that there basket."

6

Apart from a certain incident which Poppy kept to herself they had a lovely time at the fair, she and Nelly agreed, telling one another artlessly that it was the best day out they'd ever had. Since neither of them had ever been beyond the farm gate and so had nothing with which to compare it, the irony of the exchange was lost on them. Nelly had come from Myrtle Street in the little gig Mrs Goodall drove, blinded with terror as she was taken from everything she had ever known to a future hidden from her and the drive from Liverpool to Long Reach Farm had passed her by in a blur.

She often smiled at the thought of that frightened child, for could a girl have a kindlier mistress than Mrs Goodall, she asked Poppy but she hadn't known that at the time, had she? She'd never been outside the asylum walls except on a Sunday to go to church with the warden and the other girls, so the excitement as the day drew near for the fair was intense. She and Poppy, though Nelly was the elder by five years, were on good terms since Poppy was a fearless child, confident, aware of her own value even at such an early age, a natural leader, and Nelly was happy to go where Poppy led. Poppy's quick mind was a mystery to her but Nelly trusted her implicitly and would have followed her to the ends of the earth if asked. Poppy's ability to read and write and do sums put her on a different plane to the rest of them. As far as Nelly was concerned Poppy was a creature to be marvelled at since she knew about things Nelly could scarcely imagine and if Poppy said such and such a thing was so, then that was good enough for Nelly.

It was a bright golden day, the June air clear and sparkling as, dressed in their new finery, the girls set off in the stately wake of the older maidservants. Aggie and Clara, as befitted their mature years, were in the sensible colours they had chosen for their dresses, Aggie in navy blue sprigged with cream and Clara in an indeterminate green that reminded Poppy of the dandelion and burdock stout bottle she had seen Mr Goodall drink from. Both wore simple rustic bonnets of straw tied about the crown and under the chin with ribbons made from the same material as their dresses. That was one thing Poppy regretted, her lack of a bonnet. She would have loved a bonnet to finish off the splendour of her new outfit, and new shoes as well, since her stout black boots and stockings beneath the ankle-length hem of her pretty new dress played havoc with the elegance of her appearance.

May, unlike Poppy who gave what she earned to her mam, kept all her wages and she had bought herself a brand-new pair of cream kid boots at which she cast frequent admiring glances as she walked. She twitched her skirt and nearly fell over her own feet she was so enchanted with them, and herself. Poppy, who would have died for a pair of cream kid boots, hated her.

The wild roses were beginning to bloom and clamber in the hedges. Blackberry bushes were laid with their first frail white flowers and over the heads of the group of servants small yellow butterflies danced. They wandered, the five of them, down through the uncut grasses of Tom Goodall's top field in which the red spires of sorrel stood up among the pale moon faces of the dog-daisies. Their skirts brushed a path as they walked, stirring the faint fragrance of willow-herb and Poppy could feel the excitement building up, ready to explode inside her, for on the clear air carried across the fields came the "oom-pah-pah" of the Liverpool Union Crown Glassworks Brass Band which was playing in honour of their cricket team.

"It's started, it's started. Oh, do come on or we'll miss it," she screamed to the others and with Nelly by the hand, her other lifting her skirt to display her boots and even the bit of lace on her drawers, she began to run. The field was on a slope and at the foot of it and on the other side of the next field the fairground was spread out before them in a kaleidoscope of whirring, whizzing colours, of dizzying wheels and flying swingboats and rocking roundabouts. There were screams of pretended terror from those who were already participating in the fun of it; the crack of rifles from the rifle gallery where young men were bent on showing their prowess to groups of admiring, giggling girls; the hoarse shouts of vendors calling their wares, which were many and varied, the shrieks of excited children and the clamour of the hurdy-gurdy as it vied for attention with the brass band.

In the next field the cricket match was already in progress and young men clothed in the traditional white, even the farming lads managing a pair of white duck trousers, or a shirt, were engaged in the serious business of beating the hell out of one another in an effort to win the special trophy Captain Cooper was to present. A silver cup to celebrate the first match of the season, the tradition begun years ago by Captain Cooper's father and much coveted, since the rivalry between teams was ardent and to win it was considered to be a good omen for the coming season. Country teams they might be, playing each other on village greens or in fields such as this, but their enthusiasm was white-hot. The Grimshaw Arms team had spent weeks preparing and marking out the pitch and today they meant to win on it.

Poppy listened every supper-time to the Goodall boys as they vigorously pronounced on the coming game, an intercourse which was peppered with terms such as "deep extra cover", "long stop" and "square leg", none of it making any sense to her. It all sounded so childish! A crowd of grown men, most of them, knocking a ball into the air with a bat and then running between some bits of wood called stumps seemed a wicked waste of time when they could be enjoying the magic and colour that, now that she had seen it for herself, must be this fairyland she had read about in one of Mrs Goodall's books.

And over it all the blare of the band playing stirring martial music – winning hands down over the hurdy-gurdy – set her senses to racing and her foot to tapping, her pulse and heart beating with the rhythm and she yearned to run headlong towards it, leaping any obstacle that got in her way.

"Oh, Nelly, will yer look at it," she begged her panting, red-faced companion. " 'Ave yer ever seen owt' like it in all yer life?" for she certainly hadn't. The June Fair came every year to this part of the country and though it had only been a matter of three or four fields away she had never before felt a desire to go and see what went on there. There had been nothing to stop her since her mam and pa took little heed of their offspring's whereabouts or activities, but something had kept her away. Though she had not consciously thought of it in those terms she supposed it must have been something to do with who she had been then. The same girl she was now, of course, but in a totally different way. Ignorant of the world beyond Primrose Bank, the fields in which she worked had been her total sphere of knowledge. She knew a rook from a swallow, a buttercup from a dandelion, a rabbit from a fox, a horse from a cow. She knew spring from autumn only because of the farming activities at these times of the year. Her days had been filled, since a toddler, with unremitting toil, drabness, a constant, and unusual, battle for a child in her circumstances against what she called "muck and muddle". The cold and hunger she had accepted as part and parcel of her life since she could do nothing about it anyway.

Until Eliza Goodall took her by the hand and led her from the shadows into the sunlight, the sunlight of knowledge, the realisation of who she was and the worth of who she was. She had emerged from the gloom of incomprehension, blinking in the brightness into which Eliza Goodall and her own ability to read had led her. She was a person now, a person with a head stuffed full of all sorts of things, some of which she still didn't understand, a whole person who could move about among all those down there at the fairground with total, head-tilting pride at what she had achieved in just over a year. It was, there was no doubt of it, her changed appearance that helped her towards this belief in herself but the seed Eliza Goodall had sown in the parlour at Long Reach Farm during the winter evenings was well planted, well nourished, the seedling growing, flourishing with every lesson.

Confident she might be, self-reliant and unafraid but she walked through that day with the open-mouthed, wide-eyed wonder of a child. She had the few pennies Mrs Goodall had slipped her and Nelly clinking cheerfully in the pocket of her dress but there was so much to spend it on she and Nelly couldn't make up their minds what it should be. They wandered from stall to stall in a desperate attempt to choose between monkeys on sticks, tin trumpets, whips and tops, ribbons, beads, gloves, combs, lemonade, toffee apples, gingerbread – which they could eat at home for nothing – buckles and bracelets, snuff boxes and chamber pots.

There was a tent which advertised the fattest woman on earth, another the smallest man and another which beseeched them to come inside and see the two-headed calf. Poppy shuddered at this. Her contact with the placid cows at milking-time had given her a fondness for the animals and the idea of gawking at one of their kind, a freak of nature by all accounts, had her hurrying by with Nelly's hand firmly held in hers.

There was a Punch and Judy show which they watched enraptured, screaming with the rest, darting away only when the woman whose husband was the puppetmaster came among the hooting, shouting audience with the intention of collecting money.

There were coconut shies which they didn't bother with since even Poppy didn't know what a coconut was and could see no reason to win one. There was a dancing bear which Poppy ordered Nelly not to look at, poor beast, since it was evident it was illtreated and for two pins she'd tell the man who had it on a chain what she thought of him. Nelly managed to drag her away from the crowd of guffawing yokels who seemed to think the poor capering creature enormously funny. Poppy was flushed and irate since she hated cruelty in any form. She had once seen a badger chew its own leg off to escape a trap and she was sure, and wondered why it didn't do so, the bear could chew the arm off the man who held it.

The band, which had for an hour kept up a lively rendition of marching tunes, had gone off to the beer tent where a pint of ale, brought over in barrels from the Grimshaw Arms, might be had for tuppence. Though there was a raucous cacophony of sound pressing against the ears of the two girls, both still clutching their pennies in an agony of indecision on how they should be spent, they nevertheless could hear the crack of a ball against a bat, accompanied by a great deal of clapping and shouts of "Well played, lad," "Oh, good shot," followed by a concerted groan from many throats.

"It's only t'cricket," Poppy declared scathingly, taking Nelly's hand and turning back towards the still yet untouched delights of the fairground and the momentous choice of how she might spend her precious pennies there.

Nelly, who harboured a great and secret admiration for Johnny Goodall, destined to come to nothing, she was well aware of that, since, besides being the son of the house and Nelly merely a dairymaid and plain as a boot, he was handsome and fun-loving. Nelly also harboured a deep desire to see the recipient of her unrequited devotion in all his glory on the cricket pitch. From the shouts and applause coming from that direction it sounded as though a player from one of the teams was covering himself with glory beyond the hawthorn hedge which separated the pitch from the fairground and, in her love-struck state, Nelly was convinced it must be Johnny. He was so tall and fine and brave. He'd looked so splendid at dinner-time in his freshly ironed white trousers and shirt, the sleeves rolled up to show off the sunburned strength of his young arms, the neck open to display the equally sunbrowned column of his boyish throat. Her heart had jumped about quite terrifyingly and her breath had come fast in her own throat at the glory of him as he boasted to his brother that he meant to get a "century", whatever that was, this afternoon. Perhaps that was what he was doing right now and how she longed to see his endeavours as she was convinced he would achieve it.

"Sounds like summat excitin' on't cricket field, Poppy," she remarked encouragingly, striving to be casual since not even her dearest friend must guess at her attachment to Johnny Goodall.

Poppy shrugged in total disinterest, then, when Nelly, who was a couple of stone and more heavier than she was, resisted her efforts to draw her back into the crowd, turned to her in surprise.

"Excitin'? A game o' cricket? Give over. What's excitin' about watchin' a lot o' daft lads 'ittin' a ball about? I'd sooner scrub dairy floor."

"Aah, come on, Poppy. It'll tekk nobbut a minnit. Let's go an' see what's up. It might be Master Richard" – careful not to mention her darling's name – "gerrin one o' them centuries 'e were on about."

"Well, if 'e is or 'e isn't it don't matter ter me. I see enough o't pair of 'em at table." Poppy was not an admirer of boys since her own brothers weren't much cop and she judged the male sex by them. "Come on, Nelly. Let's go an' 'ave another look at them ribbons. I fancy that there bit o' red velvet . . ."

"Aaw, just fer a minnit, Poppy. See, gate's only there. I could do wi' a sit down anyroad." This from a strapping girl who spent twelve or more hours a day on her feet.

Poppy looked aggrieved. She had absolutely no interest in what was happening on the other side of the hedge, the shouts, the clapping, the cries of approval, the cracking slap of the ball on the bat. The thought of it created as much curiosity in her as the two-headed calf.

She was about to say so, tutting and shaking her head in wonder at the concern shown by Nelly when, from nowhere, or so it seemed, and missing the pair of them by no more than inches, a hard, red ball slashed between them, thudding into the rough grass at their feet. It rolled slightly as they stared at it in astonishment then came to rest in a little tuft of trodden grass.

"Well, I like that," Poppy exclaimed, her little pointed face flushed with indignation. "Did yer see it, Nelly?" though it was obvious Nelly had. "It might've killed us. A crack on th'ead wi' that'd do yer no good." She looked about her at the small but rattled crowd who, jostling in the same square yard of space as she and Nelly, and so in the path of the lethal ball and its danger, were as amazed as she was.

A young man with a pretty girl on his arm, no doubt wishing to impress her with his courage and daring in the face of such careless disregard for her safety, bent to pick the ball up but before he could vouchsafe his opinion on the madness of amateur cricketers, a white-flannelled figure flew through the open gateway from the next field, spotted the ball in the young man's hand and with a breathless "Thanks, cock," snatched it from him and dashed back into the cricket field.

"Well, I like that," Poppy said again, it being her favourite expression when riled. Her dander was well and truly up by now and her pink face confirmed it. " 'E didn't even say 'e was sorry. 'E might've done us serious injury—"

"Norrim, chuck," someone interrupted.

Poppy turned, piqued by this defence of the cricketer who'd grabbed the ball.

"What d'yer mean?" she asked the fellow who'd spoken.

"Well, 'e were only chasin' ball what feller battin' sent over," the sage continued.

"What's that supposed ter mean?" Poppy was becoming more and more irritated.

"Eeh, lass, I 'aven't time ter be explainin' finer points o' cricket to yer. Yer'd best go an' see fer yersen."

"I will, an' I'll 'ave summat ter say to 'ooever's responsible. If that ball'd 'it me or Nelly it'd 've smashed our 'eads in. Come on, Nelly, don't stand there gawpin'. Let's go an' see what the 'ell they're playin' at knocking balls at innocent bystanders. I've a good mind ter report it ter Mr Goodall," who was the man of authority in Poppy's small world.

Nelly scuttled behind her as Poppy darted like a diminutive, maddened kitten through the open gateway and into the field on which, for three or four months of the year, Tom Goodall allowed the Grimshaw Arms cricket team to play their home matches. There were wooden benches set up about the perimeter of the field on which old men with walking sticks and cloth caps, a pint of the Grimshaw Arms' best bitter in their hand, sat in the sunshine and enjoyed the game. There were children playing tig beneath the shade of the trees and women, obviously of the working class in their Sunday best, sitting in the grass swiping at the flies which buzzed about them.

In front of a tent which served as their "clubhouse" lolled the team who were at the moment in to bat, and in deckchairs among them, their parasols protecting them from the sun's rays, were the ladies, wives and daughters and sisters, who had come in their carriages to see their upper-class menfolk wear the laurels of victory this day. Among them were Captain Cooper, his handsome wife Mrs Sally Cooper, his exquisite, eighteen-year-old daughter Naomi, Farmer Tom Goodall and his wife Eliza.

The attention of one and all was riveted on the young man who had just swung his cricket bat, sending the ball delivered to him by the bowler so high and so far every eye lost sight of it. It had gone in the general direction of a clump of elm trees on the far side of the field, dropping down out of the sky where the lad had sent it and it was anybody's guess where it had landed. Or so the resigned sighs of the fielders seemed to say. Several of them had gone to rummage in the tall, uncut grass as what appeared to be another six runs were added to the young man's score.

He leaned on his bat, one hand on his hip, one foot crossed in front of the other, his tall, graceful body indolently at ease. He was a beautifully made young man with long bones and flat muscles that could be seen stretching in his back beneath the fine white cambric of his shirt.

But what drew Poppy's eyes to him was the thick thatch of his wavy red hair which gleamed auburn and roan, amber and gold in the sunlight. It was the most beautiful colour she had ever seen, a torch of brilliance among the dark and pale shadows of the other hatless players. It flowed about his head in a ripple of blazing light as he turned and lifted his bat in acknowledgement to the crowd who couldn't make enough of him and his fine play. He was grinning, his expression one of great enjoyment, his wide mouth stretched over even white teeth as the applause echoed about the field.

The ball was found and for the next half-hour, to Nelly's amazement and delight, since Johnny Goodall was the red-headed lad's partner in running up and down the pitch, Poppy stood silently watching the hero of the day knock the ball all over the field, only needing to run when it was Johnny's turn to hit it. Johnny did creditably well, scoring sixty runs before he was bowled out but no matter what they did they could not get out the red-headed demon batter.

" 'Oo is 'e?" Nelly ventured to ask but Poppy didn't answer. In her head she could hear her mother's voice repeating what she had said to Poppy only last week.

I saw him once leaning on the wall as though he'd nothing else to do but lounge about all day smiling and nodding his head at me as though he was a gentleman.

Good-looking lad, a big lad with the brightest red hair I ever saw in my life.

The description fitted the graceful young cricketer as though it had been specifically designed for him and yet how could that be? He, with their Douglas and some other lads who had apparently formed a gang, had been sentenced to three months' hard labour on the *Lahore* and that, as far as she was aware, was where he and Douglas were at this moment. They didn't get an afternoon off in that sort of a situation! There was no escaping from the reformatory ship and yet here, playing cricket, dressed for cricket, looking as though he were every inch the gentleman Dominic Cooper and his gentry friends were, smiling, enjoying himself and the afternoon's sport as though it was his right, was the lad who, her mam had said, had led their Douglas and others into the direst trouble. She *knew* it was him though she didn't know how she knew. It was him! There could not be two lads who had the magnetism this lad had, holding this crowd in the palm of his hand, not just with his dashing play but the charm and delight of his game.

There was only one way to find out.

"Wait fer me 'ere," she hissed at Nelly as though afraid of being overheard.

Nelly looked startled. "Where yer goin'?"

"Never you mind. I'll tell yer when I've bin."

Making her way unobtrusively round the outskirts of the field just as though what she did might be noticed and misconstrued, she came at last to the group of parasolled ladies, among them Mrs Goodall who sat ever so slightly apart from the others. Poppy was glad to see that Mr Goodall was deep in conversation with another gentleman, a well-set-up, outdoors sort of a gentleman who was probably a farmer like himself. Tom Goodall had come today because, his sons being in the team, Eliza had insisted upon it, but the afternoon would not have been totally wasted, in his opinion, if he could discuss fodder and milk yields and the age at which a decent heifer should be mated with someone whose interests were the same as his own.

Mrs Goodall started in surprise as Poppy dropped down in the grass beside her deckchair. She was more than a little bored herself despite her younger son's good showing in the match. Richard was batting now with the splendid red-haired lad but as soon as he was out she meant to make her farewells to Mrs Cooper and leave.

"Why, Poppy, what are you doing here?" She smiled. "I wouldn't have thought you'd have much use for cricket. Are you spent up, is that it, and where's Nelly? You know I said you were to stay together."

"Oh, us did, ma'am, she's over there," nodding at the green-gowned figure of Nelly crouching against the gatepost as though the hordes of China were after her.

"*We* did, Poppy, not *us* did," Eliza corrected her automatically. "So what brought you here?"

"That lad there," nodding casually at the bright red hair which flashed once more up and down the crease. " 'E nearly 'it me an' Nelly wi' one o' them balls of 'is so I come in ter see what 'e were up to."

"*Came* in, and *was* up to, Poppy." It was a sign of Poppy's agitation that she was reverting to the bad grammar of her first months at Long Reach Farm. Since she had begun to read properly she had corrected it and Eliza wondered what it was that was upsetting her. Surely not just a near miss with a cricket ball?

"I was . . . we were wonderin', me an' Nelly, 'oo 'e were . . . was, like. I've . . . we've never sin 'im round 'ere before."

As this was the first time Poppy had been . . . well,

Eliza could only call it *out* in society, the remark was a strange one.

"No, neither have I, my dear. He must be a local or he wouldn't be in the team."

A voice behind them spoke. It was Johnny Goodall.

"No, Ma, he's not really in our team. We were a man short, Eddie Chambers took a fall riding and Dominic" – Dominic Cooper being captain – "was cursing our bad luck when this blighter pops up and offers to make up the numbers. Damn good job, as well. Have you seen the score? We're bound to win now."

"Don't swear, dear, at least where there are ladies," inclining her head in the direction of the Cooper entourage. "But did he not give you his name?"

"Well, if he did I didn't hear it. But he's a Scottie, that you can tell from his speech."

"Doesn't Mr Cooper know?" Even Eliza was intrigued.

"Dominic wouldn't care if he called himself the Lord Mayor of Liverpool as long as we win this match."

"How extraordinary. So, there you are, Poppy, your questions are . . . oh, where has she gone?"

Poppy was skirting the assembly of deckchairs, making her way back to Nelly who was standing up in great relief when she saw her coming. She was keeping her head down, doing her best to avoid the eye of anyone who might think her actions suspicious and decide to question her. She was convinced that Captain Cooper or even Mr Goodall had only to look into her face and they would know the red-haired lad for who he was, and though there was no doubt he was wicked, a boy who had been sent to the *Lahore* for his thievery, she was strangely reluctant to be the one to point a finger at him and have him returned there.

She was looking down, he was looking at the crowd who

were applauding him enthusiastically as he came off the pitch and their collision was inevitable. She came no higher than the middle of his broad chest and when she walked into it her nose hit his breastbone with a crack that made her eyes water.

Gallantly he dropped his cricket bat and his arms came round her protectively, holding her steady or she would have gone over. She could feel the warmth of him, smell the not unpleasant aroma of his male sweat mixed with that of cut grass and squashed buttercups where he had measured his length a few minutes ago.

"Careful . . ." he said into her hair, calling her something she could not identify, still holding her and when, struggling free, she looked up at him in some exasperation, for didn't he know Captain Cooper was something to do with the Assizes, she was caught fast in the glory of the deep, blue smile in his eyes. In that moment she noticed every detail of his face. The eyes themselves surrounded by long, russet lashes tipped with gold. The sweetness of the smiling mouth, the hardness of the stubborn jaw, the high cheekbones on which golden freckles were scattered, the flat planes of his cheeks. It was a good-humoured face, a boyish face in which the harder lines of manhood were already beginning to form and on it was an expression which seemed to be telling her he was afraid of nothing. Not on this glorious summer day where his prowess as a sportsman had won him such acclaim.

But Poppy was yet a child with a child's vivid imagination who could hear the clanking of manacles if he could not and if he was not afraid, she was. For him!

"Yer daft beggar," she whispered. "What d'yer think yer playin' at? Run while yer can."

"I beg yer pardon?" he whispered back, amused and somewhat bewildered by this small girl's strange behaviour.

"Is yer name Conn?"

The smile left his face then and she knew she had been right but what the bloody hell was he doing here playing in a cricket match with half the local gentry looking on when he should by rights have been incarcerated on the *Lahore*?

"How did . . . ? But what about yer nose? Are you all right?" he asked her seriously, again calling her by that strange name. She was not to know he was thinking her dewed eyes were like rainfall. Then she darted away and he was lifted up on the shoulders of his "team mates", grinning broadly, borne aloft in triumph towards the table where Captain Cooper was waiting with the coveted trophy.

Five minutes later, when they had finished congratulating themselves and looked about for their hero, he was gone.

7

Martha Appleton had almost lost count of how many children she had borne; was it fifteen, sixteen? She couldn't remember, nor the dates of their birth. Except for their Poppy. That was one date she never forgot. It had been the year when she and Reuben, drifting in search of work with their surviving children, had almost starved. The year before Reuben began to labour for Tom Goodall and had it not been for a handy opening as a beater on some gentry's grouse moor, it would have been the workhouse for the lot of them.

Poppy had been born on the first day of the shoot and it was on her twelfth birthday that Mrs Goodall proposed that she should go to market with her on the following Saturday.

"You have proved to me in the past year that you have a sensible head on your shoulders, Poppy." Eliza restrained herself from placing an affectionate hand on the head in question, the temptation to ruffle her fingers through the short curls, glowing bright in the lamplight, almost overcoming her. Poppy was gazing at her, her soft lips parted, her breath held, an expression of what looked like incomprehension on her face and Eliza smiled reassuringly at her before continuing.

"You know what I sell as well as I do. You can read and reckon up in your head so I think it's about time we put it all to good use." She sighed ever so slightly, looking away into the corner of the parlour where she and Poppy were going over the July accounts. Poppy's absolute stillness, the sudden loss of every scrap of colour from her face seemed to have escaped her notice.

"I'm not as young as I was, Poppy, and the fact of the matter is it's either give up the stall which is very lucrative – that means it makes a good profit – or find someone to put in charge of it. Oh, you're not old enough for that yet, my dear, as I'm not yet ready to be put out to grass, but in a couple of years' time you will be old enough and experienced enough to take my place. Until then you will come with me each week and learn the ropes."

Poppy couldn't sleep the night before, almost sick with an excitement even more intense than that she had felt in June when the fair had come to Old Swan. She had spent the day washing, sorting and counting the eggs, dropping and shattering two which annoyed her intensely. She prided herself on her neatness and dexterity. She hadn't broken an egg, or a bowl for that matter, in all the time she had worked in the dairy and here she was galloping about like a stampeding pony, bumping into tables and shelves and door frames and generally making a fool of herself.

"There's quick you are, *cariad*," Dilys said, tutting and shaking her head, "but there's no need to carry on as though the place is on fire, see. We know you're excited but calm down, will you. You're fair making us all on edge, isn't she, Nelly?"

She smiled as she spoke. Dilys didn't know how she'd managed with her legs before Poppy came. Nelly would do anything, you'd only to ask, but Poppy thought ahead and did it even before you asked. If there was a job to do that could be done sitting down, like plucking and cleaning the freshly killed chickens, for instance, Poppy would beg Dilys to do it. She'd run messages, which you couldn't ask Nelly to do because Nelly would have forgotten what you'd told her to say before she was halfway there, and when it came to counting the eggs or the butter shells Poppy had it done in her head while Dilys was still busy with her fingers and the slate and chalk Mrs Goodall had shown her how to use.

All afternoon and well into the evening they spent packing the produce on to the cart, the butter and shells Poppy and Dilys had shaped draped in muslin, arranging cheeses and the fowls with their plump breasts uppermost on the scrubbed tray. They were to be up at five and off by six, Mrs Goodall told her, with a good hearty breakfast inside them since even in August the market could be cool and they would be on their feet for most of the day. Poppy was to wear her new dress covered with a snowy apron similar to the one Mrs Goodall herself put on when she got to her stall. Mrs Goodall had added, in that brisk way she had, that they must see about a new winter outfit for Poppy, something warm and practical in a pretty colour, since the customers at the market liked to be served by someone pretty and polite. She did not add that it would also give her a great deal of satisfaction to see the child in the sort of outfit Eliza's daughters would have worn had they lived.

Perhaps, she continued, if things went well, they might expand, take another stall, employ another young woman to help Poppy, or even, if Poppy had the patience to try, make something of Nelly. Not to be educated to Poppy's standard, naturally, but able to help in a practical way behind the stall.

But that was in the future, to be discussed between them when Eliza had seen the way her protégée handled herself, her attitude to customers, her ability to be calm and deal with any emergency, of whatever sort, without Eliza to support her. Poppy was a nice-looking child now that she had put some weight on her. She was as glossy as a well-polished apple, her pale honey-coloured skin and white teeth good, which was surprising when you considered her diet before she came to Eliza, her hair a tumbled cap of gleaming brown curls on her neat skull. She had a pleasing manner with those older than herself, if you didn't count May since those two were like oil and water and had to be watched, particularly May. Poppy was well liked by the kitchen servants. She was a sensible child who took her duties seriously and they admired that. She was willing to give a helping hand where it was needed even though officially she didn't work with them, and they liked that too, so if she could be trained in the proper way, not only in how to treat a customer but to make a profit while doing it, she would be an asset to Eliza Goodall's thriving little business.

As the sun rose the sky on the horizon was painted in layers of apricot, gold and a grey as soft as a gull's wing. There was still a mist lying about the fields as Eliza, with Poppy perched on the seat next to her, clucked to the placid horse, telling it to "walk on" through the yard gate which Nelly held open for them. Nelly's face as she looked up at them was filled with the wonder of what was to happen to her friend and yet, her smiling gooseberry eyes seemed to say, should anyone be surprised at Poppy's rapid rise to glory? In just over a year she had moved on from the skinny child who spent her days stone-picking or rook-scaring in Farmer Goodall's fields to Mrs Goodall's right-hand girl in the dairy. Dilys was still head dairymaid, of course, but even

Dilys could not have done what Poppy had, not with those legs of hers. Dilys had taught Poppy all she knew about dairy work but it was Mrs Goodall who had given her the opportunity to become as she was this day.

"Good luck, Poppy," Nelly's voice called out to her as she closed the gate behind them and it held no resentment or even envy.

The three-mile ride along the curving road from Old Swan towards the city took them almost an hour. The sun had dispersed most of the mist even before they were halfway along Liverpool Road. The road was hedged neatly on both sides and stretching away beyond the hedges were rich green pastures, still unwithered despite the long hot summer. Cattle stood deep in the lushness of meadow grass studded with clover or wandered in drifts of the remaining mist which lingered in hollows. In other fields reapers were already at work where crops were mature and ready for harvesting. Strong, patient horses, their heads nodding, their tails twitching against the flies, stood between the shafts of enormous hay waggons. In Tom Goodall's field the oats had already been cut, for oats were used to feed his cattle during the winter. Soon the haymaking would be finished. Hectic weeks these were, with men, women and children working from dawn to dusk for as long as the weather held. The children made bands to bind the sheaves, the women helping to bind the sheaves together while the men went before them with their scythes.

They drove past the New Cattle Market which stood between St Anne's Church and the White Hart Inn but market day was Monday and it was deserted. The smell of it was powerful, though, and it took Poppy back to the milking shed on the farm. She wondered briefly, with the naïvety that believed implicitly in her own importance, how they were managing without her, but only briefly, since her whole being, her senses, her mind, even her thumping heart were concentrating on this journey she was taking. She knew it was important, that it was the beginning of something special in her life, another step on her climb to ... to ... somewhere, but it was not that which was riveting her. It was the sheer dizzying speed with which Mrs Goodall kept the little cart on the move, a brisk trot that had Poppy hanging on for dear life. She was spellbound at the sight of so many small, neat cottages set in small, neat gardens; by the splendid wrought-iron gates which occasionally cut a hedge to reveal smoothly gravelled drives leading to some splendour she could only guess at; by the rows of tidy villas with lawned gardens in front set with colourful beds of snapdragons and delphiniums, dahlia and stock, their walls a riot of rock rose.

The narrow road was becoming more and more congested the nearer they got to the city, dense with farm waggons, drays, carts and even handcarts, pushed and pulled at great and dangerous speed among the multitude of people all going in the same direction.

The road became broader and on either side of it fields and farms and cottages became rows of mean, terraced houses, their fronts pierced at regular intervals by doors opening directly on to the pavement, by small windows and narrow passageways leading to their backs, dark and forbidding. There were threadlike streets criss-crossing the broad thoroughfare along which, at a spanking pace, their little cart progressed. The horse's rump gleamed from the attention she got from Jacko, who was in charge of the Goodall horses, her polished coat shining in and out of the stripes of sun and shadow cast by the tall buildings on their right.

It was not until much later, when Poppy had been going for several weeks to the market in Mrs Goodall's company, that she was able to separate and identify the buildings they passed that day. She was like a small mole that has spent its days burrowing beneath the earth then suddenly pops up its head to find itself cast into the blaze of daylight. She was transported from the rural peace she had always known to the lusty, brawling pandemonium of life in a big city and it overwhelmed her so that one building merged numbingly into another. Every man, woman and child was going at what appeared to be breakneck speed as though not a moment must be wasted, combining themselves into one blurred transition of drab colour.

A new and novel horse-drawn tram meandered through the mêlée, stopping without warning, since passengers had only to ask the driver to set them down wherever they fancied. Those wishing to board the vehicle, stepping out into the road to attract the driver's attention, were in serious danger of being run down by other traffic.

Great waggons drawn by horses even bigger than those which pulled the plough at the farm swayed majestically next to the cart, the waggons piled high with barrels and crates, timber and great bales, the contents of which were unknown to Poppy. Horses whinnied nervously, dogs barked, ragged children screamed in doorways, train whistles shrieked, since by now they were approaching the railway station. Old women looking remarkably like Poppy's mam sat in the gutters drinking from bottles, men in red uniforms rushed hither and thither along the pavement, coming from where, going to where, who could say? And over it all, over the great city and port which Poppy Appleton was to come to know, and love, lay the smell of it, the sea, the pungency of tar from the rigging of ships tied up in the river, the cargoes they carried, coffee beans, Indian tea, citrus fruits, nutmeg and camphor. Unconsciously, Poppy dragged it deep into her lungs.

Turning a left-handed corner into a vast and busy square, an enormous edifice loomed up before her, so magnificent it took away what little breath she had left. It was surrounded, or supported by, she wasn't sure which, hundreds of columns, all elegantly carved with steps marching up to them in regimented precision. In front of the hall was a statue of a man on a horse. It was made from solid bronze and turned out to be none other than the deceased husband of their beloved queen, or so Poppy learned later.

"St George's Hall, Poppy," Mrs Goodall remarked absently, "and that's the station over there," nodding at another splendid building that was all wide steps and fluted columns.

Poppy hardly dared move for fear she might lose her grip on the sides of the cart and tumble beneath the dashing wheels and frantic hooves of the traffic which careered about her, but she managed to nod mutely.

Another corner was turned on the far side of the square; along a narrow street and Mrs Goodall pulled at the reins and "whoa-ed" the horse to a stop.

"Here we are, my dear. St John's Market. Now get down and take those baskets of eggs. Can you carry two? Good girl. I'll fetch the chickens and then we'll come back for the rest. Good morning, Mr Clarke," she called out to a burly, florid-faced gentleman in a striped apron and a straw boater who was hurrying towards them. "How are you this morning?"

"Champion, Mrs Goodall, an' yerself?"

"The same, Mr Clarke, thank you."

"An' is this t' little maid?" The man, who turned out to be a porter, bent down so that his eyes were on a level with Poppy's, his hands on his knees. He looked seriously into her face, taking note of every feature, giving her the once-over as though she were for sale and he might be tempted to make a bid for her.

"It is, Mr Clarke. Miss Poppy Appleton."

Poppy nearly choked but at the same time she felt a great stirring of pride at being so addressed.

"That's a right pretty name an' a grand little lass, Mrs Goodall, if yer don't mind me saying so."

"She is, Mr Clarke, and will do well on my stall."

"There's no doubt about it, Mrs Goodall. Now let me give yer a 'and to get this stuff of yours inside and then Bertie" – indicating a large young man who bore a startling resemblance to himself – "can see to the 'orse an' cart."

Poppy followed blindly, her senses bombarded, not only by the noise of shouting and whistling which came at her from every side but by the sheer enormity of the building they were about to enter. It did not surprise her when Mrs Goodall told her, several visits later, since today she was incapable of taking it in, that it covered over two acres, which was bigger than the field in front of Primrose Bank. Constructed of brick and stone for one purpose only – commerce – it had no pretensions to architectural beauty. At each end there were three arched entrances and several on either side down its length. The lofty room was divided into five avenues, each lined on both sides by stalls, well lighted since there were one hundred and thirty-six windows which opened to provide not only light but ventilation. Round the walls of the building were shops and the market's offices, the shops let to butchers, provision dealers, game and poultry dealers, confectioners and bakers.

There were, in the centre of the market – Mrs Goodall had counted them she told Poppy, wanting to be aware of competition – eighty-two pork stalls, twelve fruit stalls, twenty-two greengrocers stalls, twenty-seven provision stalls and twenty-eight egg stalls and, to support this enormous superabundance of food for sale, three hundred and fifty yards of tabling.

By this time Poppy felt as though her head had been invaded by a flock of starlings, winging and diving so that her brain was incapable not only of thought but of receiving one more piece of information thrust at it. Ever since she and Mrs Goodall had passed through the farm gate which led into Prescot Road and Poppy had closed it carefully behind them, climbing back once more on to the cart, she had been assaulted by a swift series of new sounds, new sights, unfamiliar impressions, so that she felt as though she had moved into a world where madness reigned. It would pass. She would become used to it. She would come to glory in it, she knew this as clearly as she knew her own name, but in the meanwhile she clung, not quite literally, but almost, to the back of Mrs Goodall's sensible skirt and followed wherever her mistress led.

There were two distinct classes of customer who frequented St John's Market and the first, the one Eliza mainly catered to, were the respectable, hardworking, thrifty wives of the working man. Men in good, steady jobs, men associated with the shipbuilding trade, carpenters, craftsmen, sawyers, block and spar makers, sailmakers and riggers, small men in small businesses who could not afford to chuck their money about on luxuries and whose wives were disposed to come early to the market to search for the best produce at the fairest price. They were already circling the stalls in their unfashionable but decent gowns and bonnets, fingering plump chicken breasts, studying the eggs and butter, the cuts of pork and beef and mutton, the freshness of the cauliflowers and cabbage with a bargain in mind. Many of the women were cooks or housekeepers at some elegant little town house in the better part of the city, come to order provisions, which would be delivered, naturally, to the homes of the well-to-do families they served.

The second class of customer came from the multitude who existed in the sprawl of tenement houses which fanned out from the dock area, the alleys and closes, the lodging houses and rented cellars where it was not unknown for a family of fifteen to share one foetid room. They poured into the market towards the end of the afternoon, women in shawls, caps, run-down boots, who were on the lookout for anything that the stall-holder had not got rid of, food that would not keep until next market day the following Wednesday and which they might purchase at a much reduced price. Eliza was seldom still there when these gaunt and poverty-stricken creatures arrived, since her fresh farm produce, known for its quality and reasonable price, was normally all sold by early afternoon and today was to be no exception.

For the first hour Poppy kept her head down, her brain responding to the orders Mrs Goodall rapped out, her hands responding to the orders her brain sent to them.

"A dozen brown eggs for Mrs Ogden, Poppy, if you please."

"A half-pound of butter and a dozen shells for Mrs Brown."

"A nice plump chicken for Mrs Wilde, Poppy," since Mrs Goodall, who had been coming to the market for many years now, knew all her customers by name. They were as regular as clockwork, even to the time they arrived, their baskets on their arms, their shrewd faces alert and on the lookout for the very best.

"Got a little helper today, Mrs Goodall?" they all said pleasantly enough. "Shy little thing, isn't she?" and Mrs Goodall would take their money which went into a canvas bag attached to a belt at her waist. Poppy had one similar, for Mrs Goodall expected her to begin serving, and giving the correct change as soon as she had found her feet.

"A bonny wee lassie, Mrs Goodall, but can she count?"

"Yes indeed, Mrs MacDonald, as you will soon learn."

"I hope so, Mrs Goodall."

"So this is the lass, Mrs Goodall?"

"Yes, first day today, Mrs Atkinson. As soon as she knows the ropes and I retire she is to take over from me."

"Really, Mrs Goodall, you do surprise me, a little bit of a thing like her."

"Oh, she'll surprise you all one of these days, Mrs Atkinson, but don't worry. I shall be around myself for a long while yet."

"I'm pleased to hear it, Mrs Goodall."

A woman pushing a small handcart no bigger than a wheelbarrow wended her way slowly through the press of shoppers. She had two enormous copper urns balanced on the cart, each one with a tap. There was a big jug, a dozen or so mugs and a jar with a screw top which proved to hold sugar.

"Usual, Mrs Goodall?" she called out to Eliza as she manoeuvred her cart through the teeming throng.

"Thanks, Maggie, two today, both with sugar."

It was not until the steaming mug of tea was thrust into her hands that Poppy lifted her head for more than a second or two to take a furtive peep at this spectacle of noise and colour that was spread out before her. Her heart, which had been going nineteen to the dozen ever since they'd left home, its rhythm doubling as she entered the market and was told to take her place behind the stall, had slowed down to its normal pace now and she felt more able to cope with the frantic excitement of it all. There was a small lull in the brisk exchange of eggs and butter and cheese for the shillings and pence which the shoppers handed to her and from which she had been expected to give correct change down to the last farthing.

Mrs Goodall thankfully put her bottom on an upturned wooden box as she sipped her tea, turning to smile at Poppy.

"Well, my dear, what do you think?" she asked.

"Oh, Mrs Goodall!" Poppy let her gaze wander across the aisle to where a splendid array of fruit was artistically arranged, polished apples of green and red and russet, oranges and tangerines, plums and cherries, and hanging in velvet bunches, grapes of green and purple.

"Splendid, isn't it? Do you think you will enjoy coming with me every week?"

Poppy had no words, it seemed, except to repeat, "Oh, Mrs Goodall . . ."

"I take it you are impressed and that means 'yes'."

"I don't know what ter say, ma'am, except I reckon I could get used to it." There was a glint of humour in her serious young face and her eyes sparkled, a brilliant sparkle of pale blue and grey. She lowered her gaze and her eyes were shadowed by their thick fringe of dark lashes, then she looked up again. Wonderment was in them, those fiercely glittering eyes as they darted everywhere at once, her courage returned, it seemed, after the initial shock of noise and movement. The man behind the fruit on the opposite stall winked at her as he caught her eye and she blushed furiously then chanced a small smile at him.

"Right little treasure that one, Mrs Goodall," he shouted

across the bonnets of the ladies who were once again crowding round the stall.

"I believe she is, Mr Barnes," Mrs Goodall replied and Poppy's smile of pleasure lit her face.

The rush began again and for the first time without Mrs Goodall's prompting Poppy lifted her eyes bravely to a customer, asking her politely if she could help her.

"I hope so, miss. I'll take a dozen white eggs, large, and a dozen brown. A pound of butter and a nice slice of cheese, about half a pound, if you please. Now, have you got that?"

"Yes, ma'am."

"And the correct change, mind," the lady said, rudely in Poppy's opinion as she counted it out in to the large, hardworking palm.

"Of course, ma'am," Poppy answered sweetly. "Will that be all?"

"Yes, thank you, child and good morning." The customer smiled then, revealing herself to be a perfectly ordinary and pleasant woman who, faced with a small girl to serve her, had feared she might be short-changed.

Her first customer. Her very own first customer and she had managed it all by herself. She had remembered what the lady had asked her for, given it, and the right change and the lady had gone away happy.

"Well done, my dear," Mrs Goodall, who had been watching her, whispered before turning away to face the crowd of ladies who were eager to purchase what was left of her produce. The best in the market, she had a reputation for, and the way it was whisked off her stall and into wicker baskets attested to it.

Poppy was just about to count out a dozen large brown eggs when she saw him and the shock of it made her drop one. Bloody hell, she remembered thinking, that's three in two days and if she continued like this Mrs Goodall would give her the sack. The customer tutted as though to say that's what came of employing a child to do an adult's work, and Mrs Goodall turned in surprise.

The stall, which Mrs Goodall rented every week in the same position, since she wanted her customers to know exactly where to find her, was about halfway along the one hundred and eighty-three yards length of the market. The light from the one hundred and thirty-six windows was pure golden sunlight today since the building was tall and the windows all down one side got the full force of the sun. It fell on his bright head which was at least twelve inches above any other in the market, lighting his hair to a torch of blinding copper and gold, to a dozen colours of flame. It had obviously not been cut for many weeks, falling about his young, good-humoured face to his shoulders in a waving mane. As she watched him with a tremble of horror in which exasperation was mixed, for surely the fool was aware of how conspicuous he was, he lifted a hand and pushed it, comb-like, through the waves. The sleeves of his shirt were pushed up to his elbow since it was a warm day and she could see the fine sprinkling of reddish gold fuzz on his forearms and as he turned his head the first auburn prickles of a boy's downy beard gleamed as they caught in the sunlight. He was wearing tight breeches of a greyish brown colour with well-polished black knee boots just as though he were about to leap on a horse and gallop away. He was dressed so totally unlike any other male in the market, even as he walked heads were turning to look at him. In a small gap in the crowd Poppy caught a brief glimpse of his long, shapely legs, his well-muscled thighs, then the crowd closed in again and he was surrounded by shoppers, only his sun-tinted face and the bright flame of his hair still visible.

She didn't know what he took. Probably nothing more than an apple or a fancy cake from the baker's stall, since nothing incriminating was found on him but the stall-holder saw it and began to shriek. The crowd froze and turned to look in the direction of the commotion, forming a solid, unmoving block of frowning women, since nobody liked a thief, and when he began to race towards Mrs Goodall's stall they seemed to gang up on him, big as he was.

"Stop, thief," the stall-holder was shouting and as if from out of the ground Mr Clarke, the porter, and Bertie, the well-built young man who had led away the horse and cart, plus the two police constables who patrolled the market, sprang up, Mr Clarke and Bertie at one end of the aisle, the constables at the other.

He did his best, sprinting and dodging through the crowd of women and Poppy believed that if they had been men he would have managed it. It was his own reluctance to charge at and perhaps injure one of the matronly shoppers who stood in his way that was his undoing. He was weaving from side to side as they put out their hands to restrain him but he was being hemmed in and when several other stall-holders, male stall-holders who were fed up with the petty thievery that went on, losing them profit, jumped over their stalls and joined in the chase he was done for.

"Good heavens, isn't that . . . the cricketer?" Mrs Goodall asked, her jaw slack with surprise, ready to drop an egg or two herself in amazement.

Poppy willed him to escape, clenching her jaw so tightly she could barely pry it apart when it was all over, but directly in front of Mrs Goodall's stall they had him, Mr Clarke, Bertie, the two police constables and several assorted stall-holders, each one landing a fist or a boot on his unprotected body as he went down.

She simply stood there, bewildered by her own feelings of distress, her face as white as the crisp apron she wore, her eyes wide and shocked, her hand to her mouth as they hauled him to his feet.

"We've bin on the lookout fer this bugger fer weeks," she heard the constable say in triumph. "Would yer credit the cheeky young devil 'angin' about in a place like this. 'E must've known wi' that red 'air someone'd be bound to spot 'im." He seemed to have forgotten that had it not been for the cheeky young bugger's foolishness in helping himself to an apple off a stall he would have walked in and out of the place, escaping the notice of both constables.

The lad struggled, not much since there were half a dozen men hanging on to him, more to show his defiance, Poppy thought, than with any hope of freeing himself, but he earned himself a cuff about the head from the constable's heavy handcuffs and she saw his vivid blue eyes glaze in pain.

"Fetch them leg-irons from't van, Fred. I can see 'e's gonner be trouble," the first constable said to the second, as he fastened the cumbersome handcuffs to the lad's wrists, twisting his arms cruelly behind his back while Mr Clarke, Bertie and the stall-holders held on like grim death. They seemed reluctant to let go of their share of the glory. Already both his eyes were beginning to close and there was a large bruise over his cheekbone.

Eliza Goodall stepped out from behind her stall as the second constable returned with the leg-irons, her jaw jutting and angry, and it was perhaps at that precise moment that Poppy's feelings for her underwent a change. She had always admired and respected her but now she began to know the deep and lasting affection which was to endure until they were parted. Mrs Goodall didn't know this lad but she was willing to stand up for him and Poppy was deeply grateful to her.

"Surely there is no need for those, constable," Mrs Goodall snapped imperiously. "The lad is well and truly fettered beside being beaten half senseless by every man around him. He cannot escape."

The constable was incensed at what he saw as deliberate interference in what he knew to be his duty. This lad was a danger to the community, a thief and an escaped law-breaker and every means at the constable's disposal must be used to bring him to justice.

"Madam, I'll thank you ter mind yer own business. We 'ave a criminal on our 'ands 'ere . . ."

"A criminal! Why he's only a boy and even so is that any reason for excessive cruelty?"

"It's the law, madam, ter put offenders in leg-irons an' 'andcuffs an' if you'll stand aside an' allow us ter carry out the law I'd be obliged."

During the whole of this exchange Poppy and the red-haired lad looked at one another, their eyes locked in some strange communion. Though his were swollen and he could barely see through his rapidly closing lids, she felt the valiance in them cut her to the heart. Such a lovely, smiling blue they had been on the day of the fair but even now she thought she saw a hint of a smile in them, a smile directed at her. It was as though he were telling her that this was nothing, that she must not worry about him or what was to happen to him, for he was strong and well able to look after himself.

He winced as the leg-irons were fastened tightly about his ankles, the chain between them so short he could barely hobble as they dragged him away. His head was up, though, his back as straight and unbowed as a young sapling, his mane of red hair a bright signal of his defiance.

He turned back to look at her at the doorway, his mouth twitching in what she was convinced was a flicker of humour, then he was gone.

8

At the end of August, having completed his sentence of three months' "training" on the *Lahore*, Douglas Appleton came home, not exactly chastened but painfully impressed by what he had seen others suffer aboard the reformatory ship.

Just two days before he returned the kitchen servants were taken aback when Martha Appleton's youngest boy, whose name was Eustace, appeared at the back door declaring that he'd been sent for their Poppy.

The maidservants viewed him with appalled horror, allowing him to come no further than the back step, asking one another could this filthy child, his nose running, his sleeve caked with dried snot where he had used it to wipe the organ, his face and bare feet as black as the fire back, be the brother of their fastidious little dairymaid whose passion for neatness and cleanliness was a byword at Long Reach Farm?

Cook was making suet dumplings to be put into the enormous pan of stew which was simmering on the stove ready for the midday meal. Her hands were deft as she shaped the dumplings into neat round balls but, like a conjurer performing a trick she threw them both up in the air in her abhorrence at the apparition in her doorway.

May, who had answered the hammering on the door, backed away dramatically in a manner that said she had no wish to be contaminated by whatever livestock the boy was sure to carry on his person.

"Don't you come inside my clean kitchen, my lad," Cook thundered. "State your business and then be off with you. That step's just been scrubbed."

The boy showed no sign of offence, staring round the door frame with awed interest, his pug nose wrinkling as the delicious aroma of the meal being prepared assailed his nostrils.

"I've ter fetch our Poppy," he said, swallowing the saliva which gushed to his mouth and for a moment Cook was tempted to give him a bit of something to eat since he looked half starved.

"Fetch the mistress, May," she said instead.

"Yes, what is it?" Mrs Goodall asked him abruptly when she was brought to the back door from her parlour where she had been preparing the next step in the education of her protégée. She had mentioned it to no one, least of all Tom who would think she'd lost her wits, and perhaps she had, for what use, in the working world, would it possibly be to Poppy? Her pupil could write a clear, legible hand. Her spelling was correct and so was her grammar. She was reading everything Eliza put into her hands from Louisa May Alcott's *Little Women* to *The Woman in White* by Wilkie Collins, which was some achievement for a girl of twelve who had been illiterate a year ago. She had progressed from "take-aways" and "add-ups" to multiplication and division and Eliza had the fancy to start her on a bit of French. Foolish, she knew, for a girl who would never be more than a maidservant but then Eliza had private thoughts about that as well!

"Me pa wants our Poppy," the urchin declared, becoming truculent but at the same time taking a nervous step away from this tall, stern woman who their Lily had called "the witch from up yonder". He sniffed and the two ropes of discharge hanging from his nose to his top lip quivered.

They all shuddered, including Mrs Goodall.

"Can yer not blow yer nose, lad?" Cook asked him in disgust, throwing a clean cloth protectively across the bowl in which the dumpling mixture stood, as though whatever pollution the boy carried might leap across the intervening space, but he merely looked bewildered.

"Evidently not, Cook." Eliza Goodall swallowed the revulsion she felt. Her heart was already beginning to miss a beat or two in dread of what Poppy's pa might want with her, for the fear was always in the back of her mind that Martha Appleton might take it into her head to demand the return of her "good girl", particularly since this last illness. Added to that was the revolting thought that her dainty little dairymaid and gifted disciple who had brought such joy into Eliza's life was related to this snot-nosed ragamuffin. It was enough to nauseate the strongest stomach.

She drew herself up stiffly, though what effect this would have on the boy, if any, was doubtful.

"Poppy is working, I'm afraid, and cannot be spared. Tell your father I will send her over when she is free."

"Me pa ses our Poppy's ter come right away," the boy insisted.

For Poppy to be summoned at all by her father was frightening. It must be something serious, for as far as Eliza was aware the feckless labourer took little notice of what went on in his family circle.

Still she rebelled against it, her hand gripping the door

latch resolutely as though, should he try, she was ready for any move the boy might make.

Aggie and Clara were just about to go upstairs and turn out the bedrooms, and in readiness for this weekly task they were armed with a housemaid's box apiece in which were all the tools needed for the job. Dusters and brushes, bottles of turpentine to add to the buckets of hot water May would carry up for them, fragrant beeswax polish. All the furniture would be moved on to the landing, the feather beds shaken, the bolsters beaten, the ewers and jugs well scrubbed, the carpets swept, each piece of furniture polished before being returned to its proper place in the bedroom. The windows would be washed, the curtains shaken free of dust and the bed linen, which Mrs Goodall liked changed every week, brought down for the attention of the washerwoman who came twice a week to do the laundry.

They hung about by the kitchen door, reluctant to leave lest they miss any of what promised to be a bit of excitement. They all knew Poppy's mother had not been herself since the miscarriage and that Poppy went over there regularly to clean the place – and her mam – up a bit. Martha's three eldest daughters, Rose, Lily and Iris, had all left home, so Poppy had told them briefly since she was not one to gossip about her irresponsible family, Rose to get married, Lily and Iris, despite being no more than fourteen or so, to "work" in Liverpool, the type of work only to be guessed at! Marigold laboured, when there was work to be had that she could manage, mostly in the fields about the farm. Marigold was next in age to Poppy and was what Reuben unkindly called "elevenpence halfpenny in the shilling" and though a strong girl had always to be watched and told the simplest thing half a dozen times before understanding what was needed of her.

Which left Poppy. But then there had only ever been Poppy, even when all her sisters had been at home.

"What does your father want with Poppy?" Mrs Goodall asked the boy, who was already poised to make a break for it now he had delivered his message. His mam had been talking for weeks now about Poppy coming home to live. He had heard her and Poppy arguing about it, their Poppy shouting she'd rather die than return to the squalor – whatever that was – that her mam and the rest of them lived in, his mam crying and begging Poppy to give over and be a good girl. Poppy had sworn tearfully that she'd slip down to the cottage whenever she could if only Mam would let her stay at the farm, promising to scrub and scour and even give Mam a bath but it seemed Mam didn't want scrubbing and scouring and bathing, she wanted her good girl home again to look after them all, to cook them a "birra summat tasty" to eat, to keep her mam company, to change her bloody clouts and wash them, to sit and gossip when Martha felt low, which was often. Mam missed her, she had told Poppy, especially with the other girls gone, missed a bit of sensible female conversation since you couldn't count their Marigold, for, though female she might be, sensible she wasn't.

That's what his mam wanted apparently but he could not tell this forbidding woman so, could he? Nor could he tell her of the plight his mam was in, a state so dreadful his pa had sent him running over to fetch their Poppy. It was a week since Poppy had last been to the cottage and even he, young as he was and used as he was to the condition in which he had lived all his life, had been sickened by the appalling stench which hung about the upstairs room where his mam had lain for the past three days since she could no longer manage the ladder down to the kitchen.

"Me pa ses our Poppy's ter come right away," he repeated stubbornly. "Mam's took bad ways an' our Poppy's needed."

"What is wrong with your mother?" Eliza persisted desperately, doing her best to put off the moment when Poppy must be brought over from the dairy. This was Poppy's mother they were discussing, if discussing was the right word, and a mother was entitled to support from her children when in need, but Eliza longed to tell this boy that Poppy was too busy and they must manage without her for once.

There was a moment's deep silence while Eliza struggled with her conscience. The maids held their breath as though aware that this moment was one of importance in Poppy's life though they didn't know why. Cook turned away, tutting with disapproval, making sure her bowl was still properly covered, wishing she could order this lad off her clean step – which May would have to scrub again now – and close the door on him. When would the lass ever be free of this dreadful family of hers? her expression said quite plainly for all to see.

Their mistress's shoulders sagged wearily.

"Run to the dairy, May, and fetch Poppy, if you please, and be quick about it. Say her mother is . . . unwell." Her voice was bitter. None of them, least of all her, recognised the tone of deep resentment in it.

Poppy was considerably startled when May burst into the dairy, so startled she almost dropped the bowl of cream she was about to place carefully on the stone shelf to ripen.

"Yer daft beggar," she blurted out furiously, turning on May. "Is there any need ter come crashin' in 'ere as though yer were bein' chased by a bull? I might've dropped that there bowl an' then where'd we be? Cream everywhere an' the floor ter scrub . . ."

"Oh, bugger the floor, Poppy Appleton. Yer ter come right away ter't kitchen."

"May Jebson!" Poppy was visibly shocked. Like all those who have been converted any straying from the path of decency appalled her. "Yer know Mrs Goodall can't abide language. Good job she didn't 'ear yer or yer'd've bin for it." Poppy looked as though the idea of May Jebson being "for it" gave her a great deal of satisfaction. She smoothed down her spotless apron primly just as though never in her life had *she* used bad language, and pursed her rosy lips in disapproval.

"Bugger . . ." May had been just about to say "Bugger Mrs Goodall," but thought better of it. Poppy and Nelly didn't count since they had no authority over her but Dilys was a different matter and might have something to say about it.

"Look, I were sent ter fetch yer so are yer comin' or not?"

"What for?"

"Yer wanted."

"What for?"

" 'Ow the 'ell do I know? Can yer not just come wi'out all this argy-bargy. Yer mam's took bad ways, yer pa ses."

"Me pa's in't kitchen?" Poppy looked horrified.

"No, but your what's-it is. I don't know 'is name—"

"What's up wi' me ma?" Poppy interrupted though she knew full well what it was.

May's patience was wearing thin. "I don't know, do I?"

Poppy looked distractedly round the dairy as though searching for inspiration. They were just about to start churning today's butter and pails of milk stood in rows where Evan and Tommy had left them. It was a hot day and if they didn't begin soon the milk would go off. She sighed and shook her be-capped head.

"Well, I'll 'ave ter finish 'ere first. I can't just leave . . ." she began to say but Dilys tutted in exasperation.

"Look you, girl, if the mistress do want you you'd best go, see. Leave that cream. Me an' Nelly'll see to it."

"But wharrabout the butter?"

"For goodness sake, off you go. Me an' Nelly'll manage."

"I can't just beggar off an' leave it all fer you to do."

It was plain that Poppy was immensely irritated by the interruption in the smooth running of her working day. She and the others had a routine that she liked strictly kept to. She had a passion for routine, for doing things in the proper order and at the proper time. Her mam had been begging her for weeks to come home and this was probably just a trick to get her to comply, she was sure. She felt totally opposed to doing what May asked her but she supposed she had no option but to go and check. If Mrs Goodall had sent for her she could hardly refuse, could she? But it was a damned nuisance. It was market day tomorrow and there was still a lot to be done in readiness for it. Fowls to be cleaned and plucked, eggs to be packed and several dozen butter shells still to be shaped. Then it all had to be packed into the small cart. Perhaps with a bit of luck she'd be back within the hour.

"Well, I'll get back as soon as I can," she told Dilys, whipping off her apron and folding it neatly on the shelf where the clean cloths were kept.

It was a week since Poppy had been to the cottage, spending her afternoon off scrubbing and scouring and doing her best to let some light in through the dirt-encrusted windows. She had washed her mother's stained garments, after persuading her to part with them, that is, which was often a difficult feat. Martha didn't want Poppy to work, she complained, she wanted her to sit by the fire and drink Mrs Goodall's tea and and tell her old mam all that was going on up at the farmhouse. The place was clean enough, she said fretfully. After all, Poppy was at it from the moment she arrived until the moment she left and couldn't she leave it for once and sit down and talk to her mam, she said.

She had nothing to say on the matter today, or on any other matter, come to that and Poppy was shocked by the change in her in such a short time. The slow draining away of her life's blood since her latest miscarriage had weakened her already undernourished body and had it not been for the weekly basket of good food Poppy had been bringing she would have succumbed long before this.

Last night, it appeared, the slow leakage, the smell of which was so abominable her husband and sons, it being a fine night, had dragged out their palliasse and slept in the open, had begun to quicken, bringing away nasty matter which had been festering inside her since she lost her child.

It took all Poppy's strength and indomitable spirit, the steadfast fortitude she had built up in her first ten years of deprivation and poverty to get her through those next few hours. Retching drily, her face as white as that of her bloodless mother, she had stripped her and the blood-soaked mattress, then, having nowhere to put her mother's feebly muttering form, no hot water since the fire was out, no clean bed linen, no soap, in fact not one bare necessity to ease her mother's wretchedness, she had scribbled a note to Mrs Goodall on the edge of a page torn from a magazine Lily had left, thankful she had a pencil in her skirt pocket, put the note in Eustace's reluctant hand, then sat down in the filth and nursed her mother's skinny, rotting body until help arrived.

If Reuben Appleton objected to his employer's wife taking

over his poor home he showed no sign of it. It was a long time since he had felt more than a resentful pity for his wife and when, several hours later, she died in the arms of her youngest daughter, he accepted it as he had accepted everything in his deprived life. Every disaster, and there had been many, the times he had been knocked to his knees by the blows he had been dealt and got up again with the poor man's resignation, for what else was he to do? Obediently he had hurried up to the farmhouse with their Herbert to fetch a clean palliasse for the dying woman to lie on as she went. Though it was a terrible struggle and took him and Herbert and Evan, who had been called in to give a hand – much to Tom Goodall's annoyance – they managed to get Martha down the ladder to the hastily scrubbed kitchen before the doctor came. Not that there was anything the man, who would not have come but for Eliza Goodall's note, could do, but at least it eased Poppy's mind to have him there, which was why Eliza had sent for him.

Poppy refused to leave her mother's body though Eliza pleaded with her to come home.

"She will have a decent funeral, my dear, I'll see to that, and until then you must not consider working in the dairy but do come home and sleep in your own bed," she begged. She could not bear to contemplate this lovely child spending a moment longer than was necessary in a hell-hole where poverty and fertility lived side by side with festering filth, with old sweat and dirty bodies, with the stink of sewage and the sour smell of lice. She found herself taking shallow breaths and her mouth was filled with saliva that she longed to spit out since the thought of swallowing it revolted her.

Poppy shook her head gently. In her eyes was the affection and trust and gratitude she felt for Eliza Goodall but this time it was for her mam. This hour, this night, the days until Mam was put away beneath the green grass in the churchyard belonged to her. She had been as good a mam as she could be in the circumstances of her life, which had constantly overwhelmed her, and it was not her fault that in the end it had all been too much and she had given up. Since her marriage, if married they had been, to Pa, she had been carrying a child for most of the time but still working her weary body in the fields to bring in a few bob to help feed her children. And they had never gone hungry, not seriously hungry, not one of them, which was some achievement when you considered the way Pa threw his wages down his neck at the week's end. Mam had done her best and what more could any woman be asked to do? And if her other daughters cared nought for her passing then it was up to Poppy to mourn for her, to keep vigil beside her this night. Her pa was not a bad man nor a cruel man but almost before Martha Appleton was cold he was down to the Grimshaw Arms to drown his "sorrow", to accept the pints that came his way from sympathetic fellow drinkers who had heard of his loss. And when he stumbled home the worse for it, was it likely he would sit with his dead wife?

No, and as it had done ever since she could remember the responsibility fell on Poppy Appleton's valiant shoulders.

Douglas Appleton was climbing the slope of the field which led up to Primrose Bank from Prescot Road just as the small cortège of mourners was moving slowly down it. He was badly startled at the sight of it, though he had no idea at the time whose funeral it might be. The coffin containing Martha was carried somewhat lopsidedly by her husband, her son Herbert who, at nine years of age was a foot smaller than his father, and the cowmen, Evan and Tommy, who had offered to be pall-bearers for Poppy's sake. It halted at the sight of Douglas.

Poppy was dressed in the black frock and bonnet Mrs Goodall had mackled together for her. She had her hand in that of her employer who had braved her husband's irritation over what he saw as her foolishness in thinking it necessary to be there at all. The child needed her, she told him fiercely. Who else was there to stand beside Poppy Appleton as they laid her mother to rest? Certainly not that father of hers who had been in drink for the past thirty-six hours and certainly not her siblings, those who were left, so Tom could like it or not, she told him, jamming her own black bonnet on her greying hair.

Poppy honestly didn't know how she would have got through the past two days without Mrs Goodall. Food was brought down regularly from the farm kitchen and Reuben and his children told one another that, apart from Mam's death which was sad, of course, they'd never had such a good time in their lives. Plenty to eat and their Poppy to clean and scrub and wait on them hand and foot as she had done in the past and though the dead woman lay on a trestle table in the corner of the kitchen, peacefully sleeping in the plain coffin Mrs Goodall had provided, she did not unduly discommode them. Their Poppy said nowt, sitting beside the coffin, taking no notice of them and if Mrs Goodall turned up at all times of the day and night she didn't interfere with them.

She was a rock to which Poppy clung as she now clung to her hand and it was not until Douglas, his face creased in surprised consternation cried, " 'Oo's died?" that she burst into tears. To do him justice, so did Douglas, though it was more shock than grief which caused it, but he manfully shouldered Herbert's corner of the coffin as they trudged off again in the direction of the churchyard. No one but Mrs Goodall accompanied them.

Poppy was to go back to the farm that evening, she had promised Mrs Goodall. No later than seven o'clock for she'd work to go to tomorrow and she was bone tired after sitting with Mam for two nights and a day; after the relentless cleaning she had done for the last time in memory of her Mam, she told herself; after the shock and sadness she had suffered at the loss of Mam's going. Rose had turned up for the funeral to sit on her bum and drink the tea and eat the food Mrs Goodall had brought over but of the others there had been no sign. Poppy wanted to have a private talk with their Douglas before she returned to the farm and so she waited patiently until Rose got to her feet at last, saying she must be off.

"What yer gonner do, our Poppy?" she asked carelessly, not really caring since it was of no concern to her now she had a man of her own to see to.

"Do? Wharrabout?"

"Well, Pa an' the others."

"What d'yer mean?" Poppy could feel resentment stir inside her for she knew exactly what Rose meant.

"Will yer move back 'ere ter look after Pa an' the kids now that Mam's gone?"

Poppy bristled. "Why should I? Besides I've me own livin' to earn."

"I don't mean give up yer job, cloth'ead, but someone 'as ter look after 'em."

"Why should it be me? What's wrong wi' you comin' up to see to 'em now an' again?"

"I've me own place ter see to." Rose reached for her best bonnet, a battered straw which, on her labouring husband's wage, she was bitterly aware, would have to last a long time, especially as she was already in the family way and would have to give up the odd field jobs she managed so far.

"Well, it's up ter you," she added.

"I know that, our Rose, an' I'll tell yer now I've no intention o' runnin' up 'ere ter clean like I did when Mam were alive." There was a catch in her throat as she spoke. "I've done wi' that now she's gone. They'll 'ave ter fend fer themselves. Our Marigold could see to it if she was shown 'ow an' I mean ter show 'er. Anyroad, Mrs Goodall said she might find 'er a job in't kitchen. I'll keep me eye on our Herbert an' Eustace but me pa must mekk 'is own arrangements now." Her eyes glinted and her small chin was firm with resolve.

"Right then." It was obvious Rose didn't care who made arrangements, or for what purpose. She had her own life to lead.

The two sisters looked at one another uncomfortably, both aware that this could possibly be the last time they might see one another now that their mam, who had been the linchpin of the family, was gone. Rose was not yet eighteen and already headed into the deep mire her mother had floundered in though she told herself things would be different with her. Poppy, on the other hand, had a fine future ahead of her. Not for her a life on a labourer's wage. Not for her a poky cottage and a brood of children about her skirts. She and Rose had nothing in common except blood and their goodbyes were brief and cursory.

Poppy waited until Rose had moved off down the lane leading to the path across the field, shading her eyes with her hand as the bright sunlight struck the glossy cap of her brown hair. Rose did not turn. Poppy did not expect her to as she leaned her shoulder on the crumbling door frame, looking in the other direction to where Douglas was sitting, obviously at a loose end, on the top rung of the gate which led into the field. He was still in a state of shock at finding his mother's funeral cortège coming to meet him down the field that afternoon, but he'd get over it, Poppy thought grimly. They all would, even her, she was honest enough to admit, but before she made her way up the track to the farmhouse where her own future lay there were one or two questions she wanted to ask her brother about someone from the past.

"Come an' 'ave a cuppa tea an' a slice o' fruit cake wi' me before I go, our Douglas," she commanded and Douglas sighed, obediently climbing down from the gate, since at the moment he'd nowt else to do in this strange vacuum his mother's death had left. He'd be off to Liverpool in a bit, for there was no work here he fancied and he'd learned a thing or two and made a few useful connections on the old *Lahore* which might lead to something better than this. He'd no intention of finishing up like his pa just as Rose, in her naïvety, had no intention of finishing up like her ma.

In silence they drank a decent cup of tea together and ate Cook's rich fruit cake before Poppy spoke diffidently, asking Douglas to tell her about his three months on the *Lahore*, which he was quite willing to do and when he had finished she wished she'd let it alone. It was just that a bright red head and a pair of vivid laughing blue eyes had distracted her dreams, waking and sleeping, ever since that day in the market and she hoped Douglas might be able to set her mind at rest about their owner. He did not do so. Just the opposite.

"It were all right as long as yer be'aved yerself an' kep' yer mouth shut. They 'ad what were called a boatswain an' petty officers 'oo stood over us while we scrubbed decks wi' stone an' then wi' coconut 'usks. The 'usks were not so 'ard on't wood o't decks, yer see." He sipped his tea reflectively.

"D'yer know, our Poppy, we 'ad ter repair our own duds. Can yer imagine me wi' a needle an' thread? Oh aye," when she gawped in astonishment. "We was given blue trousers, a guernsey an' a cap each." He smirked grimly. "Proper little sailors we was. We even medd our own shoes, or some of us did. I were too cack-'anded so I gorra couple o' cracks round me lug'ole over that. Another job were teasin' an' splittin' old rope which were a bloody filthy job, I can tell yer. Took skin off yer bloody fingers. An' they tried ter teach us ter read an' write. Not that they managed it wi' me burr I kep' me nose clean an' they didn't bother me much. Church service an' 'ymns on a Sunday wi' what they called 'leckshers' on bein' kind, 'onest, 'ardworkin' an' leadin' clean an' Godly lives while . . . well, I'll not tell yer what some of 'em tried on wi't little lads."

He paused and his shoulders seemed to droop under the burden of some dreadful memory. "Then there were't 'Cat' fer them what tried ter escape or were . . . were . . . insub . . . insubor . . ."

"Insubordinate?"

"Aye, that were it. A dozen were the most they were supposed ter lay on since most was only kids."

"What . . . what was the . . . the Cat?" Poppy quavered, her gorge beginning to rise.

Douglas's eyes had darkened. "The Cat? A lash it were, wi' nine tails an' one stroke could tekk skin off yer back."

"Did all those who escaped an' were . . . recaptured . . . get it?"

"Oh aye. There were a bounty o' twenty shillin's an 'ead on runaways an' when they was caught we all 'ad ter watch the floggin'. They 'ad a 'floggin' 'orse' on't deck an' poor bugger were stretched across it wi' 'is arms an' legs tied by straps."

Douglas swallowed, not looking at her, his face grim as he returned to the borders of memory.

"Watchin' a floggin's norra pretty sight, our Poppy."

"No, I can imagine."

"Turned me stomach, I can tell yer."

"Who?"

"Oh, more'n one but Conn's was worse I ever sin."

"Conn?"

"Aye, a mate o' mine. 'Im what were tekken in wi' me. A bloody brave lad is Conn." Douglas's eyes glowed in respectful admiration.

"What happened?" she asked though she really didn't want to be told.

"It were when 'e were brought back a few weeks ago. 'E'd bin free fer a while burr 'e were caught in't market, 'e told me later. I . . . I seen to 'is back fer 'im when . . . they cut 'im down. God, what a bloody mess. I could see't bone. Lash draws blood right away, yer see. They was only supposed ter lay on twelve, that was orders, no more, but Conn were cocky like, smilin' as though 'e didn't give a bugger an' it seemed ter make 'em see red. 'E were always in trouble, see, givin' 'em lip, defending some little lad or interferin' when 'e saw wharr 'e thought were wrong so . . . they 'ad it in fer 'im. Thirty, they give 'im burr 'e didn't mekk a sound which medd 'em madder than ever. 'E set 'is face ter't wood an' . . . Christ, Poppy, blood were runnin' down 'is back an' . . . well, 'e musta fainted. They cut 'im down an' 'e fell. Yer should've seen skin on 'is back 'anging in strips." Douglas shook his head in wonderment, close to tears. "'E still 'ad scars yesterday when . . ."

Douglas bent his head and covered his face with his hand and there was complete silence. Poppy could hear next door's cat mewing piteously then there was a screech as some boot removed it from the doorstep where it cowered.

Douglas raised his head.

"I 'eard this mornin', just before I were rowed over to't dock, 'e'd gone again. Over't side in't night. Jesus, if they catch 'im again they'll bloody kill 'im."

9

It was Clucky who led her to him. Douglas had gone only he knew where and during the autumn and early winter Poppy had settled down to the life she had known before her mother's death. She went a time or two to the cottage in Primrose Bank which, surprisingly, since Mam had gone began to take a turn for the better, thanks to Marigold. Marigold was working at the farm now, skivvy in place of May who had been promoted to kitchen maid and who was tickled pink to have someone to boss about, particularly as that someone was Clever Clogs's sister. The work Marigold did in the farmhouse kitchen, the scullery, the steps, the stone-flagged passages, scrubbing alongside Mrs Kennaway who, getting older, was glad of the help, seemed to awaken in Poppy's sister her own desire for a bit of spit and polish at the cottage to which she returned each night. With Douglas and Arthur vanished there was only her pa and the two boys in the rooms which had once held eleven of them and, as she confided to Poppy, with Pa at the Grimshaw Arms and her brothers, once they had eaten, out heaven alone knew where of a night, she found the task of keeping the cottage in some sort of order a relatively simple one.

Cook, who got on with anyone who was respectful, clean

and hardworking, which Marigold had learned to be, had taught her how to prepare a few simple, nourishing dishes with which to feed her menfolk. She herself shared the servants' splendid meals in the farmhouse kitchen and, like Poppy, looked the better for it, so it seemed Poppy could relax and get on with her own routine of work and study in the knowledge that, for the moment, her family, what was left of it, was surviving.

She had begun to learn to play the piano. She had known for a long time what was under the shawl in Mrs Goodall's study, since Aggie and Clara, who cleaned the room and polished the instrument every week, had told her. Left to herself one evening she had taken a peep, astonished and filled with wonder at the shining beauty of the thing but she had never dreamed that it might one day concern her since she wasn't even sure what it did. It produced some sort of music, she was aware of that, but how it sounded and how one achieved it was a mystery to her.

Until one night when Mrs Goodall threw off the shawl, opened the front and began to run her fingers up and down the black and white wedges that were revealed. Poppy was enthralled. She had read about it, of course, for didn't some of the characters in the books that were familiar to her play the piano, especially Jo March in *Little Women*, but to see Mrs Goodall rippling her fingers so gracefully, to hear the mellow, rounded sounds that came from them, was a revelation to the girl.

For about twenty minutes, while Poppy leaned beside her at the end of the upright piano, Eliza played lilting songs, some of which were known to Poppy. "Greensleeves". A lullaby called "Golden Slumbers" she vaguely remembered her mam singing to her, and "Early One Morning". Other tunes which she didn't know but which moved her heart and made her shiver in delight. She was sorry when Mrs Goodall stopped, then turned to smile at her.

"Would you like to try, child?" she asked Poppy just as though Poppy had any choice in the matter! At once Poppy began to back away, for how could her rough hands, in and out of hot water all day long and which, despite the salve Mrs Goodall supplied to her three dairymaids to rub into them each night, were red and coarse, manage the lovely, intricate movements Mrs Goodall had performed?

Mrs Goodall stood up in that purposeful way she had and Poppy knew she was for it. She had done everything her mistress had taught her to do, and done it well, even to the "bit of French" Mrs Goodall had started her on. She knew she was a good pupil, quick to learn and adaptable, for Mrs Goodall had told her so, but how the devil was she to make *her* hands move in the neat and flexible way Mrs Goodall's had just done? They were cunning in the shaping of butter shells, the milking of the cows, the making of cheeses, the plucking of fowl, all the duties she performed so neatly in the dairy. A pen was as familiar in her hand now as the brush and bucket which had been her only tools last year. A book was no longer the mysterious object it had been over a year ago, though it was still her deepest joy, and really she asked for no more. She already had a dozen more accomplishments than most young girls of her age, even in those stations of life far above her, but, chewing her lip, sighing, for she knew Mrs Goodall would not be gainsaid, she sat down apprehensively on the stool Mrs Goodall had just vacated and waited.

"There," Mrs Goodall said gaily, "that wasn't so bad, was it?"

"Sittin' down wasn't. It's rest I'm bothered about," Poppy answered gloomily.

"Come now, Poppy, that's not like you. You know you can do it. Look at all the other things you were sure you couldn't do, and then did. Remember percentages? You soon got the hang of it when I told you how important they were when it came to calculating profits."

"That was different."

"Why, may I ask?"

"Well, I knew it'd be useful ter me when I tekk over't market stall."

"Does everything have to be 'useful', Poppy? Can one not learn to do something that has no use whatsoever except to give pleasure? Do you like music?"

"I suppose so." It was said grudgingly.

"There's no suppose about it. I saw your face while I was playing. You loved it, you know you did, so let us begin."

Poppy sighed again deeply but Eliza Goodall took no notice. She had set her heart on Poppy learning to play the piano and no one, least of all Poppy, was going to put her off. She didn't know what Tom would have to say – well, she did – when he heard of the latest "barminess", as he would call it, that she planned for her pupil, but whatever it was she had no intention of stopping now. It was as though she wanted to test Poppy Appleton's skills and intelligence to their utmost limit and until she reached that limit, if she ever did, she would continue to challenge the child with every endowment she herself possessed.

"Now first of all I'll tell you what each part of the piano is called. Are you listening?"

"Aye." Poppy's voice was resigned.

"Good. Now this is the top, obviously. That is the upper panel and attached to it is the music rack which will hold the music sheets from which you will read and play. The keyboard, here, is made up of black and white keys and at your feet are the pedals. Don't worry, they will become as familiar to you as your books."

Poppy looked disbelieving.

"Now I will not explain the right, or sustaining pedal, nor the left soft pedal just yet. First I want you to relax because the way you sit and position your arms and hands is very important, since it will affect how well and how easily you play. Back straight, leaning forward slightly, your upper arms vertical – you know what vertical means . . . good – your forearms and hands in a straight horizontal line with your fingertips resting on the keys. Now, assume that position for me. No, don't bend your neck and only put your finger *tips* on the keys. Yes, those are the keys. Good, that's better. Now, with your fingers slightly curved and with each fingertip on a different key, let me hear a sound."

It took many evenings of an aching back and neck, sore wrists, many fumbling, clumsy-fingered attempts even to get her hands in the correct position before Poppy could find her way round the piano and count the beat for the music, but eventually, slowly and evenly tapping her foot in time with the rhythm, she could play a simple tune with her right hand, then her left, then with both of them together.

The other servants were not at all sure they approved. It was all very well teaching a maidservant to read and write, particularly if she was to help the mistress with such things, though they were not awfully sure they agreed even with that, but what possible use would a dairymaid have for learning to play the piano? Was she ever likely to have one of her own, they asked one another, and so where was the sense of it? They were used now to Mrs Goodall and Poppy spending an hour in the study every evening, doing the accounts or whatever it was that took place there – knowing nothing of the "bit of French" – but when the hesitant, discordant, uneven tinkling of the piano keys fell on their amazed ears and, well aware that it was not their mistress playing for hadn't they heard her a time or two during the day, they were astonished and disapproving. Even Cook who had a soft spot for Poppy. Getting above herself was the kindest remark made, though really, when you considered it, it was not the little lass's fault, was it? None of it was her doing but some foolish whim the mistress had and where was it to lead?

"Yer'll be sittin' on yer bum doin' fine embroidery next, I shouldn't wonder," May sneered resentfully, "or paintin't flowers down't gardin. Is it a fine lady yer ter be then? I dunno, it fair beats all when a dairymaid is learned bloody piano."

"Button yer lip, May Jebson," Poppy exclaimed angrily. "What me an' Mrs Goodall do is none o' your concern an' I'll thank you to mind yer own business."

"Now then, you two. Poppy's right and it's nothing ter do wi' you, May, so just hand me that pie dish and you, Aggie, take that coal-box back to the parlour. It's been stood there for ten minutes and . . ."

But May hadn't finished yet, it seemed, despite Cook's warning, for a black jealousy that she had harboured ever since Clever Clogs had come to work at the farm and been given what she saw as preferential treatment now burst into flames.

"It's my bloody concern when another servant is given time off fer bloody pianer playin' while I'm still up ter me elbows in't scullery sink of a night. We don't see *you* washin' up, Poppy Appleton. Oh dear me, no, yer too busy lickin' mistress's bum ter—"

"*May Jebson*, that is enough," Cook thundered, appalled by the white-faced enmity of her kitchen maid. At the same time, being a fair-minded woman, she could understand it. Poppy *was* favoured, there were no two ways about it and though she never boasted of it or thrust her knowledge in the faces of the other servants, it must be said it was not exactly fair to the others to listen to her playing the piano, of all things, while they were still on their feet at the end of a long day. But it was the mistress's business and that was that.

"How *dare* yer talk ter me like that, yer snivellin' little toad," Poppy screeched. "Jus 'cos Mrs Goodall chose me an' not you to—"

"*Poppy Appleton*, I'm warning you. I will not have this arguing going on in my kitchen. You, May, fetch me the flour crock. I'm going to make a plum pie and you can give me a hand." Whenever Cook was upset nothing calmed her like a bit of baking, "And you, Poppy, you'd best go and cool your temper outdoors."

"What! In the dark?" Poppy's rage dared not spread itself to Cook who was the ruler here but her indignation knew no bounds.

"It's not full dark yet. There's enough light for you ter find yer way down the field. See if you can lay your hands on that dratted hen for Mrs Goodall. She was going on about it earlier. Lost again, she is. Take the lamp and put yer cloak on. It's cold out."

"Cook," Poppy protested, "it's black as the inside of a parson's 'at—"

"Don't exaggerate and don't argue. Go and cool off for ten minutes."

May smirked behind Cook's back and Poppy set her face in mutinous lines but she had no choice other than to do as she was told. She and Nelly had just come in from the dairy and Dilys had gone home to the tidy cottage she shared with

Evan. It would be half an hour before the evening meal was put on the table in front of Mr Goodall and his two sons and, foolishly, she realised that now, she had just informed the others that she would go and have a few minutes' practice at the piano which is how the confrontation with May had blown up.

Well, she wouldn't do it again, that was for sure. She'd keep her books and her music apart from the others. She'd not give it up, mind, whatever May said or the others thought, even if Mrs Goodall agreed to it, which Poppy knew she wouldn't. She would not be put off by the kitchen maid's malevolence. She was beginning to get the hang of chords, of treble clefs and staves, of quarter notes and half notes, and her own playing, though still very amateurish, was a pleasure to her.

Holding her warm cloak about her and the enclosed lamp above her head, she moved quickly through the yard and on into the rutted field which was a favourite laying place for the hen. She knew Mrs Goodall had been down here earlier in the day looking for the silly creature and had found no trace of her, or her eggs, but she supposed she'd best have another look. Five minutes and then she was off back to the warmth of the kitchen. Her belly thought her throat had been cut, rumbling away beneath her pinny but at least, as Cook had intended, her temper had cooled and as she turned to go back she vowed she'd not let that May Jebson rile her again. Did she give a damn about what the jealous kitchen maid thought, or indeed any of them really, since all that she had learned from Mrs Goodall was a gift she did not intend to be sorry over, or to waste.

She could hear the snorting and rustling of the farm horses in their stalls as she passed by the stable doorway, the top half of which was open. She could smell the animals, a not unpleasant smell and the fragrance of the oats and hay they were contentedly munching. Jacko, who had the care of Mr Goodall's farm horses in his hands, was very particular about "his" animals, especially the mares who were in foal. He was a skilled and careful horse man, knowing exactly when a breeding mare should no longer be put between the shafts. They were pampered creatures fed on oats and hay, groomed each one of them once a day, shoed every six or seven weeks and each evening lovingly tucked away in stalls no smaller than six feet wide and six feet high, their mangers on the back wall at least eighteen feet from the entrance to the stall. The stable itself was well ventilated, well lit and well built, keeping out the icy winds that blew across the flat Lancashire plain in the winter.

As Poppy was about to pass by the door on her way back to the kitchen, something else besides the smell and sound of the horses caught at her senses, an undertone, muted but very familiar since it was so unusual and she stopped to listen.

Without a doubt it was the soft "cluckee" of Mrs Goodall's prize layer.

Well, would you credit it? The stupid beggar had wandered inside the stables and was probably snuggled comfortably in a bit of dry straw thinking to itself that this was better than the old henhouse any day of the week!

Poppy was well used to the enormous gentle farm horses who worked on Long Reach Farm. Years ago she had stumbled behind them on her infant legs, picking stones with the other toddlers, stones which were chucked in a bucket and weighed at the end of the day. On more than one occasion she had ridden home on a broad back with a row of children behind her like birds on a fence.

Unhesitatingly she opened the lower half of the stable door

and stepped inside, closing it behind her, pacing out the aisle down its centre. After the chill of the raw November evening it felt warm and cosy. The heads of the mares turned to look enquiringly at her as she walked between them, calling to the daft hen in a soft voice.

"Clucky . . . Clucky . . . where are yer, yer balm cake? Come on, lass, speak up. Yer know yer shouldn't be here, don't yer? This is fer horses, not hens, so come on, show yerself ter Poppy."

There was no reply from the hen though a small drift of dust and bits of hay fell through the beam of the lamp from between a crack in the floor of the loft above. Probably the daft creature strutting about in search of a cosy nest.

"Aah, come on, Clucky, have a heart," Poppy called. "Don't mekk me come up there after yer. That ladder's bloody steep." She pulled a face as she used the word Mrs Goodall didn't like but she was cold and ready for her supper which by now would be being laid on the kitchen table.

Still no response from the hen. Not that she expected the dratted thing to call down, "Here I am," but she had been known to come running at the sound of a human voice, which usually promised food. With a resigned sigh Poppy moved to the foot of the ladder. She was tempted to leave the hen, who would come to no harm up there where it was warm and safe from foxes, returning to the kitchen to say there was no sign of her, but she knew Mrs Goodall was fond of Clucky and could Poppy do less after her mistress had been so good to *her*?

She was about to put one foot on the bottom rung of the ladder, having hung the lamp on a hook on a post, when a soft sound, not one made by a hen, she was certain, came from above. It sounded like a groan, a groan from human lips and her foot froze in mid-air and so did her hand which she had just placed on the ladder. Cocking her head, she listened intently but the sound was not repeated. She must have imagined it, she decided, or it had been one of the horses blowing through its nostrils. She took another step up the ladder.

She was halfway up when it came again. A whispering sigh really, as though a sleeper had turned and breathed deeply in a dream and there was a rustle as though loose hay had been moved upon.

Again she froze, not only her body paralysed but her mind as well. She didn't know what to do in her shocked state, go up or down or stay where she was, clinging to the ladder as if it were a lifeline in stormy seas, or an escape to safety from whatever threatened her, if anything did. There was someone up there! Dear Lord, here she was about to climb blithely up into the hay loft after Mrs Goodall's barmy hen and waiting up there for her was . . . was . . . well, it could be anybody. A tramp looking for a dry, warm bed for the night. Some itinerant worker moving from one part of the country to the other, but then how could whoever it was have known of Tom Goodall's splendid stable?

She dithered, which was not like her, but then this was unusual, not only unusual but very scary. And why hadn't the dogs barked, those who were kept to deter intruders? Perhaps it would be best if she let go of the ladder and ran over to Jacko's place and fetched him to investigate, but then if there was no one there but the bloody hen – no compunction about swearing now – she'd look a right fool, wouldn't she, and there was nothing Poppy Appleton disliked more than being made to look a fool. Afraid of her own shadow, May would sneer when she heard the tale. Poppy Appleton who boasted she was frightened of no one.

So, don't be daft, Poppy Appleton, she told herself, there's nothing up there but Mrs Goodall's best layer and if you don't get up the ladder and fetch her down soon you'll miss your supper.

The lamp, placed high on the post, lit up the ladder and, when she poked her head through the opening of the loft, it spread its glow a good distance round it. And there, looking for all the world like their own plump little queen on her throne, sat Clucky, small sounds of contentment chirruping from her throat as she settled herself more comfortably in the sweet-smelling hay.

Poppy snorted irritably, a sound somewhere between a sigh of relief and a laugh as she moved up another rung of the ladder and prepared to step off it on to the floor of the loft, but as she did so something moved just beyond the circle the lamp cast, and someone moaned.

Oh, Jesus . . . oh, dear Jesus, there *was* someone there . . . or something. She could see a vague shape, dark and shadowed, half buried in the hay: an animal of some sort . . . or, or a man . . . a man lying down but making no move towards her, nothing that could be called threatening. In fact there was utter stillness and silence except for a sort of bubbling sigh which she was unable to recognise.

Stepping slowly back towards the opening and the ladder she put out her left hand to grasp it. When she had a good grip, steadying herself, still not taking her eyes off the recumbent figure just outside the circle of light, she slid one foot on to the top rung itself. She'd go down quietly and then slip across the yard for Jacko. He'd soon have this intruder off the premises and on his way, probably going wild if he thought someone had threatened the peace and rest of his beloved horses. Funny about the dogs though. Great big ferocious things they were, at least with those they didn't know. Why hadn't they barked? Perhaps this chap had harmed them in some way, though she couldn't see how, for they were not animals any man would like to tackle.

As her foot found the second rung of the ladder the lamp on the post to which the ladder was attached moved a little, widening its circle of illumination momentarily as it swung and she saw, as clearly as though the sun had shone on it, a gleam of vivid red among the hay. No more than a brief swaying glance but it was enough to point out the identity of the lad who lay as though poleaxed in Tom Goodall's hayloft.

Conn! It was Conn, she was sure of it. Who else had she ever seen with hair that colour, like a bright beacon leading whoever was after him, as someone surely was, for why else was he here, straight to where he lay? Douglas had told her that Conn had "gone over the side" again almost three months ago so where had he been since then? What was he doing here sleeping the sleep of the dead in Mr Goodall's hayloft? How had he got past the dogs but, more importantly, why was he still lying there out for the count when he must have heard her calling the hen, heard her thumping up the ladder, seen the light from the lamp?

For several minutes she crouched on the ladder, uncertain what to do, the top of her curly head and her wide eyes the only part of her showing above the opening where the ladder rested, and when he opened his eyes and lifted his head they were the first thing he saw. For a long moment they looked at one another with that silent communication they had known on two other occasions. They were no more than a boy and a girl who were just about to move towards adulthood but that look they exchanged, that they had exchanged before, was not the youthful glance of interest between children. It had in it the maturity of a man and a woman, for in truth neither had ever been a child or known a childhood in the true sense of the word. That look spoke to each of them, linking them in some strange way and Poppy sighed as though with heavy despondency. The sigh said he had been in trouble again and there was no one else but her to help him. Would she have it any other way? a fleeting thought in her head asked her but she had no time to consider it.

He was lying on his stomach, she could see that now that her eyes had grown used to the dimness and as he twisted his head to look at her a groan was wrenched from between his lips and he fell back among the straw.

"Jesus," she heard him whisper and it was then she knew he was badly hurt.

"You'll be Douglas's sister. He told me . . . about you. Could you fetch . . . me a drink, lassie?" His voice was hoarse and muffled as though his mouth were covered with something, his hand perhaps, to keep in further groans of pain. "A sip o' water. I'd be . . . grateful."

For several seconds she remained motionless on the ladder then, when he agonisingly raised his bright head again, she lost her paralysis.

"I'll fetch help," she said firmly to him as though to tell him his suffering was over, but at once he twisted into a sitting position, his voice as strong and determined as hers had been.

"No, no, ye mustna." He tried a grin, which was more a grimace, twisting his young face into a mask of pain that must have hurt him a great deal, for his face was sadly knocked about. "I'm no' badly hurt, just a wee bit . . . damaged here and there. A drink of water and I'll be on my way."

"But you can't . . ."

"Aye, I can, lass. A bit of a rest is all I need and I'll be as right as ninepence."

"Who . . . who damaged you?"

"You mean this time?" His tone was ironic.

" 'Ave there bin others?"

"A few. When I was recaptured they gave me a lick or two but this . . . well, some bullies who didna like what I said to them. They were . . . handling a boy, a wee boy and when I objected they . . . Oh, lass, I surely crave a drink if ye've such a thing about ye." Then, just as though a light had been blown out inside him he slumped back in the straw and lay still.

So, after escaping on the very day in August before Douglas was released Conn had been caught again and by the look of him his punishment had been greater than ever. For a nasty moment her brother's words came back to her, describing this lad's last flogging and she shuddered. She knew she should run for help for how was she, no more than a lass, to get this big red-haired lad to his feet? Jacko or Tommy between them could carry him down the ladder and with Mrs Goodall's help they would soon have him restored to health again. But something held her back, perhaps the look of anguish on his face when she had said she'd run for help, the desperate appeal he had directed at her not to give away his hiding place. That desperation kept her standing on the ladder peeping over the edge of the opening as the boy called Conn, Douglas's friend, lay on his face in the hay. There was something badly wrong with him. She didn't know exactly what but some instinct told her to do as he bid. To let no one know he was here. To keep him hidden. Help him, oh yes, but keep him hidden.

Slowly she stepped up into the loft then very carefully leaned down into the opening and retrieved the lamp from its hook. Bess, one of the mares, whickered uneasily and there was a heavy stamp of hooves on cobbles. Poppy held her breath but all was quiet again except for the sound of the animals' strong jaws munching their feed. Clucky made that soft noise in the back of her throat and her beady eye winked and stared at Poppy as though to ask her what she was going to do now.

His shirt was in shreds across his back. He had been flogged, striped from his neck to his waist with weals criss-crossing his flesh in almost symmetrical neatness as though whoever had done this to him had taken a great deal of trouble to make a decent pattern of it. There was blood congealed along every weal but when he had moved he had opened some of the wounds and fresh rivulets of red ran down his sides into the hay.

She sank to her knees beside him and began to cry, not because she was only twelve, a young girl who had never witnessed such cruelty, such violence, such deliberate inflicting of pain by one human being on another, but because she felt such anguish for him who had suffered it. She bent her head, her sobs muffled in her chest and he stirred again as though her weeping had disturbed his painful drifting in and out of his semi-conscious state. He turned a glazed blue eye in her direction and his voice was soft.

"Dinna cry, *mo donn falt caileag*. It's no' as bad as it looks, honest, but if ye could . . ."

At the sound of his voice she lifted her head, sniffing and wiping her nose with the back of her hand and the shining look of resolution with which Eliza Goodall was very familiar glowed in her face. This was no time for crying. There was much to be done and whatever it was it must be done secretly, quietly, and by her, that look said. Water for him to drink at once. That could be got from the dairy before she returned to the kitchen. Blankets, salve for his back from Mrs Goodall's medicine chest in the study,

bandages, lint, food, a new shirt – and who at Long Reach
Farm had such a thing to fit him? – a dozen things to make
him comfortable and safe for the night, but first she must
hurry back to the kitchen to eat her evening meal as though
this night was no different from any other and she must go
soon or they would be out looking for her. She didn't know
how she was to get one mouthful down, she felt so nauseated
at the sight of the oozing pulp which was the flesh on this
boy's back, nor how she was to escape Mrs Goodall and
her evening studies without questions. How could she lie
in her bed until they were all asleep, for that was what she
must do before she could silently gather up all she needed
and creep back here to tend to this dreadfully injured lad
who needed attention right this minute and not in a few
hours' time.

But if she was to be any good to him, she must.

As though he read her mind he raised himself painfully
on one elbow, wincing as the movement rippled his flayed
back, turning his bright head to look into her face. He grinned,
showing even white teeth and she saw that his lips were bitten, the cracks ready to bleed again as he stretched them.

"There's no need ter grin like a bloody Cheshire cat," she
told him tartly. "That mouth o' yours looks badly."

"Aye, it's been better, I'll admit, but I reckon I'll live for
another hour or two. You'd best get off, lassie, before they
miss ye. Perhaps later . . . a bite to eat, if ye can manage it."

"I'll get yer a drink first then I'll go burr I'll be back as
soon as I can. Now you lie still, d'yer hear me," she told
him sternly as she got to her feet.

He flopped back on to his belly with a groan.

"Aye, lassie, I'll no' be going anywhere just now."

She leaned down and touched his cheek fleetingly and
he smiled.

10

The house lay in total darkness and though she strained her ears to catch the smallest sound, there was none, not even from the mice who lived in the walls. Poppy stood beside the deliberately wide-opened window of her bedroom, breathing deeply of the cold draught of air that lapped about her, glad of it to keep her awake, since her tired, over-excited body craved sleep. She was weary with the exhaustion that afflicts those who have laboured from dawn to dusk. She was burdened with the intensification of all that had happened during the past few hours but she knew she could not rest. She longed for her bed and the deep slumber that she fell into at the end of every day but in the stable across the big, cobbled yard lay the boy who had no one but Poppy Appleton to help him and as soon as she was convinced that all who lay beneath the roof of Long Reach Farm were asleep she would creep out and go to him.

It seemed as though fate, smiling kindly on Poppy, if not on the victim, had decided to give her a helping hand in the shape of an accident to young Richard Goodall. Apparently he and his father and younger brother, who, according to his furious parent, had been acting the bloody fool, and with the help of the cowman and a couple of labourers who worked in the fields, had been doing their best to pen the bull which served Tom Goodall's cows. It was a bad-tempered beast at the best of times but particularly so at that moment since, as Tom crudely put it, the animal had not yet had a chance to use his "tackle" in the manner it was meant to be used and as a result was in as vile a mood as any hot-blooded and lusty male denied his "conjugals" has a right to be. And it had not helped when Johnny Goodall, thinking he was one of those Red Indians in the wild west of America they had read about, had whooped and hollered like some bloody clown in a circus ring.

The beast had bellowed in outrage, its outstanding "tackle" attesting to its willingness, nay, eagerness, to use it on the herd who stood docilely beyond the farm gate waiting for him. A rope had been attached to the ring in its nose and with Tom and Richard and the cowman hauling on that, doing their best to avoid the beast's tossing horns, and the rest pushing on the bull's massive hindquarters they had eventually and successfully penned the animal but not before Richard's foot had been stepped on. Tom swore, as he delivered his hopping, groaning offspring to the ministrations of his mother, that he would get rid of the bloody thing before the week was out, meaning the bull, of course, though the look he directed at his younger son said he wouldn't mind if he didn't see *him* again for a while, damned young fool. As bulls get older they become more and more difficult to manage, every farmer knew that, and as this particular dairy bull had several daughters who had reached breeding age and a second sire was required to mate with them, the present bull's days were numbered. Tom couldn't afford to keep two, so all in all the animal's fate was sealed that night.

Everyone in the kitchen from Tom himself right down to Marigold was absorbed with young Master Richard, exclaiming in horror over the state of the badly bruised and swollen foot – no bones broken, thank God, the mistress said – ready to run here and there at Mrs Goodall's bidding and the white-faced, glitter-eyed state of Poppy, if they noticed it at all, that is, was put down to the general concern they all shared for Master Richard. Hot poultices followed by cold compresses, plenty of hot, sweet tea, tight strapping, curses from Tom who was also concerned, but not with his son's injury, since it did not appear to be serious, but with how long it would keep him from his work on the farm. A good, reliable lad was Dick, and his father depended on him, unlike his daft and irresponsible younger brother whose fault, in Tom's opinion, this was. A steady worker, with the makings of a decent farmer and shaping up nicely to be the next owner of Long Reach Farm, he would be sorely missed.

"How long, d'you reckon?" he asked his wife anxiously as the lad was carted off to his room.

"As long as it takes, Tom Goodall, and that's the best answer I can give," and so they had all retired to their beds, servants and family alike, worn to a frazzle by the upheaval, the worry and concern for Master Richard, for though he hadn't the impish charm of his brother, he was a nice lad and was held in high esteem by them all.

The massive, richly carved oak clock which stood in the downstairs passage struck the half-hour with a deep-toned gong. It had come with Eliza on her marriage to Tom, a glory of a thing with highly chased brass mountings at the top, fretwork in its base, brass weights and chains and a silvered dial. A devil to polish, Aggie and Clara complained, but its regular voice was a part of their lives, warning them that time was passing and must not be wasted.

Half past ten! Four hours and more since Poppy had come in from the stable and what state would Conn be in now? He had been barely aware of her then, slipping in and out of consciousness, his waking moments filled with pain, so heaven only knew what condition she would now find him in. And there was so much to do before she could creep out and tend to his needs. Thankfully, the accident to Master Richard this evening and what the mistress had said and done for him had given Poppy an insight into how she must deal with Conn. In her own head she could hear Mrs Goodall's calm voice repeating her instructions to the clustering servants. Warmth, she had said, plenty of hot, sweet tea for shock, bathing of the injured foot – back in Conn's case – the application of Mrs Goodall's own home-made panacea for what seemed to Poppy to be practically every mishap human flesh could suffer. Cleanliness to avoid infection and what was obviously of great importance since Poppy had seen Master Richard respond to it, a calm, soothing presence, compassion, an abundance of caring which had worked magically with the son of the house.

She was still dressed in her working clothes. Throwing her warm cloak about her shoulders she crept across the room, thanking whatever gods had put the idea in Mrs Goodall's head that Poppy Appleton should have her own room. She opened the door a crack and listened. Nothing except, from a bedroom on the floor below, the gusty sound of Farmer Goodall's snoring and the faint but sonorous tick of the hall clock. Once more she went over the list of things she would need, the list she had stored in her head in that methodical way Mrs Goodall had taught her, and as she tiptoed down the stairs, past the clock and into the warm kitchen, still lit by the banked-up fire, she began with the first thing on it. A warm blanket, just one, a clean one from Mrs Goodall's linen cupboard at the back of the range and off the kitchen where sheets and blankets were kept aired. There were horse blankets – why hadn't she thought to throw one over him earlier? she anguished – horse blankets by the score in the stable but she'd need something clean to wrap him in. A drop of whisky in the hot tea she meant to prepare since she had noted the reviving effect it had had on Master Richard. A lamp to see by, hoping no one would be awake and notice it bobbing across the yard and Mrs Goodall's medicine chest, which was small, thank God, and had in it the decoction made up of boiled roots of comfrey which had been applied to Master Richard's foot. She had heard the mistress say times that it was invaluable in helping tissue knit together, which meant skin, and if there was anything more in need of knitting together than Conn's back then Poppy couldn't imagine what it could be. Look at the way the comfrey had healed Aggie's hand when she had burned it badly on the flat iron and the ulcer Cook had on her shin had cleared up in next to no time, thanks to its marvellous efficacy. She would need clean cloths and hot water, something nourishing for him to eat. Lord, the list was endless. She'd have to make two trips, she thought distractedly. Fresh clothes for him to wear when he left but that could come later.

The dogs growled warningly and rattled their chains on her first trip across the yard, but recognising her they lay down again, swishing their tails lazily in greeting. The horses stamped their feet and Master Richard's fine bay, which was in the first stall she passed, whinnied uneasily. A high-strung animal and very handsome as was Master Johnny's roan who was also, in their father's opinion, on the wild side, like his son.

She had the lamp in one hand and in the other a deep basket containing the medicine chest, a blanket and the precariously balanced jug of hot tea which she prayed would not spill on to the blanket. It took two trips up the ladder, first with the lamp to light her way, placing it by the opening, then the basket, panting slightly, her heart pounding, her face flushed and yet cold with terror that someone might spot the light. She couldn't think why anyone would be up and about at this time of night, since life on a farm was hard and those who laboured on it were inclined to drop like logs at the end of the day. She knew, she was one of them.

He was icily cold when she touched his cheek and for a dreadful moment she thought he was dead but when she held the light over him she could see the slow tick of a pulse beneath his chin. He stirred as the light fell over him but did not waken. Taking the lavender-scented blanket from the basket she carefully placed it across him, resisting the temptation to stop and chafe his hands and feet to get some warmth in him. Instead she slipped down the ladder and, fleet as a deer, accustomed by now to the dark, went back for the rest of the things she had packed in a second basket. All would have to be returned, the medicine chest, the jug in which the tea was keeping hot, a second jug containing hot water, the dish in which she had scooped a dollop of Cook's nourishing but unfortunately cold broth and a thick slice of fresh bread, the baskets, everything except the blanket which, if it was missed, would have to be explained. She would think about that later.

He woke with a mumbled, moaning gasp when she began to apply cloths soaked in hot water to his back. Her chief concern was to get him warm, so before he had time barely to register what she was about she poured an almost full cup of tea containing the neat whisky, the sharp smell of which took her breath away, down his throat.

"Bloody hell . . ." He choked on his own words and on the drink but Poppy could see it was bringing him round. He lifted his head and stared blearily at her, his neck muscles quivering under the strain of holding his head up.

"Bloody hell, lass," he said again, "are ye trying to choke me to death?"

"Don't you swear at me, lad," she whispered to him fiercely. "Mrs Goodall don't like language an' neither do I. Now lie still while I bathe yer back. I've got summat ter purron it that'll mekk it feel better."

"Yes, nurse," he groaned.

"An' have another sip o' this hot tea. There's some whisky in it. It'll do yer good."

"Yes, nurse."

"An' don't you cheek me. One more crack about nurses an' I'll leave yer ter see ter yerself." She was ready to burst into tears with the strain she was under, worrying about the lamp and the horses and if Jacko should come and check and found her helping an escapee from the *Lahore* she'd lose her job and what would happen to Conn who could not stand another flogging like this one? She blinked rapidly, doing her best not to let fall the tears which sparkled on the end of her lashes.

Alick MacConnell was instantly contrite. He didn't know what would have become of him had this lovely young girl not taken pity on his appalling state, but it was his nature to make light of adversity, to joke as though the misfortunes which had plagued all his young life were no more to him than the buzzing of a troublesome fly. It was his nature to be good-humoured, easy-going, though he was not irresponsible. God knew, for a lad of his age he had had thrust upon him more responsibility than grown men twenty years his senior and it was his conscientious awareness and acceptance of it that had landed him in the wretchedness and agony he now suffered. This last flogging had nearly finished him. He was not quite fourteen and though a big lad for his age the man who had administered his punishment, the man he had "cheeked", had lost his head a bit, wanting to hear Conn cry out. To beg for mercy. To say he was sorry. Conn had done none of these things and had it not been for one of the other men present who began to be alarmed that his fellow officer might kill the lad, the man would have laid on many more than the forty or so lashes already delivered.

The hot tea laced with a great deal of whisky, since Poppy was not familiar with its potency, burned down to Conn's stomach, creating a warm fire which spread to his arms and legs, to his icy hands and feet. The little brown-haired lassie, which was what he had called her in Gaelic earlier, was spooning something into his mouth, something cold but very tasty, with frequent sips of the warm tea in between each spoonful and he began to feel considerably better. Quite light-hearted, in fact, not realising that he was rapidly getting very inebriated indeed. She had removed his shirt, apologising for hurting him, but as matter-of-fact about it as if she did this sort of thing every day. Then, with gentle hands and a sort of soft cooing in the back of her throat, applied something cool to his back. It hurt like hell at first, but he didn't mind, then it began to soothe and he could feel himself slip, heavy-eyed, into a natural sleep. He was warm for the first time in days. His belly, though somewhat uneasy for some reason, was full, his back was eased and, lying face down in the dry straw with several blankets about him, one of which smelled of the lavender his mother had once used, he could feel himself slipping dreamily away. Her voice pulled him back.

"How did yer get past dogs?" she whispered.

"Oh, animals seem to take to me, *mo donn falt caileag*. Dinna ask me why."

"But they're terrible fierce." She didn't know what *mo donn falt caileag* meant but she had the feeling it was something nice. She'd ask him when they had a minute to spare, though when that would be was not clear. She tucked the blanket more cosily about him, resisting the strangest desire to drop a kiss on his freckled cheek. She who had never kissed anyone in her life, not even her mam.

"Aye, I suppose they are and I dinna ken why it is but animals mind me and when I told those dogs to be still they did as they were bid."

"Really?" Her voice was respectful.

He opened weary blue eyes, then gave her a wink accompanied by a smile.

"Aye, really, but now, my lass, you'd best get back. Ye've done more than enough and I'm grateful. I dinna want to get you into trouble so best get back to your bed. I'll be gone in the morning so . . ."

At once she was filled with alarm.

"Oh, no, Conn, no, yer not fit," she protested hotly. " 'Sides, I've not gorra shirt or 'owt fer yer yet. Yer can't walk about in that thing," indicating the tattered heap of rags which lay in the straw. "Promise yer'll wait, at least till tomorrer night. There's some more o' Cook's broth here. I'm sorry it's not hot burrit was best I could do, an' a bottle o' water ter see yer through't night then termorrer, as soon as I can, I'll fetch yer some porridge or summat, 'appen a bacon butty an' a clean shirt. P'rhaps a jacket an' all," though how she would come by such a thing was as yet not clear.

"How can you do that, lassie? Someone'll be bound to find out."

"No," she objected, "I'll be careful. Oh, please, Conn, don't go while yer've seen me again, please, promise."

He was suddenly hot now, wanting to throw off the blankets she had so tenderly wrapped about him but he knew this fierce little girl would only pile them on him again. Besides, he was too bloody worn out to argue. He wanted to sink down into the pain-free sleep his body craved. She was glaring at him, wide-eyed, not far from tears, he thought, and he hadn't the heart to deny her. He supposed he was as safe here as anywhere, although he had got a fright when one of the stable lads had come in earlier. To check on the horses, he supposed, which, sensing his presence with that instinct animals have, had been restless.

"What's up wi' you?" he had heard the man say. "Yer jumpy ternight. Is it that bloody fox what 'angs round the 'en coop? Don't you worry about 'im, my beauties. Jacko'll mekk sure the old bugger don't worry you none."

He had gone, closing the doors carefully behind him and the animals had settled. No, it was this lass he was worried about. He didn't want her to get into trouble but it was very tempting to stay here and have another day's rest before he went on his way. God knew where that might be. Glasgow probably, a destination he had been considering ever since his mother died, but at least it would be as far away from Liverpool as he could, for if they caught him again it'd not be the *Lahore* this time.

"Promise me, Conn," she entreated him, bending down close to his face so that her sweet-scented breath fanned his cheek and her hair tickled his brow.

"You're a pretty lass, *mo annsachd*," he murmured, his eyes drooping in exhaustion.

"Promise me . . . promise me."

"Aye, I promise."

She didn't know how she got away with it but, somehow, get away with it she did. Probably because, being who she was and trusted implicitly by Mrs Goodall and Dilys they did not question her strange absences from where she should be. The trouble was, though she had not before realised it, every part of her day was taken up with some task or commitment that took place under someone else's eye. Apart from when she was in her bed she was always with another servant or Mrs Goodall. She hadn't even got the excuse that she was off down to the cottage in Primrose Bank to check on the state of her family. Marigold was making a grand job, despite her childlike nature, not only of her work in the kitchen but in her care of her pa and two brothers and had no need of Poppy except in the case of an emergency and as none arose it was some weeks since Poppy had been there.

It seemed no one except Dilys had noticed anything unusual in her behaviour, which was quite amazing since she had had the greatest difficulty in preventing herself from nodding off at the breakfast table, and again at dinner-time. Whenever she sat down, which, luckily, was not often, she could feel her eyelids begin to droop and her shoulders to slump. Fortunately Master Richard was still the focus of his mother's attentions and so Poppy's conduct was not noticed, at least by her, though Dilys, surprised and irritated, was forced to speak sharply to her on a couple of occasions.

"Now then, girl, there's daft you are. Put the wrong pattern on this yer butter, so yew have and it'll all have ter be done again, see. That's not like you, and if I see you yawn again I'll have words with the mistress about yew staying up late."

"Sorry, Dilys, but . . . well, last night was a bit chaotic. I didn't sleep well."

Chaotic! The child was always using words that amazed them all but she was right and really you couldn't blame her, could you?

"No, well, from what I yeard, none of yew did up there but that's no excuse to loll about," then, sorry to have chastised her good little worker who seldom put a foot wrong, Dilys sat down heavily in the old wicker chair she kept in the dairy for such a moment and smiled forgivingly, ready for a bit of a gossip about what had happened at the farmhouse last night. "And how is the boyo this morning?"

For a horrified moment Poppy thought Dilys was referring to the red-haired lad who lay in the straw in the hayloft. She almost gave herself away by asking her how she knew but just in time she realised that Dilys was talking about Master Richard.

"I dunno, I haven't seen 'im. Mistress medd 'im stay in bed. Took 'is breakfast up to 'im on a tray though Master were none too 'appy."

And neither was Poppy Appleton who would have given anything to have been carrying that laden tray of hot food across the yard and up the ladder to the injured boy who waited there for her and whose need was so much greater than the pampered Goodall son. It wasn't that she disliked Master Richard or anything like that, in fact he was a nice young man, serious, kind-hearted and steady and always polite, even to the servants. He was seventeen now, a man in Poppy's eyes, celebrating his birthday only last week but he always had a quiet word of encouragement for Poppy, that's if there was no one about, for he was a reserved young man in complete contrast to his laughter-loving younger brother. She had found herself to be the focus of his scrutiny lately, she didn't know why, his grey eyes studying her with something she was at a loss to understand. Perhaps it was because he himself liked to read, different kinds of books to the ones she devoured, naturally, but she supposed it gave them something in common, if a servant, a dairymaid, could have something in common with the son of the house.

"No, I'm not surprised," Dilys was saying, easing her aching legs into a more comfortable position, if such a thing was possible. "Master do depend on that lad an' with him laid up it'll put extra work on him, Mr Goodall, I mean, see. Master Johnny's a lovely boy, look you, but when it do come to work an' getting down to things he's a right monkey an' no mistake. Now, be a good lass and hand me that tray of fowl. I'll pluck an' dress 'em while I'm sitting yere. Oh, an' run to the milking shed an' tell Nelly to look sharp with that milk. It should be in the churn by now, see."

It was the opportunity Poppy had been waiting for. Cook had been astonished at breakfast when Poppy announced to the assembled company that she was absolutely famished and would be grateful for a second helping of Cook's delicious porridge, which disappeared so quickly from her plate, just like the first, Cook swore she must have fed the lot to the cat. Then, to cap it all the child begged for a second bacon butty, refusing a fried egg, but yes, perhaps a slice of fried bread would go down nicely. Mind, Cook thought she looked a mite peaky and drawn about the eyes, which was not surprising after the drama of last night and then again, girls of her age who had reached that time in their lives which was dominated by the moon, and Cook happened to know that Poppy Appleton had, were a bit out of sorts once a month.

The porridge, wrapped in one of Mrs Goodall's napkins and from which Poppy was convinced it must be oozing, with the bacon sandwiches and fried bread in another, was stored, uneasily it might be added, in Poppy's capacious apron pocket. For the past couple of hours she had done her best to keep her back to Dilys so that, should the food stain her apron it might go unnoticed. She was famished now since she had had nothing but a cup of tea since her supper last night but Conn's need was greater than hers and besides it would soon be elevenses and she could eat then.

Dilys was dextrously plucking the first chicken and did not notice when Poppy drew a surreptitious can of water from the dairy tap.

He was asleep, or at least had his eyes closed when, keeping her own eyes skinned for the men who might be working in the vicinity of the yard, she ran, her head bent against the bleak drizzle which fell from a low, grey sky. Praying that Jacko would not be in the stable, worrying over what she would say to him if he were, she crept between the stalls and climbed the ladder to the hayloft. It seemed the bull, which she could hear bellowing from its pen, was keeping them all occupied and she thanked God for it.

He had pushed the blankets which she had tucked so carefully about him down to his hips and his flayed back looked worse than ever in the hazed daylight which filtered into the loft. It was a dreadful sight with barely an inch of flesh untouched by the lash, the damage inflicted with a viciousness that made her stomach heave. Such cruelty should surely not be allowed, but Douglas had witnessed and described it to her and this big, red-haired lad had suffered it. She wanted to sink to her knees beside him and weep for him but there was no time for that, and it would do him no good, she told herself as she bit sharply on the inside of her mouth to bring herself under control. She had, last night, before she had put Mrs Goodall's medicine chest back in precisely the position she had found it, extracted a small amount of the comfrey potion ready for this morning and, taking a square of clean white linen cloth from her skirt pocket, one of those she herself used for her "monthlies", boiled and scoured, of course, by the laundry woman, she applied the cloth gently to his back. She tried to be as light-handed as she knew how but at once he opened his eyes, rearing up sharply, and a strangled moan rippled his taut throat and was torn from between his lips. He stared at her for a moment or two, his eyes wide and panic-stricken then, recognising her, flopped down again on his belly with a deep sigh. His hand, which lay beside his head, quivered and without thinking she reached out and took it, holding him steady, willing her strength and compassion through their linked hands from her to him. She wanted to ask him how he felt but knew how ridiculous that would sound since it was obvious he was in great pain and very weak from his ordeal.

"I've brought yer summat to eat, an' a drink," she whispered close to his ear, just as though anyone could hear her over the noise the bull was making.

He cleared his throat and licked his dry, bitten lips. "Thanks, lassie." His voice was hoarse. "I dinna think I could eat just now but I'd be glad of a drink."

"Yer must force yerself to eat or you'll never get yer strength back," she admonished him sternly, "an' I'll not leave yer till yer do," hoping to God that Nelly had not yet returned to the dairy with tales of wonderment over Poppy Appleton's disappearance.

He groaned again, this time in resignation and his wide, torn mouth twitched in what was almost a smile. "Lassie, ye're the most inflexible wee girl I've come across. D'you ken what inflexible means?"

"Of course I do," she answered indignantly, "and I'm not. I'm only thinking of what's best for yer."

"I know that, *a muirninn*, but you like your own way, don't you and as I've not the strength to argue wi' ye just now I'd best do as I'm told. A drink first, though."

He baulked at the porridge but Poppy insisted, assuring him it was made with rich cream and oats and would do him the world of good and to get it down him or she'd do it for him. All this in a fierce whisper with her hair tickling his cheek in a way, despite his condition, he found most pleasurable. She smelled lovely, too. Some sort of soap, he thought, with lemon in it, and of newly baked bread mixed with what he decided was the tang of fresh butter. He hadn't smelled anything so lovely since his mother had died.

Rolling his eyes, such a vivid blue despite the deep and sunken shadows about them, he managed a few mouthfuls, then ate the whole of one bacon sandwich.

"I canna manage another bite, lassie."

"You sure?"

"I'm sure, really."

"Then I'll finish it," biting hungrily into the cold, fat-congealed sandwich.

"That was your breakfast I've just eaten, wasn't it?" he said accusingly.

"Oh, don't be daft," starting on the slice of fried bread. "I can have something at elevenses and there'll be plenty at dinner-time."

"Lassie, how can I . . ."

"My name's Poppy."

"Aye, I know that, *annsachd*. Dougie told me. Poppy, a pretty name an' it suits ye. Now, a drink of water and you must go."

His eyes were glazed with the painful effort he had made

and he sank back into the straw with a sigh of relief. The food had done him good though and a touch of colour tinted his pale, freckled skin. He allowed her to bathe his back again, lying on his belly in a state of dreamy detachment which, though he was not aware of it, neither of them were, was brought on by shock.

The shock his young body had suffered at the mutilation of his flesh. He had borne the flogging with stoicism but now the aftermath of it had dragged him into a place which nature creates for those who need healing. The girl helped, of course, her compassion and courage giving him something to cling to as every nerve in his body seemed to crawl with pain. He was aware in some part of his mind that she was taking a terrible risk in helping him in this way and yet, thinking back to that moment when he had dragged his tortured body from the heaving waters of the Mersey, it had been her he had been making for. He had not forgotten the two encounters he had had with her. At the cricket match and in the market. Poppy Appleton, Dougie's sister who, according to Dougie, had the guts and fearlessness of a young lioness. Dougie hadn't put it like that, of course, when, after he himself had been knocked silly by the brutal petty officer who had flogged Conn, had confided to Conn that their Poppy was the only person he would trust in a pickle. Tongue on her like an adder and a beggar for what she called "method" but in a fix she was the only one he would turn to, he had told Conn.

She had gone when he awoke the next time but beside him was the can of water, two thick slices of fresh bread spread with creamy butter and a wedge of roast beef. This time he managed to sit up as he ate it and when, later that evening, she crept like a sure-footed shadow up the ladder, his white teeth gleamed in the darkness as he grinned at her.

11

She was to look back on those few days spent caring for Alick MacConnell, though they had been fraught with risk, as the happiest, so far, of her young life. Their conversations, when he was capable of it, were held in whispers, and during the daytime she anguished on how she was to get through her work she was so weary, but those couple of hours, snatched after the rest of the household had retired, were unique and satisfying.

It was the first time in her life that she had someone to talk to, not only of her own age and therefore ready to laugh at what she sometimes recognised as foolishness, but of the same level of intelligence and education as herself. And he was well educated, she recognised that, since so was she. He knew so much about . . . well . . . *things*. About animals and ships, about Liverpool and faraway Scotland from where he came, apparently. About books and music and pictures, even the theatre, though he professed to a liking for what he called "music-hall". He had been taught about faraway places like America and Canada where some of his Scottish relatives had gone to make a new life for themselves and he told her about them. About birds in the sky and the creatures who lived in the sea. He could play the piano and the violin, he admitted, though he had often been rebuked for being too light-hearted in what he played.

He had wanted to be off on the evening of the second day but some time before noon he had developed a fever, a shivering which rattled his teeth so loudly she feared Jacko would hear him when he came into the stable to feed and groom the horses and lead out those which worked in the fields. Conn's skin was dry and stretched, hot to the touch and Poppy was afraid, knowing that if it continued and the fever did not break she would be forced to give him away to her mistress. Well, she couldn't just let him burn away, could she?

Again Richard Goodall's encounter with the bull and the injury he sustained to his foot came to her aid. Despite Mrs Goodall's passion for cleanliness and her unceasing attempt to maintain it, the foot festered and for a day or two her son was flushed and feverish. Tom began to worry.

"What's to do wi' the lad?" he asked Eliza anxiously, meaning what measure was the lad's mother to take to restore his strong and sturdy son to the blooming health he had known all his life.

"It's nothing to worry about, Tom," she soothed him. "When the bull stood on Richard's foot it broke the skin and you know yourself the muck that lies about on the floor of the pen."

"I'll have you know it's cleaned out every single day," Tom protested hotly.

"And every day the animal deposits more. Some of it, unfortunately, must have got into the wound and infected it. But I've the very thing to heal it."

Turning to Aggie who was, apart from Cook, the most reliable of the servants and who was preparing a tray of nourishing broth for the patient, Eliza told her, "I know it's late in the year but slip out into the garden and see if there are any raspberry leaves on the canes. I have some dried but fresh would be more effective. Bring as many as you can find, Aggie. I'll make up an infusion at once."

Eliza Goodall had a well-stocked herb garden where she grew many of the plants that she made into lotions and infusions to dose those beneath her roof. Her own father, who had been a somewhat unconventional doctor, had been a great believer in the benefit of herbs and indeed many of the plants which grew in his garden and the surrounding woods. He had passed on his belief and his knowledge to his daughter.

"Not only will it bring down Richard's fever, Tom," she continued, "but soaked into a compress it will help to ease the wound." She smiled at her husband and put a calming hand on his shoulder, not allowing her own concern for the boy to show. Tom, like most men, could not abide illness and was inclined to panic at the slightest sign of it, in himself, or his lads.

Whatever was done for Richard Goodall was carefully noted and the same done for Conn. Poppy hung on every word Mrs Goodall spoke, storing it all away in her head and following as best she could the treatment her mistress gave her own son. It was strange really, for if Master Richard had not sustained the injury to his foot it is doubtful that Poppy would have been able to nurse Conn as she did. For one thing, had they not all been so distracted by Master Richard's injury, Mrs Goodall and indeed any one of the servants would have noticed at once Poppy's furtive behaviour, her short absences, her inclination to hang about at Mrs Goodall's back while she prepared the infusions to treat her son, and her strange tendency to drop off into a deathlike sleep in the kitchen chair after supper.

Mrs Goodall, though she did not speak of it before her husband, confided her worry to Cook in a low voice when the others were occupied, but Poppy, whose nerves and ears were strained in her mistress's direction whenever she was in the kitchen, heard her and followed whatever she spoke of to the letter. She was not surprised, nor sorry, when the hour or so each evening she spent with her mentor was cancelled. Mrs Goodall was absorbed for the moment with getting Master Richard back on his feet and had no time for music lessons; or French lessons, or indeed the work she herself did about the farm and dairy. What would happen on market day was yet to be revealed. And it was this eavesdropping that enabled Poppy to look after and restore Conn to health without being discovered. His own youthful strength helped, of course, since he had never had a day's illness in his life, he told Poppy weakly when the fever broke. Ths scars on his back had scabbed over nicely but the fever had taken its toll and they were both aware, should he go now, as he had intended, he would not get very far in his sorry state. Another day or so then he would be off, he told her. He would walk eastwards until he hit a main road and then, with a bit of luck he would get a lift, beg a ride on a farm waggon, or indeed any vehicle that was going north.

"Where'll yer go?"

It was the fourth night he had spent in the loft and Poppy knew he meant to leave soon. She could not bear it but really, it would be for the best. How they had managed so far without being discovered was a miracle and it could not last much longer. Conn was still far from recovered. While the fever had him he had eaten nothing and though she had done her best to get as much nourishment into him as he could take, he had lost weight. His tall, lanky frame, a boy's frame which had not yet achieved the muscle and flesh and bone of a mature man, was all elbows and bony shoulders, scrawny neck and knobbly knees. The handsome, graceful young athlete he had been at the cricket match, racing up and down the pitch to the roars of approval from his team, had disappeared, burned away by the punishment he had received and the fever which was the result.

One thing he could keep down was milk with eggs beaten in it, a remedy which had been easy to get hold of since she had the ingredients in her hands all day long. It was one of Cook's suggestions, though not for Conn, of course.

"He doesn't want anything to eat, Cook," Mrs Goodall had whispered, shaking her head as she carried her son's untouched tray into the kitchen. "Says he's not hungry. He'll never regain his strength at this rate. It's the second day he's refused food."

Eliza's face was drawn with worry. Though she loved naughty Johnny, for who could stand against his charm, Richard was her first-born, the one most like her, the one she loved the most and she did not feel she would ever recover if anything happened to him.

"Now then, Mrs Goodall, don't you worry your head none. A healthy chap like Master Richard'll take no harm for a day or two wi'out his grub but just to be on the safe side you beat him up a couple of eggs in a glass of milk. Put a drop o' whisky in it an' all. That'll put hairs on his chest."

Whether it did so was never revealed but within a day or so Master Richard was bellowing downstairs for a bit of decent food and indeed three days later he hobbled down the stairs to find it for himself.

But then Richard Goodall had not been flogged. He had not flung himself from a ship's deck into the River Mersey on a cold November night and swum half a mile to the shore.

He had not walked, soaking wet and running with blood, the three miles from the docks through the bitter night streets of Liverpool and the wind-filled blackness of country lanes to get to the hayloft at Long Reach Farm. He had not spent hours on his own with no one to cosset him until Poppy Appleton could slip away with the scraps of food she could save from her own meals and from the larder. Already Cook was wondering what on earth had happened to that half a raised game pie she could have sworn she had left on the pantry shelf and if anyone told her the cat had had it then she'd call them a liar.

" 'Appen it were a burglar, Cook," Marigold said helpfully.

"Don't talk daft, girl," Cook retorted, then was sorry, for Marigold Appleton *was* a bit daft and couldn't help it.

The remark served to distract her from her suspicions, of what she didn't know, but Poppy wondered desperately how much longer she could keep this up. The creeping out of the farmhouse after the others were asleep. The ingenuity needed to achieve hot tea, hot water, the comfrey and then the raspberry infusions, the clean cloths which, horribly soiled, must be made clean again, and all to be carried across the yard, past the dogs who had become quite used to her nocturnal wanderings and didn't even raise their heads from their paws, and up the ladder to the loft.

And she herself was beginning to show the strain. The plain fact was that no matter how hardy you are, how well fed and cared for, a few days on short rations, which she was, and without proper rest, which was again the truth, was enough to sap the strength of the most robust twelve-year-old. Dilys was beginning to look at her with narrowed eyes, not exactly sure herself why she did so, only vaguely uneasy for, though she did her work as she always did, there was something wrong with their Poppy. Dilys had had cause to scold her a time or two when she had disappeared, God alone knew where, and then reappeared with only a vague and unsatisfactory explanation of where she had been. Tommy had stopped her. Mrs Goodall had sent her for some eggs for Master Richard. She had helped the laundry woman to carry a heavy basket of laundry. All possible but not very likely in Dilys's opinion.

That night Conn told Poppy he would leave tomorrow as soon as it was dark.

"Burr I 'aven' gorra jacket yet," she protested, instinctively reaching out to tuck the warm blankets about his thin, bare shoulders. "An' wharrabout that hair o' yours? Yer'll have to have a cap o' some sort to cover it or yer'll be recognised before yer get ter't end of lane." She couldn't stand the thought of him setting off with nothing to wear but the tattered shirt and breeches in which he had arrived. Truth to tell she couldn't stand the thought of him leaving at all but if he had to go, which of course he had, then she meant to make sure he was as well equipped for his journey as Poppy Appleton could make him. She had racked her brain over what she could do about it but though she had managed to steal – yes, *steal* – so many other things which so far had not been missed how could she help herself to one of the Goodall males' overcoats? Go into the boys' or Mr and Mrs Goodall's bedrooms and rummage about in the wardrobes? Hardly! Mr Goodall had an old coat he called his "yard coat" hanging on a peg just inside the back kitchen door but it only needed to be raining tomorrow and he'd be reaching for it.

"Where's my coat?" he would thunder if it was not there and surely the missing raised game pie, the clean woollen blanket, the jug with a lid on it which she kept filled with water beside Conn, the bucket from the laundry into which he relieved himself, would all be remembered, questions would be raised and Poppy Appleton would have to answer them.

Conn took her hands gently between his and peered intently into her distressed face. He had become greatly attached to this small girl who had, he was well aware, given him back his life. Had she not helped him, had he not come here seeking her help, he would have been picked up before the first day was out. Picked up and taken back, this time into a harsher, more confining prison than the *Lahore*. Put in a cell with brutish men who, after they had used his fair boy's body, would have turned him into one of themselves. Made him into a *real* felon, a hardened criminal and not the petty thief his circumstances had forced him into. It was time to move on but first he must tell her his story.

"Where will yer go?" she asked him tremulously.

"Come here, *mo bideach eun*," drawing her towards him. He put one arm about her shoulders, tucking her into his side beneath the blankets. Resting his cheek on her dark curls, he told her who he was.

"My name's Alick James MacConnell but as ye know they call me Conn."

"Aye, I know." Poppy snuggled more closely to him, liking the warmth and solidity of him, even if his ribs and elbows did stick into her. She had brought him a small piece of soap she herself used and it seemed, while she was working, he had washed himself, for she could smell the lemon on his skin. They had doused the lamp but a sliver of moonlight shone through the small ventilation hole in the side of the loft, touching his uncombed curls. They were no longer red as they were in daylight but a deep browny grey and his blue eyes were as dark as charcoal. While he had been in the grip of the fever his breath had been sour but now, as he recovered, she could feel it on her cheek and smell its sweetness.

"I've told no one my proper name, ye ken, only you. I was Conn to all the lads, all the ones who used to go out thievin' wi' me."

He broke off to sigh deeply. "Ye ken . . . I stole, Poppy."

"Yes, I saw yer in the market."

"That was only a wee bit o' bravado, a bit o' cheek, if ye like, but I paid dear for it."

"Same at the fair, an' all."

He moved to look down into her upturned face.

"The fair?"

"Aye, that was bravado when yer played cricket wi't Goodall lads just as if yer'd every right to be there an' wi' Captain Cooper who's a magistrate lookin' on, an' all." She shook her head as though beyond words at his foolishness.

He laughed softly. "I didna ken that."

"No? I bet yer'd a still done it if yer had."

"I suppose so. Anyway, let me tell ye the rest. My mother . . ." He paused and swallowed, his boyish Adam's apple bobbing up and down in his slender throat before he went on. "My mother and father were Scots. From Glasgow. My father was a good, honest man who worked in a shipbuildin' yard on the Clyde. They met and fell in love, but my grandfather owned the shipyard and in his opinion his daughter was too good to waste hersel' on an engineer, even a marine engineer which my father was. He was an educated man, though not a gentleman, ye ken, so my grandfather forbade my mother to associate wi' him. That's how he put it, apparently. She was eighteen, and bonny. There was money, a lot of it and she was expected to make a good match, but she and my father loved one another so they ran away. They fetched up on the Forth, near Edinburgh, where shipbuilding was expandin' an' beginnin' to overtake the Clyde. They were married and my father found work. They rented a wee house and in 1860 I was born. I was eight years old when we moved to Liverpool where my father had been offered a better job, so he told me, and we settled in Walton-on-the-Hill. My mother was the loveliest, sweetest, gentlest woman you could ever wish to meet and my father and I adored her. She was gifted too, and taught me all I know. She'd take me, when I was old enough, to art galleries, libraries, to concerts and museums and I was brought up to be a perfect little gentleman."

He laughed softly, his wide mouth, healing now, stretched across his even white teeth. "I was a bit of a 'Mama's boy', truth be told. I didna mix wi' many children, bein' taught at home but . . . well, my mother was friend as well as mother so I felt no lack. We were happy, the three of us until . . . until they came to tell us my father wouldna be coming home again."

There was a long, painful silence and Poppy was reluctant to break it. She who had never known the love and commitment this boy had didn't know what to say to him in what was evidently still a searing memory. Her instincts told her words would not help him so instead she took his rough hand in hers and held it wordlessly.

"My mother began to die from that day, Poppy. I didna ken ye could really die of a broken heart, but she did. I was eleven years old, brought up gently, knowing nothing of the harsh world outside my mother's parlour but, by God, I soon learned. There wasna any money, ye see, and we had to eat. We nearly starved that first month after my father's accident and it wasna until I began to accept that not only had I to look after my mother but I had to provide for myself that I started to thieve. I had my first fight soon after. I was stealing food. From shops and market stalls, taking it back to my mother and doing my best to get her to eat it. To please me, I used to say, and she would try. But some lad, probably wonderin' why another dressed like a big jessy in a velveteen jacket and cap with a tassle on it was stealing a loaf of bread, took exception to it, and to me. I was a big lad, strong, tall, like my father. I get this hair from him and a temper to go with it" – running his hand through his mop of moon-silvered curls – "and somehow, though I knew nothing of brawling, I got the better of him."

He paused again, his chest rising beneath her cheek as he drew in a deep breath.

"But we needed more than food, ye ken. There was the rent of the house, doctor's bills, medicine for my mother. Och, 'tis strange, ye ken," he said reflectively, "how people accept situations. Or perhaps they just dinna want to know. To get involved. Those men, the doctor and the rent collector, neither questioned the amazing fact that an eleven-year-old laddie was handling the money of the house, paying them what they were owed. I . . . I had begun to wear my father's clothes by then, being so tall, those he had worked in, turnin' up cuffs and the like. And havin' become friendly wi' the lad I'd beaten, since, strangely, some boys admire those who can overcome them, we teamed up. I was clever, crafty. I could plan and carry out schemes I had thought up and he had the experience. Soon we formed a small gang organisin' ourselves so that while one of us went into a jeweller's, say, another would keep watch in the doorway and another at the corner of the street. Whoever went in, usually me, takin' the shopkeeper by surprise, would grab whatever was on the counter and run like hell. It worked. Sometimes we did houses. At night, ye ken. With a small gang ye can work out a strategy to eliminate a great deal of the risk. My friend, I never knew his real name, just called him Dicky Sam because he said that was what they called those who were born within the sound of parish bells, was well acquainted with a fence so we had no trouble getting rid of the stuff. So . . . I survived. My mother died a year later."

His voice became flat and toneless. "It was then they caught us for the first time. I . . . I had no one but Dicky Sam and your Dougie and the others but . . . well, ye know the rest, *mo donn falt caileag*. It was not what . . . what my mother would have wanted for me but I've no regrets. I'd do it all over again to get her what she needed, providin' she never found out. Which she didna." He hesitated then said, "She, at the end, confused me with my father. Called me James which was his name, and mine too, and I think she was . . . happy. She was a great lady," he said simply.

Poppy was still for a moment then she sat up and turned to look at him. A curiously adult look which he returned. They still held hands.

"So . . . yer ter go back ter yer mam's folk then?"

"Aye. My grandfather, if he's still alive, is Alaric Swainson. Our people came from Denmark, many generations ago, my mother told me. He builds iron ships on the Clyde. He had no sons, only my mother and . . . and" – his voice quivered but he went on defiantly – "as I am his legitimate grandson I mean to . . . well, lassie, I dinna ken quite what I mean to do but unless I try I'll never find out. I canna see myself in a life of crime, ye ken. I'm not cut out for it." He grinned and moved his shoulders slightly, wincing as he did so. "I've always loved ships so I reckon it's in my blood. All ships except the *Lahore*, of course. My father used to take me down to the docks and tell me what each ship was, sailing and steam. He was a designer and he showed me his plans, talked to me of . . . of what we would do together when I was old enough and, well, I thinks it's worth a try, wouldn't ye say?"

"Course it is an' I'm glad for yer."

"Ye dinna judge me? Condemn me for what I've done?"

"Well, it was wrong, Conn, but ter be 'onest," since Poppy Appleton was not only honest, but realistic, "I don't see wharr else yer could've done. Yer 'ad ter feed yer mam, didn't yer and you only eleven. I were ten when I came ter work in the dairy."

"So we've both had to get on with life in the best way we know how. It gives us something in common."

She smiled. "I suppose it does. Now then," becoming brisk, "there's one thing I want yer ter promise me."

"What's that, *mo donn falt caileag?*"

"Well, first of all, what the 'ell does that mean? What yer just said? What language is it?"

"It's Gaelic. My mother and father both spoke it. My mother taught me and *mo donn falt caileag* means 'my brown-haired lassie'."

"Oh aye." She bent her head and, with the hand not holding his, picked at a loose thread in the material of her skirt. Suddenly she felt shy, she didn't know why, unable to meet his deep blue eyes which were searching for hers.

"How old are you, Poppy?" he asked abruptly.

"Twelve."

"Aah, an' I'm not quite fourteen. My birthday's in January."

"Mine's August." She glanced up quickly and was surprised by the look in his eyes.

"We're not old enough yet, *annsachd*," he whispered, "but I'll come back. D'ye believe me?"

"Promise."

"Aye, I promise. Will ye wait?"

"Yes."

He said something else then, a long sentence in what she took to be Gaelic and though she could not understand the words she was woman enough, even at twelve, to recognise what was in him, and herself.

They both smiled and sighed, satisfied by whatever it was that had passed between them.

"I'll fetch yer jacket termorrer. Wait fer me in the spinney at back o't stable. About eight. Yer'll not go wi'out . . ."

"No, I'll no' go wi'out sayin' *au revoir*."

"That's French."

"Aye, *mo duinne*."

On the following day it was fine. One of those days that come just as winter is settling in, not exactly warm, but sunny with a clear blue sky stretching away to the horizon. They were all delighted when Richard Goodall announced that he was sick of being cooped up in the house and if Aggie would pass him that stick he'd have a wander across the yard.

"It's cold out there, Richard," his mother warned, her heart glad to see him recovered. "Don't forget you've had a fever."

"Oh, Mother, really," her son protested.

"Look, put your father's yard coat about your shoulders."

That was the last anyone ever saw of Tom Goodall's yard coat though Richard swore he hung it back on the hook beside the kitchen door. Tom was furious. He'd been very fond of that coat, he kept repeating over and over again. It was long, reaching to his ankles. It was weatherproof and had a warm woollen lining. It had deep and handy pockets in which he could keep the innumerable small farming tools he carried about with him and he'd miss it. He'd never get another like it, he fretted, and if he ever caught the bugger who'd taken it he'd see him hung.

Cook shook her head in bewilderment. There was something very peculiar going on in this household. There was the question of her raised game pie which had never been accounted for and it still caused her disquiet; and had anyone seen her good jug, the one with the lid which was so handy? And she could swear she had more linen squares than those on the shelf in the linen cupboard at the back of the range. She and Aggie had a good root round in it and the rest of the servants lolling at the kitchen table nearly jumped out of their skins when she screeched, "There's a blanket gone, a good woollen blanket, one of the mistress's best ones. Would someone like to tell me what's going on?"

No one could. Certainly not Poppy Appleton who dozed and dreamed in the chair by the fire. Dreamed of a tall, red-haired lad who strode out towards Knotty Ash, a jaunty cap, which had once belonged to Evan and which he had worn to milk the cows, slung on his head and with Tom Goodall's warm coat buttoned across his chest. Beneath was strapped the blanket and in his breeches pocket jingled a few coins with which to buy himself a second-hand shirt from a market stall.

"I canna take it," he said stubbornly. "It's your money. You earned it an' I'll let no lassie—"

"Oh, give over, yer daft 'apporth." She was just as stubborn. "What 'appens when yer tekk yer coat off an' yer bare-chested underneath it, tell me that. Yer see, yer can't. Go on, purrit in yer pocket before I box yer ears."

He began to chuckle. "Oh, Poppy, *mo annsachd*. Was there ever a wee lassie like ye. If there is I've yet to meet her, but very well, I'll 'borrow' it until we meet again. One and elevenpence halfpenny. Remember."

"Course I will. Yer'll have ter come back now ter pay yer debt." It was said with great satisfaction.

In one pocket of the greatcoat was a jug of sweet tea and in the other was a loaf, sliced and buttered and sandwiched with cheese.

He put awkward, boyish arms about her when they parted, tucking her beneath his chin, pressing her face into his bony chest and resting his cheek on her soft, sweet-smelling hair. She had wanted to cry then because suddenly parting with him was like parting with a vital bit of herself. She didn't know which bit but it was a part she needed in her day-to-day existence and she could not imagine how she was to manage without it. She had never taken to anyone, not even Mrs Goodall, like she'd taken to Conn and she felt the ache of his going even before he'd gone.

"I'll write," he whispered into her hair.

Her heart leaped joyfully and she looked up into his face, her smile dazzling. His features were indistinct in the dark beneath the sighing trees of the spinney but she caught the gleam of something in his eyes.

"Will yer, Conn, will yer?"

"Aye, bonny lassie, I promise, and when I've an address ye can write back."

Oh, thank you, God, and thank you, Mrs Goodall, for teaching me to read and write. I'll never lose him now. The link between us will be nourished with words on paper and we'll always be together because of it, even if he is far away in Glasgow and I'm in Liverpool. Then she thought of something.

"Conn?"

"What, my lass?"

"Yer'll not write in that old Gaelic, will yer?"

There was soft laughter in them both as he swung away down the path to the future.

Part II

12

Dominic Cooper thought she was quite the most exquisite creature he had ever seen as he watched her climb gracefully down from the gig. She had driven it into the stable yard with a flourish, handling the reins expertly, evidently well used to them, clucking encouragingly to the little brown mare which pulled it before bringing the equipage to a smart halt.

He had been just about to leap up on to Piper's back and head off for a brisk gallop across the parkland, perhaps calling in on his cousin Marcus who was always more than ready to throw up whatever he might happen to be doing, which was never very much, and join in one of Dominic's "escapades", as his own mother and father tolerantly called them. He had heard they were rook shooting over at the rookeries at Fullingham, which was owned by Sir Thomas Avons, a friend of his father, and there was bound to be some fun there. Sir Thomas was a hospitable old cove who liked young people about him and would greet Dominic and Marcus with the open-hearted welcome that made him so popular. Guns, not rifles, would be used and after luncheon the shooting would start. If he could winkle Marcus away from his mother, who was a trial and tribulation to them all, including her own husband, Dominic's Uncle Freddy, in her belief that her son would surely come to some dreadful harm when there were guns about, they might ride over there and see if they could find a bit of excitement. Excitement was the breath of life to Dominic Cooper and he would go anywhere to find it. And, of course, there was always Dulcie!

He would have to be home no later than four, though, or his mother would throttle him since today was his and Naomi's twenty-first birthday and there was to be a big party tonight at Coopers Edge to celebrate their coming of age and his engagement to Dulcie. That was why he wanted to get away to be honest. It was nothing but fuss, fuss, fuss at the house with servants galloping here and there at his mother's bidding, with Naomi moaning that her gown was not right and did he really think Andy Lowood would come, as if Dominic knew or cared, and it was all driving him to distraction. A couple of hours potting at rooks, a couple of stolen kisses from Dulcie, who was a sweet little thing, and a couple of glasses of Sir Thomas's fine claret would pass the day nicely until the time came for him to fulfil his obligations as the dutiful son and husband-to-be.

It all slipped away with the speed of a bullet from a gun as he stared at the girl in the gig, his left foot in the stirrup, his right still on the ground. It was as though the blood that pumped to his brain, keeping it in its usual sharp and witty state, had drained away to some other part of his body leaving him stunned, dry-mouthed, speechless for the first time in his life.

She was dark, her glossy hair short and curling riotously about her neat head. She wore no bonnet and whether it was her natural colour or had been brought about by exposure to the sun, her skin right down into the modest neckline of her summer gown was the faintest golden tint of an apricot. She was looking down as she secured the reins of the gig and he could not see the colour of her eyes but the lashes which shaded them were long, fine and dark. There was a flush on her cheek, a faint carnation, and her lips were the same colour, only deeper, parted and full and moist.

She looked up then and caught his eye. Hers were the palest blue-grey, the pupil very dark with a curious black line edging the iris. It did not seem to disconcert her, being goggled at by a handsome young man, for if he was nothing else Dominic Cooper was a perfect specimen of truly magnificent manhood.

"Good morning," she called out cheerfully. "I've brought the eggs and butter and chickens that were ordered and Mrs Goodall says if you want any more cream it's no problem. I can fetch it over later. And Dilys is making some more butter shells, just in case. I'll go and find Mrs Clayton and let her know I've arrived. Glorious day, isn't it?"

She was dressed in some sort of cotton muslin, simple but charming. A pale blue-grey like her eyes and about her waist was a broad sash of scarlet which whittled her already tiny waist to nothing and emphasised her small, round breasts. The sleeves of the dress were short and puffed and edged in the same colour as her sash and her dainty boots of kid were a pale sand colour. In her ears were what looked like gold ear-bobs which shook and jingled as she turned her head.

She leaned into the back of the gig, dragging out a tray on which were arranged a dozen or so plump-breasted chickens, then turned and smiled mischievously.

"Are you to get up on that animal, or is it that you're climbing down? Perhaps I could lend you a hand?"

Jimmie, who had been a groom at Coopers Edge since before Master Dominic was born and who had just saddled Piper for him, hid his mouth behind his hand or he would have laughed out loud and Master Dominic didn't like to be laughed at. Not unless he meant to be. He'd never seen the lad in such a pop-eyed state, he was to tell the other servants later. Struck dumb, he was, and paralysed too by the look of it with one foot up and the other down and if he didn't look lively and shift himself, one way or the other, the grey would become nervous and fidget, dragging the lad off his feet.

It was July and the sun shone from a sky the colour of lapis lazuli, a sky which stretched on for ever, merging completely with the heat-misted heights of the Pennine Chain. To the north a procession of fat white clouds drifted lazily towards the river and the Irish Sea, looking for all the world like a meandering line of fluffy and very clean sheep. It was warm and Dominic had left his jacket off, rolling up his shirt sleeves to his elbows. His cravat was in his pocket and if he and Marcus decided on Sir Thomas and the rook shooting he would put it on but his amber throat was bare at the moment as were his arms, brown and muscular.

The outline of the house, Coopers Edge, could be seen beyond the tack room and harness room and the row of loose boxes which sheltered Captain Adam Cooper's tall thoroughbred hunters. The house was honey-coloured in the golden sunshine, its stone draped with ivy. Its many chimneys pierced the vivid sky and at each corner was a small turret, the roofs of which were tiled in a pale green. It was a lovely old house, even from the viewpoint of the stable yard, with a look of patient endurance about it, its age and beauty declaring it to be the heartbeat, the pulse, the fulcrum of the family who lived beneath its roof. Even the stable block had a grace and charm which matched the house, the entrance being crowned by an enormous clock turret.

With a start which clearly alarmed the grey on whose back he had been about to climb and causing the groom to leap forward and grab its bridle, Dominic came out of his tranced delight, dragging his foot from the stirrup and hurrying – almost running, Jimmie decided – towards the gig.

"Here, let me carry that for you," he exclaimed eagerly, nearly tripping over his own elegantly booted feet as he strode across the yard. "It's far too heavy for you to manage."

He took the tray from her, giving her the smile Jimmie had seen him give a dozen pretty young ladies who came to Coopers Edge to join a riding party, or a picnic, or who landed up in the yard after the hunt. A rare lad for the ladies was Master Dominic with a reputation for breaking hearts throughout the county of Lancashire. So far he had managed it without too much damage to his family name which was respected hereabouts, but he was a bit on the wild side, spoiled by an indulgent mother and father. Well, perhaps marriage would calm him down which was why they had agreed to it, he suspected. He was very young, only just twenty-one, and they did say Sir Thomas Avons's little lass, who was as pretty as a rose, would have her work cut out to keep him reined to domesticity. In Jimmie's opinion being husband to the daughter of a baronet would have little effect on his young master's need of constant and varied amusement.

The girl laughed, throwing back her head and revealing her perfect white teeth. Master Dominic was hypnotised, it seemed, standing there with the tray of chickens in his arms and on his face a look Jimmie had never seen before.

"Really," the girl said, "there's no need. I loaded the gig all by myself since the others were busy and I can unload it just as easily. I may not look it but I'm strong and I'm used to it. I've been doing it for almost six years, after all."

"Not while I'm about you don't," Dominic answered gallantly. "No lady should be expected to carry such things," even though as he said it he knew this was no lady.

"Thank you, but I can manage," she interrupted firmly, reaching for another tray, "but if you insist you can carry that one to the kitchen door."

"Put that down at once." His voice was curt, the sort of voice one used to a servant or to a person of lesser social standing and she turned to him, surprised and not a little displeased. There was a frown on her face and her eyes had darkened and it was plain she did not care to be told what to do, or not do, by this young squireen, even if he was Dominic Cooper, son of one of the most illustrious families in Liverpool.

At once Dominic smiled. He had gone too far in his fancy that, as he always had done, he could get his own way with any woman, including this lovely girl, and his interest deepened. His face assumed an expression of innocent penitence and Jimmie watched with fascination to see what effect it would have on the dairymaid from Long Reach Farm. There had been a few dairymaids, laundry maids and parlourmaids in young Dominic Cooper's life, all falling under what were considered to be his charming wiles, ready to flirt with him and even allow intimacies he would not attempt on girls of his own class. Fair game they were among fellows like him and his friends. Jimmie had heard the rumours but so far the young master had kept his behaviour hidden within the accepted bounds of what a gentleman might be allowed.

"Why don't you carry in that small basket." He smiled. "What's in it? Butter. Well, then, I'll bring these" – looking down hastily to see what he was holding, hiding a small shudder of distaste at the sight of the plucked pink flesh – "er . . . chickens, and you fetch the butter. Please, I beg you, could I call myself a gentleman if I allowed a young lady to heave all this lot across the yard? It's far too heavy." He broadened his wicked, devastating smile, the one which weakened the knees of every woman whether she be sixteen or sixty. "Where are they going, anyway?"

She sighed resignedly, evidently considering him to be a bit simple since it was hardly likely she would be delivering two dozen herb-stuffed chickens, six dozen butter shells, three pounds of best butter and four pints of cream to the front door, would she?

"Oh, very well," she said, "but I must get on. It's market day tomorrow and I've the eggs to wash and count out yet and though Dilys is there while I'm away, I can't leave Jinny too long on her own with Nelly or they'll both get confused. I'm teaching Jinny to read and write, you see, but she still gets her Cs and Es mixed up. To speed things up I just write the capitals – C for chicken, you see – though I know she'll master it soon, being a bright child, but it can be confusing."

He hadn't the faintest idea what she was talking about and didn't care, either. He could not tear his eyes away from her soft pink mouth as she spoke and would have been quite happy, for the moment, simply to stand and watch her and listen to her babble whatever it was she was babbling but, with a basket in each hand she began to walk towards the arch which led into the kitchen yard.

The servants were all busy at some urgent task set them by the cook, Mrs Clayton, with not a minute to spare for even a word or two on this important day. There was much brisk whisking and pounding, stirring and chopping, a frenzied tumult of activity which always preceded any entertaining done at Coopers Edge. Mrs Clayton was delicately stirring a rich sauce, her expression absorbed, for she was a mistress of her craft, and when the knock at the back door heralded a visitor she tutted irritably.

They all stopped whatever they were doing as one man – or woman – and stared, slack-jawed and wide-eyed when young Maggie threw open the door to reveal their handsome, elegant young master standing on the doorstep with a tray of chickens in his arms. He was grinning absurdly. Next to him was Poppy Appleton, head dairymaid at Long Reach Farm.

"Oh, Cook, there you are," Master Dominic called out imperiously, "would you send someone to fetch the rest of . . . whatever is in this young lady's gig," for though he had been most pressing in his determination to help her he really had no intention of carting the remainder of the trays and baskets this gorgeous young creature had brought from . . . well, wherever she had brought them from. He had made this effort simply to impress her and for no other reason, but there was no need to go too far, was there? Not when there were a dozen servants in the kitchen who were paid to do such menial tasks.

He had not reckoned on Poppy Appleton, whose heart was engaged elsewhere and had been for almost four years and had no time for gentlemen of leisure besides, especially those she considered to be fools. He was piqued, if only for a moment, when she totally ignored him and placed her baskets with the greatest care on the table.

"There's no need, Mrs Clayton," she called out, not at all bothered that he might be offended since he meant nothing to her. "You just get on with whatever you're doing. I know how busy you are today. I can manage. After all I've been doing it for years now and need no help. If you'll just leave the back door open I'll . . . "

Dominic thumped his tray down next to the eggs, oblivious to the culinary magnificence of the creations that stood there and Mrs Clayton hissed with annoyance, for it would all have to be done again. Her painstaking work with whipped cream flavoured with rosewater – a tip passed down to her from her mother who had had it from *her* mother, come supposedly from as far back as Elizabethan times – strips of angelica and strands of sun sugar, had been knocked sideways by the careless clattering of the heavy tray but Master Dominic had not even noticed as he chased after Poppy Appleton.

"Well, would you credit it?" Betty Forbes, who was head parlourmaid, announced in disbelief, "and her nought but a farm labourer's daughter," for they all knew Poppy's history.

"She's head dairymaid now, Betty, you know that, and them's the sort the lad likes. I've heard he's tumbled a few in his time. She'll not be the first, nor the last, even if he is to be married soon." This from Alice Cowper, who was next in rank to Betty, both of them unmarried and likely to stay that way.

"Eeh, gi' me 'alf a chance," sighed young Maggie, fourteen years old, romantic but plain. "He's that 'andsome . . ."

"Handsome is as handsome does, my girl," Mrs Clayton snapped, her mouth pursed in disapproving lines, her face like thunder, "and come away from that door. Fetch me some cream from the pantry – I hope Poppy's brought some more – and start whipping it. That lot on the table are ruined and will all have to be done again and I've not yet started on the marchpane cake. While you're there bring the caster sugar, the ground almonds and that flask of rosewater. And I'll not have talk like that in my kitchen, you two, so think on," glaring at Betty and Alice. "It's a good job Mr Winston's not here or you'd both be for it. That's Captain Cooper's son you're talking about and what he gets up to, if he gets up to anything, is nothing to do with us. And don't you sneer at that young lass in my hearing. A good, hardworking girl, she is, else she'd not be such a pet of Mrs Goodall's. Now then, back to your work and not another word."

Suitably chastened, the maids did as they were told.

Poppy, despite the smiling, winsome "help" Master Dominic insisted on giving her, since, as she had asked, no servant came to her aid, emptied the gig, delivered her message to Mrs Clayton about the cream and prepared, being as patient as she could with the persistent son of the house, to drive it home, but it seemed he had other ideas. A saunter in the woods at the back of the house perhaps, as it was such a glorious day, or would she like to see his mother's rose garden which was quite magnificent at this time of the year, understanding privately that it would be deserted on this day of days. Apart from the gardeners, that is, and they hardly counted. Could she not smell their wonderful scent, the roses, of course, and was it not heady? Or there were the hothouses where it was said grew the most beautiful orchids and would she not like one to take home with her?

Poppy could feel the irritation grow in her. What was this beautiful young man thinking of, doing his best to tempt a working girl like herself into what she recognised would be a compromising position and, if the rumours were true, him about to become engaged to the pretty, wealthy and well-bred daughter of a baronet. Was he quite mad, or just the spoiled brat they said he was, unable to resist whatever pretty toy his immature mind seized on? Here he was smiling and smirking and treating her to what she supposed he thought of as his masculine charm when all she wanted to do was to tell him to grow up and behave himself. Silly little boy!

"Sir, I am a working girl and haven't the time to—"

"Dominic, please."

"Pardon?"

"I would be honoured if you would call me Dominic since I am sure we are to become good friends."

She almost laughed aloud but managed to keep her face straight and without expression.

"Dominic Cooper, at your service," he continued. His handsome face was flushed as he bowed and the deep aquamarine of his eyes, which he had inherited from his father, glowed with admiration. He didn't know when he had been so ... so taken with a woman; well, girl, he supposed he should call her since she could be no more than sixteen or so and he must find the opportunity to get to know her better.

"Mr Cooper ..."

"Dominic."

"Mr Cooper." Poppy's soft pink mouth firmed with annoyance. Really, did he think because of who he was he could say and do whatever he liked, keep her from her work to trail about his mother's rose garden and generally behave like one of those silly young girls who, it was said, his mother had invited to Coopers Edge? It had also been said that nothing but the daughter of nobility would do for Mrs Adam Cooper, who had once been Sally Grimshaw of the Grimshaw Arms, the inn on the road from Old Swan. Well, she had got what she wanted, by God. There was some mystery surrounding the family, whispered rumours of a first wife who had gone mad and died in an asylum for the insane but not before Sally Grimshaw had given birth to twins, this man and his sister Naomi. A hurried marriage and some legal jiggery-pokery had made the children legitimate, probably helped by Captain Cooper's great wealth come from his first wife and it was perhaps this which had made the second Mrs Cooper so determined on only the very best pedigree in a wife for her son. A strong woman, it was said, who ruled her household and her husband with a velvet glove, but ruled them just the same. There were also two spinster sisters, half-sisters of this man, still living there, in their thirties but, despite being as beautiful as the first Mrs Cooper was supposed to have been, not interested in husbands. No wonder this grinning young man was as he was, brought up in such strange surroundings.

"Miss . . . do you know you haven't told me your name yet?"

"And I'm not going to either," she snapped, putting her little booted foot on the step of the gig, ready to climb into it and drive away but before she knew what he was about his strong, horseman's hands were at her waist, offending her beyond measure and he had lifted her with perfect ease on to the seat of the one-horse, two-wheeled gig that had replaced the cart once used by Eliza Goodall. Eliza had been reluctant to buy it since gigs were considered to be the most dangerous of carriages. If the horse fell the shafts went down to the ground with the animal, sometimes catapulting the occupants to injury or death over the horse's head and Eliza would have been devastated had anything happened to the neat and pretty child who had become, in all but blood, her daughter. The girl had grown as she was cherished. Her cheeks had filled out and though she was small her bones were well covered and she was straight and healthy. Eliza wanted her to stay that way. She took full credit for what Poppy had become and loved her, she was sometimes ashamed to admit, even to herself, more than her own sons. But Poppy adored the gig and could Eliza refuse her anything? She drove it well. The vehicle had enough room in the back for the trays of fowl and all the other dairy produce Poppy and Jinny took to market every week, and the two of them, pretty as a picture and as smart as paint in the well-made outfits Eliza provided, made a lovely sight as they drove into Liverpool to their stall.

They sold over twice what Eliza had once done, not only because Long Reach Farm had a reputation for quality and value for money but simply because they were two smiling, pretty and polite young girls who drew all eyes, male and female, to them and the stall. They were seemly, naturally. Eliza trusted Poppy to be no other way and the business, and therefore profits, grew every week.

"Thank you, Mr Cooper, I can manage," Poppy said icily, taking up the reins and clucking to the mare to walk on. She turned her head for a moment. "May I offer my congratulations to you and your sister on your coming of age and to yourself on your forthcoming engagement." There, that should shame him! "I hope your party tonight is a great success. I bid you good-day."

She nodded coolly, heading for the gateway, thankful to be away from his impudent stare, but the stamp of horse's hooves on the cobbles behind her made her look round and there he was, throwing off the hand of the groom who had been holding the horse's head, and coming after her. She could hardly believe it!

"I'll ride you home. Er . . . please, won't you tell me your name? I can't keep on calling you 'er', can I?"

"You need call me nothing, Mr Cooper. You and I are unlikely to meet, our stations in life being so far apart, so there is hardly need for introductions."

"Oh, come now, my pet. You see, I *have* to call you something so 'my pet' will do and I shall find out your name, you realise that. Cook must know who you are since you came from some dairy with that produce."

"I would be obliged, sir, if you would not discuss me with your servants," tossing her head angrily, for who knew what interpretation they would put on it. "Now, I must get on."

He was alongside her by now as she drove smartly down Knotty Ash Lane towards Prescot Road. He rode his grey like a young nobleman, easy and erect in the saddle, one hand holding the reins low down, the other in a fist on his thigh, the toes of both feet pointing towards the horse's nose in the correct way. He was smiling, not at all put off by her frosty manner. There was an enquiring look on his face.

"It seems from what you tell me that you're a dairymaid so how is it you don't speak like—"

"Like a dairymaid," she challenged, her eyes like pale blue crystal in her flushed face.

"Exactly. And you're obviously well educated. I can tell by the—"

"By the words I use, is that it? You are quite rude, do you know that, Mr Cooper, and if you don't leave me alone and go back to where you belong I shall be rude too and say a thing or two that might give you a clue as to my antecedents."

"Really, how delightful." He grinned broadly, highly diverted. "I'm waiting with bated breath." It seemed whatever she said, or how nastily, he was not to be put off.

Poppy slapped the reins on the mare's back as though hoping by doing so she could make the animal go faster and leave Dominic Cooper and his thoroughbred grey behind.

"Don't tempt me," she snarled viciously. Poppy Appleton, a ten-year-old illiterate waif had been left behind a long time ago and in her place was a well-spoken, well-informed young woman who could hold her own in most company. Five years and though she was, since Dilys's poor legs had finally let her down, head dairymaid at Long Reach Farm she was much more than that now.

"Look, I mean you no harm, really," he coaxed, leaning

down to peer into her furious face. "Stop and talk to me." He honestly couldn't understand why she refused to do so, it seemed. "You're a real mystery, d'you know that?" And only slightly less than he loved a challenge, Dominic Cooper loved a mystery. Especially if it had something to do with a pretty woman.

"I am not a mystery but if it will satisfy your bloody curiosity and make you leave me alone and go back to where you belong I will tell you that I am head dairymaid at Long Reach Farm. There, are you happy now?"

"Oh dear, is that part of your ancestry, the bloody word, I mean?"

Poppy was mortified that his persistence, his belief that he had only to bedevil her and she would respond to him, perhaps laugh up at him with demure submission, had made her swear. She wanted to turn round and lash out at his smug, smiling, beautiful face with the little whip she had on the seat beside her, wondering at the same time why she had allowed herself to get into such a temper, but instead she urged the mare on into a headlong gallop. The gig bounced and swung along the dusty rutted lane and in a field beside it a man, and even his dog, who were herding some cows towards a farm gate and the milking shed, stopped and turned to stare. The quickthorn hedge was as tall as the grey in the lane and the man recognised the high and mighty Master Dominic Cooper at the canter on its back, but who was that going hell for leather in some vehicle hidden by the hedge?

Poppy determined she would not say another word to him. She had already lost her temper and sworn at him which had seemed to amuse him no end, so perhaps if she ignored him he would give up and go away. She was not to know that everything she did made him more bewitched.

Her spirited refusal to have anything to do with him, he who had had females swooning at his feet ever since he reached his thirteenth birthday, intrigued him. Her show of temper, her way with words which were not those of a servant girl, the very clothes she wore said she was no ordinary dairymaid. The set of her haughty head, the snapping brilliance of her eyes as she turned to glare at him, the flushed, rather dishevelled look about her, caused by the furious pace of the gig, the absolutely delightful bounce of her young breasts as the gig jumped into a pothole, then crashed over an unhandy stone, all excited him beyond measure. But what had she said about a farm? Long Reach Farm? Wasn't that where the Goodall boys lived and were not the Goodall boys in Dominic Cooper's cricket team? Well, the cricket team of the Grimshaw Arms of which he was captain. Richard and Johnny Goodall who, though they were not among those he called friends, since he was a gentleman like his father, and they were not, were worth cultivating if it got him close to this little beauty.

"So, you're with the Goodalls, are you?" He grinned. "Good friends of mine, the Goodalls," lying easily. "I shall have to contrive an invitation . . ."

"Don't you dare, you . . . you . . ."

"Please, feel free to swear if it will make you feel better. I don't mind."

"*Leave . . . me . . . alone*," she snarled at him over her shoulder. Her arms were aching with the effort of driving the gig and keeping the terrified mare from leaping into the deep, flower-clogged ditch at the side of the road. God knows what they would think when she drove into the yard, if she ever got there, looking, she was sure, as though she had taken part in a steeplechase, her hair all over the place and her face sweated and flushed. The corner which she must turn into

Prescot Road was coming up in a minute and if she was to take it at this desperate speed she would have herself over the hedge and poor Belle with a couple of broken legs. She was livid, murderous in her rage and need to hit back at this insufferable devil, to sneer at him, to show him her contempt and absolute abhorrence at his attentions, but at the same time she felt a prickle of alarm at his persistent belief that she did not really mean it. What was wrong with the man? He had everything any young gentleman might envy. Wealth, good looks, indulgent parents and, so it was said, a beautiful young lady of the highest social standing ready to marry him. So what in hell did he want with her? She had been perfectly pleasant with him at the start, patiently accepting his help with the produce, though she had not needed it, but the arrogant sod seemed to think she was merely teasing him. Leading him on like some coquettish young miss pretending to be disinterested in the young master of the house. A flirtatious female of the sort no doubt he mixed with who was playing him at his own game. Damn him to hell and back, she hissed through gritted teeth, getting ready to pull back on the reins and slow down the gig for the corner.

Ahead of them a horseman paused and turned in the saddle, evidently wondering who the hell was coming up behind him at such a lick and with a surprising, even alarming flash of relief, for why should she be alarmed, she saw it was Richard.

At once she drew on the reins, bringing the little brown mare to a quivering halt, both of them, she and the animal, breathing harshly. The expression on Richard's face was comical since it must have looked as though she and Dominic Cooper were having a race, but she had never been so glad to see him in her life and her manner, which was always polite and pleasant with him, became warmer than she intended.

"Richard, how nice to see you and where have you been on this lovely afternoon?" she panted, ridiculously, she knew.

Richard Goodall's expression became even more surprised and he dismounted, going to Belle's head to fondle her ears and pat her nose with a comforting hand.

"You know I was to ride over to Moss Farm to look at the bull they have for sale, Poppy. We talked of it at dinner-time." His pleasant, but serious face was disapproving as he bowed coolly in Dominic Cooper's direction. He loved his animals and so did Poppy and to see her abusing the little mare in such a way bewildered him.

"Well, I'll be off then, Poppy." Dominic grinned impishly. "I've enjoyed our little chat enormously, and by the way, Goodall," turning to Richard with that imperious charm not many could resist, "why don't you and your brother come over tomorrow. We've a new tennis court and as we're all beginners it should be fun." It would not do to invite the dairymaid, of course, but the sons of a well-to-do farmer who already played cricket with him would be perfectly acceptable.

Leaving the astonished Richard and the seething Poppy staring after him, Dominic Cooper turned his grey and made off up the lane at a wild gallop.

13

"I'm just walking down to Primrose Bank, Mrs Goodall. I thought I'd take Ellen a few eggs in exchange for those scones she sent over. I know she's always glad of a bit extra. Is that all right?" For after all the eggs belonged to Mrs Goodall and though Poppy knew she'd not begrudge them it was always her practice to ask.

"Of course, sweetheart." The endearment slipped out easily, neither woman showing the slightest surprise at the use of it. "Thank her for me, will you? Mind you, I have a fancy we upset Cook by praising them so extravagantly."

Eliza Goodall was smiling as she spoke. She draped one arm affectionately over Poppy's shoulders and walked with her to the front door of the farmhouse which led into the sunny garden. The astonishing fish standing on its tail spewed a delicate fan of water into the air, the sunshine turning it into a million hazed diamond droplets in which the colours of the rainbow were reflected. Recently Eliza had planted white waterlilies in the pond over which the fish ruled. The floating, glossy green leaves supported the exquisite, cup-like blossoms, three leaves to each blossom, and though her husband and sons thought her to be quite mad, she had an ally now in Poppy who loved and enjoyed the garden as much as she did.

The sunshine washed over them as they stepped out into it, gold-edged and brilliant and the fuchsia, which was in full bloom, frothed scarlet bells against the cobbled wall. There were lupins, vividly pink, roses, their scent dizzying, massed stock and in hanging baskets on either side of the doorway, lilac-hued, lemon-scented verbena and the bright red of geraniums. It all thrived under the loving care of Eliza Goodall and her "daughter" Poppy Appleton.

For some unspoken reason she and Poppy no longer walked casually through the kitchen past the servants and out into the yard as Poppy once had done and it all stemmed from the time when Poppy became, and the servants were aware that she had become, more to her mistress than her dairymaid.

She had been favoured from the start, of course, when Mrs Goodall had taught her to read and write with the excuse that there should be someone other than herself to do the orders. But the reading and writing had led to piano lessons, to French lessons and to hear the pair of them jabbering away like a couple of monkeys with no one having the faintest idea what they said had silenced the kitchen staff as effectively as if they had all been struck dumb. Well, they couldn't join in, could they, so best keep their traps shut.

"We must practise and practise, Poppy," Mrs Goodall had told her dairymaid in the early days, "even while we are going about our everyday duties. It's the only way to learn to speak a language fluently. The grammar is important, of course, and the reading and writing of it but the spoken French, which is really what I want you to learn," they heard her say, wondering *why*, for God's sake? "can only be accomplished by speaking it to one another at every opportunity."

Poppy had felt embarrassed, watching as the others, particularly the master and his sons, exchanged glances and pulled faces, casting their eyes to the ceiling, until finally Tom Goodall had put a stop to it, and in front of the open-mouthed servants too, thundering that English was good enough for him and if Eliza wanted to jabber in a foreign lingo she must do so when he was not present.

Which they did, she and Poppy, and the servants, having no say in the matter, were forced to put up with it. They could all see the difference in Poppy Appleton as time moved on. She began to have an air about her which none of them could have described since they were not familiar with the word "polish" unless it was to do with furniture or windows. A certain style and grace, a confidence, a finish that her education and grooming under the guidance of the mistress, who herself had been brought up as a lady, had given her. It got to the stage when they could no longer tell whether the piano music floating from the small parlour was brought to life by Mrs Goodall or Poppy and the mistress was heard to say to the master that Poppy was a better pianist than she had ever been.

"Well, don't think she's going to have more piano lessons, Eliza Goodall, because she's not. She's a dairymaid, no more, and if you go on like this she'll be neither use nor ornament about this farm. Think on."

That was in the early days.

It was when Poppy had just turned fourteen that poor old Dilys, who had been a dairymaid for over thirty years, fourteen of them at Long Reach Farm, collapsed one day as she was hobbling painfully across the yard to the milking shed for the second milking of the day and the true and shocking state of her legs was revealed.

When she went to her bed that night Poppy Appleton, shocked and yet exhilarated, had become head dairymaid at Long Reach Farm with three dairymaids, one of whom was Nelly, under her charge. But she was to be more than just head dairymaid, Mrs Goodall told her, for she was to run, alone and unaided, the whole dairy business. From the moment the cows were milked and the eggs were laid, the chicks reared and the chickens plucked, until the produce was attractively laid out on the market stall at St John's each Saturday, it was all to be in the more than capable hands of Poppy Appleton. As though Dilys's collapse had reminded Eliza that she herself was not as young as once she was and had slowed down imperceptibly with the years, she declared that from now on she would leave it all to Poppy who not only knew dairy work as well as anyone in the county, or indeed the *country*, but had a good business head to go with it. Dilys would come over from the cottage she shared with Evan and "potter about" – Mrs Goodall's words – in the dairy whenever she and her legs felt like it and her assistance and experience would be greatly appreciated.

Dilys and Evan, childless and working in tandem ever since their marriage twenty-six years ago, were Welsh and thrifty and their nest-egg, a tidy sum tucked away on Mrs Goodall's advice fourteen years ago when they came to work on the farm, was in a bank in Liverpool. It had grown through the years and was enough to enable Dilys to sit back and enjoy her freedom at last from the long, back-breaking, leg-throbbing hours she had spent in the dairy.

But Poppy and Nelly could not manage it on their own, capable as they were, Mrs Goodall said firmly, particularly if she was to put the reins of it in Poppy's experienced, but still very young hands, and another couple of girls, as bright and hardworking as herself, must be found. Nelly was a worker, a work *horse*, who, given an order, would perform it to the letter, labouring until she dropped, cheerful and willing and where would they be without her? Mrs Goodall told her so affectionately which made Nelly's plain face split into a gratified grin a yard wide, but she was no replacement for Poppy, though Mrs Goodall would not voice this last. In view of the success that Nelly had turned out to be Eliza thought she might go back to the Female Orphanage at Myrtle Street to see if she could find another just like her, she told the dazzled dairymaid, which she did, and Bess, thirteen years old and shy as a violet but a beggar for work, was taken on.

Two years after her mam died, Poppy had been surprised, and pleased, if she was honest, since she was beginning to worry about their Eustace and Herbert who were running wild and threatening to go the same way as Douglas, who had never been heard of from that day to this, when her pa told her bashfully that he was to be married again. A widow woman with one child, a daughter, from over West Derby way. She did the heavy cleaning at the Grimshaw Arms and one day, when she had finished scrubbing the front step, the back step and every inch of stone floor in between, he had treated her to a glass of stout. They had taken a shine to one another, he said. Poppy's stare of astonishment that any woman could take a shine to her uncombed and far from spotless pa went unnoticed, but it seemed the bride-to-be had seen something in him worth having. One thing led to another, he went on, and on Saturday, if Poppy and Marigold could get an hour off, he and Elly would be glad to see them at St Anne's Church on Liverpool Road where they were to be wed.

Well, you could knock her over with a handful of mist, Poppy said in an aside to their Marigold when she saw the woman who had won the affection of their pa enter the church. She was flabbergasted, not that the woman had won her pa's affection but that her pa should have won *hers*! She was probably about thirty-five or six, Poppy decided, a strong, big-breasted, wide-hipped woman with an apple-cheeked, good-natured face that never seemed to stop smiling. She had shining brown hair drawn back into a heavy bun, revealed when she removed her worn but well-brushed black bonnet after the ceremony. She had kissed her two new stepdaughters and told them they were always welcome in her home, which turned out to be the cottage on Primrose Bank, naturally, and if they ever needed a chat or anything, them being motherless girls, they were to come right over, she beamed.

That had been two years ago and in those two years Ellen Arkwright, called Elly, Elly Appleton now, had made an unbelievable metamorphosis on the cottage in which Martha Appleton had once wallowed. Poppy had never seen her pa so industrious and could only think her mam's indolent ways had made him the same. Perhaps he had been indolent too and with no one to stir him they had both fallen carelessly into the state of disrepair and filth which Poppy had fought so hard against.

Not so Pa's new bride. She stirred him up until he didn't know whether he was on his head or his elbow. She had him whitewashing every vertical surface, inside and outside the cottage. Roof tiles were mended, new window frames were put in, doors re-hung, sagging door frames straightened and all at Tom Goodall's expense since after all it was his property and Reuben was putting value on it, she told him to his face. Tom was so beguiled, never having had a tenant in Primrose

Bank who cared a tinker's toss for the state of their home, he did as she asked without argument. The chimney was swept, broken chair and table legs mended, the front path resurfaced and the doorstep replaced so that rainwater no longer flooded into Elly's kitchen. She herself scrubbed and scoured and blackleaded, polished and double polished until every facet of the place twinkled merrily. She liked flowers, she said, wildflowers would do, so there were jars of them everywhere, even on the windowsill of the bedroom she shared with her bemused husband. She was gratified when, hearing of her liking for plants, Mrs Goodall sent her over some cuttings from her own garden and flower boxes began to bloom at the windows, filled with geraniums and sweet william in the summer, crocus, snowdrops and hyacinths in the spring.

And not only the cottage was gone over but all those who lived beneath its roof. Poppy's pa became almost dapper, turning up for work each day with a clean, well-ironed shirt, well-polished boots and what looked to be suspiciously like a crease in his work trousers, to the amused astonishment of the other men. A parting in his carefully brushed and greased hair, freshly shaved and an embarrassed but well-satisfied grin about his good-humoured face, for Reuben Appleton had never been so well looked after in his life. He had a warm and amiable woman in his clean bed each night, good, well-cooked grub put before him at every meal, a home which had been transformed from what could at best be called a muddle, despite Marigold's best shot, into a bloody little palace and two sons who jumped to attention every time their stepmother spoke. It was not that she was unkind, far from it, for Elly lavished good-hearted affection and generous care on them all but she did like youngsters to know their place, to be mannered and polite and her commanding presence and absolute conviction in her own rightness won it for her. Her lass, who was just coming up eleven and ready to start work when work could be found for her, was all of these things and it had not taken Poppy long to convince Mrs Goodall that Jinny Arkwright was the perfect replacement for herself.

And so it had proved. Marigold had been found a little cubbyhole in the farmhouse attic to call her own, her bed at Primrose Bank being needed by Jinny, and had become, in Cook's own words, Cook's "right-hand man". She had gained a reputation for hard work, honesty and good humour and if only, Cook had confided sadly to Mrs Goodall, she had been "all there" would have worked her way up any servants' chain to the top. She was clean to the point of obsession, like her younger sister, and it only amazed her that two such fastidious girls had come from such a terrible home. It took spunk and Cook admired spunk and both Poppy and Marigold had it.

Jinny had begun work at Long Reach Farm in the dairy soon after and now, almost two years later at the age of thirteen, was as adept, as painstaking, as conscientious, as skilful and hardworking as the girl who trained her. She could milk cows and churn butter, weigh, shape and stamp it, fashion butter shells and cones, clean and scour and scrub as well as Nelly and Bess, but best of all she took to market days like a duck takes to its habitat, the water. Which was why Poppy was teaching her to read and write. She was bright and plumply pretty, like her mother, sensible and practical, also like her mother, with the same passion for method, order and cleanliness.

Little by little, when her own lessons were over and really, Mrs Goodall told her fondly, there was little else she could teach her, Poppy, instead of remaining in the kitchen with the other servants, including her own sister, after their evening meal, began imperceptibly to become a part of the Goodalls' own activities in the big parlour. Mrs Goodall had decided that the piano was wasted in the small parlour and Richard and Johnny had moved it under her direction into the larger one.

"Play us a song, my dear," she would say, "one we can all join in," and the cheerful notes of "Believe me if all Those Endearing Young Charms", "Cockles and Mussels" and "It was a Lover and his Lass" rose up to the blackened beams with great gusto, the deep baritone voices of the master and his sons joining in with what seemed to be great enjoyment.

"Come and hold my wool while I wind it, will you, Poppy?" Eliza would say after the evening meal was finished, or "My sewing box is in a terrible state with silks everywhere. Would you be a dear and unravel it for me?"

"I've just obtained a copy of *Tom Sawyer* by Mark Twain. Now I know you'll enjoy this, my dear," speaking to her husband, "so Poppy will read it out loud to us all."

It began to be accepted that Poppy would move with the family at the end of the day into the big parlour when they did. It was a pleasant room with pieces of solid, good-looking furniture which had been part of the farmhouse since its first owners way back in the distant past. Oak for the most part, with gleaming horse brasses, copper bowls of flowers in season, a dresser crammed with the best china, rich, red plush curtains to keep out the draughts, three deep armchairs to match for the menfolk and two low but comfortable "Grandmother" chairs made of walnut and upholstered in a deep red brocade in which Eliza and Poppy sat.

On the enormous sideboard rested a silver tea and coffee

service, richly chased and engraved, a fruit stand with a cut-crystal dish, a four-light candelabrum, also of silver, and a pillar candlestick with a glass shade. There was a wine and biscuit stand on low table, just to Tom Goodall's hand, silver-plated and engraved, and a claret jug with a cut-glass body with silver-plated mounts and lid. All speaking silently of the comfortable, well-to-do existence of Farmer Tom Goodall and his family. There were ornaments in fine art pottery and a dainty French gilt clock looking slightly out of place above the enormous fireplace, with a hand-painted porcelain dial brought by Eliza from her first home.

There was also a magnificent set of ivory chess pieces laid out on a fine hardwood board decorated with ivory inlay. It was Tom Goodall's one concession to frivolity, if the serious playing of chess could be called such and it was perhaps this more than any of her other accomplishments that gained Poppy her full and final acceptance, taken for granted now by all three of the Goodall males, into the heart of the Goodall family. She no longer fitted into her old home, despite its changed condition, for there was a new mistress there, nor in the comfortable relaxed atmosphere of the kitchen where her skills set her apart from the servants. It was not until she revealed her interest in Tom's passion for chess, which none of his family shared, that Tom, who was not at all convinced he should sit down at his fireside with the daughter of one of his own labourers, was won over.

He and Richard were playing one night, Richard merely to please his father, since he would much rather be poring over the new farming manual he had borrowed from the William Brown Library in Liverpool. Eliza dozed with her finger as a marker in the book she had been reading and Johnny lovingly tended to some urgent ministration needed by his cricket bat, getting it ready for the season. The child, as Tom called her, was squatting on a stool beside him, her elbows on her knees, her chin in her hands. Her eyes watched every deliberate move he and Richard made. Richard was a fair player, despite his only slight interest in it and on this night Tom knew Richard was winning. He sighed as he reached across the board for a piece, but some small movement to his side caught his attention. The child had flickered a glance at him, her eyes narrowed and as he watched her she gave her head a slight shake. For some reason, he was never to know why, he left the piece which was his first choice and moved another and in a moment had seen a way to checkmate his son. Tom and Poppy had exchanged triumphant smiles.

The next evening she, and indeed Eliza and the boys, had been astonished when Tom had casually asked the child if she fancied a game. Though he would not have admitted it, even if put to the torture, it was then he began to dote on her almost as much as his wife did. Anyone who could play as crafty and clever a game of chess as she could must have something in her worth admiring, he told himself.

The day was fine again. It was Sunday and as he had done last week Johnny Goodall had ridden over to Coopers Edge to play tennis. He had thoroughly enjoyed himself, he had told them all at supper that night, making Nelly, Bess and Marigold laugh with his description of the game which they had heard of, of course, but had never seen played. The idea of ladies and gentlemen hitting a ball over a net with a bat – called a racquet – backwards and forwards to one another seemed a sorry waste of time, but then it was no dafter than two men running up and down a bit of grass after knocking a ball into the back of beyond, was it? Nelly, who still harboured a secret passion for Master Johnny, was sure he would be as superb at tennis as he was at cricket. Two years ago lawn tennis had been introduced into the All-England Croquet Club and was becoming as popular as croquet among the English upper classes, especially the ladies, who longed for a less sedate physical game than croquet. They wore the encumbering clothes they wore for every day, long trailing, bustled skirts, tight corsets, blouses with voluminous sleeves, flowery hats and shoes with high heels and Johnny was amazed, he confided, that they could move about at all, let alone do it at speed.

Richard had not been so enthusiastic about the afternoon's activities but then he was not so easy with folk as his brother. He was a serious young man who cared for little but the farm, and cricket, of course. He liked a bit of shooting now and again and was a good horseman, having won the Wavertree Steeplechase three years running on his handsome bay, Rowland, to the chagrin of Dominic Cooper. He was also partial to fox-hunting, for foxes were the natural enemy of the farmer, but he had not taken to tennis at all, which he thought to be an unmanly sport and he would not bother with it again. Had he met up with some gentleman who had the same interests as himself, particularly farming, he would have felt very differently, talking the hind leg off a donkey, as his mother said, but it had evidently not happened at Coopers Edge.

"Was the bride-to-be there?" Poppy asked, doing her best to sound casual.

"Oh, yes, and a proper little beauty she turned out to be and with all that cash which comes with her." Johnny, with his usual lack of tact, grinned impudently.

"John, that is not a nice thing to say," his mother rebuked him.

"Well, it's true and Cooper's a lucky dog." Johnny was unrepentant

"Was . . . did they seem . . . very much attached?" Poppy ventured, again doing her best to sound only slightly interested, her mind's eye seeing the flushed and admiring face of Dominic Cooper turned towards her as it had been on the Friday of his birthday.

"Well, Mrs Cooper was there and several other older women, chaperoning, you know, so it was hard to tell but I did catch a glimpse of them behind a tree and he had her in a most ardent embrace."

Yes, that's just the sort of sly thing he would do, Poppy thought bitterly.

"Johnny, really!" His mother was appalled. "That was uncalled for and most . . . ungentlemanlike."

Johnny was unabashed.

"Maybe, but give me half a chance," winking at Nelly who nearly fainted and Marigold who began to giggle.

But now, as Poppy strolled down the field which led to Primrose Bank she pondered on the contradictions of the male creature. What had got into that daft beggar from Coopers Edge the other day? Pestering the life out of her to accompany him into the woods, or the rose garden, telling her they were to be friends, begging to know her name and where she came from. On the very next day, having become the fiancé of one of the loveliest, by all accounts, and wealthiest young ladies in Lancashire, he had led her behind a tree and, breaking what Poppy knew was a strict code of conduct among their class, kissed her. Not that Poppy gave a damn about that but what astonished her was the fact that, having such a gorgeous creature so soon to be his own, why had he talked such utter nonsense to Poppy Appleton?

She paused, coming to rest in a knee-high rippling carpet of summer grass. There was a slight breeze, warm with sunshine and it moved the grass, the colours of thrift and cowbane and wild thyme which grew in it, making a drifting pattern of pink and green and lilac. Part of Farmer Goodall's herd had been put in the field that morning and the cows lifted placid heads to watch her. She knew them all by name, for she had milked them a hundred times but they were mindless creatures who, if she moved towards them, would back away from her in alarm.

Her feet had bruised the plants she stepped on and the sweet aroma from them filled her nostrils. High in the sky a blackbird broke the silence, singing its joyous song as it dived towards the spinney on the far side of the field. The notes which filled her head, as the scent had filled her nostrils, were as sweet and pure as any she had ever heard and her heart was shaken with a sudden aching hurt.

The contradictions of men. Contradictory! Inconsistent! Fickle! Were they all the same, the male of the species and did she ever think she would apply any of these words to a man called Conn, for he would be a man now? Conn! Alick James MacConnell who had walked away from a twelve-year-old girl almost four years ago and taken her heart with him. Off to make his way in the world, he had told her, but he would be back and though he had not said exactly what he meant to do when he did, it would certainly include Poppy Appleton, he had implied. She had believed in him. She had waited for his letters and they had not come. She had waited for *him* and he had not come. Almost four years. She had nursed him, herself no more than a child, giving him back his health, giving him back his life, he had told her, with no thought for herself, taking great risks but ignoring them in her compassion for him. His hurt had hurt her. His pain had been hers and he had taken what she had willingly given and walked blithely away with it. Yes, his life she had given him, he had said so, but it seemed what she had done to return it to him had not been worth dwelling on, for from that day to this she had never heard a word of, or from him.

She sank down into the grass, a fluid, almost boneless movement, putting her arms about her bent knees, her forehead on her arms, her eyes wide and staring, but blind. Her heart ached with the betrayal she felt, for she had steadfastly believed in the big, red-haired, brave young lad who had marched off in Tom Goodall's yard coat that night. She had believed there was something binding them together. That life had taken her, put her in Mrs Goodall's careful hands so that she would be – what was the word? suitable? – worthy of someone like Conn. Not someone *like* Conn, but *Conn*. She had been taught to read and write for the simple purpose of keeping in touch with him, for had she been illiterate there was no way they could have done so. If she could not read, then she could not reply when his letters came, it was as simple as that.

She could not say she was actively unhappy. She had Mrs Goodall to thank for that. Her life was full, and fulfilling. She had responsibilities and power not given to many girls of her age and class. She had a good home now, a proper home with people who were fond of her, but . . . but . . .

Her heart shifted heavily. She lifted her head and looked to the far horizon where the heat merged the land into the sky. Plucking a blade of grass she put it pensively between her teeth, biting on its sweetness. Leaning back on both hands she stretched her legs out before her, crossing them at the ankle and tipped back her head, her eyes narrowed and unfocused as though she sought some image in the azure arch of the summer sky. She sighed and lowered her gaze to the field of wildflowers which ran down to Primrose Bank.

Where was he? What was he doing now? Had he got to Glasgow and his grandfather or had he fallen back into his old ways and been picked up by the police and jailed, this time for far longer than three months? She didn't think she could bear it, or forgive it if he had. He had broken the law as a boy of eleven but there had been an altruistic reason for it. With a mother who lay dying, in his child's mind he had no choice but to do what he had, short of putting her and himself into the poorhouse. But now he was a man with no one but himself to think about. A strong man capable of work of any sort and with no excuse to force him into a life of crime. She could find out, she supposed. She could write to the man he said was his mother's father. Alaric Swainson, she had not forgotten, who lived in Glasgow. Send a letter to the shipyard on the River Clyde, the position of which was as well known to her on the map now as the River Mersey. Has your grandson Alick MacConnell arrived? She could ask, but what was the use for if Conn wanted her to know he would have written and said so. Perhaps he was dead.

The thought scoured her painfully and she bowed her head again but it was a fact that boys and men who lived the life he had led after his mother's death, encountered savagery and evil, dangerous criminals who would think nothing of cutting his throat for Tom Goodall's good yard coat. Would she ever know and what was her destiny now?

Destiny! She remembered the first time Mrs Goodall had spoken the word and she had not known what it meant then. Destiny. It had had a lovely ring to it, an importance that had pleased her despite her ignorance of its meaning.

"It's not your destiny to be no more than a dairymaid, Poppy," Mrs Goodall had said to her one day as Poppy was scouring out the setting dishes in the dairy and Poppy had been so amazed she had almost dropped the pan of boiling water she had just carried from the boiler. "Nor to be the wife of a farm labourer," the mistress had added.

"What's that mean, Mrs Goodall, destiny?" Poppy had asked when she recovered from her surprise.

"It means what is going to happen to someone in the future."

"Well then, I don't mean ter be neither." Poppy had lifted her neatly be-capped head imperiously, for she believed every word that Mrs Goodall uttered though at the time her one ambition had been to be head dairymaid at Long Reach Farm. It was as far as her childish ignorance could carry her.

And the thing was, she still didn't know what life held for her, though it was becoming very obvious what Mrs Goodall hoped for. She was not blind, nor was she insensitive to the fond looks which were cast in her direction, not only by Mrs Goodall but by Richard himself whenever they were alone together. Not that they spent a great deal of time in one another's company, at least not alone, but for a long while now she had been aware of Richard Goodall's interest in her. She had caught him watching her when she played chess with his father, or when she was at the piano and she knew that he made excuses to meet her, pretending it was unintentional, when she returned from Primrose Bank. He approved of her, he let that be known quite plainly, to her and to his mother, for she worked hard and, with the education and grooming she had acquired from his mother, was eminently suited to be the wife of a well-to-do and successful farmer. And could she do better? she asked herself. She liked Richard, she trusted him and he would always treat her kindly, so why did a big, red-headed lad with the soft burr of Scotland in his voice still invade her dreams and stand between her and a safe and comfortable future?

Elly was baking bread when Poppy reached the cottage, knocking hell out of a lump of dough as though she had a personal grudge against it. She would knead and fold it in on itself until she was satisfied it was ready to stand, covered by one of her spotless cloths, by the warmth of the fire until it had risen sufficiently to be divided into loaves. It would then stand again before it was put into the oven. The batch she had done earlier stood cooling on the window bottom, its fragrant, mouth-watering aroma meeting Poppy as she came up the path. Elly's bread was the best Poppy had ever tasted and the saliva rushed to her mouth at the thought of a slice, still warm from the oven, spread thickly with the butter she herself had churned.

"Aah, there y'are, my lamb, come in an' sit yerself down." Elly was always the same, placid, even-tempered, never out of sorts and Poppy marvelled every time she came to her old home at the change in it. Why had her mother not been capable of making a home as clean and cosy as this? She was well aware that there had been many more occupants then than there were now, creating much muck and muddle and Mam, who had worked in the fields all day, could not seem able to get on top of it. She had been weary to the bone when she came home of a night but then Elly had a job and she managed it. She still scrubbed every day for Mrs Hawthorne who ran the Grimshaw Arms and yet this home she had fashioned for her new family was as bright and spotlessly clean as Poppy's dairy. There was still very little money, for Pa's wage as a farm labourer was small and the few coppers Poppy and Marigold had sent over before Pa had married Elly had been courteously refused by his new wife, who said the girls had earned it and were entitled to *all* of it. Elly eked out what there was and made it go so far with her talent for good management, for making a penny do the work of two, or even three, it was a miracle.

Poppy kissed Elly's cheek with great affection, for she had become fond of her stepmother and was eternally grateful to her for what she had done for Poppy's family, pulling it together as she had. Both boys, though they were fourteen and twelve now, had been persuaded to enrol for evening classes at the Mechanics Institute in Mount Street. They laboured in Farmer Goodall's fields during the day but three times a week after work they undertook the three-mile hike into Liverpool and were, with Poppy's help, learning to read and write and do simple arithmetic. Poppy had high expectations for them and they themselves were excited at their own improved prospects for the future. Boys with a bit of education had so much more to hope for than those with none. After what had happened to Douglas, whatever that now might be for nothing had been heard of him for four years, and Arthur who, it was rumoured, had gone to sea as a deck-hand on one of Hemingway's steam ships, Poppy was proud and grateful that Herbert and Eustace, thanks to Elly's good influence, were not to go the same way as the rest of Poppy's brothers and sisters who had vanished as though the earth had opened up and swallowed them.

"I've brought you a few eggs, Elly." Poppy put the basket on the corner of the table, pushing to one side a crock of flour. A small kitten stirred on the cushioned chair which stood beside the table, leaping up frivolously between the crock and the basket and with a "tutt" of irritation Poppy picked it up and placed it in the fireside chair where it began to give itself a good wash. "Mrs Goodall says to thank you for the scones, they were delicious," she went on, "better even than Cook's though we daren't say so."

Elly preened and gave the dough another gratified thump.

"Gerraway, t'were nowt. Just a birra flour an' an egg or two. Mrs Goodall's bin that good ter you an' Marigold an' now my Jinny, wharrelse could I do?"

"Well, they went down a treat, thanks. Now, is there a cuppa tea in that pot," indicating the brown teapot which stood, as it always did, on the hearth, for Elly was partial to a good "brew" and thanks to Mrs Goodall's kindness, could afford it.

"Aye, just medd, pour me one an' all, will yer, lamb?"

The two women sat companionably, one on either side of the fire which was never allowed to go out no matter how hot the day. The kitten purred on Elly's lap while they chatted of this and that, at least Elly did, for there was nothing she liked more than a gossip over a cup of tea, especially with Poppy who was a sensible lass. Her next door had given birth to another girl, had Poppy heard? and himself with a face like thunder since he had set his heart on a lad. Eight girls and who was he to pass on his family name to? he'd whined to Reuben, as though he were an earl or summat, with a fortune to his name. And there was to be a wedding – oh, yes, she'd heard of Master Dominic's engagement – but this was Mrs Hawthorne's lass, Hetty, a bonny young thing of eighteen and promised to a chap said to be first mate on one of them steam ships owned by the Bradleys. A wedding in spring, Mrs Hawthorne said and she and Job, her husband, were made up . . .

Poppy smiled and nodded and sipped her tea but Elly knew she was not really listening. Sometimes she was like that, Elly had noticed, wondering why, for if anyone had reason to be pleased and proud of herself, and her life, it was Poppy Appleton. They had all seen the way young Master Richard looked at her, but now and again, like now, Poppy seemed to be miles away, in another place, another world to the one they all knew. Perhaps one day she'd tell Elly why. Her face looked so sad though what Poppy had to be sad about was a wonder and a mystery. Elly sighed as eloquently as Poppy had done half an hour ago.

14

The atmosphere in the kitchen was electric with the charged tension that is created when one stubborn male goes up against another, particularly if one should be the elder with the right, or so he thinks, of obedience from the younger. The silence was breathless. The servants, snatched from whatever they had been doing when it began, by the snarling anger of their master, melted away into the corners of the room, attempting to become invisible and Eliza looked frantically at Poppy as though begging her to think of some way to separate her husband from her younger son. They waited. Cook, her expression one of resignation. Aggie, Clara, May, Nelly, Bess and Marigold, all watching with open-mouthed and fearful interest the contest of wills that was taking place between Farmer Tom Goodall and his younger son, Johnny. Their master would have the last word, for didn't he always, but the truculent expression on Master Johnny's face said he would not give in easily.

It was the glorious twelfth of August, the first day of the grouse-shooting season and Poppy Appleton's sixteenth birthday. Johnny Goodall had just announced, to everyone's alarm and amazement, that he had been invited by Dominic Cooper to join the shoot which was to take place over Sir

Thomas Avons's grouse moor at Fullingham. The invitation extended to Richard, of course, as though that made it all right and the statement had taken, for a moment only, the breath from Tom Goodall's lungs and the speech from his lips. He couldn't believe the nerve of the lad, really he couldn't his expression said. He was a farmer's son and as such his day was filled from dawn till dusk with the endless tasks that a mixed dairy and arable farm demanded. Autumn was approaching and the cornfields were changing colour, turning to rippling seas of gold. Wheatfields which were to provide the grain that would be used for winter animal feed were ready for harvesting and before very long cutting would begin, and how in God's name could the lad expect to go frolicking off with Captain Cooper's spoiled son who had nothing to do all day but play the fool? He said so, bellowing across the table like the very bull which had once stepped on his elder son's foot.

"You can put that right out of your head this minute, my lad, and you can take that look off your face an' all. What d'you think this is? Some sort of game where, when you've had enough you can knock off and go and try something else? If you do then you're sadly mistaken. Grouse shooting! What the hell next? Damnation, boy, there's fields out there" – flinging his arms wildly in the direction of the window – "with grass and corn and wheat waiting to be cut. There's the potatoes ready for lifting and them cows need moving again if we're to plough Downside Pasture and put in the next crop, and it's to be manured first. God's teeth, I don't know why I'm wasting my time standing here telling you about it when we should all be out there doing it. Now get your boots on, both of you," snapping his head sharply in the direction of his elder son as if he were as much to blame as his brother, "and don't let me hear another word.

And you lasses," turning on the frozen, speechless figures of Poppy and Nelly, "shouldn't you be down in the milking shed by now? We'll have Evan shouting up the yard for you if you don't look lively."

In his longing to gallop off with his sudden and surprisingly cordial new friend, surprising since Dominic Cooper had shown not the slightest interest in him except as a player in the cricket team, Johnny would not give up and his mother sighed deeply, for was it not all a waste of his breath. Even she who indulged him far more than she should knew that the farm came first.

"Father, just this once couldn't I be spared to go on the shoot? I promise I'll be back by tea-time," her son went on, "and I'll do all my work before it gets dark. This is a special day, you see," he pleaded, "and it would be churlish to refuse." And after all he was not a child to be ordered about any more, was he? Twenty and no longer a boy, no matter what his father might think. Besides, why should he sweat his guts out on this land which would never be his? He'd always have to take second place to Richard. Never out of a job, naturally, and a good allowance in his pocket as befitted the son, or brother, of a comfortably-off farmer but never, never his own man. Always having to toe the line, take orders, as now, bow to the decision of the man who owned Long Reach Farm and that would never be Johnny Goodall. True, he didn't relish the responsibility Richard would have thrust on him when Father died but it would be grand to be able to please himself when he took time off to pursue the country sports which were so dear to his heart. After all there were a dozen or more men to work the farm and one day off now and again wouldn't bring the bloody place to a standstill, would it?

Tom Goodall's face had become an alarming shade of

puce and Eliza was convinced he was about to strike his son or have an apoplectic fit, or both. His hands twitched and he hunched his shoulders as he did his best to control his temper. His breathing deepened and even Cook, who had seen many a set-to in this kitchen, between brother and brother, between father and son, stepped back in alarm. The servants shuffled uneasily from foot to foot, doing their best to fade into the whitewashed walls of the kitchen and Bess began to whimper deep in her throat.

"Tom . . ." Eliza said warningly. "The boy—"

"The *boy*, Eliza! He's no boy, he's a man and if he can't act like one at his age then it's a poor lookout for his future. Adam Cooper's son may have time to frolic about the countryside with those friends of his, and why he wants to make one of mine is a mystery to me, but this is my son, a farmer's son and I need every pair of hands I can get at this time of year and he knows it. If we don't get the corn, the wheat and grass cut before the weather breaks . . . Bloody hell, boy, you know what will happen. Now, all of you, before my patience goes completely, get to work. I never saw such an idle-handed lot in my life, standing about as if any time of the day will do. Jump to it."

Though they were deeply affronted by this last remark, for in truth they were hardworking and conscientious, the women "jumped to it" returning to the tasks they had been performing before Master Johnny had put the cat among the pigeons with his preposterous demand to go grouse shooting with the gentry. May began to side the table of the breakfast dishes, making as little noise as possible since she did not want the master's attention drawn to her. Miss Clever Clogs might, and did, get away with blue murder now that she was the spoiled pet of not only Mrs Goodall, but him as well, but that did not extend to the rest of them who were no more than a pair of hands, at least to him, easily hired and just as easily fired, and jobs as comfortable as this were hard to come by. She was a lucky cow, that Poppy Appleton, but then, given half the chance couldn't May Jebson have been just as successful? Taught to read and write, couldn't she have risen to the same dizzying heights? Of course she could and if she could manage it somehow, she didn't know in what way, she'd do Miss Clever Clogs a mischief, bring her down and grind her face in the muck. She'd longed to do it for years now but the trouble was Poppy never seemed to put a foot wrong and it was difficult to think of something bad enough to turn the Goodalls against her.

None of this showed in May's smooth, averted face. Aggie and Clara went off with their housemaid's boxes, heading upstairs to turn out the bedrooms and Cook began to murmur of a nice bit of pork for their dinner, happen with roast potatoes and apple sauce and when Marigold had washed them pots would she run down to the orchard and get her some apples.

It was already well past the time when Poppy, Nelly and Bess should be in the milking shed. Jinny, Evan and Tommy would wonder where they were. Master Richard and Master Johnny, with their father behind them like a dog herding a flock of reluctant sheep, tramped off across the yard to the dozens of jobs that a farmer might expect to be employed with at this time of year. The casual hired labourers, taken on to help with the haymaking, with the lifting of the potato crop which should, Tom hoped, yield approximately ten or twelve tons to the acre in the rich farmland which lay to the east of Liverpool, much of it his, were already hanging about the yard gate waiting for orders, their scythes sharpened in readiness beside them. They were surprised and not a little aggrieved when Farmer Goodall asked them what the hell they thought they were doing, lolling about as though it were a public holiday, and the cause of it all, his face set in lines of white temper, almost knocked Herbert Appleton over. Herbert, at fourteen, was a big lad and didn't take kindly to being jostled, his expression said, since he didn't intend remaining a farm labourer for ever, not with his learning, but he buttoned his lip since this was his master's son.

Nevertheless within ten minutes every man jack of them was at his allotted task, Johnny Goodall among them.

Just as Poppy was about to blow out the candles, sixteen of them, on the splendid birthday cake Cook had made for the occasion, the clatter of horse's hooves sounded in the yard. It brought Eliza Goodall to her feet at the kitchen window, for who could it be at this time of night and her heart dropped when she saw who it was. There was a great commotion as a dozen hens which pecked there scattered in panic. The rooster squawked indignantly and the dogs barked in frantic agitation.

They were having a small party, the servants and the Goodalls – it being their custom to sit down together unless the Goodalls had guests, which was not often – and with the help of Eliza's cowslip wine, which had a bottle of brandy added to every three gallons, it had become very lively, which was just as well, for Eliza didn't know how Tom would take to the cause of all the commotion earlier in the day riding up here perhaps to cause some more. Johnny had got over his sour humour at being refused permission to go grouse shooting and was thoroughly enjoying himself since he had every reason to believe, due in part to the amount of wine she had drunk, that May, who, though not exactly pretty, had a magnificent breast which Johnny had high hopes of getting his hands on, might not be averse to a cuddle in the stable loft later. Or perhaps more! She had come with Clara down to the hayfield at noon, bringing the customary "noon-pieces", jugs of tea and ale, bacon wedged between thick slabs of fresh bread, jam pasties and a basket of Cook's apple cakes, the apples left over from the apple sauce since Marigold had picked far too many. The harvesters, men, women and children, had fallen on the feast with great gusto since it was not often they ate such delicious food and in such abundance. It had been hot, a lovely mellow summer's day in which the air seemed to stand still in a golden, midge-filled haze and they had all sprawled in the shade cast by the great, leaf-laden branches of the oak trees which edged the field, sheltering from the fierce heat of the midday sun. Even Farmer Goodall was in a cordial mood, for they had made good time this morning, smiling and nodding at the quips and good-natured chatter that went on among the company. He was a fair man on the whole, father and employer, but his temper was quick. He was sorry now that he had had the clash with Johnny earlier, since the lad had worked hard and willingly all morning, bearing no grudge, it seemed, at being denied the day off he had asked for. Still, he had to learn that a farmer's son did not gad about with those of the gentry. Tom had made no objection when May sat down for a moment beside his younger son, his own eyes, for was he not a man also, dipping appreciatively, as his son's did, into the swelling cleft of May's young breasts. The top buttons of her prim blouse were undone since it was so hot and she fanned herself with the cotton bonnet she had worn as she and Clara came down through the fields to the haymaking.

May had not been unaware of Master Johnny's interest, then and now, and as long as it might lead to some advantage to herself she was not averse to a bit of "fun". Master Johnny was a good-looking chap. She was eighteen last birthday and had still not landed herself a husband, which was no surprise, at least to her, for she looked a great deal higher than the rough and ready labourers who worked Farmer Goodall's fields. Not that she had any hopes in that direction with Johnny Goodall but you never knew where an inch given might lead to a mile won.

"Dear Lord, it's Dominic Cooper." Eliza put her hand to her mouth in consternation. The unpleasantness this morning appeared to have been forgotten by both father and son but should Dominic come out with some further daft scheme for Johnny to go gadding off with him and his friends it would only be raked up again and Tom's temper would not be so easily calmed this time. They were making a special evening for Poppy who looked as bonny as a hedge rose in a new dress, Eliza's birthday gift to her. Totally unsuitable for a girl who was really no more than a dairymaid, of course, but then was she not the darling of the Goodalls now, treated, despite the work she did, as the daughter of the house would be treated. The dress was of tarlatan, the colour of apple blossom with a pale rose sash which was tied in a bow at the back. The neckline of the bodice was lower than normal, revealing the soft upper swell of her breasts. It had short sleeves and the rose and honey tint of her skin was like satin in the glow from the lamps which Aggie had just lit. Her eyes were silver-blue and brilliant with excitement and as she smiled her long brown lashes meshed together, half an inch long. There was a flush at her cheek and in the semi-dusk her white teeth gleamed between her full poppy lips. She had tied a ribbon in her hair to match the sash on her dress and the ends fell down her back to her shoulder blades.

It was this delightful picture that met Dominic Cooper's

eyes as he stepped through the doorway and into the warm
kitchen at Mrs Goodall's gracious invitation. He bowed to Mr
Goodall, apologising for intruding into what was obviously
a family party. As soon as he had reassured himself about
his good friend Johnny, who he had missed at the shoot,
grinning in Johnny's direction, he would, of course, be on
his way.

Tom Goodall grunted disbelievingly. He was not pleased
that the perpetrator of all that rumpus this morning should
have come interfering again in what Tom considered to be
none of his business. Why didn't he leave the lad alone?
his expression said. Tom did not like disagreements with
his younger son, who was very dear to him, as he was
dear to them all, being such a good-humoured, likeable
lad. Easily led, of course, which was half the trouble. And
here, standing in the middle of the room looking about him
as though captivated by the quaintness of a farm kitchen
which he had evidently not met with before, at least at close
quarters, was the nincompoop who had started the bloody
row in the first place. What in hell's name did he imagine
he was doing? Though Tom was proud of his heritage and
the line of yeoman farmers from which he came, they and
the like of Captain Cooper's arrogantly smiling lad did not
mix. Oh aye, a game of village cricket. That was customary
and happened the length and breadth of the land where any
chap with a talent for batting or bowling was welcome to
play beside, or against, the gentry. But this, this cultivating
of Tom Goodall's lad by the son of the man who could really
only be called the squire, for that was what Captain Cooper
might claim to be in this district, had something behind it.
Poppy Appleton could have told him, of course. No, Tom
was not a bit pleased to see Dominic Cooper and though
no one noticed it, neither was she.

Though she did not look at him again after Dominic had bowed courteously in her direction, she was conscious of his eyes on her as he was asked – for what else could she do? – by Eliza Goodall to take a seat, to sample a piece of birthday cake which Poppy was about to cut, and perhaps take a glass of wine. He was pressed to make himself comfortable in Tom's own chair by the open fire but instead he insisted, providing Mrs Goodall had no objection, on placing himself on the bench where the servants sat, squeezing in between Nelly and Bess, to their awed gratification, smiling his radiant smile until the pair of them, glancing shyly at him with great humility, were ready to fall in a grateful heap at his feet.

The maids, at least the younger ones, despite the glass of cowslip wine Eliza had allowed them and which was strong enough to give a bit of courage to the most timid, were all of a flurry, casting overwhelmed and admiring peeks at the handsome visitor, vying with one another to fetch him a plate, a napkin, a fork, a glass of wine, begging him wordlessly to allow them to serve him, while at the far end of the table where the family sat, Poppy's lip curled and it was all she could do not to storm up to him and ask what the hell he thought he was playing at. She had hoped his behaviour on the day of his twenty-first birthday might be a whim, just the sort of high jinks the upper classes, having nothing better to do with their time, got up to. A spur-of-the-moment lark, the last flirtatious fling of a man about to be married but it seemed she was wrong. He was officially engaged now to the daughter of Sir Thomas Avons, to be wed in spring, it was rumoured, and yet here he was like some rampant stud, still sniffing about *her* skirts. She was not imagining his interest in herself, she was perfectly certain of that. She might be only sixteen with no experience of men but she was perfectly able to recognise admiration and desire in a man's eye, since it was not the first time she had come across it. Bertie, one of the porters at the market, the one who had given Mrs Goodall a hand with the horse and cart years ago, and now helped Poppy, was always trying it on, though he was now a married man with children. She dealt with him as she did them all. The man with the fish stall who called her his "poppet", thinking himself to be extremely witty, and tried to lure her round the back of the stall among the fish boxes. The cheeky beggar who collected the rent for the stall who begged her every week to go to the Music Hall in Bold Street with him, not at all crestfallen when, week after week, she refused. They were all after the same thing and she and Jinny, who was a bonny lass and whom she watched over like a mother hen with a chick, feeling responsible for her, were well versed in the feminine art of saying "no" without giving offence.

If Eliza was surprised by Poppy's unsmiling, averted face, her tart answers when Dominic put some urbane question to her, in fact her complete turnabout from the lively, laughing young girl she had been half an hour ago, she did not show it. There were presents to open, small things from the other servants. A cheap brooch with a blue stone in it from Nelly, a lace handkerchief from Bess, a comb of tortoiseshell from Dilys, a tiny box stuck with seashells from Jinny.

There was a copy of the recent publication of *Anna Karenina* by Leo Tolstoy from Richard and Johnny, prompted by Eliza, Poppy was aware. All affectionately given and vastly appreciated, so that when Dominic, his face set in suitably rueful lines, began to pronounce on his lack of a gift and his mortification that he had not known it was her birthday she answered him coolly.

"Don't give it a thought, Mr Cooper. I have so many I would be quite overwhelmed to have one more."

"Nevertheless, having so rudely interrupted your celebrations and been so kindly treated by you all I do feel that something would be appropriate. I shall ask my mother and will ride over again, if I may, to deliver it."

Poppy's eyes narrowed and her face hardened. "Nonsense, I would be insulted if you thought it necessary." She did her best to be firm without being downright rude, which would have amazed the company, but it was hard when all she wanted to do was box his ears and tell him to grow up!

He departed eventually, fulsome in his thanks for the hospitality shown him; the magnificence of Mrs Goodall's cowslip wine which he likened to the best served at his father's table; the miraculous lightness of Cook's cake which could not, he was sure, be bettered by his mother's own cook who was remarkably talented. It seemed he had a word of praise for everyone in the kitchen right down to the cat which sprawled in front of the fire, swearing he had never before seen such a handsome animal. Poppy felt a great need to vomit, so sickly sweet were his condescending words which were obviously as false as himself, at least to her who knew his true purpose in being here. Perhaps, it was his upbringing that led him to believe that most people, at least in this part of the world, were beneath the notice of Dominic Cooper and only when he wanted something from them, as he did with his own servants, did he deign to speak or even notice them.

As he rode out of the yard, turning to wave cordially to the group in the doorway which did not, Dominic noticed, and with little concern since he did not require her to like him, contain the dairymaid, his mind was busy with where and how quickly he could meet her again. He trusted he would not have to act out this bloody charade again with these plain and boring folk in order to get to know her. The

Goodalls, though of good farming stock and well-to-do, had not the breeding he himself had, at least on his father's side, and in the ordinary way of things would not have come within his supercilious sight.

But what he felt for Poppy Appleton, who, though only the dairymaid, was evidently highly regarded by the family, was no ordinary thing. It was ordinary *lust*, naturally, but a lust he had not felt to such white-heat passion for any female, and it was going to be more difficult than he thought to douse it. He had been quite amazed this evening to see the way she was treated and had he not known differently would not have been surprised to learn that she was the daughter of Mr and Mrs Tom Goodall which, of course, would have forced him to alter his tactics. Even he, self-serving as he was, knew that a man did not pursue the daughter of a decent family no matter how badly he desired her. Not unless he had marriage in mind! They appeared to dote on her, even that clodhopper of an elder son of theirs and was it any wonder she acted the way she did. It certainly explained the way she spoke and her wide vocabulary. Not that she had much to say this evening, leaving the pleasantries to the farmer's wife but then he was not interested in what she had to say, was he? Only in the graceful, shapely sway of her young body, the lift and movement of her breasts, the unusual rosy gold satin of her skin which he was itching to find out whether it was the same glorious shade all over, promising himself it would not be long before he did so.

He began to whistle softly as he guided his grey down the track towards Prescot Road.

Poppy had got over her annoyance an hour later as she sprawled on the step of the cottage at Primrose Bank, a cup of tea in her hand, her shoulder pressed companionably against that of her stepmother who sat beside her in the last rays of the setting sun. Behind them the cottage was as clean as a new pin, brasses polished, floor scrubbed, walls whitewashed and a good fire on the well-swept hearth despite the heat of the evening. There was a smell of freshly baked bread, of stew and apple dumplings in the oven ready for her pa's meal when he got home from the Grimshaw Arms, and of clean garments recently ironed.

The other occupants of the cottages were doing the same on their own doorsteps as Poppy and Elly, enjoying the fading warmth of the day, watching the crows croaking across the sky overhead as they made their way to their nests. A dove was calling from somewhere, sending a plaintive message to a mate and in the hedge opposite wild roses and woodbine closed their buds against the coming night. A barn owl hooted and, attracted by the rushlights which shone in the windows of the cottages, moths danced crazily.

The sky in the west created a vast dreaming languor in Poppy, its beauty so glorious it even silenced the starling chatter of the Primrose Bank inhabitants who normally noticed nothing unless it was to eat or posed a threat to them. Deep blue velvet above them shading imperceptibly to pale lilac, to dove grey and silver and blush pink where the orb of the sun had slid down behind the horizon. The hush went on and on and Poppy was reluctant to end it but she knew she should get back before total darkness fell or Eliza would worry. She had walked over with Jinny to display her birthday presents to Elly and had received what she knew must have cost her pa and his wife money they could ill afford. A shawl of fine cobweb wool, probably bought second-hand at the market, in a delicate shade of heather blue but so pretty and light and elegant Poppy was delighted. Elly must have gone to a great deal of trouble to find a gift so appropriate, for she was well aware that Poppy was no longer the daughter, or at least only biologically so, of a farm labourer. The shawl reflected this and Poppy was immeasurably touched.

Throwing it gracefully about her shoulders in a whirl of pale blue mist, she kissed her stepmother warmly before stepping out up the slope towards the farmhouse. She could smell the faint aroma of woodsmoke from the kitchen chimney and see the glow of welcoming lights in the downstairs windows. They would be waiting for her, her family, for that was how she thought of them now and a warm tingling of content lit itself just beneath her breastbone. Eliza would be in the parlour window, fiddling with the curtains, ostensibly drawing them against the growing dark but in reality watching to see Poppy come up the field. Mr Goodall would have lit his pipe and in front of him would be set out the chess pieces, a game, complicated and of long standing, waiting to be finished. Even Richard might be fidgeting, glancing at the clock on the mantelshelf in the parlour, waiting for her return, pretending an indifference she knew he did not feel. Only Johnny, irrepressible Johnny who had been so sorely disappointed today, would show little concern. In fact, what Poppy thought to be likely, since May was not as discreet as she might have been, nor as responsible as she should have been, he might at this moment have the kitchen maid in his ardent embrace in the stable loft.

The shadow stepped out from behind the thick mass of the hawthorn hedge and Poppy felt her heart constrict and miss a couple of beats, plunging down and then up again in alarm. The shadow was tall against the lights from the farmhouse, tall, lean, coatless, lounging with hands on hips just where the hedge met the yard gate.

For a dreadful moment she felt a shaft of terror pierce

her, for it seemed that what every young woman out alone after dark fears above all else was about to happen to her. On her own doorstep almost, she was to be thrown to the ground, held down and forced into an act of gross indecency and with her mouth so dry and frozen she could not even cry out.

The shadow moved towards her and at once, as his white teeth gleamed in his brown face and his eyes, pricked by the stars which had begun to shine, sparkled in obvious enjoyment, she recognised Dominic Cooper. The arrogant, self-centred young man she had seen canter off a couple of hours ago, presumably making his way home in the summer twilight. Dear sweet God, what was the bloody idiot up to now? her maddened thoughts asked, standing there grinning as though she were as pleased to see him as he was to see her. He must be pixillated, or drunk, or so thick-skinned he couldn't recognise her total lack of interest in him, no matter what she said or did. Her fear turned at once to fury, for there was nothing in this fool that could possibly harm her, was there? He was just a damned nuisance and should go home to his well-bred fiancée and stop bothering Poppy Appleton, who had better things to do with her time than waste it on a simpleton such as him.

"So, we meet again, Poppy," just as though this encounter had come about by chance. "How very pleasant to be able to talk without . . . interruption." His voice was soft, no more than an intimate murmur against the sounds of the night creatures which were beginning to whisper in the air. "I felt I couldn't leave without a private word of congratulation for your birthday. Your sixteenth, I believe. Johnny, who, as you probably know, is inclined to chatter" – making of Johnny Goodall no more than a prattling infant – "told me so I thought, if we could be alone I might . . ."

The furious speechless paralysis which had held her in its grip for the time it took him to utter these words left her as suddenly as it had come and though she wanted to shriek and stamp her foot in temper, for how *dare* he treat her this way, the way the sons of the gentry treated a common servant, she took a step away from him, speaking in a voice of icy control.

"You have gone too far, Mr Cooper and I must ask you to let me get by. What do I have to do, or say, to let you know that you and I can never be . . . friends? Indeed your advances are abhorrent to me."

"Oh, come now, Poppy, that is no way to talk to a man who admires you enormously and would like to—"

"I have no wish for your admiration, Mr Cooper, nor for this attention you persist in paying me. I am head dairymaid to Farmer and Mrs Goodall and as such can think of no reason, except the obvious one, why you should pester me like this. I do not care for it, sir, and so would ask you to stop it at once."

He smiled winningly, not at all put out, it seemed, by her coldness. He was Dominic Cooper who had for years had his pick with no trouble at all of every young maid in Lancashire. They fell before him like corn beneath the scythe, sighing and dropping their drawers, honoured to do so and, given a few compliments and perhaps a small gift or two to show his approval, had never failed to thaw before his charm. As this one would. Perhaps he might go at a slower pace than usual, for was she not more delectable than those he had known in the past. The idea pleased him. He would *court* her, win her and when she succumbed it would be all the sweeter and besides which it would pass the time nicely until his marriage in the spring to Dulcie. His thoughts showed in his face and Poppy felt her murderous rage grow.

He took a leisurely step towards her, not with any intention of touching her but it seemed she did not care for it.

"I should like to remind you, Mr Cooper, that I have only to shout out and half a dozen men, including Farmer Goodall and his sons, will come running down here to protect me. I am not some poor defenceless maidservant who has no option but to allow liberties lest she lose her job, you see, and they will want to know why, after leaving a family party to which you were not invited, you are still hanging about here like some vagrant up to no good. They believe you to be a gentleman but it appears they are wrong. Now, stand aside, if you please. I wish to go home."

"Home? Long Reach Farm is your home? I was led to believe you were come from one of those labourers' cottages down there," nodding in the direction of Primrose Bank.

Poppy could feel her temper getting away from her. Her scorn, her contempt, her total lack of fear seemed to wash over this man like a small wavelet on a beach, making no impression whatsoever. His total belief in himself and his attractions, which he was convinced no woman could resist, was becoming dangerous. His languid mind, which had had nothing more to contend with for many years than how best to enjoy every hour of every day to its full capacity, could not comprehend a rejection. Well, she was rejecting him and if her politeness had failed perhaps a bit of downright contemptuous rudeness would do the trick. God, she hated the bugger and she would tell him so, leaving him in no doubt as to her feelings for him.

"It seems you are as dimwitted as you are rash, Mr Cooper. I may come from Primrose Bank as you say, but I have travelled a long way since then. I am from labouring stock but that does not mean your advances are welcome. You are insolent and insulting. I will say no more for now but by God if you don't stop pestering me I shall complain to Farmer Goodall."

"Really, Poppy, you are making far more of this than you need." His tone was bantering and not at all offended. "And has anyone ever told you how very attractive you are when you are cross. Your eyes, even in the dark, shine like twin stars and as for your" – his own eyes dropped boldly to her heaving breasts, for in her anger she was breathing deeply – "well, you look quite exquisite."

"I'm warning you, Mr Cooper."

"Oh, Poppy, don't be absurd. I mean you no harm. It's not against the law to pay a compliment to a pretty girl." It was obvious from the way he smiled that he still believed he had her. He was sure, even now, that given a few secret meetings where he could overcome her reluctance with his charm, his good looks, his upper-class breeding, he would have her eating out of his hand. He would treat her graciously, flatteringly, impressing her with his not inconsiderable skill as a lover for as long as it pleased him. She could not resist, not if he persevered. He was Dominic Cooper, the indulged son of an illustrious family, with looks and wit and charm and it was inconceivable to him that the daughter of a farm labourer could resist him.

"Look," he said, smilingly, placatingly, "we seem to have got off on the wrong foot, Poppy, but I'm sure that if—"

"Mr Cooper." Poppy could barely speak through the thin white line of her compressed lips. "We have got off on no foot at all and I would advise you to turn round, get on your horse and ride away. If you don't I shall scream so loudly they will hear me in your mother's parlour. Now, get out of my way."

She pushed past him, doing her best not to touch him but he made no move to stop her. His soft, *pleased* laughter, which seemed to say he had enjoyed their encounter, followed her across the yard.

It was at that moment that a strange fear touched her and for an incredible moment she felt a great and sorrowful need for a big red-haired lad with an engaging grin and the kindest, bluest eyes she had ever seen.

15

He set out deliberately to charm the Goodall family and though Tom was a blunt, outspoken, down-to-earth country man, already wary of the intentions the squire's lad had towards his son, and Eliza had a cool and sensible head on her shoulders, both of them were gradually taken in by Dominic Cooper's clever resolve to ingratiate himself into their lives.

Tom was suspicious at first whenever he found the young man lounging in Eliza's parlour, drinking Eliza's coffee, or cowslip wine for which he vowed he had formed a strong attachment – that was how he talked! Tom believed that the lad had come to lead *his* lad, who needed a tight rein kept on his fun-loving spirit, into bad ways. It was the grouse-shooting season and following it from October to Christmas there would be pheasant shooting and, of course, fox hunting during the winter months. Tom knew that Johnny longed to join Dominic and his gentry friends in the sport that took place over Sir Thomas Avons's moorland but it would not do, in his opinion, for the son of a farmer to become involved with young men who were the offspring of landowners, gentlemen with no occupation other than to be gentlemen. Sport was the foundation upon which country house parties, of which there were a great many at Coopers Edge and Fullingham, Sir Thomas's place, were built. Winter sports which involved killing something and summer sports where hitting a ball was their only aim and his Johnny was good at both. He was a fine shot, a fine sportsman in every pursuit he set his mind to, indeed a fine fellow all round who seemed able to mix comfortably in any level of society. He was amiable, easy-going, confident, due no doubt to his mother's rearing of him, seeing no difference between himself and Dominic Cooper, which was what worried Tom Goodall.

Now Richard could be trusted to know where the line was which separated the Goodalls from the Coopers. In fact, where his place lay. Not that Tom Goodall, nor his elder son, had the slightest difficulty in believing themselves to be as good a man as Captain Adam Cooper any day of the week, but they were born into different worlds with different lives behind and ahead of them, lives which did not overlap. Just as he would no more expect to hobnob with any of his own farm labourers, so he would no more expect to be a guest at the Cooper dinner table. Each man had a position in life where God had put him and Tom believed firmly that each man should keep to it.

So did Richard. He could think of no reason why, suddenly, Dominic Cooper should take it into his head to make a "chum", as Dominic put it, out of his brother Johnny. Dominic had friends and to spare among his own sort and though Johnny was a good-natured lad – well, he supposed he was a man really, no longer a lad at twenty – and made an entertaining companion, it struck him that there must be some ulterior motive behind Dominic Cooper's frequent visits to Long Reach Farm. Especially after what he had seen on the lane leading from Coopers Edge a few weeks ago when he had found the fellow doing his best to engage Poppy in some kind of conversation. What other conclusion could he come to? he asked himself in those early days, the poisonous fangs of jealousy sinking into his heart. Had the comeliness of his mother's protégée caught Dominic's eye and with the gentry's total disregard for anything but his own satisfaction was he about to pursue her with the wholehearted enthusiasm of a male in rut?

But the strange thing was he paid no more attention to her than he did to Richard's mother. He was scrupulously polite to both of them, apologising for disturbing their evening – he soon learned that that was when Poppy would be there – saying that the weather was so fine he could not resist riding over to see if Johnny, and Richard too, of course, would care to come for a gallop while the light lasted. And it had occurred to him as he rode over that the brothers might like to be included in a tennis party his mother was getting up this weekend. It would probably be the last before the autumn and winter set in. Since its emergence several years ago tennis had become wildly popular. Particularly mixed doubles where the prospect of a charming partner of the opposite sex prompted young ladies to practise their game with great enthusiasm. The tennis court was what some mamas considered to be a mating ground and many and varied were the items of advice given to daughters who were in the marriage market.

"White shoes should be avoided as they make the feet look large; the prettiest of white underskirts should be worn under a frilled and flounced white skirt and bodice, showing off to perfection a trim, graceful figure, fleet of foot and terribly attractive to the masculine eye," were but two of them. Gentlemen were honour bound never to serve with strength at a lady opponent and were to endeavour always to return the ball which fell at any distance from their lady partners, for should she run, and fall, decorum would suffer.

For this reason many gentlemen who were keen on the game, Dominic Cooper included, preferred to play in gentlemen's doubles and singles – he had no need to angle for a lady since he already had one of his own whom he was to marry in the spring – and though Johnny Goodall, for lack of practice, was nowhere near the standard Dominic had reached, what did it matter? It was not to play tennis that he sought him out but to insinuate himself into the Goodall family and get close to the dairymaid. Her rose-honey skin, the lustrous and unusually short cap of brown hair which swirled and bounced in curls about her gracefully held head, her slanting, luminous blue-grey eyes, her full, poppy red mouth which thinned grimly whenever they met, which amused him, her breasts that moved provocatively as she did were all driving him to distraction. Her trim waist and hips and the turn of slim ankle and foot, revealed as she had climbed into the gig on the day he first noticed her, filled his dreams, waking and sleeping, and he had become obsessed with his need to have her, naked and willing, or unwilling, he didn't care, beneath him. He wanted to subjugate her, humiliate her, since her disapproval of him was not concealed, and if, afterwards, she ran home to the Goodalls crying rape it would only be her word against his. A dairymaid, one of those who were known to be obliging, to accuse the son of Captain Adam Cooper, a blameless young man who was to be married to the daughter of a baronet very soon and who would hardly risk his future happiness for a tumble with a servant, would hardly be believed, would she?

Her total lack of interest in him, indeed her barely hidden contempt for the fine fellow he knew himself to be, were spurs which raked him on to this one deep-seated goal. There were other young women in his life, cooperative maidservants, shop girls, chorus girls, who would oblige him at need and then there was a certain place in Juniper Street where a gentleman with money in his pocket might find any sort of sexual gratification that took his fancy. But, for the moment, they had no appeal for him. He wanted, lusted after the dairymaid, the golden-skinned beauty who stepped out like a queen and treated him as if he were one of her lowest subjects. It could not come soon enough and yet he found he quite enjoyed seeing the look of uncertainty, of apprehension on the milkmaid's face every time he rode over to Long Reach Farm or sometimes, to whet his already lusty appetite, he sauntered through the market on a Saturday, watching as her face tightened when she spotted him. Once he had followed the gig home, walking his grey just behind, smiling whenever she glanced over her shoulder, keeping up with her when she lashed the small mare to a faster pace.

He was careful not to make a nuisance of himself to the family. He kept his visits infrequent and short as though to say to them that he knew Long Reach was a working farm and its sons did not have the free time he did. He surprised himself with his own restraint, popping in, as he called it, to visit his new friend when he was certain he would not interrupt some vital bit of farm work. He made no suggestion that might interfere with their labour, particularly of the farmer's sons, both yokels in his arrogant opinion, hinting, as the fox-hunting season approached, that they might be interested in a bit of sport some Sunday, or perhaps, if their father did not mind, an evening at Coopers Edge with him and his friends. They played cards, or board games, he said winningly, presenting a picture of innocent domesticity in which the Goodall boys would be completely at home and in which their parents would certainly find no harm. Eliza and Tom relaxed their vigilance and Eliza at least was pleased that her sons were to mix in company suited to their lineage, for her father, though a professional man, had come from gentlemen.

He brought the promised birthday gift the following week, saying it was no more than a trinket, worth little in monetary value but a small token of his appreciation of the kindness shown him by all those at Long Reach Farm. A fine gold chain for her neck with a tiny charm to hang just between her breasts fashioned in the shape of a poppyhead. He'd seen it in a second-hand shop in Bold Street, he told them, and had known at once that it was meant for Miss Appleton and if she and Mrs Goodall had no objection to her receiving it he would be very pleased. In his eyes and on his face was an expression of innocent unawareness that what he was doing could in any way be construed as a breach of etiquette. No gentleman gave a gift of jewellery, no matter how inexpensive, to a young, unmarried woman and so, knowing full well what he was up to, though they, it seemed, did not, he presented it to her before them all, the Goodalls and their servants.

Had it come from any other source, Poppy would have been enchanted. It was tasteful, a delicate thing to please the heart of any girl, but the thought of having it round her neck, placed there by this narrow-eyed speculatively smiling impostor who was charming and deceiving them all, even Tom Goodall, turned her flesh cold and crawling.

She could not accept it, she told him coldly, aware of the surprised stares of the servants though she was conscious that Eliza agreed with her, if not for the same reason. Eliza knew that it was too much. A handkerchief perhaps, or a posy, some innocuous gift which meant nothing, she was surprised that Dominic did not know better though she said nothing.

"Thank you for . . . for your generosity but it's out of the question," Poppy told him, handing him back the lovely thing in its equally lovely box. "I cannot accept it."

"I'm sorry?" Dominic's face was a bewildered mixture of consternation and hurt.

"It's too much, Mr Cooper." She refused absolutely to call him Dominic no matter how many times he asked her. Richard Goodall was seen to nod his head in agreement.

"Oh, please, Poppy, it cost nothing, really."

"I still can't accept it." Her tone was curt and Eliza and Tom exchanged glances.

"Well, though I don't understand, Poppy, since the gift was meant in the most sincere way, I will, of course, not press you."

He had been like a small boy who has been cuffed through no fault of his own and they all, even Eliza, who knew the present was not suitable, felt sorry for him.

When he left, the small box with the chain inside was found behind the clock on the mantelshelf in the parlour where someone would find it. When it was brought to her by Clara Eliza shook her head and said perhaps it would be churlish to return it but it was noticed that Poppy never wore the chain.

Poppy began to feel the strain of constantly swimming against the current of Long Reach Farm's total approval of Dominic Cooper. He was Master Johnny's friend, his winning ways, his smiling courtesy adding a warmth to their day whenever he rode over and they were bewildered by Poppy's cool reception of him. Poppy was amazed that they could not see through him, but then he only revealed that acquisitive, self-seeking, self-deluding, shamelessly bold side to her who was the object of his desire. To the Goodalls and their servants he was polite, quietly spoken, self-effacing and unassuming. Tom's only complaint about him was that he did not seem to realise that his sons were working men and did not have the time nor the choice to go jaunting with him whenever he suggested it.

But by this time, as Christmas approached, Johnny was off every Sunday, joining the Fullingham hunt, or shooting pheasant over the moor after he had finished the several tasks necessary to a farmer on a Sunday. They were not a church-going family, fortunately for Johnny, and so, with no reason to keep him at home, Tom Goodall had no choice but to let him go. He was only glad, he said to Eliza, that their Richard had a more sensible head on his shoulders and while he was on the subject of Dick, was it his imagination but had she noticed, as it seemed Tom had, that the lad had a soft spot for Poppy? Though the lass was not exactly what he would have wanted for his son, had he the choice, he had come round to thinking what a splendid farmer's wife she would make. Didn't Eliza think so? She came from poor stock, none knew better than he, but then look what a grand little family the Appletons had become since Reuben married that woman from over West Derby way. The bad apples sorted out and chucked away and the four who were left, those lads, Marigold and their Poppy, scarcely aware that he had used the possessive "their" when speaking of his wife's dairymaid, had turned out grand. Marigold, though a bit simple, was the best little worker since Eliza had taken on Poppy, Cook said. Both boys able to read and write and do quite complicated arithmetic so Poppy had told him proudly, and beginning to look round for jobs suitable and to the standard of the education they had received. Old Reuben a changed man and the cottage they occupied as neat and attractive as Poppy herself. They'd certainly improved out of all recognition and really, if anyone was to be introduced to Poppy, meaning the successful folk who were Tom Goodall's equals, would they believe that the lass had had such poor beginnings? Smart and pretty as a picture, well-mannered and better spoken than he himself and yet set her to running the farmhouse, the servants in it, the dairy, the market stall and everything else Eliza did so well and he'd like to bet a guinea to a farthing she'd make as much a success of it all as Eliza herself.

He drew contentedly on his pipe, lounging in comfort opposite his wife in his deep, well-cushioned chair in the parlour. He had stoked the fire halfway up the chimney, for his bones were a bit on the creaky side at his time of life and it was a bitter, frozen day on this Sunday just a week before Christmas. He had his stockinged feet on the fender. He knew Eliza did not care for it, since a real gentleman would never remove his boots even before his own fireside, but Tom was his own man in his own home and did as he liked and Eliza made no objection. He had just eaten a splendid dinner of saddle of lamb prepared and cooked as only Eliza's cook knew how, with crisp roast potatoes – home-grown, of course – brussels sprouts and cauliflower with mint sauce made from the mint in Eliza's own herb garden. A plum crumble to follow made from the plums picked in his own orchard and bottled by Cook in the autumn, with thick, creamy custard and a pint of his own home-brewed ale with which to wash the lot down. He felt grand and his genial, smiling face said so to anyone who cared to look.

The only shadow darkening his pleasant Sunday afternoon was the absence of his younger son who was off up yonder with Dominic Cooper, involved in "summat and nowt", as

Tom liked to call the games the gentry got up to and where would it all fetch up, he often wondered.

Poppy and Richard had set off up the fields towards the spinney where a dense and berry-laden bush of holly was looked for. Poppy meant to decorate the kitchen and parlour with all the Christmas ornamentation that was traditional at this time of the year, she had declared, and Dick, his serious eyes as grey as a snow-filled sky, shining and silvery with the anticipation of an hour alone with her, had offered to take the wheelbarrow to carry what she gathered. The holly, the mistletoe – under which the maidservants would hang about hopefully – the ivy, the laurel and myrtle, the aromatic evergreen boughs Poppy had decided would mix beautifully with the everlasting flowers and the coloured and gilt paper chains she and the servants meant to make. Richard was to cut a fir tree to stand in the corner of the parlour and on its boughs would hang wax candles, fruit, flowers, pretty little trifles such as bon-bons and crystallised fruits which Cook had promised to make. Poppy had the whole household already in a state of pleasant excitement which Tom found he enjoyed, acting like a small girl who is to attend her first party, flushed and quite lovely as she made up for the first miserably deprived years she had known as a child. There was to be carol singing in the parlour, spilling out into the hall on Christmas Eve and as a concession to the time of the year Tom had agreed that the household would walk down to St Anne's Church on Christmas Day morning to hear the parson's Christmas sermon.

Eliza eased herself more comfortably into the nest of cushions she had arranged for herself in the armchair, doing her best not to breathe too deeply or move too sharply lest it bring to life the pain which savaged the inside of her chest and trailed down her left arm to the tips of her fingers. It had been getting steadily worse for many weeks now and even the infusion she stealthily made up from the plant of the figwort family, the foxglove, no longer seemed to help. She knew what was wrong with her, naturally, since had she not been a doctor's daughter and had she not seen her father suffer in exactly the same way? He could not heal himself and neither could she and her only ambition in life now was to see Poppy and Richard settled together. Had Poppy not captured his heart, which it seemed she had, her elder son would have found some suitable young woman in the farming community, a young woman brought up to be a farmer's wife. But where in God's name would he find one as perfect for the job as Poppy? And if he did and married elsewhere, what would become of the girl who was as dear to Eliza as her own daughter? No woman would care to share her home, her dairy, her market stall, which was very profitable, with a girl who, though probably more capable than she was at running the household, was really no more than a farm labourer's daughter. So was Poppy to return to her own roots, to Primrose Bank, improved as it was, usurped from the position where Eliza herself had placed her? No, dear God, no! Far better that she and Richard make a match and a continuing success of Long Reach Farm and, longingly, while she was still here to witness it.

No one, except perhaps Cook, who missed nothing, had noticed that little by little, à fraction at a time, Eliza had begun to ease more and more of her own duties on to Poppy's strong young shoulders. She encouraged her to take more of an interest in the housekeeping accounts, the ordering of provisions, conferring with Cook, of course. To make decisions on the management of the servants and the work they did. It was such an imperceptible shift of responsibility it scarce caused a ripple, since by now the maids had become used to Poppy's elevated position in the Goodall family and it had become quite natural for any household emergency to be laid before the erstwhile dairymaid, who dealt with it in the way Eliza had shown her, mainly by example. In the dairy itself, Jinny, Bess and Nelly, with the occasional bit of welcome help and advice from Dilys, which Eliza encouraged, formed a splendid team, held together by Poppy who still supervised the running of it, and, of course, spent Saturday with Jinny at the stall in St John's Market.

Though she herself was not aware of it since it did not occur to her that she was actually doing it, Poppy was slowly taking into her own steady hands the reins laid down by her beloved mistress and friend.

"I'm having a couple of hours in the study, my dear," Eliza would say, "sorting out some papers. See I'm not disturbed, will you?"

"I'm just going to steal an hour or two with *Middlemarch*," since George Eliot was a great favourite of hers. "Keep them away, will you? I might even lie on the bed."

"I didn't sleep very well last night. That dratted vixen would keep barking in the spinney," though no one else had heard it, "I think I'll have a nap. Can you manage for half an hour?"

These were but three of the many excuses she made to go off by herself and rest, thinking artlessly that she was pulling the wool over all their eyes. She was surprised, and relieved, when Poppy herself began to urge her to get away for a while, to have a nap, or put her feet up for an hour and it had occurred to her just lately that she was not as clever as she thought herself to be. Poppy was attuned to her every mood, to her every requirement, but covertly so, as though she respected Eliza's need for privacy. She was kind without being fussy, indispensable, always at her elbow but not pressing her. Did Poppy guess, she wondered, and if she did should Eliza be surprised? She knew she had lost weight and her skin had taken on the pallor of the grey ash in the fireplace but if she could just keep on her feet until Poppy was settled that was all she asked.

"Would Poppy suit you as a daughter-in-law then, Tom?" she asked him now in a deliberately casual tone.

Tom pulled on his pipe for a moment before answering, then looked up at her to find her watching him closely.

"She's a good clever lass, Eliza, and virtuous. You've trained her well and she's a credit to you. But are we putting the cart before the horse here? Nay, we don't even know what's in the lass's mind so I can't give you an answer. What do you think? D'you think she has warm feelings for our Dick? She's only sixteen and as far as I can tell – mind, I'm no romantic so how would I know? – she's shown no sign of it."

"No, but she could be . . . persuaded."

"What the hell does that mean?"

"It wouldn't be hard to point out to her, not directly, of course but in a subtle way, what a good match it would be."

"Aye, for her."

"True, but Richard couldn't do better, Tom. Think about it. Think what an asset Poppy would be to him. She knows the farm and everyone on it and what they all do. She's bright and intelligent and would help him no end in the business side of it."

"Like you've done for me, lass." Tom was not a demonstrative man, nor an observant one, but the look he bestowed on his wife was fond. "Anyroad, let's wait and see."

"You're right," she agreed, while her thoughts were busy in her head. Think about it, they told her. Say nothing to either of them yet, for she still had a bit of time before her. "But you won't discourage it, will you, Tom? You'll need someone steady when . . ." She had almost said, "when I'm gone" but stopped herself in time. "You know what a happy-go-lucky lad Johhny is. He'd be little support for his brother. He'll probably take up with some pretty lass who hasn't the faintest notion how to run this farm. But Poppy, as Richard's wife, would hold it all together. Don't you agree?"

"Aye, lass, happen you're right." Tom reached out and threw another chunk of sweet-smelling applewood on the still enormous fire, then settled back to enjoy his well-earned Sunday rest. "But there's plenty of time for that yet. Sixteen and twenty-one's no age to be wed. I was thirty when you and I got hitched. Anyroad, let's see which way this particular rabbit's to run."

Eliza slowly let her shoulders relax, unaware until now how stiffly she had been holding them. The pain stayed at bay. She was satisfied. The first hurdle, though perhaps not the biggest, had been cleared. Poppy herself could be difficult, for Eliza knew she did not love Richard as a woman truly loves a man but if she could be steered towards it, made to realise how suitable it would be, she would be safe and cared for in a quiet way by Eliza's son and that was all that mattered.

They had been successful in their search for decorative Christmas greenery, rummaging about in the almost bare, frozen spinney, their breath smoking on the icy air, until they had found what they were looking for. Or at least what Poppy was looking for. Laurel, or sweet bay, grows happily in the shade of other trees and was planted because of its broad, evergreen leaves to provide protection for game birds in coverts. The spreading lower branches gave the birds shelter from the wind, the rain and the snow and the berries supplied food in abundance. The smell is sweet when it is cut, filling the room which it decorates with enchantment and Poppy explained to Richard, who was no scholar, that the ancient Greeks knew the tree as Daphne because a nymph, so called, had turned herself into a bay tree to escape the attentions of Apollo, the Greek god of music, poetry and healing.

"Sounds a bit drastic to me," Richard answered, ever practical as he cut and stacked branches into the wheelbarrow, layering them methodically so that there would be room for the holly, the ivy and the Christmas tree. "Couldn't the lass just say 'no' and have done with it?" He was a man very much like his father, insisting that everything be done in order and at the proper time. He was honest and hardworking but with little sense of humour and no understanding of sensitive emotion. Nevertheless his heart was true and faithful, if not imaginative. He was what his mother would have described as a "plodder" and to herself she often likened her two sons to the tortoise and the hare.

Poppy, who had caught sight of a blaze of red berries on the holly bush on the far side of the spinney and was walking towards it, stood stock still on the faint track which led between the denuded trees. The spinney was all that was left of the great forests which had once covered this tract of land before farming took over. The sun was already sliding down the midwinter sky, turning the pale blue above it to lavender and dusky rose and gold. The sun itself hid behind the bare, slender branches of a beech tree, the outline of the tree a dark brown tracery of lace. The hoar frost which had gathered during the night still lay white and crisp over every bush and tree and underfoot, and the grasses crackled beneath their boots. It was quite lovely, still and silent and mysterious as the short day drew to a close. It was here, years ago, that she had said goodbye to a tall, broad-shouldered lad whose copper-bright hair in the dark had been no more than a colourless halo about his proudly held head. She could remember it, though, as it had looked in the light of the lamp, a dozen different colours of cinnamon and gold and copper like a newly fallen autumn leaf. His eyes, soft and deep with an emotion he could not articulate, had been so dark as to be almost black and yet she knew them to be as blue and shining as the sapphire brooch pinned on Mrs Goodall's bodice on special occasions. His tall frame had swung gracefully away, his long legs striding out to his future in Mr Goodall's yard coat and he had left her behind. Where was he, that good-humoured, courageous, bright-spirited lad who was hidden in the deepest part of herself for safekeeping, there for ever, it seemed?

Poppy did not realise that she had frozen as stiff as the branches of the trees as Richard spoke. At the sound of the words an instant picture shouldered aside the sweet memory of Alick MacConnell, a picture of the arrogantly smiling face of Dominic Cooper. Impudent, insolent even, full sensual mouth parted to reveal even white teeth and though she knew they were perfectly normal, the right size and shape, why did they remind her of the fangs of the wolf in the story of Red Riding Hood? God, how she loathed him. Even when he was not present he had the power to make her skin crawl; to spoil her pleasure in what she was doing. She had been enjoying the afternoon. Enjoying the anticipation of decorating the farmhouse, looking forward to the warmth, the laughter, for Johnny could be guaranteed to play the fool. Looking forward to Christmas and though cows must be milked no matter what time of year it was, to the few hours the household would spend together in a festive mood.

Now, with a few innocent words Richard had shattered it, bringing her back to the remembrance of what had been hanging over her for months now.

"Poppy?" Richard's voice was anxious. She felt the hesitant touch of his hand on her sleeve and knew that she had only to turn, to look into his pleasant face, to allow her own to crumple into the tears which often threatened her these days and she would be cradled against his broad, sheltering chest. She knew how he felt about her. How could she not, for his pale grey eyes followed her about the parlour and in them shone his feelings no matter how he fought it. She also knew what was stopping him from declaring himself. He was the son of a well-to-do farmer, conventional and true to the belief that like must marry like. He was not a pretentious young man who put himself above others but he knew his own worth. The farm would be his one day and he was expected to take as his wife a woman from his own level of society. His mother's dairymaid, no matter how well educated she might be, would not be one of those. She could persuade him otherwise, she was well aware, with the wiles known to woman since Eve, but she did not love him and never would and could not bring herself to win him with deception. He was too fine a man for that. She loved no man and never would.

"What is it, Poppy? Are you unwell?" Richard knew nothing of female ailments and was faintly alarmed at the idea that Poppy might be about to succumb to one.

"No, it's just . . . what you said."

"What I said? What did I say?" He frowned, not liking the idea that it was he who had upset her.

"Oh, nothing really. Just about a woman saying 'no' to a man who . . ."

"What? Tell me." His face turned a furious crimson. "Has someone been bothering you? Because if they have you've only to say and I'll deal with him." He flexed his brawny shoulders in readiness. "It's not that bloody buffoon from Coopers Edge, is it?" his suspicions flowering suddenly to unendurable proportions.

"Oh, no, Richard . . . please, of course not." Dear God, if Richard was to hear the full truth of the cat and mouse game Dominic Cooper was playing with her, quiet and peaceable as he was, he'd thunder over to Coopers Edge and thrash him to within an inch of his life. Like most men who are slow to anger, once he was roused he could be dangerous. Dominic was the son of a prominent and influential man and anyone who threatened him or any member of his family, for whatever reason, would be in serious trouble.

"He's always hanging about—"

"No, not after me, Richard, believe me," she interrupted frantically, ready to clutch at the lapels of his jacket and shake him. "I know he bought me that chain on my birthday but it meant nothing. It's just the sort of daft thing he would do, you know that. Ask your mother. He's just a fool who believes every woman from sixteen to sixty should fall in love with him. His conceit is prodigious. I do believe he has a girl in every village in Lancashire and him about to be married. But then that's nothing to do with us, is it, so let's put it out of our minds and concentrate on this holly."

She was smiling and herself again, or so she would have him believe, and it appeared he did. "Just look at that bush over there. It's positively bursting with berries and see" – pointing with a gloved hand to the right of the bush – "isn't that just what we need for our Christmas tree? It's exactly the right size for the parlour. Bring the wheelbarrow over here."

She darted away, bright and beautiful as a robin in her vivid scarlet cloak, her cheeks on fire with the cold, her eyes shining like pale crystal in her animated face. Not a care in the world, her manner said as she turned to smile at Richard, and wanting to believe her, he did.

16

The ground was frozen hard, still as solid as it had been all winter and the two grave-diggers grumbled as they struggled to cut into it to make the last resting place for Eliza Goodall, wife to Farmer Tom Goodall.

"They do say that lass, the one she fetched up as 'er own, 'as bin struck terrible 'ard. Tha' knows 'oo I mean, Reuben Appleton's girl what went as dairymaid. Missis medd a right pet of 'er, they say. Put 'er above 'er own, learned 'er ter read an' write."

"Gerraway!"

"Nay, 'tis true. I did 'ear as 'ow she can play't pianner an' jabbers away in some foreign lingo an' t'other servants can't understand a bloody word. Only't missis an' she'll do no more jabberin', in foreign nor in't Queen's English."

"Thass true."

"So 'oo's ter see ter't farm'ouse now, tell me that, at least until young maister's took a bride."

It was a question the whole farming community was asking and when, on the day of the funeral it was revealed that the dairymaid was to be that bride, it caused a ripple of amazement that spread outwards in ever widening circles stretching as far as St John's Market in the west and to Prescot in the east.

Poppy herself was stunned, not only by the unalterable fact that she was to marry Richard as soon as it was proper to do so after the funeral, but by her own acquiescence to it. She had spent the last eight weeks nursing Eliza Goodall, sitting with her day and night – except for market day – only falling into a light doze now and then when Dilys, or Cook, who were the only two she trusted, took over from her.

It was on Boxing Day that Eliza collapsed. They had spent a happy Christmas Day, house and farm servants and family mixing all together, protocol forgotten on this joyous occasion. There was a great uproar of talk and laughter, Mrs Goodall's wine and Farmer Goodall's ale loosening tongues and shattering inhibitions, casting shyness to the winds. There was a great clattering of cutlery and moving of plates heaped with turkey and goose and pork, each man and woman jostling their neighbour in great good humour. The enormous table in the dining-room seated a dozen or more which included the Goodalls and the head servants, Aggie and Clara, when they were not refilling someone's plate or glass, Dilys and Evan, who had parted reluctantly from his beasts in their winter stalls. Tommy who had no wife. May plus Farmer Goodall's second cowman and his nervous spouse, and a couple of lads who could squeeze in on a bench. In the kitchen were the rest, Marigold and Bess and Nelly – Jinny was at home with her mam, stepfather and stepbrothers – Jacko from the stable and indeed anyone who worked on the farm and cared to find himself a place at its groaning table. For weeks Cook and Poppy had been closeted in earnest consultation of how much to prepare, Mrs Goodall begging Poppy to take over since she felt like a rest from the upheaval Christmas always brought. The larder and storeroom and game-house had bulged with roast fowl and pig, with sides of beef and mutton, great smoked hams decorated with frills, flagons of cider and one could be forgiven for thinking a siege was about to take place. There was a Christmas cake and a plum pudding and a mountain of mince pies, all good, hearty stuff to please the appetites of those who did not often eat much beyond bacon and pease pudding, stews and apple dumplings for the rest of the year.

Dinner proceeded, uproarious and merry. Songs were sung. "The Holly and the Ivy", "Good King Wenceslas" and so lively was the enjoyment, no one, not even Poppy, noticed Mrs Goodall's extreme pallor, nor the bird-like amounts she picked off her plate. When nobody was looking she slipped what remained on to the already full platter of the big-eyed, silent lad who was learning the art of cowman from Evan and who had been placed beside her, to his consternation.

As was customary, and had been for generations, Christmas presents were given out to the house servants on Boxing Day. Again Mrs Goodall had asked Poppy to stand in for her in the choosing of them, relying on her good taste and good sense to pick what was suitable for each one. Lengths of dress material were popular with the women, stockings and shawls, a pair of gloves or a bunch of ribbons to redecorate an old bonnet. Poppy had purchased them, the best quality, mind, for Mrs Goodall did not like shoddy goods, from Mrs Girvan who had a splendid shop on the Upper Arcade in Bold Street.

It was just as Marigold was bobbing a respectful curtsey to the mistress who was handing her a prettily wrapped gift that Eliza Goodall felt the agony rip across her chest and down her arm and the gift dropped to the parlour carpet with a small thud.

"Oh, ma'am, I'm that sorry," apologised Marigold, who

always believed that whatever went amiss it must be her fault, but as she bent down to pick up the present Mrs Goodall fell against her and they were both flung to the floor.

For a second or two no one moved. The servants were unsure whether Marigold, who could be clumsy, they all knew that, had tripped, catching her foot in her skirt perhaps and, clutching at the mistress, had brought her down too but at once Marigold was on her feet, her face crimson, ready to weep for what had happened though the fault was not hers.

Poppy's heart floundered erratically in her breast as though already it knew that disaster had struck. Her mind froze, appalled and stupefied at the same time, then her crisp, practical brain took over and she sank to her knees beside her mistress. All about her the company stood, shocked and frightened, including the fallen woman's husband and sons, not knowing what had happened or what to do about it.

"Ride for the doctor, Johnny," Poppy ordered briskly, aware that he was the best man to put up on a horse. He'd had enough bloody practice, hadn't he, galloping all over the county with that bastard Dominic Cooper? "And be quick about it. Don't stand there with your mouth open. *Fetch the doctor.*"

Eliza's face was a contorted mask of pain but her eyes blazed into Poppy's, sending her some message and when Poppy bent her head, putting her ear to Eliza's blue lips, the whisper, no more than a sighing breath, reached her. She looked up and even in the midst of this devastation which had them all in its thrall she chose the one person who desperately needed to be doing something.

"Mr Goodall, will you fetch the mistress's medicine box, please. She needs something from it."

Before she had finished speaking he was lumbering away

up the hall until it occurred to him that he had no idea where the thing was kept.

"Where . . . ?"

"In her cupboard on the landing."

"Right," pounding up the stairs in great relief at being told what he must do. Eliza had been peaky for a while now, resting more than she used to, not eating much, but always cheerfully smiling as though to tell him he was not to worry about her. So he hadn't. Now look at her, measuring her length on the parlour carpet, her head in Poppy's lap, her throat an arch of twisting, painful tendons, her hands like claws as she tried to draw breath.

It seemed she had managed to convey to Poppy what it was she needed and when it was administered the servants all let out a great sigh of relief when it had the desired effect, relaxing their mistress's body to what seemed to be manageable pain. Cook knelt beside Poppy, holding her mistress's hand and on the other side Farmer Goodall and his elder son dithered helplessly, trapped against their wishes in this dreadful female catastrophe that had struck down Eliza. They had no idea what it could be, since illness was unknown, and therefore feared, by both of them, but thank God for Poppy who seemed to know just what to do. How would they have managed without her?

The doctor came, driven on across the frozen fields by Eliza's frantic younger son, the doctor's horse flagging as they approached the farmhouse, despite the short cut Johnny had taken. Eliza was examined where she lay, the doctor shooing the servants back to the kitchen, all except Cook who was steady and the dairymaid who would not be parted from her mistress. He looked grave and when, after they had carried her gently up to her room and seen her comfortably in her bed, he called

Tom Goodall and his sons into the parlour, closing the door behind them.

It took her eight weeks to die. Her glorious spirit, captured in the frail shell of her body, would not let her go, not until she had achieved what she had set out to achieve on the day Dominic Cooper had given Poppy that necklace. Poppy must be safe. Poppy must have the place in life that had been Eliza's and was now to be hers. Poppy had given Eliza almost six of the most satisfying, joyous years of her life and she loved her because of it. Even close to death as she was, Eliza knew she must protect Poppy. She had made the farm labourer's daughter what she was and so it was up to her to see that Poppy *remained* as she was. She had not long now, her husband's bewildered, grieving eyes told her, her sons' awkward, shuffling visits to her bedroom told her that. Poppy's falsely cheerful smiles and devoted, caring concern told her that. She dozed under the effect of the drugs the doctor gave her, in no pain, drifting in and out of consciousness, her eyes turning towards the bedroom door whenever it opened.

One evening it was her son Richard who peeped cautiously round it and though she was aware that he had hoped to find her asleep since her condition saddened and embarrassed him, she raised a weak hand to summon him to her.

"Dilys" – for it was her old dairymaid who sat peacefully beside the fire – "leave us a moment, will you, dear?" Even these words tired her but Dilys heaved her increasing bulk from the chair and shuffled from the room, closing the door quietly behind her. She knew Poppy slept the sleep of the exhausted in her room at the top of the stairs but would be down like a shot if she thought she was needed. Thin she was now, poor little lass, like a stick, all her lovely golden rose paled to an almost yellow fragility and what was to happen to her when her mistress had gone? Dilys wondered. Would she still be treated by the Goodall men as if she were a sister, a daughter, a valued and loved member of their family or would it be back to Primrose Bank as seemed likely? She'd still be head dairymaid, of course, which was a grand position for a girl of sixteen but not as fine as that she had known here at Long Reach farmhouse.

"Mother, how are you feeling?" Richard asked awkwardly, treading with wary steps towards the bed where his mother lay dying.

She smiled with her old humour when she saw the expression on his face. "Son, don't be afraid of me. I'm not dead yet."

"Mother!" His conventional soul was horrified.

"I'm sorry, Richard . . . but I can't abide this false manner which you all put on, even Poppy, which is meant to tell me I am to . . . get better. We know that's not true, don't we, my son?"

"Oh, Mother . . ." Man that he was he hung his head in shame and tears filled his eyes. He sank to the chair beside the bed, took her skeleton hand in his and put the back of it to his cheek.

"Don't weep, Richard."

"Mother, what else can I do?"

"There is something . . . if you want to please me."

"Anything, you have only to ask."

"Poppy . . ."

He looked startled. "Poppy?"

"I know you have . . . a fondness for her, lad. I've seen it in your eyes."

"Mother, don't let's talk about such things here," for Richard Goodall was awkward with his emotions and did not want them on display for his mother to see, not here, nor anywhere.

"Where else, my son? I am stuck here . . ."

"You know that's not what I meant, Mother." He was vastly embarrassed.

"Richard, you know I am to . . . I won't be here . . . much longer . . ."

"Mother, you must not talk like that."

"Stop it, Richard. Face the truth, about me and about Poppy. You love her . . . don't lie to me, not now when I am to . . . to . . . Do you love her . . . please, Richard?"

He looked into her anguished face and his own gentled, truth shining from his crystal grey eyes.

"Yes, I do, but . . ."

"There are no buts, my son. Marry her. Don't lose her. Don't let this family lose her. She is needed. She is very precious to me. I'll die content if . . ."

"Mother, I beg you . . ."

"Promise me . . ."

"She is . . . Father won't like it – a dairymaid and his elder son."

"Fiddlesticks. Leave him to me."

"And Poppy?"

"She is very . . . fond of you, Richard," and he knew that she was telling him that a woman on her deathbed has great power over those who will grieve for her.

Her conversation with Poppy went much the same way though it took place over several days. She had mulled it over in her mind, furious with its inability to function, drugged as she was, in its usual clever fashion but struggling with it nevertheless. She felt no guilt at arranging the lives of two people to suit herself, for she genuinely believed that what she did was best for both of them. Best for the family, best for the servants, best for the farm. Richard needed a steady, reliable wife to help him and guide him in the years to come and yet she must be attractive, good-humoured and well educated or she would not hold him to her. Not that he was light-minded or likely to be unfaithful, but a man who is content in love is a happy man and will be good to the giver of that love.

And what could be better for Poppy, who was at present, and Eliza took the blame for it, neither fish, flesh nor fowl in the level of society in which she moved. Neither servant nor family, and yet both, and there was only one way to make sure she remained in the situation that suited her best.

"Poppy," she whispered to her that first time as Poppy sat beside her bed. She feebly searched for the girl's hand. Poppy took hers between both her own. She leaned on the bed and looked lovingly into Eliza's waxy face, then bent her head to kiss her cheek.

"What is it? Do you need something?"

"Yes."

"What? Tell me."

"I need to know you will be . . . safe, when . . ."

Poppy's face spasmed in anguish for there was no one in the world she loved more than this woman and the thought, the *reality* that she was to lose her could scarce be borne.

"Don't . . . don't," she murmured, much as Richard had.

"We must be truthful with one another, sweetheart. You and I."

"Yes, I know," Poppy's throat worked on the tears that jammed it. "But you see I cannot face . . ."

"I know . . . but we must. What is to happen to you . . . after . . ."

"After?"

"You know what I mean . . . To you?"

"To me . . . why? What should happen?"

"You are . . . you mean a great deal to me . . . and to . . . Richard." Eliza's breath rasped painfully in her throat. She closed her eyes and her hand between Poppy's grew limp so that for a terrifying moment Poppy thought she was dead. Her own face became blanched. Dear God, oh sweet Lord, how was she to manage without this good woman in her life? But then a small sigh escaped from between Eliza's lips and her breast rose and fell. She had only slipped into sleep, exhausted with the strain of talking, even for so short a time. The words she had spoken about Richard had barely registered in Poppy's tired, sorrowful mind but they came back to her on the next occasion.

The room was hushed, as sickrooms are. It was the end of January and piercing winds swept across the Pennines and over the frozen fields, shrieking round the house, searching for a way in. But Long Reach farmhouse and all the buildings that surrounded it were solid, well built, sturdy – with the exception perhaps of the cottages at Primrose Bank – and all who sheltered within its walls were snug and warm. Animals and humans alike.

Poppy and Jinny had been to market that day which had been as busy as always with its usual lively bustle. She had been overwhelmed with enquiries as to how Mrs Goodall fared and with messages of goodwill to take back to her. They knew by now they would never see her again and the sadness seemed to deepen each week. She had brought back gifts of flowers, great big chrysanthemum blooms in cheerful yellow and white and bronze from the florist. Fruit packed in a dainty basket tied with satin ribbons, and cakes, light as a feather, to tempt her appetite, the confectioner said hopefully.

The flowers made bright splashes of colour on the

dressing table and the mantelshelf above the fireplace in which a glowing fire crackled. The room was soft, comforting, a place of peaceful repose in which to end a life, and every day, one or other of the servants came to smile at their mistress, to recount some small event that had happened since they saw her last, careful not to tire her, or upset her, though they themselves were upset and wept grievously when they got back to the kitchen.

"Poppy, my love, did you . . . have you given any thought to . . . what I said the other night?"

"The other night?"

"Mmm, about . . . Richard?"

"Richard? Oh, Mrs Goodall . . ."

"He loves you, child . . . as we all do."

"Please, don't tire yourself."

"I must, dearest girl. I must know that you will all be safe . . . when I am gone."

"Don't . . . don't. I can't bear it . . ." Poppy's tears, always so close to the surface these days, coursed down her face on to Eliza's hands.

"Sweetheart, promise you'll take care of them all . . . please."

"You know I will."

"Take care of my family."

"Yes, oh yes."

"And . . . Richard?"

"Anything . . . anything that will make you happy."

Eliza let out her breath on a long shuddering sigh and a look of utter peace softened her face. "Thank you, dearest girl. I will speak to him."

Poppy, desolate with the knowledge of what was to come, scarce in her right mind with grief, nodded, agreeing to what

Eliza asked, though it was doubtful she fully understood what it was.

And again, as though Eliza was suddenly fearful of what she asked of her son and her protégée, she spoke of it.

"My dearest girl . . ."

"Yes, I'm here."

"When we talked . . . the last time . . ."

"Yes, darling."

"About you and . . . Richard."

"Yes?"

"Are you quite sure . . . of what you do? Are you happy to look after him . . . and Tom and Johnny?"

"You know I am," perhaps only hearing the words which made sense to her. She would continue to give everything she had in her heart to make the lives of the Goodalls as trouble-free and contented as Mrs Goodall had. They were her family, all she had now, though she was fond of Elly and Pa.

Later that evening Richard Goodall, with a nod of approval from his father, drew Poppy into the small study where she and Eliza had known such happiness and formally asked her to marry him.

"You are aware that I have held you in high regard for a long time now, Poppy," he said somewhat pompously, his serious face stiff with the emotion he held well hidden. "I . . . we . . . are all fond of you and you know it is my mother's dearest wish that . . . well . . . that we be wed, you and I. It is mine too. She has spoken to you about it?"

"Yes, she has, Richard, but . . ."

"Do you care for me at all, Poppy?" He swallowed painfully and if she had been in her right mind instead of out of it with worry and grief, her ears attuned for any sound that might come from above, she would have seen the need in him to crush her to him and kiss her with the passion of love long denied. He had been brought up to be kind to children, females and animals and so he was. He was twenty-one and still a virgin and the thought of getting into bed with Poppy Appleton caused his heart to thud, the blood to run hot in his veins, his mouth to dry up and his breeches between his thighs to become distinctly uncomfortable. He loved her and he wanted her, though he allowed none of this to show, which was just as well for it would have frightened her badly. He might have been asking her to put up a dozen eggs or half a pound of butter, he was so impassive, and it was perhaps this which persuaded Poppy to tell him she would marry him right gladly. It was all so unreal. At the back of her mind shone a small light of thankfulness that as Richard's wife she no longer need fear Dominic Cooper. She had not seen him since before Christmas, for even he, probably at his father's insistence, no longer plagued his friend Johnny Goodall to join the hunt. Now, the game he had played with her was over.

Eliza died a week later, her face serene, her eyes, for she could no longer speak, telling Poppy, with no conception of the disaster she was creating, that she was happy to leave her and Richard in one another's care. Tom would be sorrowful for a while and her sons would grieve a little but being young and active they would take up their lives again. And watching over them all, secure herself, would be Poppy Appleton. Poppy Goodall in the spring.

There were many at the graveside, folk from St John's Market, customers who had been honestly dealt with by the dead woman. Men and women from the farming community, some of whom had cause to thank Tom Goodall's wife for a kindness. Mourners crowding in and outside the little church, spilling over into the pale sunshine. There were crocus underfoot, pools of white and yellow and purple, and her grave made a bleak hole in the midst of them.

Poppy held Richard's hand, her head drooping tiredly against his shoulder and if she saw Dominic Cooper standing respectfully with his parents it made no impression on her. She was too dazed, too crushed, exhausted and dragged down with sorrow to notice anyone, wanting only to have this done with and go home. She had said goodbye to Eliza in that last moment of her life, kneeling with Tom and Richard and Johnny at her bedside, her future as Richard's wife assuring her of her place there. This was merely a formality, a rite demanded by society, a respectful farewell to a woman they had all known.

Poppy's grieving would be done in private.

17

If the community thought it unseemly that Richard Goodall should marry his mother's dairymaid – and that alone gave cause for talk – the speed with which he did it, so soon after his mother's death, scandalised them all.

It was a bare eight weeks later that they watched the lovely young bride step numbly, just as though she were not awfully sure where she was, or so it seemed to them, from beneath the porch which had so recently sheltered her mother-in-law's coffin. Their faces were sharp, for hadn't the sly minx done well for herself? Oh, aye, pretty enough as all could see and demure as a dove on her husband's arm but what went on in that clever head of hers they wouldn't like to guess. They had been shocked and disapproving when Eliza Goodall had raised her up years ago to be what they could only call a daughter of the house, but now, with Eliza gone and Eliza's son as her husband, she was mistress of Long Reach Farm and, if what they heard rumoured was true, the inheritor of a tidy sum of money left her in Eliza's will.

Poppy had worn black during the eight weeks since Eliza's death but now, on her wedding day, she was dressed in a simple gown of soft pearl grey challis, which was a fine twilled mixture of silk and wool. She had purchased it with her own money, the money which, astonishingly, Eliza had bequeathed to her, not only the money astonishing her, but the amount of it! The bodice was plain, buttoned high to her throat, the skirt following the slender lines of her body to her hips where it fell into ruffled frills, each one edged with a band of narrow white broderie anglaise and draped into a small bustle at the back. Her bonnet of pale grey silk to match her gown had rows of white fluted broderie anglais beneath the brim, enfolding her unnaturally calm face like a bright flower in a bouquet. She carried nothing in her grey-gloved hand but one single, unopened, white rosebud, said to be an offering from her young husband, a romantic gesture that surprised them all. She was elegantly and yet simply dressed, plain enough to please Eliza, for everything that Poppy did in those weeks after her death was done to please Eliza.

As though she had been born to it, brought up for her sixteen years for no other purpose, she took over Eliza's place, running the house and presiding at the head of the table next to her future father-in-law, acting with youthful dignity, and the servants, even May, knowing of her forthcoming marriage to their master's son, had no choice but to accept it. For many months while Eliza had been ill, Poppy had virtually had charge of the housekeeping and its accounts, and of them. Of the dairy and the market stall and they had become used to her, to taking orders from her which, they believed, came from their real mistress. To them Mrs Goodall was still in charge even if she was confined to her bed and Poppy Appleton was merely the carrier of orders and the one who supervised their completion, or so they told themselves, and each other.

It was different now and that first evening on the day of Mrs Goodall's funeral after the departure of the mourners, who had fortified themselves with Eliza's wine and Cook's rich fruit cake, one and all had been taken aback when Mr Goodall said to her, "You must sit here by me now, my lass," indicating the chair which for the past twenty-five years had been occupied by no one but his wife.

Poppy, still wading through the black shadows of her grief, her mind fixed numbly on her great loss, not knowing in which direction to go since, without Eliza, they all seemed dark and mysterious, did as she was told. If she was aware of the wide eyes and open mouths of those at the other end of the table it made no impression on her. If there were nudges and whispers they passed her by, and when Richard, who had been so kind and attentive to her during the last few days, took her hand in his and in plain view of them all folded it in the crook of his arm as he led her to the chair, she was as flummoxed as they. In the back of her sorrowing mind she dimly remembered Eliza's plea to her to look after her family, and even, though it didn't seem quite real, Richard's proposal of marriage. He had kissed her on the lips then, a gentle kiss which touched her not at all but somehow it added up to the astonishing fact that, as soon as he thought it fitting, Tom Goodall meant his son to take her to wife.

"You all right, my lass?" Tom asked her gruffly, his face stern as he looked along the table as though to say she'd better be, at least as far as *they* were concerned, or he'd know the reason why.

"Yes, sir." Her voice was steady and Richard squeezed the hand he still held.

"There's no need to call me 'sir', lass, not now. If you're to be wife to my son, and you are" – again casting a warning eye along the table – "then you must call me Father, as the lads do."

A small hiss escaped from the group of servants – was it disbelief, outrage or just amazement? – but it did not alter the truth of what their master had said. What *they* thought was of no consequence. On the whole they liked Poppy, indeed most of them were fond of her. She had proved her worth, to them and to her mistress. She had never flaunted her position in the mistress's affections and they could not fault her who had climbed from such depths to such heights. It was just that it would take a bit of getting used to, to be ordered about by a lass who had once been no more than a skivvy. To have as their new mistress a starveling waif from Primrose Bank. Were they still to call her Poppy, for instance, or, when she married the master's son, as it was obvious she would, were they to address her as Mrs Goodall? And if so would that include Marigold who, though a scullery maid, was still her own sister? It was a right facer, as Aggie was to say to Clara later and Cook was inclined to agree, but for the moment she held her tongue, telling the others sharply to do the same.

Strangely it was Poppy's own grief and the fierceness with which she missed Eliza Goodall that got her through those weeks preceding the wedding. She existed in a shadowed world of pain which noticed nothing outside that pain, which was concerned with nothing but the filling of her day and the duties that were hers. She rose at the same time each morning when the cocks crowing told her it was time, washed and tidied herself to the standard Eliza had demanded and went downstairs.

"Good morning, Cook," she would say. "Good morning, everyone. Have you slept well?" just as Eliza had always done.

Then they had answered, "Good morning, Mrs Goodall.

Yes, thank you, ma'am," bobbing a curtsey and a smile in their mistress's direction.

They still answered, but stiffly. "Good morning. Yes, thank you," but it was noticeable, if not to Poppy who noticed nothing much, that they gave her no title.

Not until Cook, who was a practical woman, took a hand. Cook was different to the rest of them. Cook was her own woman and would stand no nonsense from anyone, not even Poppy Appleton who must not be allowed to get above herself. A sensible way of addressing her must be found, one all the servants could get their tongues round. Cook accepted that Poppy was to be her new mistress and was perfectly sure that when everything settled down and some time had passed it would all work out sensibly. It would take a bit of doing being told what to do by a sixteen-year-old who had until recently been at *her* beck and call but she and the rest of them would manage it somehow. Cook had been at Long Reach Farm for twenty years and at the age of fifty-five didn't fancy looking for a new position just to avoid calling Poppy Appleton "mistress". At the same time, when the lass became Master Richard's wife she'd be damned if she was going to call her Mrs Goodall. Mrs Goodall was dead and buried. Her mistress was gone and if she was to work amicably beneath this lass a compromise must be reached. This was Cook's domain. This kitchen. In it she performed the job she was hired for and which she knew she did well. She was cook here, in charge of the kitchen staff and the future Mrs Goodall must be made to recognise it. In return Cook had no objection to Poppy continuing to consult with her, if she felt so inclined, on menus and accounts, on what needed doing in the house and when, and in exchange she was prepared to recognise Poppy's status, to accept her as mistress and to give her a title that the others would follow. What Cook did would influence the rest.

Having decided on a course that she felt they could all manage she began it on the day of the wedding. As Master Richard brought his bride over the threshold of the front door of the farmhouse, carrying her high against his chest in a most romantic way, Cook, who had walked back from the church with the other servants ahead of the wedding party, was there in the hallway to meet them.

"Welcome home, Mrs Poppy," she cried, ready to shed an enjoyable tear, for she did love a wedding and she was fond of the lass. "And you too, *Mister* Richard," elevating them both at the same time from the status they had known before they set out across the fields to the church an hour ago.

It was then, as Richard put her down on the polished wooden floorboards of the hallway, as her pa and Elly with Jinny and Herbert and Eustace, as Mr Goodall and Master Johnny crowded at her back followed by the wedding guests, and the servants hovered in their Sunday best in front of her, that the merciful veil of shocked sorrow began to lift from Poppy's mind.

The spring sunshine fell in a pale golden beam from the open front door along the hall, touching the whitewashed walls to a warm primrose glow and bringing the shining floor to an even deeper gloss. An enormous copper urn stood in the corner filled with a profusion of wild cherry branches, the delicate white of the blossom hanging thickly in green, leafy clusters along each branch. Wild daffodils from the orchard, picked only that morning by Jinny, Nelly and Bess, were a vivid yellow in the delicate cut-glass vases which had been Eliza Goodall's but which now belonged to Richard Goodall's young wife. It was all so lovely, a welcoming loveliness which smelled of home, a familiar smell which was of beeswax polish, lavender, fresh baking from the kitchen, clean and fresh and calling back to Poppy's memory the woman who had created it all years ago, a creation that was carried on though she was no longer there to see it.

The ice in her veins began to thicken and she had the feeling she would never be able to move again.

"Come through then, come through," Tom Goodall was urging his guests, frowning slightly when he saw that one of them was that damned pup from Coopers Edge. How the devil had he got himself an invite? he asked himself, knowing full well the answer, since Johnny was putty in his hands, wondering at the same time why Dominic Cooper should want to witness a farmer's son wed a dairymaid. He was smiling that cat's smile of his and bowing his head in the direction of the excited servants, looking no end a dandy in his well-cut, superbly tailored morning coat and waistcoat of the same colour and material, as was the current fashion. His necktie was white and his gloves were lavender, his trousers tapered and tight to his well-shaped leg, his button boots immaculately polished. He carried a top hat, not quite as tall as the "chimney pot" favoured at the beginning of the decade, and quite outshone them all, even the bridegroom.

The dining table groaned with the weight of Cook's ribs of lamb, platters of tongue, roast fowl, veal and ham pies and cuts of lobster come fresh from the market that day. There was charlotte russe and savoy cake and in the centre the magnificence of the bride cake, all of which Poppy had helped to prepare, the reason for it all, despite Cook's and the other servants' talk of a wedding, of Master Richard, of new dresses and bonnets, meaning nothing to her for she was buried by a weight on her spirit that would not lift.

Now she viewed it all with considerable amazement as though she had stumbled on some private party, some feast which was to take place and to which she did not remember being invited.

"Come along, Poppy, my dear," Mr Goodall encouraged her, "you must sit at the head of the table and your husband beside you."

There was general laughter as Poppy hung back in the doorway, since it was only natural for a bride to be shyly overcome by her new status, her new family and her new husband, especially a girl who, some six years ago, had been no more than a farm labourer's daughter from Primrose Bank. Cook did hope there would be none of the bawdy country customs that sometimes accompanied weddings of this sort, like the lighting of the happy couple to bed and the old tradition of throwing a stocking over the bed as the young couple sat side by side in it. Poppy, who was a private sort of a person, would be appalled, and so too would Mister Richard since he was a man who did not care for show. He was embarrassed enough now just leading his reluctant bride to the table.

Poppy sat down where she was put, her face a pale mask of incomprehension. Mr Goodall was making such a fuss of her, handing her this and that, to tempt her appetite, he said, an expression on his face that seemed to hint at something where strength might be needed. He piled her plate with veal and ham pie and a slice of tongue, urging her to eat up and enjoy herself. Richard would keep holding her hand and several times, under the table, she felt him grip her in a most familiar way just above her knee.

She became aware that on the opposite side of the table Dominic Cooper sat between Jinny, who as her stepsister was a guest, and Edith Broadbent, the daughter of a farmer whose land lay just south of Tuebrook. Poppy wondered dazedly how the captain's son came to be there. He was charming them both, Jinny and Edith, dividing his time equally between the plumply pretty but tongue-tied Jinny and the equally plump but voluble Edith who was so overcome by his attentions she couldn't stop talking. He looked so out of place in this room full of well-fed country folk, yeoman farmers and their families, Tom Goodall's servants and Poppy's lot from Primrose Bank, she could see that several guests were, like herself, asking one another what he was doing here.

The afternoon wore on and the company grew more boisterous. The food was stolidly got through, for these were, on the whole, country folk, strong and hearty and they had appetites to match. The savoury dishes disappeared like snow in the sun, washed down with ale, cider and the last of Eliza's cowslip wine. The charlotte russe and the rest of the desserts followed the main course and the heat and clamour increased. Most of the men and women who worked on the farm were there, those who were not needed in the care of Tom's animals, the lowliest of them seated in the kitchen where howls of mirth and talk in the broad vowels of the North Countryman grew in volume with every pint that went down each throat. Evan and Nelly had gone off to see to the milking and she'd have given ten years of her life to have gone with them. As Evan explained, glad to be out of it, "Cows didn't know t'was a wedding, look you."

They laughed and called to one another across the room and Herbert, not used to such rich fare nor the ale he had consumed, was sick out of the window on to Poppy's recently planted spring bulbs. Reuben, as father of the bride, was pressed to make a toast but his sensible wife, knowing the state of him when he had drink taken, declined on his behalf.

The bride and groom were prodded to their feet to cut

the cake and Tom, well in his cups by now and having no sensible wife to deter him, made a long, meandering, maudlin speech in which his Eliza's name was repeated again and again and Poppy could feel the dam waiting to burst inside her.

Cook's face was grim. This sort of thing should never have happened, *would* never have happened in Eliza Goodall's day. This rowdy clamour, this deafening hullabaloo would never have got to such dramatic proportions had she been present. It was totally out of place in her old mistress's gracious home. A real lady Mrs Goodall had been and the white-faced, glitter-eyed girl who kept drinking the mistress's cowslip wine as though it were water was no replacement for her. She'd done right well in the past eight weeks, quiet and dignified in her grief but coping with it, but now she looked as though she had no idea what was going on and if she did had no idea how to deal with it, or even how it had come about, poor lass. The festivities were going on too long and needed ending and the new Mrs Goodall had obviously no idea how to bring it about. And her new father-in-law was no help, neither. They'd have it dark soon and the men who were drinking in earnest, many of them come from as far away as Walton-on-the-Hill, West Derby and Everton, would have to be carried home if someone didn't bring it to an end.

The solution came from an unexpected quarter.

"I think it's about time that we gentlemen claimed a kiss from the new bride as is our right," a smooth and cultured voice declared, its clear, upper-crust tones cutting through the commotion like a hot knife through butter and, as he intended, bringing the whole company to total silence. "It is the custom, I believe, and if I may" – or even if I may not, his arrogant expression told them – "I shall be the first. Come along, Richard, let's have no argument. Stand aside and let your wife step forward."

The silence continued, a deadening silence which hurt the ears, even those who were too drunk to stand up remaining mute as the full implication of what the squire's lad had just proposed filtered into their somewhat befuddled minds. Kiss the bride! Kiss that pretty little lass with the enormous eyes and the luscious poppy red mouth which stood out in her pale face as though it had been stung by bees. Into their drink-excited, male minds crept the indelicate notion that, later on, there'd be a deal more done to her than kissing, but there was no harm in keeping up the old customs, of which this was one. Though she was small and a bit on the thin side the sight of her fear and dread seemed to excite them and there was not one there, with the exception of those who were related to her in one way or another, who would have argued if asked to change places with the bridegroom when darkness fell.

The quiet flowed on and they all turned to look at Dominic Cooper as he slowly stood up. Tom Goodall, who had attended a country wedding or two in his time and knew what sort of thing went on, despite his inebriated state looked uncertain, perhaps the gradually fading image of the lady who had been his wife touching a raw nerve. Kiss the bride! Kiss the silent, curiously pleading little thing who was now his son's wife and who was cowering like a cornered doe against his shoulder. Treat her to the coarse and humiliating experience of being handed about among the red-faced, loose-lipped yokels, his own farm hands among them, who, though they were at heart good fellows, had not the sense nor the sensibility to be satisfied with the chaste peck on the cheek that was called for. And the expression on Dominic Cooper's face was very strange. Even

Tom, tipsy as he was, could see that. There was a glitter in his thickly lashed eyes and a curious twist to his mouth. Tom didn't like it and he meant to say so but before he could get to his feet to put an end to the good-natured shoving and guffaws which were beginning to erupt as men jostled for their turn, Tom's son, the new bridegroom, stood up. His hands rested on his wife's shoulders. His own face was pale, whether with nerves, or anger, none of the company could tell, but he looked directly at Dominic Cooper as he spoke.

"That custom does not find favour with me, Cooper, and I'm sure my . . . my wife" – looking down at her as he attempted to lighten the atmosphere which was somewhat charged – "would not care to be the centre of such attention. She is the mistress of this house now and it would not seem proper to me for the mistress to be treated in such a way."

" 'Ear, 'ear," a deep voice from the doorway said and they all turned to look at Evan who had milked his cows, seen to their feed and settled them for the night just as though they were his children, returning to the wedding party unnoticed. Beside him was Nelly who looked bewildered.

Evan's face turned a furious scarlet under the scrutiny of Farmer Goodall's guests but he did not back down. "Little mistress do look spent to me, is it. This be a 'appy day but a sad 'un, too, see, rememberin' the lady who's not by 'ere."

"Well said," another voice chipped in, this time from Edith's father, Billy Broadbent who, a moment earlier, despite his wife's tight-lipped disapproval, had been about to shoulder aside those who got in his way as he made to kiss the bride. Evan had brought them all back to their usual down-to-earth good sense and kindliness and they were glad of it, for the new Mrs Goodall was a taking little thing and not meant for vulgar handling.

They resumed their seats good-naturedly, all except one.

"Oh, come now," his voice drawled, "what harm is there in it, I ask you? A kiss for good luck, they say and I'm sure Mr and Mrs Goodall would not refuse a good-luck token on their wedding day, would they? Come now, Goodall, hand her over."

It was very evident that, conscious of the importance of the day, Richard Goodall was doing his best to hold his anger in check. This was his wedding day, his and Poppy's, and he did not want it ruined by this silky-voiced bastard's stupid attempt to inject something into it that was unwholesome. There was nothing wrong in a bride allowing a gentleman to brush her cheek with his lips but this was nothing like that and Dominic Cooper's strange smile said so. He wanted to distress Poppy for some reason, to humiliate Richard, to force him into allowing a bit of horseplay, but for the life of him Richard couldn't understand why. Well, understand or not, he would not allow it and his jutting jawline said so.

"I don't think so, Cooper. In fact I think it is time that—"

"Good God, man, you're not going to throw us all out just because I suggested a custom that has been carried on for generations? Why, I am to be married myself in a few weeks' time and I can assure you that my bride will be more than willing to perform her duties in that respect. Perhaps we are a bit more . . ."

It was not certain what he had been about to say but the implication was that the level of polite society in which he moved would not make such a fuss over something as trifling as kissing the new bride. His lips lifted in a sneer and he turned to smile at the company behind him who had frozen into stunned amazement. Half of them hadn't the faintest notion what was going on, or what was being said, not with words but with some nasty underlying meaning that most could not make head nor tail of. Young Master Richard was hanging on to his temper by the skin of his teeth, they could tell that, and his new little bride looked as though she were ready to break her heart crying. And what the hell was wrong with the captain's lad, making all this rumpus and, what's more, unwilling to back down when the new husband, as was his right, was unprepared to allow his bride to be kissed by one and all? What the devil did it matter? Best get their hats and leave, the expressions on most faces said and one or two stood up as though they were ready to be off.

"I think you've said enough, Cooper," Tom Goodall's lad said through stiff lips and they all had to admit they admired his self-restraint since it was obvious he wanted nothing more than to smash his fist into Dominic Cooper's face. Then he made a mistake, one that was to cost him dear. "Your wife may be willing to share her favours with one and all but mine isn't and so . . ."

The roar from Dominic Cooper's mouth nearly lifted the roof and Cook was to say later she distinctly saw the tablecloth lift even with its burden of left-over food. The women all shrank back and the men shot to their feet but not quickly enough to stop Captain Adam Cooper's son as he launched himself in a rugby tackle for which he had been famous at his well-known public school. Across the table he flew. His arms reached out and wrapped themselves about Richard Goodall's unprepared body. His head took him full in the chest. He was still roaring, presumably as he did when he was on the rugby field and when he went down he took Tom Goodall's son with him. The windowsill on which Nelly had tastefully arranged a bowl of daffodils was at exactly the right height and exactly the right distance for Richard's head to hit it and even among all the uproar there was not one person in the room who did not hear the snap of something in the young bridegroom's body.

18

Tom Goodall insisted that the doctor came every day to poke and prod at his son's rigid body, unable to believe that with a bit of effort and goodwill, not only on the doctor's part, but his son's, they couldn't get him out of his bed and on his feet again. There were no broken bones, the doctor said after a careful examination of the young man's body, or at least none that he could see, though he did not voice this last to the young man's father.

"So why the hell can't he move a muscle then?" demanded Tom, badly frightened by his son's total inability to do more than roll his head restlessly on his pillow. "If there's nothing wrong with him what's he lying in that bed for, tell me that?"

"I didn't say there was nothing wrong with him, Mr Goodall. There must be or he would be able to get up and walk about but until we know what it is we cannot cure him."

"We? Who's this bloody 'we'?" Tom asked rudely.

"I think it might be a good idea to get in another doctor. A second opinion, if you like. There's a man in London who is spoken highly of."

"A man in London?" Tom was clearly astonished. "Why in hell's name should we need a man from London? You're the doctor. Surely you know what to do for the lad. He's broken something . . . somewhere . . ." Tom's voice trailed away uncertainly. "We all heard it go . . ." remembering that moment of horror at the wedding feast.

"So I believe, but, it's not just a case of putting on a splint as one would a broken arm or leg. Wherever it is, we must wait for it to heal. In the meanwhile keep up with the hot baths I recommended which will help to bring out any hidden bruising. Keep him warm and . . . well . . ."

What else was there to say or do? Fetched by the patient's frantic brother, the ride reminiscent of the one he had taken on the day the boys' mother had collapsed, the state of affairs at Long Reach Farm, normally a place of well-ordered calm, a peaceful haven of domesticity, had badly shocked him. The place was positively seething with people, like an overturned beehive into which all the bees are doing their best to re-enter. It was the poor fellow's wedding day, for heaven's sake and his guests seemed unable to tear themselves away from a drama that had them in a grip thrilling, and yet at the same time appalling. Their morbid interest did not allow them to leave in case they missed something, that much was obvious. There were groups of them sitting about the kitchen table, to the consternation of the Goodall servants, where the remains of a meal was still scattered. Their heads were shaking, their faces were grave.

"Poor lad, and on his wedding day too . . ."

"So young to be struck down . . ." as though he were already in his grave.

"Should be locked up . . ."

"Always was wild . . ."

These were some of the snatches of conversation the doctor overheard as he was ushered up the hall to the dining-room. Maidservants were weeping and some chap was repeating over and over again that if only he'd been quicker he could have prevented it.

"There's daft you are, Evan," a plump, elderly woman told him tartly. "You were nowhere near him, boyo, an' didn't the . . . the . . ." It was clear she was doing her best to call the attacker by some name acceptable in mixed company. "Didn't he move so fast we were all taken by surprise. There was nothing anyone could've done, see, so stop carryin' on about it, there's a good lad."

There were guests loitering in the yard and farm workers, by their dress, lingered at gates and along the track, gratified and yet sorry to be part of this disaster which had again struck at the Goodall family. Like a felled tree he had gone down, it was said, and like a felled tree he could not get up again. Though not as outgoing as his younger brother, who liked nothing better than a good laugh, and therefore was easy to warm to, Master Richard was well respected for his qualities of leadership, of fairness and a certain benevolence, despite his youth, to those in need. He was strict, hardworking, expecting others to be the same and could spot a malingerer at a hundred paces. But he treated his workers and his animals without harshness and would be a good master when the time came.

They had all witnessed the arrival of Captain Adam Cooper, for it had coincided with that of the constable Tom Goodall had sent Jacko for. He'd have that bastard arrested and in gaol within the hour. Tom had been shouting, doing his best to reach the white-faced, trembling figure of Captain Cooper's son who had been shut in Eliza's study for his own safety with two stalwarts to watch over him, one of whom was Tommy, the second cowman. Attempted murder were the anguished words on Tom's white lips but Captain Cooper and the constable between them had removed the assailant to safer quarters, presumably at Coopers Edge and who were they to try and stop him, despite Tom's ranting. The captain promised he would get to the bottom of it and Mr Goodall was to see to his son and let the captain deal with his.

What the bloody hell was there to get to bottom *of*? Tom had snarled. They had all witnessed it, looking round for confirmation from Billy Broadbent and the others who were inclined to look away, for some of them were tenant farmers on the captain's land. Tom would not give up. The bugger had gone for Richard and struck him in the most vicious way and there he was, Tom's lad, lying like a log on the dining-room floor with only his eyes moving, the rest of him as lifeless as a corpse.

Tom, nearly driven out of his mind by the sight of the supine and apparently paralysed figure of his elder boy who, let's face it, had always been his favourite, appeared not to notice the still, blank-faced figure of the bride who, since her husband had gone down beneath the savage attack of Dominic Cooper, had stood without moving beside the window. She had risen from her chair, the crash bringing her to her feet as it had the rest of the company, but while women shrieked and men shouted and Tom Goodall's hoarse voice entreated his son to get up, which he didn't, she stood to one side in a state of frozen shock. It was as though her numbed mind, which had been doing its best to get to grips with the fact that this was her wedding day; that she was no longer head dairymaid but *mistress* at Long Reach Farm; that all these people gawking at her were wondering how it had come about, that Dominic Cooper was causing trouble again and that for some reason the men were all intent on kissing the bride, which was *her*, not to mention what was to happen to her later upstairs, could not unravel itself and she felt herself to be in a nightmare. She could not take it in, any of it, and now, for some reason best known to himself, Dominic Cooper had lunged at Richard and knocked him down. None of it made sense. Richard had not got up though Mr Goodall begged him to in a most heartbreaking manner and for the next hour it was as though she existed in a vacuum, or underneath one of those glass domes from which she could see what was happening, hear what was happening but could not herself be reached.

No one seemed to notice her. Mr Goodall was ranting and raving and cursing. The doctor arrived and under his direction Richard was lifted by four of the men and removed from her sight. Captain Cooper came and went and she thought she saw a policeman hurrying Dominic Cooper out of the side door and into a small gig which drove away at speed.

Johnny Goodall, his usual high spirits knocked out of him by his friend's attack on his brother, the reason for which he could not fathom, hung about at the bottom of the stairs, waiting for someone to tell him what to do, where to go and indeed how to act on this happy day that had all gone so horribly wrong.

Reuben had taken his sons home since there was nothing any of them could do here and perhaps, Elly had whispered to him, if someone started a move the rest of the guests would follow.

Nelly and Bess, under Nelly's direction, had changed and taken themselves off to the dairy where Nelly meant to give the place, the already immaculate place, a damn good scrubbing for want of something better to do. Her training by Eliza Goodall always seemed to tell her what was the right thing, the best thing to do in times of trouble.

It was Elly who brought Poppy round. It was as though the wise and kindly woman her pa had married knew what was in store for the young mistress who had been that for no more than a few hours and was already preparing her for it.

"Poppy, come in't kitchen an' 'ave a cuppa tea, chuck. They've all gone at last, thank God. Ghouls, the lorra them, 'angin' round in case they missed owt. I told Cook ter get shut o' them an' though they didn't like it, they went so thi' an' me an' Cook'll 'ave a brew an' then tha' must go up an' see ter tha' 'usband."

All the time she was speaking Elly was guiding Poppy, still in her pretty wedding bonnet, out of the dining-room, along the darkening hallway and into the familiar comfort of the kitchen. She was placed in a chair by the fire and a cup of tea, hot, sweet and strong, was pressed into her hand. She was vaguely aware of several people, women, hovering on the fringes of her consciousness. One of them was weeping – was it their Marigold? – and Cook remonstrated with her to "give over now".

Hands patted Poppy's shoulder gently, for how was any lass to get over this, her wedding day that should have been so happy and had turned out so tragic. None of them knew what Master Richard's injuries were, of course, but he'd looked real badly, Aggie had reported, for she'd gone up to light the lamps as Evan and Tommy, Jacko and Master Johnny had carefully got him up the stairs and into the bed which, by rights, he should now be sharing with this little grey ghost who was his wife. No wonder she looked so mesmerised, poor little lass. It was enough to rattle the strongest and Poppy was still frail from the loss of their mistress to whom she'd been devoted.

"We'll start clearing the dining-room now," Cook told them all sharply. Cook was a firm believer in the maxim that there was no better remedy for taking the mind off trouble than hard work. Her attitude was, let this lot hang about dwelling on what had happened, discussing it with the freakish curiosity that prevails at times like these and they'd be wailing and loitering about for days, deliberating on the whys and wherefores which were nothing to do with them, especially that May who seemed entranced by the whole thing.

Reluctantly, for their lives were uneventfully tedious, each day exactly like the one before, though they were genuinely sorry for Master Richard and what had happened to him, Aggie, Clara, May, Jinny and Marigold prepared to begin the herculean task of clearing up the remains of the wedding feast. At once, still inclined to tremble but relieved to be about something she understood in this world of madness, the creating of calm and order and cleanliness out of chaos, Poppy stood up, took off her bonnet and reached for the big white apron which hung behind the kitchen door, watched by the thunderstruck servants, but Cook's voice, gentle and compassionate, put a stop to it.

"Nay, Poppy, there's no need for that." It seemed that her plan to address her new little mistress by the name of Mrs Poppy had been forsaken. Well, it wouldn't do, would it, not now. Not now when the lass was already in a state of confusion and shock.

Poppy looked at her, startled, then turned as Elly took her by the arm.

"Lass, tha' place is upstairs wi' tha' 'usband now. We'll see ter this. Tha' faither-in-law'll be waitin' on thi' an' the doctor'll want a word."

Poppy continued to look bewildered, though deep within her the real Poppy, the true, strong, practical Poppy who had been hiding from reality ever since Eliza's death, began to stir.

"See, put on tha' pinny if tha' want" – for perhaps dressed in her customary, everyday wear she would come more quickly to herself – "an' go an' ask after Master Richard. See if owt's needed."

"Yes . . . yes, I'll do that." Colour tinted her chalk-white face for the first time that day. It was as though the performing of a familiar task, one that had nothing to do with weddings and brides and the amazing behaviour of Dominic Cooper, had given her some inner strength and she moved slowly towards the kitchen door, watched by the pitying servants. She turned, her hand on the latch, perhaps for the last time as Poppy Appleton, as servant, as a young girl who, though she had achieved marvels in her young life, had always been directed by others.

"Will you . . . d'you think you might . . . come with me, Elly?" she asked, her face so young and vulnerable Cook was seen to turn abruptly away.

Elly shook her head. "Nay, my lass. Master Richard don't want me. He's tha' 'usband and'll need only thee."

They lived in hope at first, even Richard, who railed interminably at this unfamiliar inertia which he hoped to God would not take long to disappear. A few more days of this and he'd go out of his mind, he told his young wife. This bloody failure of his strong, young body to act as he wanted it to, commanded it to, was enough to try the patience of a bloody saint, he groaned, furious at the prospect of having to spend hour after hour in the enormous bed on which for weeks before the wedding his mind had been centred but with Poppy lying beside him in it. She did lie beside him every night ready to tend to his needs but in a narrow trundle bed which was pushed beneath his during the day. He was effectively stranded in their marriage bed with no movement beyond those which nature demanded of his body and even those were not within his power to control. He managed to smile, though, when she and Elly between them devised a kind of napkin, the sort babies wore. He would not allow her to put it on him, of course, nor change it when it was soiled, for she was his bride, an innocent girl who knew nothing of men's bodies. Then he had still had his young man's dreams of taking her to bed and changing that status. He still believed, as did Tom, otherwise he would have run mad, that this was a temporary thing. He did his best to be patient.

Poppy bore his frustrations with good humour, flying to do his slightest bidding as soon as they were made known to her. Her former insensibility had vanished, it seemed, dispersed by the necessity of caring for her injured husband, her home, her family, the servants and the hundred and one tasks that were hers as a farmer's wife. The day-to-day running of the household was performed by Cook, and by Elly who had given up her job at the Grimshaw Arms and came in each day to take a turn with Richard, but it all needed direction, leadership, and Poppy gave it, modelling herself on Eliza Goodall and the training she had received at her hands. It ran smoothly, as did the dairy and, though she had had misgivings at first on the wisdom of it, the market stall which Nelly, who was, after all, twenty-one now and had the experienced Jinny to guide her, took over. Nelly had been almost speechless with the wonder of it but in her green gooseberry eyes had been an expression which had told Poppy she would never forget this wonderful trust Poppy had put in her and she would not let her down.

But Poppy's main task was caring for her husband. He was not obviously ill but his need of her, not just for his bodily comfort, which she oversaw, but his peace of mind, the lifting and keeping up of his spirits, his hope, his belief that soon, when whatever it was that had gone wrong righted itself, and which could only be achieved by absolute bed rest, he would be up and about again. His father and this farm needed him, everyone knew that, for though Johnny worked as hard as the next man, he was not truly a farmer at heart. Tell him what to do and he did it but he did not see things that Richard saw. He could not recognise instinctively the need for planning, for method, as Richard did; for the round-the-year care and nourishment and maintenance, the seasonal rhythm that kept a farm well run and profitable. He knew these activities were required but his light-hearted attitude of "tomorrow will do, for what difference will a day make" did not hold out the promise of a good farmer. With his father or his brother beside him he fitted into a pair, a team, forming one half of it successfully, but on his own, a state Richard's accident had brought about, he was like a man with one arm, unbalanced, going round in circles and creating nothing but muddle.

Tom Goodall could not be everywhere at once. Spring-time is so busy in the farming world there were never enough hours of daylight to get through all the jobs that needed doing. Tom's fields were bound by dry-stone walls. Over the past year his cattle, reaching for some delicacy that lay on the far side, had knocked off the stones, breaking the walls down in places. These had to be repaired or the animals would wander into fields where crops were sown. The care and management of his bull calves, especially those intended for breeding. It was a full-time job for one man to see to these beasts, for they had to be well exercised and fed correctly so as not to become fat. Their coats were attended to, and their hooves trimmed, their yards kept swept and clean. The servicing of his cows at fifteen months was important so that they would calve at two years old. There should be constant attention to dairy yields, to the feeding and fattening of animals best suited to beef production. All this was just one part of Tom Goodall's farming day. Crops had to be planted, kale to be used as winter feed for his herd, early potatoes, oats and barley, his grassland controlled for grazing, the waterlogged fields drained, for Lancashire was a wet county.

With only one man to lead it all instead of two it became apparent, at least to Tom, Evan and Tommy who were the two mostly concerned with the herd, that unless the lad was up and about again soon, Tom was heading for disaster. Hardworking as Reuben and Ernie, Jem and Willie and the rest of the men and boys were they were only human and take your eyes off them for half an hour and they'd be leaning on their shovels or spades or hoes, lighting their pipes and having a good laugh and a chinwag. And Johnny Goodall likely to join them at it! Evan and Tommy and Jacko and others with responsible jobs on the farm, like the farrier and the wheelwright, were more conscientious but it all needed holding together and Tom Goodall, who was getting older, had relied on his elder son to do it.

"What in hell's name are you to do about my son, doctor?" he hissed every time the doctor called. "As far as I can see, bugger all."

"Patience, Mr Goodall, and rest. We can do no more at the moment."

"What the devil does that mean? He does nothing else but rest. You've been saying it for two . . . four . . . eight weeks now" – as summer took the place of spring – "and he's still lying there."

"Now, now, Mr Goodall, it is early days yet."

"Early days! Early bloody days! It's eight weeks and him still flat on his back. And what about those men from London you were on about?"

"I was under the impression you were not in favour of the idea, Mr Goodall. When I first mentioned it—"

"Never mind that. Fetch them up here, and never mind the cost, neither. I want my boy out of that bloody bed and on his feet as soon as may be. See to it."

The doctor saw to it, bringing from London two eminent-looking gentlemen in black frock coats and wearing full grey whiskers. They were suitably grave, stroking their beards and speaking in low voices to one another in the corner of the bedroom. They had stripped him naked and looked him over, turning and twisting him like a rag doll from which the stuffing had leaked. Though it did not appear to hurt him physically, Poppy, who was there against his will since her young husband did not want his new bride to see him as he was, knew he was mortally humiliated at being treated not only like some unfeeling figurine but like an imbecile who does not understand what is being said.

He cried for the first time that afternoon as she and Elly re-dressed his increasingly frail body. Tom had stumped off somewhere in despair, needing to be alone to come to terms with the truth that his strong, hardworking, conscientious, engaging son, whose young life had stretched out before him in a shining path of promise, might as well be dead.

When Elly had diplomatically followed him out of the bedroom Poppy lay down for the first time with her husband. She stretched her warm supple body alongside his lifeless one and drew his head to her breast, cradling him as his anguished tears soaked into her bodice. He wept hopelessly, helpless as a child in his mother's arms. He wept for his young manhood which, though they had not said as much in as many words, was gone for ever. He wept in defeat that though he was in Poppy's arms, his face to her breast as he had yearned for it to be, she would never be in his. He wept for the children he would never have, for the life he would never have as the dread canker of doubt that had begun to take a sly hold of his intelligent mind became a certainty.

"Hush, my darling, hush," she whispered to him, doing her best to soothe him, speaking softly, lovingly, holding him, kissing his drowning eyes, his dark, tumbled hair, even his lips with a passion she would never have shown him if he had been whole. Her body and mind were on fire with compassion, with a love of sorts, with a desperation that tried to show him that she would, to the end of her days, spend them making his life as whole, as sweet, as fulfilling as his paralysed body would allow. He would not be left to wallow in the empty life of a cripple. She had no idea how Tom was to manage without the strong, reliable son he had lost but that was his concern, not hers. She would hang on to Richard, the somewhat pompous, somewhat humourless but always kind and well-meaning man who was her husband, helping him to live as decent a life as she could. She would not let him slip into the pit of despondency which the doctors' solemn faces had told him was to be his fate. He had missed the spring, the froth of blossom on the wild cherry trees up by the spinney, the budding of the hawthorn trees which bordered the lane down to Prescot Road. The massed cranesbill which had been a shimmering lilac-blue carpet moving in the breeze across the unploughed top field, the lady's bedstraw, the palest yellow of delicate lace blending with the fresh green of the new grasses. He had missed the fully leaved burgeoning of the sycamore and beech, the yew and the ash and the oak which had stood in a lake of bluebells lapping in a magical wave from one side of the spinney to the other. The first cry of the cuckoo and the plaintive calling of the new calves for their mothers.

He had lost the enchantment of spring but he would not lose the summer, nor autumn, nor indeed anything that was in the power of Poppy Appleton, *Poppy Goodall*, to give him, she vowed. She held on to her injured husband with all the strength of her young arms. She would make his life worth living, she promised herself and if she could do a mischief to the man who had caused all this, she would.

Tom's despair deepened to hatred, black, corrosive, destroying hatred when it became clear that, whether through influence, money, or knowing who to call upon for favours that could be returned, Dominic Cooper was not to be charged with the attempted murder of Richard Goodall. The Chief Inspector of Police himself called to see Tom, presumably to make him aware of the fruitlessness of carrying on with his charge, saying that at present there was not enough evidence to bring the case to court. There had been a fight, certainly, young Mr Cooper had not denied it, but had Mr Goodall not caught his head most inopportunely on the windowsill, thereby breaking some bone in either his neck or his spine, or so the doctor had told them when interviewed, he would have got to his feet and returned Mr Cooper's blow. Mr Cooper had not meant to injure Mr Goodall. Not at all. There had been words exchanged, so he had heard. Mr Goodall had insulted Mr Cooper's then fiancée – yes, she was now his wife, had not Mr Goodall heard? – and Mr Cooper, being a man of honour, could not let it pass. A heated moment had led to tragedy but there had been no premeditation on Mr Cooper's part.

It was an indication of Tom's state of mind that at that moment as the inspector's voice droned on, he seemed to switch off the spirit, the strength, the essence of what had once been Tom Goodall and give up the fight. Not only for Richard, not only for justice, but his life's work on the farm.

As he had in the beginning they had expected him to roar his outrage and tell the inspector to bugger off. To inform them one and all that they hadn't heard the last of this. That he'd see Dominic Cooper behind bars if it was the last thing he did, no matter *who* his bloody father was, or who he knew in the Courts of Justice.

He did none of these things. In fact he did little of anything after that, sitting for hours on end on the wall that surrounded Eliza's garden, his back to his farmyard, watching the water spout merrily from the fish which stood on its tail in the centre of the pond. When one of the men approached to ask him what he should do about this or that; could he come and have a look at Clover's udder which Evan didn't like the look of; did he think it was time they started to lift the early potatoes planted in the spring; should they start ploughing the top field, he would turn and stare at whoever spoke as though he did not recognise him, even his son Johnny, then say absentmindedly, "Nay, do as you like, lad," or worse, "Ask our Richard, he'll know."

It was at this last that those who had worked the acres of Long Reach Farm under the experienced guidance of its owner, some of them since he himself had inherited it, began to know the truth. That along with his elder son their master had lost the will to go on.

At first it was thought he would recover. When he had accepted it, tackled the truth that Johnny was all he had now and the lad must be trained as Richard had been trained, he would pull himself together and do it. Stand up and shout for Evan, or Jacko, and go stumping off with his younger son beside him to see to his land, his cattle, his crops, his *life*. It had been a terrible six months, enough to knock any man sideways. He had seen his wife buried in February and though it had not been recognised during the years they were married, it began to dawn on them slowly that it was Eliza Goodall who had been the guiding force, the strong mind, the will, the brains and ingenuity behind Tom Goodall's success as a farmer. Without her to turn to and without his son to take over, to carry on, to keep Long Reach safe and growing in prosperity, he did not seem to be able to pick up again and grasp the nettle of life.

Now and again he would throw on his yard coat, the one Eliza had bought him to replace the one that had gone missing, and stride off as though he had no time to waste and must be about something of great importance and with the utmost speed. They would watch him go with great elation at first, thinking he had recovered from the double blow he had suffered, but when he got beyond the farmyard gate he would hesitate, stop and stare about him as though wondering where the hell he was, then plod slowly home, his face bewildered.

"Let me help you, Father," his son Johnny pleaded, doing his best to be his brother but they all knew, as he did, that he was no farmer and it seemed his father did too.

Tom would pat his hand vaguely. "Good lad, there's a good lad, but Richard will put it right. You go and . . . well . . ."

Had it not been for Evan and Tommy and Jacko who, through years of obeying Tom's orders, of imbibing his vast practical store of farming experience and knowledge, and who carried on their daily routines, which for the moment sufficed, the farm would have faltered to a stop for want of someone to guide them. No use asking the young feller-me-lad who, on top of his other shortcomings, was badly affected by his brother's accident. He had been allowed, foolishly it was now realised, to drift along at his brother's coat tails. He had always been made to put in a full day's work or Tom Goodall would have wanted to know the reason why, but Richard had been the inheritor, the one to whom one day it would all belong and Johnny had absorbed the fact from the first day he had been put to work. He was a country lad. He loved country pursuits and would have made a splendid son for a gentleman landowner, shooting and hunting in season, riding to hounds, fishing, seeing to his game with his gamekeeper beside him. He would not have the slightest notion, of course, how the estate was run, for his land agent would see to all that for him, but what a benign landlord he would have made.

He did his best for a while but soon, with no one to order his comings and goings it began to be noticed by the men working the fields at haymaking and where he himself should have been, by Evan who now had full responsibility for the welfare of Tom's herd, by Jacko who had the care and saddling of Master Johnny's roan, Chestnut, that the son of the house was wont to vanish for hours on end, God alone knew where, though they could guess, of course, and were appalled by it.

They shook their heads and sighed, wondering where it was all to lead. How was that little lass to manage it all? A crippled husband, a broken-hearted, mindless father-in-law, and a feckless son of the house who could neither cope with it nor even wanted to try.

What else was in store for them in this sad year?

Part III

19

The station platform was acrid with smoke, noisy with the hiss of steam, the shriek of engine whistles, the clattering of wheels and the excited voices of the purposefully moving swarm of passengers who were intent, or so it seemed, on travelling from one end of the country to the other, and in the shortest possible time. There were trains drawn up at every platform, each one with its rows of doors open to debouch or admit passengers. The platforms themselves were dense with travellers, with uniformed guards and porters, with gentlemen in top hats and bowlers and men in cloth caps; with fashionably dressed ladies in bustles, and on their heads toques trimmed with fur, some with a "three storeys and a basement" hat which made the wearer eight inches taller, and bonnets on which dead birds jostled for space with dried posies. Flower sellers in shawls, their voices drowned in the flood of noise, hopefully called their wares, pinched faces blank with boredom. Luggage was strewn everywhere, in tall, teetering monuments and small neat piles, cases and boxes being conveyed from one place to another by sweating porters.

The station clock stood at quarter to two.

The enormous young man with the bright red hair swung

lightly down from the railway carriage on platform one, then turned to reach back inside for his large leather Gladstone bag. It was of excellent quality and had the initials A.J.M. stencilled on the side. Lifting it down as easily as though it were a sack of feathers he placed it on the platform and then turned back to the first-class compartment.

"Wouldna it be a good idea if I was to fetch ye a porter, ma'am?" he was heard to say courteously as he emerged again, this time hefting two hatboxes followed by several pieces of hand luggage which included two fitted dressing cases and which were placed beside his own bag on the platform. Across the seething mass of people, having spied the amount and quality of the luggage being unloaded from the train, a sharp-eyed porter hurried towards them with a trolley.

"Aah, here's one now, ma'am," the young man continued, his handsome face breaking into a good-humoured smile which revealed the white perfection of his teeth.

"Will you inform him that there are trunks in the guard's van and we are to be met by Mr Hornby's own carriage. Mr Hornby is the chairman of the Dock Board, did I tell you, and we, my daughter and I, are to be his guests during the festivities. We shall, I'm sure, be presented to their Highnesses, did I mention?"

"Aye, ye did, ma'am, an' I ken ye'll have a fine time. I might even walk down to the docks myself to see the royal family." His smile deepened and his eyes, the glorious vivid blue of a cornflower, were clear and fathomless. He held out a large hand and the well-dressed lady who had spoken put hers in it, surprised at its warmth as he helped her down from the railway carriage. As he did so a stray beam of sunlight, which had managed to creep through the high, smoke-blackened roof windows of the station, touched his hair which he wore rather long and at once it was a blaze of gold and copper, of amber and tawny russet, a flame of glory that made his travelling companion gasp.

"Young man, you have the reddest hair I have ever seen," the astonished lady said, turning to the young woman who, in her turn, was being helped down from the carriage. "Don't you think so, Margaret?"

The young man smiled whimsically. "Aye, so they tell me but I cannae do a thing about it."

"Oh, please, it really is . . ." Suddenly she was overcome by her own lack of manners in speaking to this total stranger in such a familiar way. She began to fuss with her gloves, wondering what it was about this young man that had such an alarming effect on someone of her age who should know better and indeed on the rest of the female occupants of the carriage. Even the imperious lady of advanced years by the window had watched him openly and listened as though mesmerised by his every word.

Margaret cast down her eyes shyly and blushed. She was no more than fifteen or so, pretty in an insipid way and completely bowled over by the large and engaging young man with whom she and her mama had travelled down from Preston, and though it had been a relatively short journey she had fallen in love with him as totally as only the young can do. Come from Glasgow, he had told them in his soft and pleasing Scots brogue, travelling through Dumfries and Carlisle, Lancaster and Preston to Liverpool, a journey of over two hundred and fifty miles which he had set out upon the day before. They had been startled and somewhat reluctant, having seen the size of him, to join him in the first-class compartment at Preston but there were three of them and he had proved to be a perfect gentleman, obviously of sound breeding from an old Scottish family and such a help to them, a positive mine of information regarding the journey so that they could hardly bear to part with him at the end of it.

Again he held out his hand, this time to the third lady with whom they had shared the carriage, helping her gallantly with the steps, begging her to be careful, holding her handbag and the small dressing case which he had lifted down from the rack for her until she was safely on the platform.

When they were all assembled with their luggage, the porter, who had called another, fussing over which bag belonged to whom, the young man picked up his own bag and turned to them, bowing slightly. He was immaculately and expensively dressed in a double-breasted morning coat and narrow trousers to match in a mid-grey over which was slung a black Inverness cape. He wore it open. His collar was stiff with turned-down points and he sported a trim-drawn tie in a rich, ox-blood red. His buttoned boots were of patent leather with suede tops and had he not been so overpoweringly, so completely masculine might have been taken for a "masher", which was the fashionable term for a dandy.

"Well, ladies, it has been a pleasure to travel wi' ye." His eyes twinkled and his wide, tender mouth moved in another heartwarming smile and they all three felt their hearts beat faster. "I hope ye enjoy your stay in Liverpool and may I wish ye all a pleasant journey home. Good-day to ye."

He carried a top hat which he lifted in salute then turned and walked away from them with his bright head a foot higher than any other man's, his broad back straight and supple, his carriage graceful, his long stride carrying him towards the ticket collector and whatever it was that awaited him beyond the pillars of Lime Street Station. He exuded a masculine vitality, an enthusiasm, a drive which seemed to say he could hardly wait for whatever it was he was seeking to appear.

They all three sighed simultaneously then, as though conscious of how foolish they must appear, the two older ladies began to speak sharply to the porters as though to illustrate their total indifference, nay, even contempt for the male of the species. At the same time, though they would not have admitted it if put to the torture, they could not help remembering what a personable young man he had been and wondering what he was doing in the great sea port which was tomorrow to play host to His Royal Highness, the Prince of Wales, Her Royal Highness, the Princess of Wales and the three little princesses, Louise, Victoria and Maude.

"I think yer'd be a fool not ter go, chuck. Yer never go anywhere except ter't bank an' besides, it'd do yer the world o' good ter gerrout a bit."

"What d'you mean, I never go anywhere. I went to the market with Nelly only last week when Jinny wasn't well."

Poppy and Elly were sitting on the bench in a patch of sunlight by the kitchen door shelling peas, their backs resting on the sun-warmed wall. Hens moved carefully about their skirts hoping for scraps, picking their way here and there, muttering comfortably to one another and darting their heads to the ground as they spied something delectable.

"That's not whorr I mean an' well yer know it, my lass," Elly went on. "Oh, I know yer enjoyed it, seein' all yer old customers again burra proper day out'd put roses in yer cheeks."

Not that Poppy Goodall needed roses putting in her cheeks, Elly Appleton was inclined to think as she turned to her stepdaughter, admiring her sleek look of golden good health and the soft blooming maturity had given her. She had a glow about her, a shining look of innocence which was not surprising in the circumstances, of course, which drew all male eyes to her. And she had acquired a poise, a confidence which seemed to say that there was no problem too complex for her at least to try and resolve.

She had been not yet seventeen when it began but from the first she had been forced into the position where she was not only mistress but *master* of Long Reach Farm, for when the servants in the house and the men who worked the farm had finally come to the unhappy conclusion that there was no one else to turn to for the last say-so on any matter, they had begun to turn to her. She was a steady, sensible lass. Not that she knew anything about the care of cows beyond cleaning their udders at milking time, nor the planting and harvesting of crops beyond the weeding and stone-picking she had done as a child, but she could *read*, couldn't she, and Richard and Tom had shelves filled with books and manuals on farm management which she pored over for hours on end. She had been raised on a farm and the daily involvement with all living things, human, animal and plant, had been unknowingly absorbed by her, giving her a feeling for its tempo, its rhythm, a sense of familiarity with its production which helped her to understand its needs.

She was nineteen now and she'd put that practical common sense and feeling for the farm to good use over the last three years. Ask any of them how she'd done it and they could not have told you, but somehow, with an equal measure of hope, determination and, as Evan put it, almost in tears, sheer bloodymindedness and the refusal not to be beaten which she had shown since she was a nipper, she had kept it going, and *added* to it. The farmhouse under whose roof her young husband had managed to hold on to his sanity and where her father-in-law had found some kind of "other-worldly" peace. The dairy and the market stall which Nelly, despite her inability to read and write, and Jinny, who could do both, ran with a high degree of efficiency, and the farm, the land, the crops, the dairy herd, all in Evan and Tommy's capable experienced hands, of course, but under her sharp and intelligent supervision.

"Look what this farming manual has to say, Evan," she would enthuse, "and tell me it doesn't make sense. If we planted sugar beet in Sweetacre field which is well drained – it says here the ground has to be well drained – it should do well. Spread the farmyard manure, and we've plenty of that, before ploughing, it says, which should be deep, the ploughing, I mean, sow in mid-April, keep it well manured and hoe and hand trim it after twenty days when the shoots should be through. It should be lifted in September. Fifteen tons an acre . . ."

"But what's it for, lass? Farmer Goodall . . ."

"They extract the sugar from it, Evan, and the pulp after the sugar has been taken out can be used to feed the animals. We sell the sugar."

"But . . ."

"And then there are turnips and swedes and carrots which we could send to the market with the cabbages and potatoes."

"There's mop-headed you are, Poppy. Runnin' afore you can walk, an' what will Mr Goodall say to all this? 'Tis a dairy farm, see."

"And that's another thing. If we can produce an extra thousand gallons of milk, it says here" – shoving the book into Evan's bewildered face – "though it costs more to produce, the total profit will increase. And then there are pigs."

"Pigs! Now hold on, lass, tell me how we're to . . ."

"I'm not telling you, Evan. It tells us here. We've a hundred-and-seventy-five-acre dairy farm, right?"

"Aye." Reluctantly from the little Welshman.

"But might it not be practical to turn it into a mixed farm?"

"Eeh, master'd not like it."

They had just finished their midday dinner in the kitchen, the table crammed about with house servants, with Dilys who was helping in the dairy since there was a rush for shells, with Evan and Tommy and even Johnny Goodall who, it appeared, was today not off on one of his myterious errands, whatever they might be. They had partaken of Cook's vegetable and barley broth soaked up with her freshly baked bread, followed by mutton stew and dumplings, a deep apple pie and cheese from their own dairy. It was spring again and a busy time on the farm – when wasn't it? Cook was often to ask philosophically – and they had all worked hard, needing the good food which was stoked into them three times a day.

They had become somewhat used to their little mistress's enthusiastic approach on how to get the best out of this farm by now, but sometimes they were thunderstruck by the daring, the . . . well, you could only call it effrontery with which she interfered in the management of Tom Goodall's farm. She was, despite her headlong elevation to a position of authority due to her marriage and its consequences, a farm labourer's daughter and yet here she was changing this, that and the other and what was more, with Evan's steadying hand on her, making a success of it. Of course the farm had been in good shape when she was forced to take it over, which helped, but really, they were constantly amazed at how well she'd done.

At Evan's last remark they all turned to look at Tom Goodall who sat in the chimney corner peacefully puffing on his old pipe. He was clean, shaved, tidy and looked well, his ruddy face attesting to the days he spent working out of doors side by side with his own labourers. He was sensible for days on end, not the old Tom, of course, for he had gone with his son's paralysis, but moving about the farm and doing as he was bid by Evan or Tommy or Jacko, for he was good with the horses, even by Reuben who seemed to take him under his wing. But ask him to do more, ask him what he would advise should be done about such and such and his face would become blank, shuttered and he would tell them to "ask our Dick, he'll know," stumping off as though he were mortally offended.

One of the more distressing outcomes of the tragedy that had struck Long Reach Farm was that Poppy had been forced into setting up with the bank manager and Tom Goodall's solicitor the means whereby she was now in partial control of the financial management of the farm. There were wages to be paid, household bills, accounts with seed merchants and many others to be settled. Animals were sold along with the yield from the crops and the dairy produce and someone had to deal with it all. There had been a great coming and going of men in sober suits and solemn faces. Men who spoke to Tom, to Richard and even to Johnny Goodall who was, after all, the logical person to take it all over in place of his brother. They had been astonished, by his almost hysterical denial of any interest in the farm, his manner intimating that as long as he continued to receive a decent allowance commensurate with his position as a son of the house he was perfectly happy to work as . . . well, no more than a common labourer really and leave all that side to his sister-in-law.

There were restraints, naturally, on what monies the young Mrs Goodall could withdraw, but Mr Hilton and Mr Gibson agreed that she had turned out to be practical, thrifty and willing to be advised by their more experienced minds. Someone must have a hold of the purse strings and who else was there in the family but her?

Now, nearly three years after she and Richard were married, the farm was doing so well she had even persuaded Mr Hilton and Mr Gibson to give a raise in wages to the servants, in the house and on the land, for had it not been for them and their support of her during these three years none of it would have been possible. They were all tickled pink, agreeing among themselves what a marvel their little mistress had turned out to be and who'd have thought it nine years ago when Mrs Goodall had brought the pale little scrap with the over-large hat to work in the dairy. Scrawny she had been, all eyes and hair, illiterate and speechless and look how she'd turned out. A real beauty but with a head on her shoulders that could only be attributed to their old mistress whom they still missed.

Poppy realised that she was content. Mr Goodall had settled down to an untroubled old age, shuffling about the place with no apparent signs of distress or puzzlement over the inclination of his elder son to remain in his bed, or sit in the sturdy wooden chair the men carried him out in when the sun shone and the day was warm. The chair had straps to hold Richard securely at the chest and thighs and ankles and the old man was often to be found sitting beside him, conversing with him about everyday events he himself found interesting. Old Bessie had been delivered of her fourteenth calf that day, had Dick heard? A lovely little bull calf who had the look of a champion and when he felt like it perhaps Dick might care to walk over to the cowshed with him to see it. The kale was doing well and so was whatever was growing in Sweetacre field, referring to the sugar beet, though don't ask him what it was. Some new-fangled thing Evan had thought up, no doubt. Old Reuben was becoming a bore about those two sons of his who were, it seemed, training to be teachers, of all things. It was coming to something when the sons of an illiterate farm labourer could become teachers, didn't Dick think so and where would it all end, he asked his quiet son, sucking contentedly on his pipe.

Richard Goodall listened but had no answers. The whole sum and substance of him was concentrating on the moment when his wife would come out of the kitchen and smile at him and, though it was pleasant to feel the sun on his face and see the activity of the farm going on around him, he lived solely for, and through the young woman who kept him alive, and sane. She was his heart, beating in love. She was his soul, for the rest of him was dead. She was his eyes, seeing and describing life outside himself. She was, in all but body, *him* and only through her did he exist. He got through the days somehow, either in her care or Elly's, eating what they put in his mouth, answering quietly when asked a question, listening when Poppy read to him, his eyes avid on her expressive face, waiting for her to look up and smile at him.

But it was the nights he lived for. It was the nights that brought to him the nearest he was ever to know of normality between a man and his wife. She would take off her clothes for him, stripping them away one by one, acting out for him the fantasies and dreams in his head, moving about the room in the lamplight, her naked body smooth and slender, a lustrous shade of pale, polished honey, her lovely golden body which had been touched by no man's hand and never would while he lived. Her breasts were rich as cream tipped in rose, bouncing delightfully as she moved. She allowed him to look at her in poses which, in normal circumstances, he might himself have thought indecent but all he had were his eyes to make love to her with, his eyes and his mouth. He went to sleep with his lips at her breast, the taste of her nipple on his tongue and when he woke in the night the weight of her body against his, though he could not feel it, was the greatest joy he knew.

He took little interest in the farm, in any of the things she

spoke of, for it was not of his world. *She* was his world and
only in her did he find the will to live. What did he care
if they planted kale, sugar beet or bloody begonias in the
fields over which he had once tramped? What did he care
if Evan was beside himself with excitement at the prospect
of winning a prize at the County Fair with the new bullock?
What did he care if his feckless brother was cavorting about
the countryside and the city of Liverpool with the sons of
the privileged classes? No names were mentioned in his
hearing but it was of no interest to him in any case. If it
did not concern his wife it did not exist.

"Elly thinks I should go to town tomorrow – take Jinny
as a chaperone, did you ever hear the like? – and watch the
opening of the new North Docks."

He watched her as she sat before her mirror brushing
her hair, which had grown over the years to a curtain
of rippling silk that now reached her bare buttocks.
The mirror was of a size and was deliberately placed
so that he could see her from the bed from the parting
of her hair to the parting of her thighs and he sighed
contentedly. For the next few hours she was his. His mind
was concentrating on that fact and her words seemed to be
of no importance, merely an accompaniment to the rhythmic
lifting of her high, round breasts as she plied her brush. He
was mesmerised by her softness and roundness, the supple
grace of her back as, in the only way she could, she made
love to him.

"Oh," he said dreamily, "and would you like to?"

"Well, it's not often you get a chance to see a real live
prince and they say the princess is very beautiful."

"Not as beautiful as you, my darling."

She turned and smiled, careful to let him see the rosy
bobs of her nipples through the curtain of her hair since

she knew how it pleased him and she would do anything to please him.

"Well, I don't know about that, Richard, but, if you think . . . if you could spare me I would like to go and see their Royal Highnesses and the little princesses. There's to be a procession from Newsham Park, it said in the *Echo*, down through the city to Bootle then the royal party are to go aboard a boat and steam to the new dock. Oh, and there's to be a twenty-one-gun salute, our Herbert says."

"Does he indeed. It sounds a bit noisy to me."

"Mmm, that's what I thought but it should be splendid. The new dock is to be called Alexandra after the Princess of Wales. There'll be banners and flags, Venetian masts, streamers, bands and . . ."

Suddenly aware that she was becoming carried away with the exciting prospect of an outing on which her husband could not come she hesitated. "But I won't go if you'd rather I didn't. It wouldn't be the same without you," she went on loyally. "Oh, I wish . . ."

"Don't, sweetheart, for God's sake, don't. I'd rather you didn't go but that's only me being a selfish swine. I can't bear you out of my sight for an hour let alone a whole day but of course you must go and when you get back you can tell me all about it. Now come here and let me put my mouth where . . . just here. God, you're so beautiful . . . beautiful . . . and mine."

"Wear t'frock you was wed in, yer daft 'apporth, an' stop all this bletherin' about 'avin' nowt ter purron. It's never bin outer t'box since then an' could do wi' an airin'. Just like you!"

"Oh, Elly, d'you think it would be all right?" Just as though sacrilege might be committed by wearing the gown she had worn only once on the day she married Richard. It was true. It had been folded away in tissue paper with the pretty bonnet on that very night and had never seen the light of day since. She had been off the farm only on the occasions when she had visited the bank manager and the solicitor and then she had worn one of the dresses Eliza had thought suitable, those that had been made before she died, good quality and plain of style, though she had allowed Poppy to choose the colours she herself liked the best. One was the colour of heather which put the same tint in her clear, blue-grey eyes. Another of saffron yellow with a bonnet to match with silk crocuses scattered round the brim, and a deep plum trimmed with the palest grey which she had worn to the market last week with Jinny. It was not as though she could not afford to buy new since the staggering amount, over three thousand pounds, left her by Eliza, sat doing nothing but accruing interest in the account Mr Hilton had shown her on her last visit. It was her intention next time she went to town to collect the cash needed for household expenditure and wages to withdraw some of it, which Mr Hilton had assured her was very easy, and buy a present for everyone on the farm, even May who, though her tongue was still sharp as a knife, had mellowed somewhat over the years.

' 'Course it would, fer God's sake. Yer could tekk tram from old Swan, one o't lads could drive yer down there in't gig . . .''

"Oh, Elly . . ."

". . . an' pick yer up later."

"Oh, Elly . . ."

"Stop 'Oh, Ellyin'' me an' go an' put yer ruddy bonnet on. Our Jinny's goin' mad wi' excitement."

"What about Nelly and Bess?"

"They're excited an' all."

"I didn't mean that. I meant will they be able to manage without Jinny?"

"Give over, lass. Dilys'll give 'em a 'and if they need it an' I'll watch over Master Richard."

"Oh, Elly, I don't like leaving him. Not for something as . . . as . . . frivolous as this. It's different when it's the bank."

"Eeh, if yer don't gerron yer'll feel back o'me 'and. Talk about fuss! 'E'll be as right as rain. You 'eard 'im. Now go an' give 'im a kiss an' be off with yer."

They were all aware of the devotion which the little mistress lavished on her damaged young husband. It was a poor do that a lovely young woman should be forced to live the life of a nun, for they were all sadly aware that he could not be a true man to her even if she did share his bed. They could not praise enough the way she looked after him, patient as a mother with a sick, sometimes fractious child, so they waved her off, quite overcome by the expression of unbelieving wonderment on her face, as though she herself were a child off to enjoy a treat she had never thought to experience.

A dashing squadron of the 18th Hussars was acting as escort to the royal family, a dazzling procession of colour and glitter and music beneath triumphal arches all the way down from Newsham Park and along Castle Street to the docks. Everyone had a Union Jack so that the day seemed to be a blur of moving red, white and blue. Their Royal Highnesses bowed and nodded graciously from their open carriage and the little princesses waved their gloved hands to the delighted, exhilarated crowd. On arriving at the landing stage the illustrious guests were ushered on board the *Claughton* with much bowing and scraping by Mr T.D. Hornby, JP, who was the chairman of the Dock Board.

They saw it all, Poppy and Jinny. They had managed to squirm their way along Langton Street and right down the waterfront, smiling and fluttering their eyelashes in the most outrageous fashion at every gentleman who stood in their way. How could they be resisted, two pretty, rosy-faced girls in their stylish dresses and demure bonnets and the general cry of "Let these two young ladies through now" was treated with great good humour by the dense crowd. Over a million of them, it was reported in the newspapers at the end of the day. The Blue Coat boys from the famous school of that name, the *Indefatigable* boys, the Royal Naval Reserve who stood to attention along the route, the vast crowd which cheered itself hoarse when the rather pop-eyed, bearded and portly figure of their dear queen's son turned and raised his hat to them in acknowledgement.

There was a sudden hush as His Royal Highness moved a handle ingeniously connected to some hydraulic mechanism and magically the dock gates opened. The royal ship steamed through them and the Langton Dock was opened. Two adjoining docks were honoured with the same treatment, this time by the severing of a silken cord by the Princess of Wales and a bottle of champagne was broken over the bows of the *Claughton*. The three branch docks were collectively named Alexandra and the *Claughton* steamed away with its party to partake of luncheon in the tastefully decorated North Dock sheds. There was to be a march past by the Volunteers later with massed bands. The weather was glorious and this being a public holiday Liverpool had turned out in force and was bent on enjoying it.

She and Jinny waited with hundreds of others to cross Regent Road with the intention of making their way to the Town Hall where the royal party was to appear on the balcony. They wanted to get a better look at Her Royal

Highness's outfit, they told one another, for the maids at home would be bound to ask and would be highly indignant if a full description was not forthcoming.

The road was busy, crammed with ladies and gentlemen making their way back to their carriages, mingling with the working classes who, having no carriages, were intent on fighting their way on to a horse-drawn tram at the Pier Head. They had all come to see their future king and queen and their mood was cheerful as they jostled one another. For a moment, as the passage of people thickened, Poppy and Jinny were stranded on the kerb.

It was the sunlight that picked him out, for even with his considerable height it is doubtful she would have seen him among the massed parasols which bobbed gracefully about him. His head stuck out above them and his hair was like a beacon, a torch of flame illuminating the space about it with a brilliant halo. He was at least a foot taller than anyone in the crowd and from across the busy road his eyes met hers. The intense blue shock of them flowed through her entire body and for them both, time stood still. They looked at one another, encapsulated in the moment, their faces serious and wondering. It was as though they were caught in a hollow void, a timelessness which stretched on for ever and ever though it could have been no more than seconds. She was conscious of sound, a man shouting to another to "mind your bloody feet", of the squeals of gulls cutting sharply across the commotion, of a mongrel snapping at a man's ankles in fear of being trampled on, of a bird alighting mistakenly on a parasol and darting off in fear, of Jinny's hand on her arm doing her best to draw her across the road towards Conn MacConnell. And of Conn MacConnell on to whose face had come an expression of incredulous joy which she knew matched her own.

20

Poor Jinny! She didn't understand what was happening to her stepsister, nor to the enormous young gentleman who, short of actually holding her in his arms, seemed to be embracing her. He was the most impressive young man Jinny had ever come across, not only in his dress, which was quite splendid and obviously very expensive, but in his physical appearance. He was tall, well over six feet, broad in proportion, and striking of feature, with deep-set eyes so blue they were impossible to describe. Jinny's mouth fell open and stayed that way as the chap, the gloriously handsome chap who looked as though he would like nothing better than to sweep Poppy into his arms, just kept repeating, "Poppy . . . Poppy . . . Poppy . . ." over and over again.

Poppy was dazed with the suddenness of it, the delight of it, the happiness that had swept through her at the sight of this man whose memory had long been buried and barely thought of during the past three years. He had gone from her as surely as Eliza, the remembered sweetness and bravery and humour of him nothing at all to do with her life, she had decided, even before she married Richard.

Now it rose to the surface of her like a balloon that has been held down by an anchor, leaping up to the surface and escaping before she had time to get a grip on it and hide it away again. He was experiencing the same emotions as she was, she could see it, his eyes a blaze of blue in his face, his wide, sweet mouth trembling on an uncertain smile, almost as though he could weep with joy.

"Poppy, I didna think I'd find ye so soon. I meant to look, ye ken that fine, but so soon." His strong hands held her arms just above the elbow, bringing her face up to his so that her toes barely touched the ground and all about passers-by had begun to notice, bumping into one another as they stared in slack-jawed amazement. His mouth was only inches from her own and she could feel herself beginning to respond to the warmth of him, to the strength of him, conscious that if he did not put her down, if she did not get away from him, the sheer masculinity and wonder of him, she would kiss him, allow him to kiss her and with Jinny standing in shocked amazement at her elbow.

He saw it in her eyes, in the paleness of her face which had been rosy with excitement, in her imploring expression and reluctantly he set her carefully down, removing his hands, although it appeared he didn't know what to do with them when he had for they fluttered about her longingly. She stepped back, her gloved hand to her bonnet which had become dislodged, then to her throat which spoke of her shock.

"Conn," she managed to say, conscious of Jinny, whose mouth was still open but in whose eyes was the same bemused admiration the big Scot seemed to arouse in all females.

Poppy cleared her throat and blinked furiously as though her eyes could scarcely believe what they were seeing, which they didn't, and he studied her intently as if he were determined not to miss any change in her expression, or any word she was to say to him.

An enormous brewer's dray, held up by the royal procession and anxious to make up for lost time, rumbled by, scattering the surging crowd that had been in the road on to the pavement, a wave of them jostling against Conn but he stood firm. The dray, which was heavily laden with barrels, was pulled by four massive, broad-backed Shire horses, beautifully decorated for the occasion in red, white and blue, and their hooves struck sparks off the cobbles. The clatter rang in Poppy's ears.

She was beginning to regain her equilibrium somewhat, though her heart still banged in her breast and a pulse beat frantically in the hollow of her throat. She could see one doing the same in Conn's, just beneath his jaw which he had clenched tight as though afraid of what he might say, for he too had become aware that Poppy was not alone.

"This is . . . a surprise," he managed to mumble at last, more for Jinny's benefit than anything. His eyes were clamped on Poppy's face and had you asked him to describe her companion he could not have done so. When he and Poppy had last met they had been children, at least she was and he scarcely more, but a bond had been mysteriously forged between them which, now that they had met again, appeared to have remained intact. She had aroused something special in him then and though he could not admit to pining for her, or even giving her much thought over the years, he knew now it still rested in him. He had spoken the truth when he had said he meant to look for her but it had, until now, been no more than to thank her for giving him his life all those years ago, to see how she had got on at Primrose Farm and what had happened to Douglas who had been his friend. But the sight of her, grown so lovely, so poised, had shattered his casual intentions and to his own amazement he could not seem to get a hold of his emotions, his need to have her on her own where he could unburden himself of the past seven years or so, of his reason for coming back to Liverpool, which he had to admit had nothing to do with her. To share with her the aspects of his own life and to learn about hers. She had obviously done well. She was exquisitely dressed, a lady, it seemed, with what looked like a lady's maid to accompany her, so what had happened to Poppy Appleton since that dark night he had waved goodbye to her wearing the coat she had stolen for him?

They still continued to stare incredulously at one another, their little group seriously impeding the progress of the crowds who were making their way up to the Town Hall where a good view of the proceedings would be at a premium and not until one burly chap told them truculently to "get outer't bloody way", did they come to their senses.

He regained his first. "Tea," he said jerkily. "A cup of tea would be nice. Let's get out of this crowd and find a café. Perhaps ye'll know of one nearby?"

"Tea . . ." Poppy dragged her gaze from his and looked about her as though a pot of such a thing might be found conveniently to hand, while Jinny watched fascinated the expressions which chased one another across the big chap's face. She was not awfully sure what some of them were since Jinny knew little about men but he certainly seemed to be very confused. She was still waiting for Poppy to tell her who the dickens he was. They obviously knew one another from somewhere, but where? As far as Jinny knew Poppy had been at Long Reach Farm for ever and no mention had ever been made of a tall, red-haired gentleman with an accent she decided was not from around here.

Poppy gazed distractedly at Jinny, her blanched face

harassed, then, as though remembering the manners Eliza had instilled in her, turned back to the big chap, her eyes deep and troubled with something Jinny could not fathom.

"Oh, Conn, this is Jinny. Jinny . . . er . . . Jinny . . ." She couldn't for the life of her remember what Jinny's surname was but it didn't matter. "Jinny's dairymaid at Long Reach now that I'm . . ." She faltered to a stop, for how to tell him what she did now?

"Long Reach?" A strange stillness came over Conn and he bent his head questioningly to Poppy.

"Yes, the farm, you know, where . . ."

"Long Reach! *Long Reach?*" He seemed dazed by something and both women stared at him uncomprehendingly. The crowd still continued to surge round and past them, those in it irritated by this obstacle in their progress, but taking one look at the width of the shoulders and the height of the young man who was blocking their path decided to say nothing.

Conn MacConnell made a sudden decision. Turning them about he took both women by the arm and using his size to blast a way through managed to get them to the hansom cab rank at Clarence Dock further along Regent Road.

"The Adelphi," he told the cab driver, bundling them both inside and Jinny, who had never been in a cab before, let alone the Adelphi Hotel, nearly burst into tears with the excitement of it all.

"That's a fair way in this crowd, mate," the cabbie said.

"Is that my concern?" Conn answered coldly.

"No, sorry, sir," and they were away, swerving through streets still swarming with people, along Waterloo Road, Bath Street, Strand Street, the vast panoply of the crowded river on their right until they turned into Hanover Place. The smell of the river, the docks, the ships and their cargoes filtered into the hansom cab. A dozen smells which were made up of timber, coffee, tobacco, tar, nutmeg and other spices from the east.

No one spoke. The big man, as Jinny had named him in her own mind, seemed lost in his own thoughts, his long legs stretched out before him, his eyes turned to the window. His fingers beat a rapid tattoo on his knee and whatever was in his mind did not seem to include making conversation with Poppy or her.

The Adelphi Hotel was at the foot of Mount Pleasant and it was as they approached its imposing façade that Poppy exploded. The cab door was opened by a splendid uniformed personage in a top hat and when Poppy erupted on to the steps of the hotel the surprise on his face was comical. Poppy did not laugh. She was scarlet-faced now and her hands were trembling with some deep emotion which looked very much like rage as they adjusted her pale grey, white-ruffled bonnet, smoothed down her full skirt and pulled firmly at the cuff of each glove.

Conn followed her, his face a picture of amazement, both of them forgetting about Jinny who was forced to find her own way out of the cab. The cab driver was intoning in an aggrieved fashion, for he was losing money hanging about here, "That'll be three an' six, sir, if yer please," while the doorman looked about him as though seeking reinforcements.

"What the hell . . .?" Conn began, his face still carved in the grim lines it had worn on the journey.

"Don't you 'what the hell' me, Conn MacConnell, and you can take that surly look off your face," she said sharply, not caring as he stiffened in outrage.

"Surly! I've never had a surly look in my life and what's the matter wi' ye all of a sudden?"

"Because if you think you can turn up after seven bloody years" – there was a sudden shocked silence all around them – "drag me into a cab without so much as a by your leave, let alone an explanation, and trail me through town as though I were some stray you had found abandoned but which has no need to be bothered with, then you're sadly mistaken. Not a word of what is happening here. No apology and if you can catch that cab, Jinny, we'll go home at once."

What it was she wanted an apology for was not clear. The silent seven years just gone? The abduction into the cab, the total lack of conversation during the ride? Whatever it was she was hopping mad, mad as she had not been for years in the invalid atmosphere at Long Reach Farm.

Conn's voice was desperate. He put a placatory hand on her arm. "Poppy, if ye'd calm down a bit and just let me explain."

"I have never met such rudeness, such inconsiderate ungentlemanly behaviour in my life and I'll thank you to take your hand off my arm."

"Poppy, if ye'll . . ."

"Is this gentleman bothering you, miss?" the doorman asked anxiously. Guests, influential and wealthy guests, did not care to witness unpleasant scenes on the very steps of the hotel for which they were paying a great deal of money. Several had gathered, staring as the crowds at the docks had stared and the doorman was resolute in his determination to have it over and peace returned to his domain.

Poppy turned a withering glare on him. "And you can go to hell an' all."

The small, well-bred crowd gasped.

"Poppy, will ye no' come inside and have some—"

"No, I will not. I am not some serving girl to be ordered about." God, why had she said that, appalled at her own insensitivity with Jinny standing next to her but she could not seem to be able to stop.

"I am not ordering you about. Let me take you and your friend . . . Jeannie, is it?" turning frantically to her "friend".

"Jinny."

"Yes, Jinny. Let's go into the restaurant. They do superb teas and I must talk to ye, ye do see that, don't ye, Poppy, and ye must talk to me. We canna continue like this, here on the steps of the hotel. No . . . hush, *mo annsachd*," as she would have argued further. The endearment slipped out unconsciously and though Conn did not notice it, Poppy did, and became quiet with memory. "I must tell ye what has happened to me," he went on. "I havena been idle and will ye look at yourself. A fine wee lady. Ach, please, Poppy, dinna argue any more. It willna take long and it canna be said in the street."

Jinny was mesmerised. What was taking place was a dark mystery to her, better than one of those plays they put on at the Theatre Royal. Not that she'd ever seen one but they could surely not be as exciting as this?

Poppy raised her head regally, still disposed to be infuriated at the way Conn had acted, though probe her as to why and she could not have said with any degree of logic.

"Very well, but we can't stay long. We are expected home."

The doorman breathed a sigh of relief as they disappeared inside the hotel. If they caused a disturbance within it would be someone else's problem, not his.

The Adelphi Hotel was described as the most palatial in the world. It was a recognised stopping place for members of the royal family visiting or passing through Liverpool. Distinguished foreign visitors made it their headquarters and it was said that many years ago ambassadors from Washington in America had made it their temporary home. Only five years ago it had been entirely rebuilt on a much larger, even more luxurious scale, incorporating all the modern comforts of the civilised world. There was an elegant French restaurant, a grill room for more informal dining, a magnificent ballroom and banqueting suite, spacious lounges, public rooms and drawing-rooms in which ladies might take tea, and it was to one of these that Conn led the two silent, open-mouthed and completely overwhelmed young women, settling them into deep velvet sofas, ordering tea from the polite and hovering waiter, "And perhaps cakes?" turning to the ladies who looked at him as though he spoke in a foreign tongue.

There was soft music in the background, come from three gentlemen on a small raised dais in the corner playing, respectively, a piano, a violin and a cello and Poppy was to remember later thinking to herself that the pianist was not as good as she was.

The silver teapot was set before Poppy but, it being very clear she was too overcome by the splendour of her surroundings to do anything with it, Conn poured three cups, inviting the ladies to drink up which, obediently, they did. They did not look out of place as far as their dress was concerned, for Elly's daughter, taking a lead from Poppy whom she greatly admired, was simply but fashionably gowned in a shade of pale coffee, her small bonnet of brown velvet as tasteful and becoming to her as any lady in the room. Poppy might have just driven up in a carriage from the well-bred home of the highest in the county, her pearl grey and white outfit, which though it was three years old was still stylish, comparing favourably with the other ladies drinking tea in the room, but it was their stares of awed astonishment which gave away the fact that they were not used to such magnificence.

"Now then . . . er, Jinny, ye dinna mind if Poppy and me have a wee chat, do ye? It's a long time since we saw one another and there's a lot to say." He smiled, his eyes glinting to the deepest blue, his ruddy eyebrows raised questioningly.

With a great effort Jinny regained some of her self-possession and shook her head.

"Thank you." He turned to Poppy, finding himself wanting to reach for her hand. He paused, then said quietly so that Jinny could not hear him, "Ye're a bonny wee lass, Poppy Appleton."

She blushed and bent her head, her long eyelashes hiding the expression in her eyes but he had seen it, recognised it and it brought gladness to his heart.

He sighed deeply, half in pleasure, half in pain. "Ye say the name of the farm where ye live is . . . Long Reach?"

"Yes." She lifted her head and her eyes narrowed warily.

"Then it's no wonder I havena heard from ye in all this long time. Not that I've written in many years."

"You wrote?" She leaned forward eagerly, her hand reaching to touch his then drawing back.

"Aye, I did. I said I would and a promise is to keep, is it no', but it seems I didna write to the correct address, I ken that fine now. Ye see I had it in my head that it was called *Primrose* Farm. Dougie took me there and I thought . . . well." He shrugged his shoulders at the irony of it.

"We lived at Primrose *Bank*." Her voice was no more than a whisper, a sad whisper of what might have been, for they both recognised now what had been done to them by a twist of fate, a quirk of chance, a slip of memory in a youth who, in his weakened state, had got the name wrong.

"I wrote a dozen times to Poppy Appleton of Primrose Farm," he went on, "but I didna get a reply so . . ." He sighed again. "I couldna even remember the district. Put me on the road now and I could find my way to it blindfold, which I meant to do, but . . . well, I couldna understand why ye didna reply. We'd . . . I dinna know . . ."

For the first time he took his eyes from her face and gazed over her shoulder at the remembered hurt a young man, scarcely more than a boy, had known. A hurt on top of all the rest he had suffered. She remembered his back which had been a physical agony and his anguished eyes when he had spoken of his mother. So much to bear when he was scarcely out of childhood and yet here he was, a man grown, a successful man by the look of him, and it was all too late. She didn't know quite what might have happened had his letters reached her. How her life would have changed for they had still been only children. She only knew how it *might* have been and it broke her heart.

"I found my grandfather, Poppy." He was becoming animated again, for what did it matter if his letters had not reached her years ago since he was here now and so was she. "There's so much to tell ye. How it was with him and me and what I'm doing in Liverpool but . . . well . . ." He looked at her almost shyly. "We've time for that later."

When we're alone, his eyes told her. When this friend of yours who is listening avidly to every word we speak and will probably report back to your mistress is not with you. He was astonished himself by the feelings which swept through him. How could he have known that despite the lapse of time, the children they had been, the young emotions they had shared would remain inside them, buried by the years, but still bright and strong. Only God knew where it would lead, if it led anywhere, for there was a great deal standing between them, a great deal to be discovered and spoken of. He had come to Liverpool to further his career but one day he would return to his home on the Clyde and all that he had left behind there. When he had set out, Poppy Appleton, though he had meant to look her up, had not been included in his plans.

But he had been bowled over by the sight of her elegant little figure on the opposite side of the road, the part of his brain that was not totally dazed, wondering how, after all this time, he had recognised her so quickly. She had been a pretty child of eleven or twelve, he supposed, barely on the brink of adolescence, but the vision today which had filled his eyes and his heart and his senses was so obviously her he had been amazed. He had seen her at the cricket match, a golden-skinned, brown-haired child with thickly lashed eyes of pale crystal, the blue washed out as they glittered in the bright sunlight and her own vast annoyance at what she saw as his foolhardiness. That day in the market her face had been paler, anguished, her eyes a soft blue-grey of horrified concern. Now would you look at her, a young lady of fashion and some breeding, that was the impression she gave and he must make immediate arrangements with her to meet again without the big-eyed, silent and obviously fascinated young person with her. Surely, *surely* she could not still be a dairymaid at – what was it? – Long Reach Farm, not with that air of being *somebody*, that air of distinction, of confidence and dignity which sat so strangely on one so young. She had been able to read and write on that bitter day in November when her determination and courage had kept him alive. That much she had told him, the implication being that her mistress was teaching her to be more than a servant. She had been singled out by the farmer's wife for some reason and now, here she was, transformed, and dammit it all he could hardly wait to hear her story, and to divulge his.

He smiled at her and her heart fluttered like a trapped bird in her breast. She felt herself to be breathless, he was so . . . beautiful. His fair skin, on which golden freckles were scattered, was flushed with emotion. His face had the high cheekbones and flat planes of a Viking she had seen in a story book. He was fierce and yet gentle, challenging and yet compassionate, though she did not know how she knew, strong, stubborn even, but vulnerable. His eyes, a darker blue here in the soft light of the Adelphi drawing-room, were surrounded by long tawny lashes tipped at the end with gold. And his mouth, though it was firm, had a permanent humorous curl at each corner. His jaw was blunt, his ears, where he had pushed back the bright flame of his hair, were neat and flat to his head. She had an overwhelming compulsion to lean forward, to touch him, to put a hand to his cheek, to brush back his hair, which needed cutting, from his forehead.

Dear God, what was she about? What was she allowing to happen, even if it was only in her mind? She was letting her bemused heart wander on paths that were totally forbidden. Hadn't she a husband at home whose need of her was the most important part of their shared life, and this man, who was looking at her with an expression in his eyes that made her want to weep, had no part in that life. None! Never!

She could feel the droop to her shoulders. Her head felt heavy and she began to sag forward, to shiver and then, abruptly, she stood up. Her cup of tea, which she had barely tasted, was knocked over by the small grey silk reticule she still had on her arm, and instinctively Conn reached to retrieve it. The tea ran in a brown rivulet across the snow white cloth and a waiter leaped forward to help.

"Leave it," she said harshly and Conn, Jinny and the waiter all stared at her in bewilderment.

"Come along, Jinny, it's time we were off or Elly will be sending out a search party for us."

She began to move round the table and Jinny rose to her feet, her young face displaying her total bemusement as she fell in behind her stepsister who was also her mistress.

"Poppy, ye canna go like this. We must . . . please, dinna be in such a hurry."

Conn followed, almost running to catch up with her, his heart suddenly beating fast in what he recognised as great fear, though God knew why. "Poppy, I must . . . we havena . . ."

She turned then and held out her hand to him, a picture of ladylike breeding copied from Eliza and presented to Conn MacConnell in a manner that left him in no doubt of her intentions.

"It has been lovely to see you again, Conn, really it has and we're only sorry we cannot spend more time with you, aren't we, Jinny?" turning a brilliant, ice-edged smile in Jinny's direction.

Jinny nodded uncomprehendingly.

"Poppy, dammit to hell . . . what . . .?" he began, his face flushed with the onset of furious consternation, but she lifted her head even higher and gave him a look that a lady gives to some rude fellow who is bothering her.

"We really must get on . . . perhaps a cab, Jinny? You see my husband will be wondering where I have got to. He worries if I'm not home on time so I'm sure you'll forgive me for rushing away like this. I wish you well in Liverpool but now . . . ah, the cab. Goodbye, Conn, and thank you for the tea."

His white face and suddenly empty eyes would haunt her dreams, she knew they would, until the end of her days, and as she fell back into the confines of the cab she anguished on how just one hour could do such dreadful harm, could cause such pain, could change two lives so irrevocably. For they had been changed, hers and Conn's.

As though to offset in some way the devastation she had suffered, to place in her desolate mind a complication with which to occupy itself while it recovered, she could hear the cries from the kitchen as she and Jinny stepped down from the gig that had met them at Old Swan. Someone was weeping loudly and she could hear Cook's voice rising and falling in what appeared to be a tirade of disgust. Other voices joined in. One seemed to be that of Elly speaking in a placatory tone, mingling with Aggie's who, through the open kitchen door could be heard to shout, "I'll never believe it, never. Not if I live to be ninety."

Putting aside the feeling that her heart was being dragged down into the pit of her stomach, heavy as lead and riven with pain, Poppy stepped into the kitchen. They were all so wrapped up in whatever it was that had happened while she had been out, no one noticed her and she had a moment or two to register that the person weeping was May and that Cook, who had her hands on her hips in an accusing way, was telling her she could pack her bags and leave this minute.

"What's going on here?" Poppy asked, her voice quiet. It took a few seconds for it to register with the group of servants, Dilys among them, that their little mistress was home and they all turned guiltily and began to fiddle industriously with trays and teacups and dishcloths as though they had been caught doing something wrong. All except Cook whose face was puce with outrage.

"What is it? What's happening? What's the matter with May?" Her voice was sharp now as the cloak of her life here in this house fell familiarly about her shoulders, Conn MacConnell's pleading face fading for the moment to the back reaches of her mind.

"You'd best ask her," Cook said contemptuously, tossing her head in May's direction.

May, who was sitting at the kitchen table, her head on her folded arms, raised it and looked beseechingly at Poppy. Her face was ugly with crying, splotched and swollen and her nose was running. She wiped it on the back of her hand while the tears continued to course down her red cheeks.

"May?"

"Oh, what's the bloody use?" May moaned.

"Unless you tell me how will I know?" The servants were still again, not at all displeased that May Jebson was going to get it in the neck, for hadn't they all suffered her sharp tongue in the past.

"May, I'm waiting."

May stood up, her defiant face saying they could all go to hell, for who in this place would stand by her?

"I'm up the spout." Her voice was harsh.

"Up the spout?"

"Bloody 'ell, d'yer know nowt in that immaculate world yer live in? I'm 'avin' a kid. A baby, and though none of 'em 'ere believe me," turning to glare at the circle of disapproving faces, "it were Johnny Goodall 'oo give it me."

21

"There'll be no talk of sacking, and if there were I would be the one to do it. Is that understood? I am the mistress here and you'd do well to remember it. I will say who goes and who stays. Indeed who does what, not just here in this house but in those fields out there," nodding her bonneted head to the world outside the kitchen window. "Do I make myself clear?"

They were all speechless, even Cook for the moment, for not once since she had been pitchforked into the position of authority old Mrs Goodall had held had Poppy Appleton, as they sometimes still thought of her, made any attempt to what May would have called "chuck her weight about". Perhaps there had been no need for it. She had devised a routine that ran smoothly round the needs of her young husband and not one of them would have dreamed of going against it. Poor lass, they had said, so brave and uncomplaining, doing her best in those early days to come to terms with the unnatural life she was forced to lead and with so many relying on her. Not just Master Richard but the old master, and, for all the worth he was to anyone, Master Johnny an' all. Good sense, she'd shown. An aptitude for farming ways that Evan and Tommy had finally admitted was doing Long

Reach Farm no harm. They'd all worked to help her in it. This was a good place. She had been fair and generous and they had been fond of her ever since she'd come as a bedraggled scrap to work in the dairy.

Now, with a few icy words, none of them aware of the stunned confusion which seethed inside her and which, at the moment, drove out all the sense of obligation Eliza Goodall had taught her, she was laying down the law in a way which astounded them, sticking up for May Jebson of all people, who, let's face it, was nobody's favourite. She stood there in her lovely gown and bonnet, which transformed her into a lady, they had to admit, her mouth hard, her face carved in lines of grim determination, and her eyes all aglitter in it.

"Now, May, I'll see you in the study and the rest of you can go back to your work. I'll just go and have a word with my husband and then . . ."

"If you expect me to work alongside a slut who's to have a bastard, no matter who gave it to her, then you'd best think again, lady. She's no better than one of those women who—"

"Then you must go, Cook." The words cut through Cook's furious hostility as though she were a child in a tantrum and every last one of them gasped in horror. "If your conscience forbids you to work with a fellow servant then of course you must find employment elsewhere. That goes for all of you. I will not be told who I am to employ, or fire. Now I will go and see Richard and change and then I'll speak to you in the study, May. We'll have some tea."

"Tea," Cook shrieked. "Tea, is it, for a hussy who'd drop her drawers for any man who fancied it, which, let's face it, is probably every labourer on the farm."

"Why, you old bitch, you," May snarled, her face a vivid scarlet, her deep brown eyes glowing in their centres like hot coals. "There's bin no one, no one burrim." She began to cry again, turning away, her shoulders heaving, her hand to her face. "I love 'im."

"Give over, I've seen you giving Tommy the eye."

"*That is enough*, both of you. I will not have this pandemonium in my kitchen, d'you hear? Go to the study at once, May, and calm yourself, and then I'll talk to you, Cook. I must confess we wouldn't want to lose you, not after all these years and I hope we can settle this."

"She's always been a troublemaker ever since she came here."

"*I have said that is enough, Cook.* Until I have spoken to May, and then to you, I shall make no decisions."

They all shuffled their feet, even Elly, never before having seen this sharpness, this implacability in their little mistress. Nelly and Bess were still in the dairy and Dilys was sitting with Master Richard but Marigold was crying quietly in the chimney corner, her face in her apron. She could not bear any kind of dissension among those she loved and Marigold loved everyone in this grand life of hers. May could be sharp, and Aggie, who was getting on, a bit short-tempered when she was tired but usually there was a pleasant, even-handed feel to the atmosphere of the kitchen where Marigold worked. She had understood that May was in the family way, for hadn't her own mam been in that condition for most of her life. She had been shocked, for May wasn't married, but that she should be wicked enough to say it was Master Johnny who had . . . who had . . . Marigold didn't know the word for what May claimed Master Johhny had done to her, but it was a bad thing and had brought trouble to Long Reach and put that cold and dreadful look on their Poppy's face.

Richard was in what Elly sometimes called a paddy – only to Poppy, naturally – when she entered the bedroom, demanding to know what the hell time she thought this was and where in God's name had she been to all day leaving him alone to the ministrations of that bloody woman who had dragged him about the bed as though he were a damned doll and he'd be obliged if she'd not go off again because after all he was her husband and was entitled to her attention. Who had she met was what he'd like to know, for the procession had taken place hours ago; she'd told him herself what the timings were to be, and so where had she been until now, and with whom? His ill temper, caused by his fearful distress without her, so furious he missed her start of guilt and her sudden shift away from him so that he could not see her face which she knew must display it. Gadding about the town, he went on, and if she imagined he would allow her to do it again then she was sadly mistaken. Apart from her necessary trip to the bank each week to withdraw money for the wages and household accounts she was to stay on the confines of the farm. Had she got that? His midday meal had been atrocious, the meat unchewable, the gravy lumpy and the vegetables as soft as clarts, and as for the pudding, well, if she didn't go right down and sack the cook he'd send for the woman and do it himself.

It was so ironic she wanted to laugh hysterically, but the pale, peevish face on the pillow told her that she must be careful, patient and, the last thing she felt like, loving, if she was to coax Richard out of this. He had never been left before except perhaps for an hour when she visited the bank, and of course, a week or two back when she had taken Jinny's place at the market stall. He had seemed content enough then, as far as he could be content in the life that was his, but it was as though he sensed something about today, sensed something different about her that had got inside his head and turned him to a state of vitriolic condemnation. He was a bitter man and who could blame him? Poppy knew, though he did not bring it out into the open, that he wished Dominic Cooper had killed him on their wedding day, for what could any man find more agonising, apart from the loss of his active life, than to know he would never make love to the beautiful girl who was his wife.

Now, something had tipped him over into a state of self-pity, a state into which he was falling more and more lately. At first he had been savage in his hatred of everything and indeed everyone who could move when he could not, but recently he had begun to slide into a condition which verged on the semi-conscious, apathetic. But now he was far from apathetic in his snarling outrage and before she could attend to the emergency downstairs she must soothe him, calm his fears, hold him in her maternal arms like the sick child he was.

It took her an hour before he fell asleep at her breast, his face ironed out of the lines of pain and grief and fear that had been drawn on it, young and boyish and very frail and her heart ached for him as she quietly changed from her elegant gown into her everyday attire of plain toffee-coloured gingham covered with a snowy apron. She had sent Dilys downstairs when she returned; now she called for Elly, telling her to watch over him and call her immediately should he wake.

May was still waiting in the study and it was a measure of her apprehension that she sprang to her feet the moment Poppy entered the room. May had always teetered on the edge of insolence with her new mistress, obeying an order but with just enough lethargy to let it be known that she still resented Poppy's meteoric rise in this house. An uneasy truce seemed finally to have been declared, for May Jebson had been sensible enough to realise that she would never find a place of employment as easy as this one. For a start there were too many maidservants for a house of this size, which meant that the workday, though long, was not arduous. The food was good and plentiful, the bedroom, which had once belonged to Poppy and where May had been put when Poppy married Richard, was comfortable and the recent rise in their wages must surely have made them the highest paid servants in the county of Lancashire. Now, carried away by a madness of the blood, a passion she could not let go of, she had thrown it all away and what the devil was she to do? Chuck herself in the Mersey, she had decided, for her family'd have nothing to do with her in her present condition. She could go to one of the hundreds of back-street abortionists who thrived in Liverpool, and have a knitting needle stuck in her and bleed to death which, she decided, was preferable to the bearing of a child. There was no greater sin than for an unmarried woman to fornicate with a man and to compound that sin by bearing an illegitimate child. Though she was not one to show her feelings, especially to Poppy, her terror was very evident.

"Sit down and tell me all about it, May," was the first thing Poppy said after seating herself on the opposite side of the table in the chair that had been Eliza's.

"What's there ter tell?" May said sullenly. "Though I don't suppose yer know owt about it in . . . er . . . your position. What 'appens between a man an' a woman, I mean. Well, it 'appened wi' me an' Johnny an' now I'm the one as ter pay fer it."

She didn't care how she spoke or if it gave offence, since she expected nothing from Poppy Appleton who'd always been too big for her boots, in May's opinion, brought about by the old mistress's daft ideas for her. She'd probably only dragged May in here to gloat.

Poppy shrugged. "Well, unless I know the facts . . ."

"Facts!" May hooted. "He stuck 'is thingy in me an' now I've a bun in th'oven. Will that do yer?"

Poppy didn't care at that precise moment what kind of insulting remark May came out with, since part of her was still hidden away in mourning for a tall man with bright red hair and she could not be hurt any more than she already was. She kept remembering and being tortured by the memory of small things, endearing things like the indentation of his well-shaped lips, a tiny area of red bristle on his chin where his razor had not cut close enough that morning, his hands which were large and blunt but which performed the task of pouring the tea with such delicacy. The way his face softened to tenderness when he looked at her, the way his face hardened to irritation when they had argued and the fall of thick, copper-tipped hair which fell over his brow and which she longed to brush back.

Dragging her thoughts back to now, she sighed. This must be settled. There was to be a child. A Goodall child if May was to be believed and Poppy was inclined to think she was, for had she not herself, before her world had caved in two years ago, thought there was something between Johnny Goodall and May Jebson? So could Poppy allow Eliza Goodall's grandchild to be turned out of its rightful place?

"Look, May, before you say anything else which might influence me to your detriment, shall we agree to talk like two adult women, one who is in trouble and the other who might be willing to hold out a helping hand?"

May was not at all sure what some of the words Poppy said had meant but the last few caught her attention and she let out a long shuddering sigh. There was silence for several long moments then she shook her head and her whole body seemed to sag.

"I'm sorry," she said simply, probably the first time she had ever apologised in her life. "I were just so bloody scared."

"I know. Now, shall we start again?"

"Aye, why not? It's bin goin' on fer a while, me an' Johnny." A curiously soft look of warmth lit May's eyes to amber, clear as malt whisky, and a small smile of remembrance rested on her lips. "Before 'is mam died we took a shine ter one another. Oh, I weren't daft enough ter think it would come ter owt, nothin' like that. He's a gentleman an' I'm nowt burra kitchen maid but . . . it weren't just the lovin', though that were grand. We used ter 'ave a good laugh together an' 'e'd talk ter me about . . . about not . . . well, 'e knew 'e'd never be a real part o' this farm an' when that Dominic took a fancy to you . . ."

Poppy felt herself blanch as the blood left her head. "What?" she stammered.

"Oh, give over, Poppy Appleton, the others might not've seen it burr I did. That were why 'e kept comin' over 'ere, doin' 'is best ter mekk a friend o' Johnny. It were an excuse ter . . . well, I never said owt burr I'll tell yer this fer nowt. I reckon yer'd best watch out for 'im, fer 'e's not the sort ter forget summat 'e were after, even if you an' 'im are both married. Anyroad, like I said, I never said owt, not even ter Johnny."

"Why not?"

"It were none o' my business, lass. I know when ter keep me gob shut, an' anyroad, what good would it o' done?"

"May, I don't know what to say. You must know I never encouraged him. In fact I loathed the sight of him and still do. I don't know what else to tell you."

May blew out her cheeks in a huge sigh as though an enormous tension was being released from somewhere inside her. "There's nowt else ter tell. It all ended in tears an' this'll be the same," indicating what lay under her apron.

"Not necessarily."

"What d'yer mean?" May looked up from her contemplation of her belly and slowly sat forward on her chair.

"I have no intention of sacking you, May, and not just because you held your tongue about me and that . . . that devil up at Coopers Edge but because . . . well, it takes a woman *and* a man to make a child and I happen to believe that it's wrong for the woman to be made to suffer. Johnny is . . . well, he's been made wild by the company he keeps and though he's a good worker he's easily led by others. There has been no one in the last two years to curb him. Mr Goodall barely knows what day it is."

"Aye, poor old sod," May said surprisingly.

"And of course with Richard as he is . . ."

"I don't know 'ow yer stuck it, 'onest. Ter be in bed wi' a chap an' not be able ter . . . an' then there's rest." She shook her head and there was something in her eyes which might have been admiration.

"He . . . he needs a strong woman, May." Poppy picked up the pen Eliza had always used and studied it intently before looking up at May.

"'Oo does?"

"Johnny Goodall. A woman who will keep him at home. Who will keep him on this farm where he belongs, for it will be his son who will inherit it. D'you understand what I'm saying, May?"

"Bloody 'ell, Poppy, yer don't mean . . .?" May had gone the colour of Poppy's apron but in her eyes was a luminous joy, hope and yet disbelief, for surely Poppy was not suggesting what she seemed to be suggesting.

"Indeed I do, May, and why not? Do you love Johnny Goodall?"

"Yer must know I do, Poppy." May's voice was low and her hand went protectively to her belly which was just beginning to show the slight curve of its burden.

"And would you marry him even if he has to be . . . persuaded to it?" For both of them were aware that Johnny Goodall would not take kindly to marrying the kitchen maid whose body had been readily available to him without marriage for more than three years.

"Yes." May looked Poppy directly in the eye and squared her strong shoulders.

"Let's have him in, then."

Johnny had been helping with the harvesting, enjoying the September sunshine and the day which was beginning to wane, the laughter and camaraderie of the men, the physical exercise, and when Marigold ran down the field shouting that he was wanted in the house he tutted irritably.

"What in hell for?" he asked the breathless Marigold. Marigold had just taken a tray of tea in to Poppy and May, doing her best to ignore the look of great offence Cook directed at her, since Marigold could not disobey a direct order from her mistress, could she?

She shrugged helplessly at the question, for it was not her place to acquaint Master Johnny with what had gone on this afternoon and the dreadful accusation laid against him by May. Presumably their Poppy would and then what would happen? Cook was threatening to pack her bags and both Aggie and Clara declared that if Poppy Appleton thought they would work alongside a woman who was carrying a bastard then she'd got another think coming! What was going on in the study no one could even guess at and when it was learned that Master

Johnny was to be brought there the excitement was intense.

They never learned what was said. There was a great deal of shouting, mostly from Johnny Goodall, though May's voice was raised now and again. There was a crash and Marigold winced, exchanging glances with Dilys, who was still there, having said she wouldn't have missed this for a gold clock. Surely he hadn't knocked May down, the glances asked. No man likes to be accused of having put a lass in the family way, even if he had, and come to think of it when they cast their minds back over the past three years or so there had been many an evening when May had had "an early night", going to the bedroom where she now slept alone; how easy it would be for her to slip out and meet a man.

The door to the study smashed open, nearly coming off its hinges and across the hallway in the kitchen Marigold squeaked and the rest cowered back, for someone was in a tearing rage.

"It's bloody blackmail, that's what it is," Johnny Goodall was shouting in a high and outraged voice. "Bloody blackmail and when my father hears of this he'll not have it. He might not be in his right mind but he knows a lying bitch when he sees one and will have her out of here before the sun sets. You can be sure of that, madam. I'll not be threatened." His voice was a snarl and his furious figure could be seen hurtling across the yard towards the stable. A moment later Chestnut thundered out, Johnny on her back without even a saddle and Jacko at his tail hurling imprecations at his young master.

Threatened! Blackmailed! They couldn't even guess at what that meant, not being privy to Poppy Goodall's warning that she would cut off his allowance if he didn't do the right thing by May, which was pure bluff since she hadn't the faintest idea how to go about such a thing, nor if it was possible. They did not hear her promise that if he settled down to a proper day's work, to marriage and fatherhood, the farm would one day be his. It was only common sense, she had told him, surely he could see that and later, when he calmed down and came to see the simple logic of it, realising that from now on he would be working on his own land, he would accept it.

"Do you still want him, May?" Poppy asked her when he had gone, for Johnny had been unpleasant in his contempt for May and her claim.

"Oh, yes, an' I'll mekk summat of 'im an' all, see if I don't."

If the good folk of the district had been astonished when Tom Goodall's elder lad had married his mother's dairymaid, they were even more astonished, *and* disbelieving when his younger wed Long Reach Farm's kitchen maid. What was happening to the family, for heaven's sake? Could those sons of his look no higher than serving girls and them with a fine farm, fine prospects, a bit of cash and their yeoman antecedents going back into the mists of time and as proud in their way as the Coopers of Coopers Edge?

The wedding was quiet. The bride, though not what you'd call pretty, was handsome enough, tastefully gowned in a plain buttercup yellow silk which they thought might have been chosen for her by her sister-in-law who was known to be fashionable. She had a fine figure with a breast on her which would be pleasing, they supposed, to a full-blooded man. Not that you could really call Johnny Goodall a man, not a mature man that is, though he must be twenty-three by now. He'd spent the years since his brother's accident gallivanting about the countryside, or so it was rumoured, with the very man who'd caused it, and others of his ilk, so how would this strong-boned, dark-eyed, gypsy-like wife of his deal with that? She had a look of stubbornness about her, her full red mouth firm and her jaw resolute so perhaps she might steady him, but what about her beautiful sister-in-law who ran Long Reach Farm? What did she make of it all, they asked, not realising that she had engineered the whole thing.

Richard had been appalled.

"Send him up here immediately," he barked at Poppy, his eyes fierce in his thin, waxen face and when Johnny, defiant and yet shame-faced, stepped into the bedroom said at once: "You don't have to marry her, you know, Johnny. You're not the first man to get a serving wench in the family way and you won't be the last. It might not even be yours. Have you thought of that?" Poppy stood impassively by, her hands folded in her apron. "Give her a few bob and send her on her way," Richard continued. "A bloody kitchen maid's not for you, lad, not with your prospects."

"It was good enough for you, Richard, when you took me," Poppy said mildly. Richard turned his head stiffly and glared at her.

"This is nothing to do with you, Poppy. This is a family matter and my father and I will deal with it."

"It may have escaped your notice but I *am* family, Richard. I'm your wife and mistress of this house. And this is the kind of problem a mistress deals with. I also help to run the farm now that your father is . . . incapacitated and though you may not care for a *dairymaid* taking your mother's place, you put me there so I feel that I have a perfect right to my opinion and to take part in any decision made. May is to have a child. A Goodall child, your flesh and blood, and I will not allow it to be discarded, along with May, to finish up in the workhouse, or worse. I will not allow May to be thrown away like an old glove for which Johnny has no further use. If Johnny refuses to marry, or you persuade him that he needn't do so, then she will remain here as . . . as my companion. She shall have her Goodall child here under the Goodall roof and it will be reared here, illegitimate or no. There is nothing you, your father or Johnny can do about that, for I have made up my mind. Everyone will know whose child it is and though I have no wish to . . . to upset you, it is the only child this house will have, unless Johnny fathers another. So, there is nothing any of you can do. Your father has been told and has somehow got it into his head that May is the daughter of Billy Broadbent, God knows how, and is hugely delighted, particularly as I made it my business to whisper to him that Johnny had anticipated the wedding ceremony and he could expect a grandchild in the spring. He went striding off to spread the news."

"You bitch, you stupid bitch, what right have you say what is, or what is not to be done in this house?" Richard hissed, and Johnny's good-natured face clouded, for he had become fond of his sister-in-law, at least before this happened, and knew that had it not been for her and her diligent care of the farm they would have gone under.

"Hold on, Dick . . ."

"No, you hold on, you careless sod. If you want to marry that bovine creature who scrubs the floors and can neither read nor write then go ahead. At least Poppy was educated when . . . when . . . Oh, dear Lord, what the bloody hell do I care. She rules the roost here, it seems, so go ahead and ruin your bloody life."

He slipped away then in that unnerving way he had, retreating into somewhere, escaping from his body that held him trapped in his bed, his eyes in his ravaged face becoming flat and grey, a deep grey like unpolished pewter.

Poppy knew that nothing would fetch him back until this evening when she took off her clothes and got into bed with him and the thought made her shudder. He did nothing, could do nothing to offend her but the fleshless skeleton of his body, its pallid, unnatural frailty, though it filled her with pity, was abhorrent to her now. In her mind's eye was another figure, warm, strong, ruddy with life, with broad back and shoulders and long shapely legs muscled with health. The total maleness of Conn whose image had filled her mind since he had come back into her life was a joy she could hardly bear. It was out of reach, a chimera which was hopelessly forbidden and she ached from her hair down to her toes with the pain of what she would never have. She had known no man but Richard and then not in the way a woman knows a true man. *And never would*.

The weeks wore on and Poppy began to accept that she had to shape her life from things other than fleshly love. In the gratifying way the farm prospered, in the respect the men who worked it showed her, in what promised to be a vague but pleasing friendship between her and May brought about by May's undying gratitude for what Poppy had done for her and her unborn child, and the fatalistic way in which Johnny Goodall, with his new wife behind him, had begun to take an interest in the farm. He and May seemed to have formed a relationship which satisfied them both. She would always be the stronger of the two but she had begun to develop a knack of getting him to do exactly what she and Poppy wanted him to do without him being aware that he was being manipulated. Of course, the dawning realisation – and why had it not occurred to him before? he wondered – that Long Reach would be his, and *his* sons, was a spur which got him out of bed at five in the morning and kept him in the milking sheds, the pig pens, the bull pen, the stable, the fields until dark; those who worked alongside him couldn't get over it, they told one another. Who would have believed that Master Johnny could have shaped the way he had and that May Jebson must have a way with her that was to be admired.

At times, particularly during the hunting season, a note came from one of his gentry friends – Poppy suspected Dominic Cooper – and he would state defiantly that he was off to join the hunt at Fullingham, glaring at May and Poppy as if he knew already that it was no good. May would put on a stern face, beckon him to join her upstairs in the bedroom they now shared and there would be raised voices for ten minutes or so, then silence for a further twenty, which was a bit uncomfortable for those in the kitchen, and off he would go meekly to whatever was waiting for him and May would come down looking flushed and with a strand or two of her dark hair floating about her face.

Now that May had been made an honest woman of Cook had decided she could manage to continue working with her as long as she didn't start playing Lady Muck. They already had a mistress and one was enough, but to give May her due she made no attempt to lord it over the others despite now being Mrs Johnny Goodall and the mother to the unborn heir. She continued to do the work she had always done, despite her increasing size and they began to fuss her in that strange way women have, telling one another it would be lovely to have a bairn about the place and, if the amount of time May and Master Johnny spent in that there room of theirs was anything to go by, it wouldn't just be the one.

They just wished their little mistress would buck up a bit. She had been out of sorts for weeks now, a faraway look in her eyes and none of them connected it with the big, red-haired chap Jinny had never stopped talking about who had taken them to tea at the Adelphi Hotel on the day the Prince of Wales came to town.

"Oh, yes, he was a friend of my brother's," Poppy had said vaguely when questioned and they hadn't liked to ask which one, for Poppy had several and except for Herbert and Eustace they'd all taken to bad ways.

May's child was due in the second week in March and though she was as big as one of those elephants she had seen in the book from which Poppy was attempting to teach her to read she was still doing many of the tasks she had done before her marriage. And more besides. She would sit beside Richard after he had fallen into one of those states vaguely reminiscent of being asleep, rocking placidly, one hand on her kicking child, the other holding the book she was studying. Richard was not aware of her. In fact it was doubtful he really noticed anyone but Poppy, but someone had to sit with him and May's presence meant that Poppy could get out of the house for half an hour. He himself had not been out of doors since before that day in September when, almost from one moment to the next, he had turned his face to the wall, in a manner of speaking, and withdrawn into some dark and secret place known only to him. He had been ill during the winter, his lungs wheezing, his chest heaving, every breath a torment to him and only his wife's devotion had pulled him through, so the doctor said, keeping to himself the thought that it would have been better all round if she'd let him go.

Now it was almost spring and if it was fine she would walk up to the spinney and settle herself with her back against the trunk of an oak tree which stood on guard at the end of the overgrown track leading from the farmhouse to the patch of woodland. She would listen to the sound of the waggon pulled by Penny and Buck and the voice of one of the men as he affectionately encouraged them to "walk on, Penny, walk on, Buck". Across the field which was waiting to be planted with sugar beet she could see Tom Goodall's herd of Fresians moving slowly towards the gateway that led into the yard where, with a gentle "Coom, coom, Buttercup, coom, coom, Bessie," Evan called them for the afternoon's milking.

But her surroundings would be lost to her as she turned backwards and inwards to dwell on that afternoon in September when her heart had broken over a tall, red-haired Scot who had called her *mo annsachd* as he had done eight years ago.

22

Anything that might have been whispered about May Goodall, any grudge that might have been harboured by the older women servants over her "entrapment" of Johnny Goodall, vanished for ever when, in March, she gave birth to not one but two handsome, sturdy boys. Tom, in a seventh heaven of delight, slapped his thigh and said he'd never heard such lusty bawling, no, not even when old Bessie had dropped that champion little bull calf at the back end of last year. The house was in an uproar of joy which spread out like the ripples which are formed when a stone is dropped into a pond, moving from farmhouse to farmyard and dairy and out into the fields where the men were agreed that Master Johnny had proved himself a man at last. He was slapped on the back, had his hand shaken and his hat knocked from his head in play, their congratulations filling him with such pride he might have performed the whole procedure of conception, pregnancy and childbirth totally on his own.

It was as though the infants put the final seal of acceptance on May. For a start they were so bonny, both weighing an amazing eight pounds by the midwife's calculations, dark of hair and eye and as placid as the cows in the meadow as they took turns at May's bounteous breasts. Where their composure came from was a mystery since May could be a firecracker and Johnny, and even old Tom, had a quick temper on them. Handed down from the old mistress, she'd be bound, Cook told them as she had a nurse of first one and then the other, for May was generous and forgiving in her happiness. The babies brought some miracle of renewed life with them, they all knew that, transferring on to the quiet, saddened house an elation it had not known for years.

The only person who had no interest in the arrival of the infants was poor Master Richard. The servants shook their heads sadly, for had it not been for that tragic event on his wedding day he and their little mistress would probably have had a couple of bairns of their own by now. It was bound to bring home to him the appalling nature of his affliction and what it had taken from him. And Poppy too. Though she was kindness itself to May who received everyone's homage with a great deal of satisfaction and pride in her own cleverness. How could their little mistress feel anything but sadness at her own lack? She did her best, taking great care to give May her due, for were they not sisters-in-law, the wives of the Goodall boys? She sat with her when her duties allowed in the over-warm, over-stuffed bedroom, for May had rooted out from the attic every knick-knack, gee-gaw, picture, vase and trinket box discarded by previous Goodall ladies to furnish the room she shared with her husband.

"Well, an' what d'yer think ter that then, Poppy Appleton?" she could not help but ask triumphantly an hour after the twins' birth, already sitting up in bed, her mouth full of Cook's fruit and spice cake. She did not mean to be malicious, not now when she had so much more than she had ever hoped for and it was all down to Poppy, but her immense satisfaction could not be tethered. "Two lads an' both the spit o' their pa, which is just as well. An' look at 'em," which Poppy dutifully did, staring into the cradle where, one to each end until other arrangements could be made, the babies waved tiny fists, scowled and mewed like kittens. "Norra day old an' as strong as little bulls an' that midwife ses I've enough milk fer another four," May chortled. "See, 'ave a birra cake, Poppy. Oh, I know I'm norr eatin' fer two any more burr I'm that 'ungry an' wharrelse is there ter do? That woman ses I've ter stop in bed but that's daft. Me mam, an' yours an' all I'll be bound, was up an' about next day so I'm gerrin' up tomorrer. I'm not one fer sittin' about on me bum, you know that," which Poppy did. "I'm as fat as a pig already an' unless I get me shape back our Johnny's not gonner fancy . . . well, yer'll know wharr I mean," which Poppy did again but did not wish to be reminded of it.

Poppy was glad of any excuse to get away from Long Reach Farm after the birth of May and Johnny's sons. Though she had engineered it and was pleased with the consequences, since it now meant the future of the farm was safe, until she grew used to it she knew she would find the worshipping activity that went on about the children, and May's wallowing in it, overpowering and difficult to accept. She would have to be both patient and tolerant. May must have her share of being mistress, if she wanted it, that is. She should learn how to take charge as well as be a wife and mother, for it was only fair, though Poppy's attempts during the winter to teach her to read and write, or at least do a few sums so that she would understand the household accounts, had fallen on stony ground. May declared herself, at twenty-three, to be too old a dog to be taught new tricks. No, Poppy could continue to deal with all, May said comfortably. Her fingers and thumbs, which she'd used all her life to count, would do her just fine.

But the weeks and months ahead, even the years that stretched dismally into the future for Poppy would need fortitude and forbearance, which would be hard to find now and it was nothing to do with May. The past four years, once she had got over Eliza's death and come to terms with Richard's accident, had been pleasant, harmonious and had filled her with a sense of satisfaction over what she had discovered herself capable of. But now, now that she had met again the man who, as a boy, had won her young heart, and, it appeared, kept it over the years, it had upset the smooth, day-to-day serenity of her life and stolen her peace of mind.

He was in her thoughts, as he was whenever she was not involved with some problem or task that needed her whole attention, on that day when May's sons were a week old and Poppy boarded the tram in Old Swan to ride down to the bank to withdraw money for the servants' wages. They were paid every Friday. It had been the custom until recently to pay wages yearly but Eliza had made the decision to divide what they earned by fifty-two and pay each man and woman weekly. It was advantageous to most but the wives of the labourers often grumbled that a weekly wage was soon got rid of in the beer house.

There were bills to be paid and Poppy meant to call at Anne Hillyard & Co where good-quality baby linen might be bought. "Children's clothing of the most novel manufacture and description always on hand", the advertisement had said and that was what Poppy had in mind.

Richard had been in a deep sleep when she left. For several weeks he had been complaining of acute pains in his head and the doctor had left a draught for him, a pain-reliever, with instructions to use it sparingly. It alleviated the pain and made him sleep for a great deal of the day, which in a way was welcome to them all, for ever since Johnny had married May he had been even more withdrawn and when he spoke, especially to Poppy, whom he blamed for the unsuitable marriage, he was cold and bitter. Perhaps it was the knowledge that with the marriage of his younger brother, and the child who was coming, that child would inherit the farm. It had planted in his brain a worm of increasing vigour which confirmed the absolute certainty that he, Richard Goodall, was trapped in his wasting body until the end of his days. He had known, of course he had, that he would never escape, but his father's acceptance of Johnny as the crown prince, as it were, of Long Reach and Tom's jubilation at the approaching birth of Johnny's child, who should have taken second place to Richard's, had hammered its final vicious nails into his living coffin.

Poppy alighted from the tram outside Lime Street Station then walked through to Great Charlotte Street where the bank was situated. After withdrawing the required amount, some from the Goodall account and some from her own, she stepped out on to the crowded pavement. She felt a lift of her spirits, for though it was a cold day with a sharp, invasive wind, it was brightly sunny. The sky above the high lines of the sloping rooftops was a soft blue, a spring blue which would turn, as summer approached, to a deeper shade. It was cloudless, and down in the canyons of Liverpool's streets, sunshine and shadow striped the roads. It was, as usual, clamorous with traffic but, dodging the menacing wheels of huge drays and waggons and the dangerous hooves of high-stepping horses drawing carriages, she turned right into Ranelagh Street and then left into Bold Street where Anne Hillyard's shop lay.

She wanted to buy something special for May's babies. Though they had all stitched and embroidered during the winter's evenings none of them was what could be called a needlewoman and what had been turned out was plain and functional. Naturally, only one of everything had been made, or at least with only one child in mind. The twins, who had yet to be named since again their parents had chosen only one name, Thomas for a boy and Elizabeth, since May did not care for Eliza, for a girl, were making do with a long frock apiece and a band, beneath which would be worn a petticoat, both thirty-six inches long and five and a half inches in the body as the pattern book had instructed! All the garments were plain made of fine, dressed long cloth, gathered at the yoke and so Poppy had decided to make a present to each child of a splendid christening robe. An extravagance, she was well aware, but then May and Johnny would be bound to have more children and the robes would come in again. It would not occur to May that an infant she gave birth to might be put into such magnificence and Johnny, being a man, would be ignorant of the custom of dressing a child to be christened in muslin and embroidery, in tucks and lace insertions, in flounces and fabrics of a richness and costliness few could afford. It would please May and the tender plant of her and Poppy's relationship might be nurtured by it.

Though she knew she should, she was reluctant to return home. The sunshine had brought out the crowds as though the scent of spring had drawn them from their winter burrows. Elegantly dressed ladies alighted from splendid carriages, assisted by footmen who carried their purchases, moving in and out of the smart shops which lined Bold Street. The sun shone on the glossy coats of the horses and the polished metal buttons of the police constable whose job it was to see that the gentry, who abounded in this area, did so unhindered by vagrants or begging ragamuffins. It glittered on vast expanses of windows and on the splendid red-jacketed uniform of an officer of the Loyal North Lancashires who marched smartly along the pavement as though he were on the parade ground. Poppy wondered where he had come from, or was going to. There seemed always to be wars in some part of the British Empire: Afghanistan, India, South Africa where, two years ago, the Boers had proclaimed an independent republic and now, or so it was reported in the newspapers Poppy read, in Egypt.

It was lively, exhilarating, blowing a fresh wind through the stagnant passages of Poppy's mind. She sauntered on, looking in shop windows, enjoying the bustle, turning into Berry Street and then Upper Duke Street until she reached St James Road and the imposing setting of St James Cemetery which, though its purpose was the decent tidying away of the dead, was laid out like a park. It was built in a deep dell of what, fifty years ago, had been a quarry which had contributed its stone in the erection of many public works. Long sloping inclines led down into it where it lay like a jewel within the protection of splendid, recently painted iron railings.

The cemetery was vast, with curved pathways lined with gracious cypress trees, green all the year round, with beeches, beautiful in the purity of their spring foliage, and groves of cedars of Lebanon beneath which were seats on which the recently bereaved might compose themselves in the tranquillity where their departed loved ones now rested. There was an immense shrubbery of glossy-leaved rhododendron, not yet in flower, sloping from the top end of the cemetery to the bottom. To the eastern side were catacombs, finished in tasteful rustic masonry and though their purpose was obvious they did not seem to intrude any note of gloom on the general air of serene beauty which lay about the neat headstones. Even these were not laid out in symmetrical lines but in curves along the pathways, dotted in groups beneath the trees and following gracefully the slope of the shrubbery.

There were spring flowers planted in the grass about the graves, crocus and snowdrop and the green and gold spears of ready-to-open daffodils. There was even a little temple of Grecian Doric architecture where a portion of the funeral service might be performed for those who required it. The only affront to the eye in the perfection of the grounds was a hideous statue to the late Liverpool politician and philanthropist William Huskisson, beneath which lay the great man himself.

Poppy sighed, feeling the calm and tranquillity wash over her. It was a strange place to find comfort in, she thought to herself with an inward smile as she strolled along the curving path, making for a wooden bench that had been placed to catch the sun for most of the day. She would sit for a moment, her mind hopefully empty, before making her way back to the tram. A brief space in time just for herself with no one to disturb further her already disturbed thoughts.

There were other visitors, two ladies in the deep black of mourning sadly studying a new headstone. A lady and gentleman of obvious quality, both expensively and fashionably dressed, making their way from the temple towards the gateway where a smart brougham waited for them, a coachman holding open the door. A younger couple, the woman holding a child by the hand. Beside a plain headstone, his head bowed, his hands clasped in front of him, the tall, still figure of Conn MacConnell.

Poppy froze, every part of her body coming to an abrupt halt except for her heart which raced and banged so violently she thought she would choke. She could feel the blood drain from her head and knew that if she didn't turn and run for it she would slide gracefully to the ground in a faint. There was a strange buzzing in her ears, like a swarm of angry bees. Her legs trembled and she had time to wonder on the perplexity of how one man could have such an effect on sensible Poppy Goodall. It was shock, she supposed, and yet inside her blazed a flame of pure joy. She didn't know what to do, that was the madness of it. She knew what she should do, which was to turn and creep quietly away before Conn raised his head and saw her, and she knew what she wanted to do which was speed across the neatly cut grass and fall into his arms.

But it seemed her rapturous, bewildered heart would let her do neither and so she just stood there, pale and beautiful, waiting for what was to happen, to happen and as though suddenly aware of her Conn turned his head and his eyes met hers. He became as frozen as she was and it was clear he was experiencing many emotions at once. Astonishment, reverence, disbelief and a joy as great as her own.

His lips formed her name though no sound emerged. He was faultlessly, even elegantly dressed in a chocolate-brown frock coat and fawn trousers and in his clasped hands he carried a brown top hat. The sunlight set fire to his hair and in his face, which had turned as pale as hers, freckles stood out like tiny golden guineas and his eyes were an electrifying blue.

He moved slowly towards her, his eyes never leaving hers. He began to smile a little, a smile which told her how glad he was to see her, and yet was sad, for he knew now that a great and insurmountable barrier stood between them. It was there in his face, his longing to stretch out his hands to her, to take hers and hold them but of course he could not. Not with what was deep in them both but which could never be acknowledged.

"Poppy." This time he found his voice. "This is ... I hadna' expected . . ." He cleared his throat, doing his best to be casual. His hat twirled furiously in his hands and he looked down at it, frowning as though to ask what the devil it thought it was doing, then stilled it, dropping his hands to his sides. "What brings ye to the cemetery? Ye havena' someone here, have ye?"

His eyes, without appearing to, took in every minutest detail of her appearance. The unblemished satin of her complexion which, normally a golden honey shade, was totally without colour. The pale, pale almost silvery blue of her wide eyes and the endearing tendrils of glossy brown hair that had escaped from under the brim of her bonnet. She was dressed in a rose-coloured woollen gown which had been made for her in the winter before Eliza's death. Her bonnet matched it, trimmed with dainty pale grey feathers and over her dress she wore a dolman mantle of pale grey velvet. Her hands were tucked into a velvet muff to match. Though her face was like ivory she was exquisitely lovely, the very lack of colour adding to that loveliness.

Conscious of his grave gaze she found her voice at last. "Oh, no, no . . . I was shopping," indicating the parcel on her arm, "and . . . well, the day being so fine I began to walk and found myself here. It is the first time. And you?"

He glanced behind him and his eyes rested on the place where she had first seen him. "I come now and again. My parents are both here."

"Oh, Conn, of course. I'm so sorry." Remembering the anguish of the boy who had opened his heart to her years ago, she placed a compassionate hand on his arm. As though it was the most natural thing in the world, and so it seemed to her, he took it and placed it in the crook of his arm, turning to lead her back to the simple headstone where she had first seen him. There was an inscription. "Alick James MacConnell," it read, "the beloved husband of Margaret" and beneath that it read, "Margaret, his wife and beloved mother of Alick James MacConnell." There were no dates, nothing but the simple story of a family circle. Two Alick MacConnells and between them the woman they had both adored.

They stood for a moment, Poppy and Conn, her hand still in the crook of his arm, both with their heads slightly bowed. Hers came barely to his shoulder. There was no awkwardness now, only a shared sadness for the young husband and wife who rested together beneath the flowers heaped on the grave, put there by Conn, in the peace and beauty of the cemetery.

"Shall we sit down for a moment?" Conn said, pointing to the bench where Poppy had been heading, letting go of her hand with obvious reluctance. "Tis nae cold in the sunshine and there's things I want to tell ye. Things we didna have time for last time."

"Yes, I'd like to hear. You look so fine. You've evidently done well and I'd be interested to know what happened to you."

Their contretemps of last September had been put away. They both understood the reason for it, the vast upheaval of meeting again after so long, the trick the gods or Conn's memory had played on them and then Conn's learning of her marriage. Even now convention decreed they could be no more than civil with one another but she would like to know what had happened to him in the past eight years and why he had come back to Liverpool.

"Aah, well." He made a deprecating gesture with his

hand. "It's not all down to me, lassie. Luck played a big part."

"You were due some, I'd say." They smiled at each other carefully so as not to reveal any of the seething emotions that were barely hidden beneath the surface of their mutual politeness.

"Aye, perhaps." His eyes were very blue as he glanced away from her, scanning some far horizon only he could see. "It took its time coming, I willna argue wi' that. It's a hell of a long walk from Liverpool to Glasgow, I can tell ye, but I got there. Me and the farmer's yard coat."

They both smiled at the memory of Tom Goodall's yard coat.

"Did he miss it?"

"Oh, yes, but Mrs Goodall bought him another."

"I was damned glad of it. It kept me warm on many a cold night. I got lifts now and again, on the tails of carts, ye ken, sometimes in the van of a railway train and I got there. I found my grandfather's place, Swainson's Shipyard, just by Port Glasgow on the Clyde."

He smiled and shook his head in remembrance. "I could take all day to tell ye about me and my grandfather, for he was a stubborn old bugger who refused to believe I was his grandson even though his eyes shone in my face, though his were a wee bit faded. We might have come out of the same mould, him an' me but for the hair since his was white. Nevertheless, he had me turned out of his premises half a dozen times. What a stramash! Had I no' been so persistent he'd have disowned me but . . . well, I think he saw himself in me and finally he gave me a job in the yard. I didna do a damn thing but sweep up and run errands for a year but I knew he was watching me, ye ken, so I made sure I didna put a foot wrong. Weel . . ." He looked down into her enraptured face as she hung on his every word. Though she was not aware of it her heart was in her eyes and he stopped abruptly. His hand lifted as though it was no part of him and had a will of its own. A fingertip touched her cheek, so gently she scarcely felt it, then he looked away hurriedly and his hand fell to his lap. His voice had gone curiously flat as he took up the story.

"Weel, I went to school for the first time, for previously my mother had taught me, then to university, in between working in my grandfather's shipyard and . . ." He shrugged and did not look at her again. "I attained a degree in marine engineering. I design ships in my grandfather's shipyard. I live in his house. I am his grandson, acknowledged as his heir, so ye see, lassie, I'm a different lad to that poor sod whose life you saved so many years ago. I came back to Liverpool to spend a year at Laird's in Birkenhead. I have rooms in Upper Duke Street close by here. My grandfather is acquainted with Mr William Laird who invited me to get some first-hand experience in all the aspects of shipbuilding in their Birkenhead Ironworks. It is a great and wonderful place, Poppy, making my grandfather's yard look a mite small. The engineers' shop is a miracle, a series of five docks in which repairs and construction of ships take place. The smithy alone has thirty-two fires and yet the roofs of the shop are as beautiful as a cathedral. And their health and safety is second to none. Fireproof partitions, and you should see the men's dining-room with an enormous cooking range and the cook will heat up whatever the men bring in and then there is . . ." He stopped and a wide grin split his face. "I'm sorry, when I get going I canna seem to stop myself so I'll . . . weel, they've just completed their first order for the Cunard Line, a passenger ship *Cephalonia*, but what am I babbling on about? It's neither here nor there." Impatiently now, he pushed aside the nonsense he had been telling her as though it were nothing to do with Poppy Appleton and Conn MacConnell and he didn't know why he had rambled on so.

He sat there staring straight ahead of him, his animation gone, his shoulders squared, his back straight and yet graceful, his hat held between ceaselessly plucking hands, a strange and sudden misery in every line of him. His wide, tender mouth was held firmly as though, should he relax it might tremble. Poppy did nothing, said nothing, for what was there to do or say? Richard Goodall sat between them on the bench and though Conn was not aware of the frailty of that presence, of the insubstantial hold he had on Poppy, Poppy knew it was still as strong as the hawsers which held the great ships to their berth in the docklands.

"But what about you?" He turned his head then and his eyes caressed her face, their colour like the blubells which would carpet the spinney very soon. They told her he didn't really want to know about her marriage but politeness insisted on it. They had parted nine years ago when they were children. He had told her what he had done in those eight years and now, as people do who have not met in a long while, it was her turn to tell her story.

"Your . . . your husband?" he prompted courteously when she did not answer, though his eyes were blank. "He is a local man?"

"Yes, Richard Goodall."

"The son of . . . of the man who donated his yard coat?"

"Yes, Richard is the elder son."

"When?"

"Nearly four years ago."

"You must have been very young."

"Yes," and for God's sweet sake don't ask me how I came

to marry him for I don't know myself, she wanted to add but of course she couldn't. She only knew in her own mind that it was something to do with Eliza.

"Children?" His voice was clipped and he looked away to hide the expression on her face when she answered.

"No. No children."

There was astonishment in his voice when he turned back to her. "No children in three years?"

"No."

He could not ask her why, though the question was in his eyes so she hurried on with her tale. "Mrs Goodall died – she had been ill – and afterwards . . . I took over her place. My husband" – she saw him flinch but could not spare him – "he is a good man."

"You love him then?"

"You have no right to ask me that." There was a harsh note in her voice.

"No, I apologise. It has nothing to do with me but I canna forget that braw wee lassie who risked everything for a sorely injured boy. I will *never* forget her."

There was a brooding silence while they both stared out across the cemetery, busy with their own thoughts which, had they known it, were very similar. Long shadows were creeping over the quiet grass, for at this time of the year the days were short. There was a soft twitter of birds in the trees as they settled for the night and an early owl hooted, reminding them of the passage of time.

She jumped hastily to her feet, fidgeting with her skirt, her muff, her parcel and at once he rose politely beside her.

"Well . . ." he said, his face carved in stone.

"Well, it has been . . . nice."

"Yes, very nice," staring somewhere over her bonnet.

She held out her hand and he looked at it in surprise then

took it reluctantly, as though the idea of touching her was anathema to him.

"I wish you good fortune in your career, Conn," she managed to say with a steady voice, though her heart was breaking over and over again.

"Thank you I hope . . . well, you must go. May I see you to . . . perhaps a hansom?"

"No, really. The tram stop is just . . ."

His eyes were a deep lavender blue, like the sky above as twilight draws near, and very soft.

"Goodbye, *mo annsachd*," he said gently, then turned and walked away with a long easy stride which carried him from her as quickly as he could manage it. He was graceful, beautiful, his hair glowing like a torch in the gathering dusk.

She remembered nothing of the journey home. Though she had implied that the tram stop was nearby, it was not and she must have walked over a mile along the still-congested street until she reached London Road. She stepped out with no conscious idea of where she was going, guided by her instinct that pleaded with her to get home to safety, like a wounded animal seeking its lair. She gave no thought to those at Long Reach, who would be worried about her, nor Richard who would be awake by now, her broken spirit centred on the tall, red-haired man who had just walked out of her life. The man she loved, of course. As a boy and now as a man.

She sat on the top deck of the tram in the open air, to the conductor's surprise since ladies didn't usually like to get themselves blown about in the smart lick the horses got up. She didn't answer when he spoke, merely offering her fare then staring out at the backs of the horses and the peaked cap of the driver just below her. The conductor shrugged and ran downstairs saying to Sam that there was nowt so queer as folk, especially if they happened to be female.

She alighted at the tram stop in Old Swan, wondering without much interest where Jem was with the gig, forgetting that she had told them she would walk from the tram stop up to the farm. It didn't matter. Along Prescot Road and then on to the lane that led to the farmhouse. It wasn't far and it was not yet completely dark. Besides, she knew every inch of the way and the walk would give her another few minutes of blessed oblivion before she took up her duties as Richard Goodall's wife.

She heard the clip-clop of his horse's hooves first, turning out of Prescot Road and into the lane when she did. The lane was little more than a track with two deep furrows worn by the wheels of a hundred carts and waggons, with a grassy hump between. There was a deep ditch on either side below the neat dry-stone wall her pa and Willie had repaired only last week. Already the ditches were beginning to be submerged by a rising tide of growth, the wildflowers which came up in spring and would be waist-high in a couple of months' time.

It was strange, she was to think to herself afterwards, that even in the pit of despairing misery she dwelled in she knew who it was but she could not bring herself to care.

"Well, if it isn't the charming Mrs Goodall," he drawled as she turned to face him. "I thought it was you as I came out of the Grimshaw Arms. I said to myself, 'I'm sure that's the charming Mrs Goodall, I'd recognise her anywhere even after all these years,' and sure enough I was right. 'I must just have a word with her,' I said to myself, 'let her know I've not forgotten her or she will think me very remiss.' "

His thoroughbred mare danced and jinked on her slender dainty legs, rolling her eyes and shaking her head but

Dominic Cooper held her steady with his experienced horseman's hands.

He grinned and his teeth gleamed white in the deepening darkness. "Have you nothing to say to an old friend, Mrs Goodall? I seem to remember you had a way with words a few years ago. But that was before you married that . . . weakling who, I hear, cannot satisfy any woman, let alone one as . . . high-spirited as yourself. Well, my dear, that can soon be rectified and I can guarantee you will have no cause for complaint. Don't think I've forgotten you. I see you about the place now and again and marvel at my own patience. I am not renowned for my patience, did you know that, Mrs Goodall? But now that we meet again I'm sure something can be arranged to suit us both. Well, I must be off. My family calls, as, I suppose, does yours. Good evening to you, Mrs Goodall. We shall meet again quite soon, I'm sure."

When he had gone, when the sound of his animal's hooves had died away and total silence reigned Poppy Goodall sank slowly to her knees, wrapped her arms about herself, bowed her head and began to rock in the age-old way of a woman who is fast in the depths of sorrow.

Who was there to protect her now?

23

"Yer never walk up ter't spinney like yer used ter, lass," Elly said diffidently one warm day in June as she and Poppy worked in Eliza's garden. "In fact, yer never go nowhere beyond farm gate an' when yer go ter town yer tekk me wi' yer. Is there . . . is owt wrong?"

Poppy continued to prune delicately the Morning Glory which Eliza had planted against the wall the summer before she died. Its dainty pink and white bell-shaped flowers contrasted sharply with the vivid green of its foliage which had already grown half the height of the house. It rioted against the wall, clinging and twisting on the trellis, ready to take over the climbing rose which covered the porch. At sundown it closed its petals and at the first peep of dawn opened them again, but Eliza had liked it because on moonlight nights it remained wide awake, hospitably offering shelter to moths and butterflies.

Poppy carefully snipped another wayward shoot, then stepped back to study the shape. It was just the kind of day she liked, not too hot, just right to be gardening and she and Elly, who had begun to notice the difference between dahlias and daffodils, were working companionably side by side. They had weeded one mixed bed of delphiniums and foxgloves, in front of which was a vivid mass of old-fashioned pinks in every shade from the palest to the deepest and now Elly had begun on the one beneath the parlour window while Poppy took up her shears to attack the Morning Glory.

"Richard should be out here on a glorious day like this," Poppy said, deliberately ignoring Elly's question, pretending she had not heard it or if she had could think of no suitable answer that would satisfy her stepmother. How could she possibly tell her of that day last March when Dominic Cooper had followed her up the lane threatening her with . . . well, it would be rape, wouldn't it, and of how, since then, she had been terrified to be alone. Nor of all the other times over the years when he had menaced her, not only physically but taking her peace of mind, so that even here in the safety of Eliza's garden she sometimes felt the urge to glance over her shoulder as though he might have crept up on her and be leaning against the garden gate in that arrogant way of his. Not that even he would have the nerve to come on to Tom Goodall's land, not after what he had done to Tom Goodall's son, though surely after all this time a report of Tom's "strangeness", with a possible loss of memory, would have reached Coopers Edge.

Tom had become quite used to his elder son's affliction and the necessity for him to lie flat on his back in bed for the remainder of his days, though it is doubtful he thought of it exactly in those terms. Johnny's marriage to May, the birth of Tom's healthy grandsons and May's happy ability to keep Johnny where he belonged, on the land, had obliterated from his memory that day when Dominic Cooper had felled his elder lad, and, far worse, had not been punished for it, and Tom pottered through the days, happy as a pig in muck, as Evan described it. He spent time wherever he fancied with frequent trips back to the farmhouse to check on the progress of his grandsons, Tom and Jack, as the twins had been christened. Well, it was Thomas and John, really, but May, with her usual unconcern for anyone's wishes but her own, had soon shortened them to Tom and Jack. They were the hub of life, the centre of the universe to all those who lived beneath the roof of Long Reach Farm, with the possible exception of Poppy and Richard. It was not that Poppy objected to them but they were a constant reminder to her of her own childless state which was likely to be permanent, and sometimes the despair swamped her. Their vigorously yelling presence had every female in the house, plus Tom, running to find out what was to do and how to put whatever it was to rights. They grew and thrived, nourished at May's breast, dark and handsome and very demanding but with so many willing slaves at their command Poppy was of the opinion that, young as they were, they would soon be ruined, though May didn't seem to care. She gave them all her attention, the queen tending to the needs of princes, and nobody questioned it.

So there was nothing Poppy would have liked better than to walk up to the top field and take refuge in the spinney, especially at this time of the year when wood sorrel would be in flower hiding wood mice, bank voles and shrews, hedgehogs and rabbits and hares. Where the woodcock and pheasant and nightjars nested and butterflies went mad with joy in the sunny clearing. When the growth of hazel would be dense and dark green in contrast to the paler shade of the hazelnuts and high above it all the boughs of oak and ash would be thick with summer leaves. No matter what the time of year Poppy had found immense peace there and a welcome escape from the demands of the farm, but it was three months now since she had been near it and Dominic Cooper was to blame.

"Did yer 'ear whorr I said, lass?" Elly asked quietly. "Yer know I'm not one fer pokin' me nose where it don't belong, but yer've not bin yerself fer weeks now. Not that I don't like goin' ter town wi' yer, I do. It's a rare treat an' that outfit yer bought me ter go in, well, I feel like the Queen in it, burr I can't 'elp askin' meself, why?"

Poppy tutted and shook her head, snipping testily at another tendril of Morning Glory, cutting away more than she meant to in her agitation.

"Well, if you would rather I took Nelly it could be arranged," she said loftily.

"That's not wharr I meant an' yer know it. Tekk 'oo yer like, I don't care. Wharr I want ter know is why tekk anyone? Years yer've bin goin' to't bank on yer own, an' now, sudden like, yer must 'ave someone with yer. Summat's put wind up yer is my guess or . . . well, I dunno . . ." Her voice trailed away uncertainly.

"Stuff and nonsense. Nothing has put the wind up me. I just . . . just like company, that's all."

"Rightio, lass, if yer don't want ter tell me then that's an end to it. I'll shut me gob but . . . Poppy, if yer do need ter talk, I'm 'ere, so think on."

Something in her stepmother's voice made Poppy turn to look at her. She was very fond of her pa's wife and she trusted her above anyone, but somehow she found she could not share her fears with her. She could share them with no one. Tom would not understand if she was to tell him about Dominic Cooper's threats and might become distressed if his name was even mentioned and God alone knew what he might do. Johnny would not believe her, for despite what had happened on her wedding day she felt that Johnny still harboured the belief that it had been a tragic accident and Dominic was not to be blamed. She sometimes thought that if May had not been in his bed to keep him amused he might once again have taken to slipping out on his old jaunts with the gentry. Then there were Evan and Tommy who, should circumstances ask it of them, would defend her to the death, but they were farm workers, men of the lower class who could hardly be expected to knock on the door of Coopers Edge and demand that the son of the house discontinue his harassment of their little mistress. Her pa and brothers were the same, working men and if she told them and they acted on it, would find themselves in deep trouble. No, she must tell no one. There was no need to really, was there? As long as she kept close to the farm, for the time being at least, and made sure she was never alone when she went off it, surely, *surely* that bastard would give up and lavish his unwanted attentions – unwanted at least by her – on some other woman who would welcome them. But perhaps that was the reason he persisted, despite having a pretty, wealthy young wife and two children of his own, both girls, unfortunately. Dominic Cooper only wanted what was hard to get. He liked the pursuit of an unwilling quarry and she had no doubt that the moment he had her he would lose interest.

Elly watched her closely as she resumed speaking. "Yer know yer can tell me, lass. If summat were troublin' yer, I mean. It's not that . . ." She took a deep breath. "Well, yer've bin . . . absentminded like, ever since you an' Jinny met that chap in Liverpool last back end an' I've bin wonderin' if it were 'im you was feared of."

Poppy curbed an urgent need to burst into hysterical laughter. To have accused the very man who would defend her with his life if he knew of the situation was surely the biggest irony of all.

"No, really, Elly. There's no one . . . nothing. I've just been busy; the babies, you know, and May doesn't seem to want to share my place as mistress which she's entitled to. Besides, I enjoy your company so why shouldn't you come to town with me?" She smiled. "And you can see that Mr Hilton at the bank thinks it very suitable for a young woman such as myself to have a chaperone. Now, I must go and get the gig ready for tomorrow. Not that Nelly couldn't do it, or Jinny for that matter. They really have made a successful team, wouldn't you agree? Jinny is so level-headed and of course Nelly is a rock. Mrs Goodall would have been proud of them."

Jinny's level-headedness and Nelly's rock-like qualities were put under considerable strain the next day.

Nelly was weighing out a pound of cheese for Mrs Ogden who had once been served by Mrs Goodall, then Poppy, and was still a regular customer even after all these years.

"It's just over, Mrs Ogden. Shall I tekk a birroff?" Nelly asked cheerfully, completely at ease now in the busy commercial world into which she had – terrified out of her wits – been propelled when Poppy was forced to stay at home with her crippled husband.

"No, leave it on, dear. Mr Ogden's very partial to your cheese and it'll get eaten."

"Very glad to 'ear it, Mrs Ogden. Now, will there be owt else? Them chickens is fresh killed only yesterd'y."

"Aye, go on then. We'll have us one for us dinner on Sunday."

Jinny was counting out a dozen large brown eggs from one of the deep, lined baskets into the one Mrs Atkinson held out to her. Mrs Atkinson was another old customer from the days of Mrs Goodall. Jinny's fingers were dextrous as she tucked the eggs in the teacloth Mrs Atkinson brought with her to protect them. Mrs Atkinson had purchased two dozen butter shells, since she and Mr Atkinson were to entertain Mr Atkinson's brother and his wife and Mrs Atkinson wished to impress her sister-in-law. There were two fowls, a pint of fresh cream and a pound of cheese lying beside the eggs and butter. A good customer was Mrs Atkinson and Jinny was most careful with her purchases.

She was smiling, her plump young face rounding to apple-cheeked firmness, her eyes on her own hand as Mrs Atkinson counted out what she owed and, though she could not have said why since he made no move to attract her attention, she glanced over Mrs Atkinson's shoulder and into a pair of the brightest blue eyes she had only ever seen once before. For a moment she was totally overwhelmed, fumbling with the coins Mrs Atkinson had given her, even dropping a couple among the attractive display of cheeses she and Nelly had set up early that morning.

"Oh dear," said Mrs Atkinson, rummaging among the display, surprised, for usually Jinny was nimble-fingered, taking the money and always giving the correct change.

"Sorry, Mrs Atkinson," Jinny mumbled, dragging her gaze away from the enormous bulk of the red-haired chap with whom she and Poppy had taken tea last back end in one of the luxurious drawing-rooms at the Adelphi Hotel.

He was standing quietly, his back against the whitewashed wall, keeping out of the way of the darting shoppers, attracting a great deal of attention nevertheless as he had the last time he had visited the market, though Jinny knew nothing of that, of course. The ladies, doing their best to be discreet about it, admired his fine physique, the smooth planes of his unsmiling face, the brilliance of his hair and eyes and the excellent cut and quality of his clothes. The men eyed his size respectfully, giving him a wide berth, though he offered no threat to any of them, those pushing trolleys careful not to catch his toes.

When he noticed he had Jinny's attention he bowed his head gallantly and she could feel the blush begin somewhere inside her, rippling outwards until it seemed her whole body was flushed with it. He made no move, however, to come near the stall since it was two or three deep in customers.

For an hour he stood there. It was mid-afternoon and gradually, as time drew on, the stall's dairy produce dwindled until there was nothing left for sale. From the corner of her eye Jinny had watched him in between serving customers and even Nelly, who only managed to do what she did by dint of superhuman concentration on the work in hand, nudged her, asking if she'd noticed him, as if anyone could miss him. What did Jinny think he was up to, she hissed, wondering if he had his eye on the comely dairymaid – not Nelly, of course – and should they send for Bertie? He was a gent, that was obvious, in his light grey lounge jacket and trousers, the jacket undone. Under the jacket he wore a pale lemon waistcoat. His boots were narrow, pointed, black and highly polished, a real dandy, Nelly thought and was quite overwhelmed when he caught her staring at him, and winked!

They were beginning to clear up when he strolled over to them and both girls, seeing him come towards them, felt a great urge to clutch at one another and squeak.

"Good afternoon . . . Jeannie, isn't it?" he asked, smiling at her with such sweetness and humour she almost swooned. There was a look of quiet amusement behind his alert gaze as though he were aware of the effect he was having on her and Nelly.

"Jinny," she answered automatically.

"Of course, Jinny, I'm sorry. D'ye no' remember me, Jinny?"

His smile was a thing of such engaging but sincere charm Jinny almost fell back before it. Remember him? How could anyone, man or woman, having once met him forget him? her eyes said but she could not speak.

Those still searching for bargains among the dwindling crowd turned to stare, wondering, no doubt, what the well-dressed young gentleman, who surely couldn't be shopping, was up to talking to the lasses behind Goodall's dairy stall? There was a great deal of cheerful noise as stall-holders who still had perishables for sale called out the splendid bargains to be had at this late hour, and porters whistled the latest music-hall tunes as they began the task of clearing up the rubbish that had accumulated during the day. The sun still shone obliquely through the high windows in the roof, picking out the spread of colours on the fruit vendor's stall, red and green of apple, blaze of orange and cool lemon. Bertie went past, trundling a trolley, his small eyes curious and staring, obviously wondering, like others, what the toff was up to. It was in his eyes, should he stop and enquire? but the width of the chap's shoulders, his great height, the hard lines of his body beneath his clothes convinced him to do otherwise and he went by without stopping.

The big man cast his vivid blue gaze on Nelly, plain Nelly who had never caught any man's eye in her entire life and his smile was just as kind, just as disarming, before he turned back to Jinny.

"My name is Alick MacConnell," raising his eyebrows enquiringly.

"Aye, sir, I remember yer. We 'ad tea at the Adelphi. You an' me an' Poppy."

It was strange really how his face changed, not only the shape but the colour when she mentioned Poppy's name. She didn't know why. It was a fine face, with gentleness in it, and yet strong, with a jaw not many men would care to tackle. His lips were firm and yet smiling at the same time as he looked down at her from his great height and when she had spoken Poppy's name he had drawn in a breath which might have been surprise, wonder, or was it delight? How could Jinny know the answers since she was an innocent girl with no experience of men?

"Aye, lassie, that was me. I was wondering . . ." He paused, "If Poppy might . . ." There it was again, that strange expression on his face. "I was wondering if Poppy . . . well, I thought, you see, that she might be here. She and an older lady used to work the stall a long time ago when . . ."

His eyes became a dark, unfocused blue as though he had gone back in time to some memory that disturbed him, a sort of sad look that made both Jinny and Nelly, who was hanging on his every word and gazing at him in awe, want to say something like "There, there, never mind," as women do to a hurt child. Then the look vanished to be replaced by one of barely concealed entreaty.

"I'm going home, ye ken, back to Scotland and I didna want to go without saying goodbye to her," he explained. "I didna want tae come to the farm neither since I dinna know the family, ye ken." His slight Scottish brogue had become stronger. "Only Poppy and Dougie . . ."

Poppy's brother! What had he to do with anything? both girls wondered, for though Jinny had never met him, since he had left home before her ma had married Reuben Appleton, Nelly remembered him. A bad un', he'd been, in and out of trouble, so how did this gentleman, obviously from the upper classes of society, come to know Douglas, or Poppy for that matter? It was a great mystery and one they were eager to solve.

"So I thought I'd walk round here and say goodbye to Poppy but it seems I'm out of luck."

His face was hard to read. There was something in it, young as he was, that spoke of pain, of hardship, of dreams unfulfilled, of sadness and yet a resolution to allow none of these things to stop him moving on. Something, at the moment, was holding him back, but when he had put it behind him, whatever it was, he would get on with his life. Neither of them had the faintest notion of what it could be. They both stared at him in open-mouthed wonder, completely at sea and he almost had to snap his fingers to recapture their attention.

"So . . . she's no' here today then?"

Jinny blinked. "Eeh, no, sir, she's not 'ere any day. She's never bin 'ere since she an' Master Richard wed."

His face, already grave and still, froze to a pale marble, his golden freckles, his ruddy eyebrows and his unruly shock of red hair seeming to become even more vivid as his face paled.

"I see, of course. I do beg your pardon. I should have known. She is a . . . a farm wife now and could not possibly spare the time for the stall."

He was about to turn away, smiling his thanks, unable to say goodbye even when Jinny's voice stopped him.

"Well, it's not just that, sir, not really, though o' course she's very busy wi' May an' Master Johnny an' then there's Tom an' Jack who tekk up a great deal of May's time so Poppy 'as ter do it all 'erself. Master Richard needs a rare lot o' lookin' after, yer see. Me ma 'elps but Master Richard, 'e don't want no one ter see to 'im but Poppy an' sometimes she looks so—"

Jinny stopped speaking abruptly, aware suddenly of the total incomprehension on the big chap's face and also that she might be revealing more of the private lives of the Goodall family than she should. After all, she did not know this man. Poppy did, though, that had been evident the last time they met and though Jinny was a simple country girl with only the minimum of education passed on to her by Poppy, she was not daft. There had been something . . . something, she couldn't describe it on that day last September, between Poppy and this man. Something they had shared that had excluded her. She didn't know what it could have been, for they had not met since they were children, they had said, but he was looking at her now with such a bewildered expression she could not deny him further explanation of what she had already started, could she? And he was going away, back to Scotland, he said, so what harm could there be in telling him? It was no secret. Everyone knew about and was sorry for Richard Goodall. She didn't really know what she meant by *explanation*, for what right did he have to such a thing? But then . . . Oh Lordy, she was getting so mixed up and all the while he stood there like one of those tailor's dummies in Dawbarn and Davies' window in Bold Street, nothing about him alive except his eyes and his hair.

Then he spoke. No more than a croak really. A frog in his throat which he did his best to clear.

"Is . . . is Poppy's husband . . . unwell?" he managed to say, his face quite ghastly now. Jinny could feel Nelly leaning against her as though this chap's distress, and it *was* distress, was devastating her.

Jinny shook her head sadly and Nelly bowed hers.

"Oh, aye. Well, 'e's not poorly or owt like that, it's just since the accident 'e's . . ."

"Accident?"

"Aye, on their weddin' day an' all. It were that Cooper lad's fault."

"Cooper?"

"Aye, 'im from Coopers Edge. 'E an' Master Johnny were thick as thieves."

In her compassion – why should she feel compassion? she was to wonder later – for the big man she let her tongue run away with her again, saying more than she should about Dominic Cooper and Johnny Goodall, describing to him the trouble Master Johnny got into with his pa over his association with Mr Cooper and his friends, the wild riding and, it was whispered, though how much truth there was in it, Jinny didn't know, the gambling and Master Johnny only a farmer's lad when all was said and done and yet Mr Cooper was never off the doorstep then, she said.

"Anyroad up, I don't know why" – she shook her head sadly and so did the speechless Nelly – "Mister Cooper clobbered Master Richard at 'is weddin' feast an' Master Richard went down, 'ittin' 'is 'ead on't winder bottom. Poor Master Richard an' poor Poppy. On 'er weddin' day an' all, an' now Master Richard's bin lyin' in that bed for over four years an' Mr Cooper gorroff scot free. Old Mr Goodall never gorr over it, did 'e, Nelly?" turning her sad young face to Nelly who, despite the passage of time since the dreadful event, was nearly in tears.

The man stood as though turned to stone, his body so rigid and frozen that when a porter said politely, "'Scuse me, sir," since he was blocking the way, he appeared neither to hear nor see him and the porter, sighing, was forced to manoeuvre his trolley round him.

There was a long silence. Nelly and Jinny exchanged glances and then, when Mr MacConnell didn't speak, began to fidget with the empty baskets and trays that had to be taken out to the gig and returned to the dairy where they would be scoured ready for next market day. They couldn't hang about here, could they, or Poppy would begin to worry, fearing they'd had an accident in the gig. Jinny drove it competently but there would be a great deal of traffic moving out of the city at this time of the day.

She cleared her throat. "Well, sir . . ." she began and as she spoke he returned to them. That was just how it seemed to the two young women. As though he had been away, in his mind, at least, for several minutes, and had come back from that journey, startled to find the two of them watching him with great concern. His eyes, surrounded by thick, auburn lashes, had lost that unfocused sunken look, as though they had been haunted by bad dreams, had come alive, a brilliant life, an incredible, incredulous life in them which was awesome to see.

"D'ye mean to tell me that . . . that Poppy's husband has been bedridden since . . . that on their wedding day he . . . he became paralysed and since then he's not been able to . . . to . . . Dear sweet Christ . . ."

Conn MacConnell threw back his head in an exultant gesture neither Nelly nor Jinny could understand. Both women, still innocent virgins, blushed deeply, for just the same there was no mistaking his meaning. They were outraged, red-faced with it, turning away from him in embarrassment, crashing baskets and trays about as though to cover, not only their own awkwardness, but their deep offence. To speak of such a thing . . . well, he hadn't said it in so many words but it was more what he hadn't said than what he had. And would you look at him. He was like a dog with two tails, wagging both of them with what looked suspiciously like triumph. Poor Master Richard lying there able to do nothing at all, let alone make love to his wife and this big chap almost crowing over it. It was disgraceful and the two stiff backs presented to him told Conn MacConnell so and he was instantly contrite. It was just that – another surge of rapture jolted through him – to be told after all the heartache he had suffered at the thought of another man having the woman Conn MacConnell loved in his bed every night, doing to her what Conn longed to do, to learn that it had not happened, that she was still the untouched maid he had left all those years ago, was almost too much joy to bear. He must put it right though with these two young women. He must persuade them that he had not meant what he had, that they had mistaken his meaning and that, most important of all, they must not blab about it in the kitchen of the farmhouse when they returned.

"Poor chap," he began, "not to be able to run his own farm. After such an active life, no' to be able to walk his own fields. I canna bear to think about it," and he genuinely couldn't, somewhat ashamed now of the vast rejoicing he had felt at the news of Richard Goodall's disablement. "And so young, too. What will he be, in his twenties? Is there no hope that he'll ever recover, lassie? A fine, braw laddie wi' all his life before him."

At the sound of the genuine sympathy in his voice both girls turned hesitantly and it was evident from their expressions that they were thinking they had perhaps been a bit hasty in judging him. That he hadn't meant what they had thought he meant. Like everyone who knew the Goodalls and the tragedy of Master Richard's injury on his wedding day it was only natural that, being his wedding day, his inability to be a husband to his new wife would figure in their thoughts.

"Has he no brother?" he continued.

"Oh, aye, Master Johnny. Then there's t'master burr 'e's not bin right since, so Poppy's in charge of . . . well, most things."

Keep off the subject of Poppy for the moment.

"Then the farm continues to prosper?" In his voice was no more than the concern that a virtual stranger would show for someone who has suffered a serious setback and the women began to thaw, falling again under the spell of his smile.

"Oh, aye. We all think the world o' Poppy, don't we, Nelly?" Nelly nodded wordlessly. "Evan ses she's a brain like a man," which was evidently the highest praise a man could heap on a woman. "She decides what crops go in, sugar beet an' such."

"Does she consult her husband?" he was able to ask smoothly, a non-committal expression on his face.

Jinny was amazed. "Eeh, no. Well, she did try at first, like, burr 'e's not int'rested no more." A huge sigh. Poor Master Richard, the sigh said, who was interested in nothing and no one, his only pleasure, or so it seemed to them, baiting his wife. "So Poppy does as she likes, seein' as 'ow Master Johnny's not trained up proper yet an' maister's not . . ."

There she went again, she told herself crossly. Mr MacConnell had only to smile, look at her with his lovely eyes and she was disclosing the confidential affairs of the Goodalls which were nothing to do with him.

"Anyroad, me an' Nelly'd best be off," she said firmly. "We've a long drive ter Old Swan."

"Right, lass, and I've things to see to before my journey tomorrow so I'll say goodbye and thank you. Ye've been most kind."

They didn't know quite how but they dimpled just the same. At least Jinny did, for Nelly hadn't a dimple in her.

"May I ask a wee favour of ye lassies before ye go?" He smiled. His face had regained its look of glowing health and his teeth gleamed in it.

They both looked wary.

"It's just that I'd be obliged if ye'd say nothing to Mrs

Goodall about me. It's been a long time and, to be honest, I'd rather she didna ken I was asking after her, her being a married woman. It might be awkward for her."

They weren't quite sure how but they promised nevertheless, since it was none of their business and he *was* off back to Scotland tomorrow. Their mistress had enough on her plate without raking up the past, whatever it was.

They watched him stride away, his easy, graceful walk fascinating them, reminding Jinny of a big striped tiger she had seen in a cage at the Zoological Gardens. His bright head, as he moved in and out of the patches of sunlight, turned to red-gold, to glinting auburn and amber. A thick wavy mass with a dozen colours of red and gold in it and they both sighed as he disappeared through the wide doorway.

24

Poppy was playing the piano, a treat she rarely allowed herself in her busy day, when May came, or rather sidled, into the room, shutting the door gently behind her. In fact she was so quiet Poppy was barely aware of her standing by the closed door and continued to let the music of Chopin breathe softly round her, then drift through the open window into the rapidly falling darkness outside.

It was a beautiful night, still retaining the warmth of the day and above the roof of the stable a full moon was creeping. The sky was a deep lavender blue, darkening to purple, and round the moon was a circle of silver blue. A pale trace of cloud, like a length of chiffon, drifted across it. The night scents of stock and roses crept into the room as the music crept out and for a moment both women, even May who was not one for flights of fancy, felt the magic of it wash about them.

Her voice broke the spell. "There's a big, red-'aired chap askin' for yer at top o't lane, Poppy." May was clearly excited but her voice was no more than a whisper. Despite this, Poppy's hands crashed on the keyboard and she whirled about as though May had stood in the yard and shouted it to the rooftops. The sound of the words drowned her, deafened her, going round and round in her head, pounding against her brain until she felt herself sliding down into what she seriously thought would be her first faint. She didn't, of course, for women like her had not the time nor the choice for fainting. She held on to the sides of the piano stool with white-knuckled hands, staring at May as though she were an apparition from another world speaking a foreign language.

"I sent 'im up to't spinney," May hissed confidentially. "Well, daft thing were 'angin' about fer anyone ter see, large as life an' twice as bloody 'andsome. Yer couldn't miss 'im, silly beggar, not wi't size of 'im an' even in't dark that 'air of 'is could be seen fer miles." She smiled and waited.

Poppy felt as though a clenched fist had been rammed into her stomach, emptying her lungs of breath and making her heart crash painfully against her ribs. For a moment it hammered there then flew into her throat where it fluttered like a bird trying to free itself.

"What?" she croaked. Her face had lost every vestige of colour, even her lips turning pale and her eyes in the lamplight had the transparency of rain, all the blue faded away with shock.

May sighed impatiently. "I said there were . . ."

"I heard . . . but I don't understand. Dear God, May, how did you . . . Oh, Jesus, dear sweet Jesus. What . . ?"

She began to shake and her teeth were inclined to chatter. She knew exactly what May had said to her but she couldn't seem to make sense of it and even if she did, what was she to do about it?

"Now calm down, lass, calm down," May said in a hoarse voice which passed for a whisper. "I dunno 'oo 'e is nor what 'e's ter do wi' you but let's get one thing straight. What yer do outer this 'ouse an' 'oo yer do it with is nobody's business but thine. Bugger it, no one'd blame yer if . . . well, yer know wharr I mean but wharrever it is, no one'll know of it from me. Norr after what yer've done fer me. I owe me life ter you, Poppy, 'cos I were ready ter go down ter't landin' stage an' chuck meself in't Mersey. I'm grateful burr I don't like bein' be'olden ter no one so I reckon we're fair an' square after this, you an' me, so think on."

"But how did you . . .?" Poppy began through clenched teeth, barely aware of what May was saying she was so stunned.

"I were walkin' up ter Elly's place ter ask 'er fer that colic remedy fer our Jack. 'E's gorra real bellyache on 'im. Anyroad, I never got there. This chap looms up outer't dark. Gawd, I nearly wet meself. Don't be feared, 'e whispered, I'll not 'arm yer, I only want, if yer'll be so kind – lovely way o' talkin' 'e 'ad – ter speak ter someone in't th'ouse. 'E asked me if I knew yer and when I said yes he said could I be trusted wi' a message for yer. No one must know of it 'cept Poppy, 'e ses, an' if I wouldn't swear on summat I 'old dear, that's 'ow he purrit, 'e'd 'op it an' ferget the 'ole bloody thing. Good job it were me 'e picked on an' not one o' t'others. Well, I swore on our Jack an' Tom's lives," she said simply, for above all others May idolised her two handsome sons. Besides which, like most uneducated folk, she was superstitious and she wasn't about to tempt fate by swearing an oath and then breaking it and therefore threatening the health and safety of her babies.

"What does he want?" Poppy asked almost voicelessly, but already, no matter what he wanted, nor how difficult it might be to get to the spinney and find out, the magical prospect of seeing him again was beginning to sweep through her, singing in her veins and fluttering rapturously about her heart which was already doing handstands in her breast.

Why was he here? What madness had encouraged him to risk, not his place in life, for no one here knew or cared about him, but hers? Why, after all these months of living and working in Liverpool, of doing the honourable thing by keeping out of her way since she was a married woman, had he come sneaking up to the back of the farm, haphazardly accosting one of those who lived beneath its roof and extracting a promise from her to send Poppy out to him. God in heaven, he might have chosen Nelly, or Beth, both of whom would have come shrieking down to the house of intruders, waking everyone in it, rousing the men in their quarters and generally causing chaos in Poppy Goodall's life.

But to see him again! The joy of it melted the cast-iron shell in which her emotions hid, emotions which played no part in the life she and Richard shared, emotions she had locked up years ago. It allowed them to flood out on a great wave of gladness, a delight which left her breathless with longing and she could not resist it. Just once . . . just once, she breathed to herself. Just this once, no matter what it is he's come for, let her loosen her hold on sanity, on loyalty to her family, on the devotion she had always shown to Richard. Forget responsibility and the level-headed calm with which she ordered her life and fly on enchanted wings through the moonlight up to the spinney where love was, where joy was, where Conn was. Just once and she would treasure that once to the end of her days.

"Well?" said May softly. "Are yer ter go then, or not? I'll cover for yer. Say yer've . . . I dunno, I'll think o' summat."

Poppy lifted her head and looked at May suspiciously. She and May had not got on when they were youngsters, May's envy of Poppy's position at Long Reach souring her, making her snipe at Poppy and, if she could, do her a bad turn. She had mellowed as the years moved on and since her marriage to Johnny it had been May's opinion that she, May Goodall, was the one to be envied. Didn't May have everything she had ever wanted and so could afford to be magnanimous. Not that she knew the word but she felt sorry for this woman who had once had everything May had ever aspired to. May had a grand home on a successful farm, a husband who would one day inherit it all and two beautiful sons and it was all down to Poppy, for May was realist enough to recognise that Johnny Goodall would not have married her if he could have got out of it. Poppy had done it and so she owed Poppy. Now she was to pay back that debt. May's nature was not to be forgiving or grateful, not to anyone, but Poppy was the exception and, in an ungracious sort of way, if she could do her a good turn, she would. This was it.

But Poppy was not aware of this. She still remembered the spite, the enmity that had once existed between them. Could May be trusted? It was in her narrow-eyed appraisal and May saw it.

"Look, lass, it's nowt ter me if yer've a chap."

Poppy was horrified. "I haven't a chap, as you call it. In the name of all that's sensible, would I . . ."

"Orlright, orlright, don't go off 'alf-cocked, but wharrelse can I think when there's this big bugger lurkin' at top o't lane askin' for yer an' all this secrecy?"

"He is not my lover, if that's what you're thinking, May Goodall, and if . . ."

"Bloody 'ell, Poppy, d'yer think I care? I've got wharr I want in me bed an' if you want t'same then . . ."

"Look here . . ." Poppy's face was scarlet with indignation.

"Poppy, for God's sake, *go.* I don't know what yer arguin'

wi' me for. Now, I'm goin' back inter't kitchen an' what you do is up to you. There's a chap out there waitin' ter see yer burr I'll tell yer this. 'E were very persistent an' I reckon if yer don't go to 'im 'e'll come knockin' on't door askin' for yer."

She knew the path from the farmyard gate, which she didn't open but climbed in case it squealed for lack of oil, up to the spinney as well as she knew her own face in the mirror, better really, since she'd no time, nor the inclination these days, to be peering at her own reflection in the mirror. She'd come up here often enough. In all the seasons of the year, at all times of the day but it was not often she came at night, not since Dominic Cooper, at any rate.

The yard dogs swished their plumed tails on the cobbles as she went by, their chains clinking softly but they didn't even stand up for they had caught her scent. They were good guard dogs, fierce and noisy with those they didn't know and she had wondered idly if she could chance taking them with her on a solitary walk up to the spinney some time. Would they guard her against Dominic Cooper if he showed up and made some movement they didn't care for? The trouble was, they were Tom's dogs, obeying only him, or perhaps Evan, and could she trust them to do what she told them? It was a chance, as yet, she had not taken.

The moon was as good as a lamp, lighting her way, casting its strange silvery light across the field, draining the grasses and wildflowers of their colour so that the world was clothed in black and white, grey and silver, but the path was clearly defined, a darker thread, on the rough ground. The stars cast their own light, a brilliant scatter of sugar crystals thrown across a length of dark blue velvet and so clear was the sky even the far-off golden glow from the city could easily be seen. There were little rustles and squeaks as small night creatures sped out of her way and a barn owl shrieked. A sudden noisy commotion of birds up ahead in an ivied tree told her that the owl was hovering over them.

She began to walk more quickly, her eagerness tripping her up over clumps of rough grass and small declivities in the path, for the strange light inclined her to misjudge their height or depth. Her senses ran ahead of her, picturing him as she had seen him on the last two occasions they had met since they had become adults. His hesitant, boyish smile as though he was somewhat out of his depth. The melting blue of his eyes that told her exactly how he felt about her. The rough red tangle of his hair that she longed passionately to run her hands through, his strong body, arresting and vigorous in its young masculinity. Her mind, and now her body, called out to his and it was all she could do not to break into a wild gallop.

He must have seen her coming up the track. It had not occurred to her to change from the pale summer dress she wore, though now, as he stepped out from behind a massively broad oak tree on the edge of the spinney, she realised she must have been clearly visible.

"What the devil d'you think you're playing at?" was what she said to him, though words of love, only a moment ago, had trembled on her lips.

It was as though she had erected an invisible barrier into which he had walked, so abruptly did he stop. Despite the subdued light his face had clearly shown his own eagerness, his joy that she had come, his longing to be about some physical thing that would get her into his arms, but now it all faded away, wiped away by her harsh words.

"I'm not playing at anything. I'm deadly serious." He was doing his best to keep his disappointment in check, for he had nurtured visions of them running into each other's arms in the sanctuary of the trees. He didn't know why really, after their last meeting. He understood she must have got a hell of a shock when the servant he had frightened half to death passed on his message and though he had impressed upon the woman the need for secrecy she might easily have blurted it out in a room full of other servants.

Realising it was fright that had made Poppy so angry, he softened his tone, soothing her, he hoped, into listening to what he had to say. He had not much time. "I wanted to talk to you," he went on quietly, "and short of coming to the house, which might have been awkward for you, this was . . ."

"Awkward! *Awkward!* Good God, we . . . you understood the last time we met that I'm married. My husband is just down the meadow in our home. You understood that my life is here and . . . well, I don't know what you want from me." Her voice was high with anguish and Conn looked round fearfully in case someone should hear her. "We can be nothing to one another and yet you've come up here ready to play havoc with my life with no thought for the consequences. To me, I mean . . ."

"Poppy, will ye no' . . ."

It was caustic inside her. A raging bitterness that had nothing to do with him or this moment; with this madness in sending messages by a member of her family, for God's sake, summoning her here. It was not his foolhardiness that tore her to shreds. It was the knowledge that she loved him and always would. That he loved her, it showed in every line of his rigid body, the tremble in the hand he held out to her, and she must send him away. She must be cruel, cutting, hammer a spike into his heart, and hers, if it was the only way to make him realise that they could never, ever be anything to one another. Not in any way. He must go away and get on with his life, as she must get on with hers.

"I've come up here for one reason only," her glacial voice told him, "and that is to impress upon you once and for all that I'm not free. That I have a husband."

"Ye dinna say the word *love* when ye speak of your husband, lassie. Never, not once have ye said ye loved him, which is one of the reasons I'm here. This is the third time we've met, since we were grown, and ye've never told me the one thing that would make me go away for ever."

The intensity of emotion in his voice, the grim set of his face, the held-back, tamped-down cautious hope which he seemed to be holding on to by the strength of his willpower, cut off the torrent of words she was using to defend herself, broke down the obstacle of vast proportions she was doing her best to put in his way.

"D'ye love him, lassie? D'ye love your husband, because if ye do ye've only to say and I'll be off. Is he good to ye?"

"Of course he is," she blurted, answering the one question she could with complete honesty.

He took no notice. "Have ye a successful, happy marriage, would ye say, one that nothing could wreck, one that no man could sunder? Have ye, Poppy? And I'd be glad of the truth, *mo annsachd*."

"Don't call me that," she said wretchedly, hanging her head.

"Why not? It's how I feel about ye. Ye're my darling, for that's what it means. Ye're my blessing and I canna hide it any longer. I want ye to come with me."

"What?" Her head shot up and she took a step away from him in amazement.

"To Scotland. I'm going home tomorrow."

"God in heaven, I don't know what you're talking about. Do you? You must be mad."

"No, but I'm short of time and I want tae get this settled before I go. I'd take ye with me now, if ye'd come though . . . well . . ." He looked down shyly, studying his hands, which still yearned to reach out for her since they cared nought for the conventions. "I've only the one room . . . bed, ye ken, and I want us to be . . . I want it to be right for us . . . for you. When we can we'll be married but what I'm trying tae say, lassie, is that if ye'd rather stay a while . . . here, I mean, speak to . . . to those who love you . . . explain, make them see what you and I feel, then I'll wait for ye. I know ye for a good, honest woman so . . ."

She shook her head in violent disbelief. Her hair, fastened loosely into a heavy coil at the back of her neck, broke free and tumbled wildly about her face and down her back and she lifted both frantic hands to drag it back. When she spoke her voice was ragged.

"You must have lost your wits," she stammered, but it was merely a token remark. She should be offended by what he had just said, a man, a gentleman persuading another man's wife to desert him, to run away and live as his mistress, for what else could Poppy Goodall be to Conn MacConnell? She was married to Richard until one of them died and surely this man knew her better, thought more of her, respected her too much to believe she would just up and take off without a thought for those who loved her and relied on her.

But the trouble was, what he said was so sweet, so enchanting, so bewitching to her senses, her woman's body that would give the world to get into that one bed with him, to leave everything behind and live in the dream world she had often pictured, and the awareness of how easily she could do it, how much she longed to do it, made her want to strike out at him.

Her voice was icy. "I don't know what made you come here tonight, Mr MacConnell," she heard it say. "I'm sure I've given you no reason to believe your attentions would be welcome and if . . ."

"Bloody hell, lass, this is me ye're talking to, not some prissy women's magazine column which advises on how a lady should turn down a gentleman."

He took her by the forearms, dragging her into the cover of the trees, shaking her as he did, so that her hair swirled about her head like a thrown cape. It fell about her face, blinding her. Her feet tripped over the rough grass and she fell against him, his arms instantly going round her in a grip of steel. Her face was pressed against his chest, the warm length of his body along hers. She was dazed, her limbs useless and weak and when he spoke, his mouth in her hair, she had no strength left to push him away.

His voice was harsh. "I've no' come to take what's his," he almost snarled, "but what's mine. I know, ye see. I know about your husband and his . . . his injuries and though I'm sorry for the poor bugger I canna help feeling glad . . . glad . . . oh, Jesus . . . that he's no' a husband to ye. That ye're no' a wife to him and never have been. That's why I've come. I only found out today. Jesus Christ, if I'd known before I'd have been up here . . . oh, *caileag*, d'ye no' ken how much I love ye? It's tearing my guts out. But I'd have gone home and done my best to put ye out of my heart, if that lassie hadna told me."

She began to stir, to become aware of the dream-like state into which his hard male body had captured her. She wanted him to go on and on talking, not to listen to or make sense of but simply to rest herself against his great strength, the wonder and warmth of him, to listen to his heart, smell the scent of lemon soap on him. As old as the human race was this meeting of male and female flesh in the dark but new to Poppy Goddall who had known no man's touch, who had been joined in union not even with her own husband and she could feel herself letting her senses free to fly in the rapture of it.

"Poppy, *mo annsachd . . .*" His voice trembled, his mouth against her hair as he murmured over and over again in the Gaelic which seemed to come to his tongue when a great emotion had him in its grip. "*Mo donn falt caileag.*" One strong arm held her to him while his free hand began to stroke her hair, smoothing the rippling curtain of satin down her back and over the arm that held her. He gripped it, then, putting his hands one on either side of her head, turned her face up to his and laid his mouth on hers.

It was not her first kiss, of course. Richard had placed hesitant lips on hers before they married, correct and respectful, for he was of the opinion that a man and woman should go to their marriage bed virgin and who knew where liberties might lead? But it had been nothing like this. This was warm, soft, light, with a gentle movement of his mouth against hers. It surprised and delighted her and she found that after a moment of having Conn's lips against hers, hers parted and so did his so that they breathed sweetly into one another's mouths.

Conn had dreamed of this moment, of having her alone and willing in his arms. All through the winter when his day at the shipyard was over he had tried to form other attachments, for there was no shortage of pretty women in Liverpool, but her great silvery blue eyes, enormous in her pale golden face, the pupils black as sable, her soft coral mouth, which was like that of a child in its delicate loveliness, would come between him and them at the most inappropriate moment, making it impossible to dally with Kitty or Frances or Mary. He had tried but he had found it impossible to tear her out of his heart where she had lain, dormant, it seemed, for all these years. The neat pretty child, curls glossy, cheeks rosy, heart strong and purposeful, had grown into this honey-skinned, glorious creature whom no man had touched and he meant to make her Conn MacConnell's own. He had been introduced to other pretty women, ladies, for William Laird was a hospitable man, he and his family very willing to entertain a handsome young Scot with connections in shipbuilding and good prospects for the future and, though it had been made plain, not only by them but by the young ladies' approving mamas, that his attentions would be welcome he had been unable to go on.

Now she was here, no more than a breath away in the white drift of her dress, the warm scented silk of her hair, the depthless beauty of her eyes and the sweetness and strength he had never forgotten. He felt quite light-headed, not just by her nearness but at how closely he had come to missing her. One day! Just this afternoon the young girl in the market had told him about Poppy's husband and if he had not known he would have gone back home believing her to be . . . be *normally* married, perhaps happily married, and lost her for ever, for he would never have returned to Liverpool.

He drew her deeper into the spinney. She seemed to be dazzled, making no objection, letting him lead her by the hand until he found the tree where he had spread his jacket for her, hoping she would come. She sat down on it obediently, like a good child, then, when he pressed her, lay back in his arms. His reason, at the first touch of her body beneath his, fled away, his rampant male desires, which were young and eager and cared for nothing but their own satisfaction, gripped him fiercely and all he wanted was to do what Richard Goodall had never done, what no man had ever done, and make her *his*. The skin of her face and chin and throat was petal soft beneath his seeking hand and her lips lifted to his, eager as his and it was then, when his hand tenderly cupped her breast, when the nipple rose hard and peaked into his palm, that Poppy Goodall's brain finally heard the words that had fallen on her ears some time ago.

Scotland . . . only one bed . . . speak to those who love you . . . injuries and I'm sorry . . . husband . . . wife . . . what's mine . . . mine . . . mine . . .

With a great heave, like the one she had seen the newborn calves make when they got up for the first time on their tottery legs, she got up on hers. Her rage, her murderous rage splintered the sighing languor, the dream-like wonder, the sweetness like honey that ran through her veins, giving her the strength to push Conn's considerable weight away from her. He fell back in bewilderment and, for a moment, male pique, but a second later he had leaped to his feet and was standing before her, face flushed in the dark, his eyes gleaming, not with lust but with love.

"I'm sorry, lass," he said humbly. "I . . . ye're so lovely . . . forgive me, I shouldna have . . ."

She was trembling violently, whether in need or temper even she didn't know. She put her arms about herself, holding on for dear life as though afraid she might shake herself to smithereens if she let go.

"So that's it," she spat out, fanning her rage with false bitterness. "This is all an excuse to get me on my back with my skirts round my waist as though I were nothing more than a sixpenny whore down at the docks."

Even in the dim light cast by the moon she could see his

face turn to a dead white and he took a horrified step away from her.

"Poppy, ye'll no speak to me that way."

"Will I not? I'll speak any way I choose and it seems to me you're as bad as . . . as . . . You're all the same, you rutting bastard."

He fell back even further, his eyes blazing.

"Ye've a foul tongue on ye, lassie, and ye know it's not true."

"Isn't it? Then why is it that five minutes after finding ourselves alone you've got me on my back with your hand . . ."

He was glaring at her now, panting with emotion, but when he spoke his voice was low and ragged with passion.

"I'm sorry if ye're offended, but ye've no call to speak to me as though . . . Jesus! No man should use a woman's body uncaringly, especially that of the woman he loves, and that was not my intention. I love ye. I want ye for my wife and I swear before God I'll no touch ye again until ye are."

"*I'm already married*," she hissed, doing her best to hold on to the outrage that was the only thing keeping her from flinging herself back into his arms and begging him to make love to her, to make love to her *now*, and when tomorrow came take her back to Scotland with him.

"No, ye're not . . . ye're not." He was speaking a little more calmly now but his eyes still flashed with pain and rage. "Oh aye, ye're wed to him on paper. Ye've fine marriage lines in a drawer somewhere, no doubt, but ye're no' his. I didna come here to . . . make love to ye though I dearly want to but to beg you to come away and make a new life wi' me. I dinna know how it will come about, *mo annsachd*." He ran his hand distractedly through his hair until it stood on end, then turned away and put both hands to the broad trunk of the oak tree, his forehead pressed to the rough bark.

"I have'na thought it through properly, I have'na had time. I have'na got beyond today, beyond tomorrow, having ye with me in any way I can. I'd give it all up, lass, the shipyard, my grandfather's wealth that will one day be mine. Everything . . . to have ye with me. I'm strong. I'd work for ye so's we could be together. I'd take care o' ye, always. Ye'd want for nothing."

"Except an honest name."

"Goddammit, Poppy." His utter wretchedness was in his voice.

Her heart was near to bursting with loving pity for his wild pain but, though it hurt her so badly she wanted to moan out loud, she could not help him, for one small move on her part would have them both spiralling on the downward path to what she knew to be disaster.

"I . . . I can't come, Conn, you must see that. You make nothing of my marriage vows." *Marriage vows!* She scarcely remembered making them herself on that faraway day three years ago. "But I must stay here with my husband."

"Don't, for pity's sake, don't."

"They . . . he needs me. I am all he has. I cannot walk away from him . . . them . . . this place . . ."

"For Christ's sake, please . . . no more." He did not turn round and though she longed for just one more glimpse of his dear face she was glad.

"I'm . . ." she began.

"Dinna say any more, lassie. I canna bear it. Just go. Just go quickly. Turn round and run away home."

When he hauled himself away from the tree she was gone. He leaned his back against it, then slowly sank to his haunches, his elbows on his knees, his hands dangling between, his head bowed. He stayed that way for an hour and the man who hid deeper in the spinney was just beginning to wonder if he could creep away without being heard when Conn MacConnell stood up and strode off swiftly towards the lane which led to Prescot Road.

Clouds had begun to drift across the moon, blotting out its brightness, darkening the world, but Conn did not notice since his world was already darker than the blackest depth of a pit.

25

Conn turned on his heel, looking vaguely about the room as though he were checking that he'd left nothing behind, his eyes drifting from one piece of furniture to another, though it was very plain he did not really see them. His eyes were empty, unfocused, set in deep, mushroom-coloured sockets. His face was pale and drawn, the freckles across the bridge of his nose and his cheekbones standing out in sharp relief. He was freshly shaven, as immaculately turned out as ever, but somehow he gave the appearance of having dressed without consciously being aware of what he put on. His hair was neatly brushed, but lifting a hand he ran it through the waves and at once it fell into heavy disarray over his forehead.

Reaching for his Inverness cape he flung it about his shoulders, for despite the stunned despair the meeting with Poppy had flung him in he had noticed it was raining this morning. He picked up the leather Gladstone bag which he had left by the door, turning again to look about him, then, squaring his shoulders which, since last night had been strangely slumped, ran down the stairs to the front door.

A horse-drawn cab stood outside, the driver huddled beneath a many-caped greatcoat, rain dripping from the brim of his bowler hat. The horse which pulled the conveyance looked just as dejected, head drooping, its coat slicked with rain, one leg bent as though resting a weary foot. There was no one else about in the quiet stretch of Upper Duke Street where Conn had had rooms for the past ten months, except for a woebegone-looking mongrel which was making its way with great speed towards the corner, though what it hoped to find there in this downpour was not apparent.

"Mornin' sir," the cab driver said, touching his whip to his bowler, doing his best to be cheerful, though it seemed to him by the look of his passenger's grim face he might as well not have bothered. He did hope he didn't have to get down from his box, for where he sat was the only dry space, outside that is, on the cab.

"Is that all yer luggage, sir?" he asked hopefully, eyeing the Gladstone bag.

"No, there's a trunk and a box or two. I'll give ye a hand."

"Thanks, sir," he answered dolefully, clambering down to the pavement. "That's good o'yer. Awful day, innit?"

His passenger did not answer.

Together they manhandled Conn's luggage on to the rack at the back of the cab, the driver silently cursing the rain which by now would have soaked into his seat, then, with his passenger inside and his own bum in a puddle of rainwater, he turned.

"Lime Street, is it, sir?" he enquired.

"Aye, for the Glasgow train." That's all he got out of him and he wondered why such a splendidly set-up young gentleman, with looks, money to spare by the cut of his clothes, should be so bloody miserable. He wanted to try sitting up here on this bloody seat day in and day out, rain or shine, like he did, then go home to a hovel in Banastre Street filled with the kids his missis bore every twelve months, then he'd have something to be miserable about.

The rain continued in a solid sheet, sharp and, despite being July, cold. The pavements were almost deserted as the cab turned into Berry Street, as though wise folk who had no need to be out of doors had stayed at home this morning. The cab swayed and lurched with the slow plod of the ancient horse that pulled it. There was plenty of traffic along Renshaw Street and Lime Street which, years ago, had known the appalling stench of gases from the limekilns which gave it its name. It was frantic with cabs and carriages and people on foot making their way to the busy station.

Conn sat slumped in the corner of the cab, his elbow on the sill, his chin on his fist, making no attempt to lift himself out of his own deep misery. He'd done all that during the long endless night when he'd paced from sitting-room to bedroom and back again, his aching brain composing and rejecting one daft plan after the other, refusing for a while to be beaten, for if he was beaten he was without hope. To go back to Glasgow knowing he would never see her again was tearing him apart but what else was he to do with his sorry life? He'd even toyed with the idea of storming up to Long Reach and demanding that Richard Goodall release his . . . release Poppy from the prison he held her in, let her go and find the happiness and love he could not himself give her. How could the man, if he loved her, hang on to her in such a cruel way? He knew he, Conn MacConnell, wouldn't. If *he* had been injured in such a way that he was of use to no one, not even his wife, especially his wife, he'd end it all, releasing the woman he loved. What man would want to live as a cripple? Certainly not he, but it seemed this Richard was doing so, his injured body holding Poppy with strong, relentless if useless arms.

His thoughts were like a seesaw, lifting to hope and falling to despair. If Richard Goodall couldn't have her, he had mused at one point, then that meant no other man could, so at least he was spared the agony of picturing her in another man's arms. He was ashamed when this thought drifted through his mind, for it was unworthy, dog in the manger since his Poppy, *his* Poppy! – dear Christ, where had that come from? – should not be forced to lead the life of a nun, and he should not be glad that she was. She was a woman, warm, vital, vivid, loving and he'd have loved her fine if she'd been his.

Another tempting idea had wormed its way into his tired brain during the black night and that was a secret note passed on by the same woman, if he could spot her, who had given her his first message, a note to Poppy saying that if she found herself free – a widow, in fact – that she must let him know at once.

He'd laughed out loud at that one, the appalling picture of Conn MacConnell waiting patiently for the death of another man, perhaps for years, perhaps until they were all old and grey, with no love in his life, no woman, no children, no warmth nor joy . . . like Poppy was forced to do, his exhausted mind reminded him.

The wide shallow steps leading up to the entrance to the station were wet and slippery and he and the cabbie almost went over a couple of times as they struggled with his trunk. There were no porters available, though one, his trolley loaded, indicated that he would be free in a moment if the gentleman wouldn't mind waiting.

"That'll be one an' sixpence, sir," the breathless cab driver told him, holding out his hand, eager to be off, for there would be fares galore to be had in this crowd where there were as many coming into Liverpool as going out.

The big chap, his red hair scattered with what looked like diamonds where the rain had fallen on his bare head, looked down at the cabby's hand and as he did so some miraculous change took place in him, though what he saw there, the cab driver could not have said if his life depended on it. As he stared down, the rain drenching them both, his hair dripping raindrops on to the cabby's hand, the big fellow's face became flushed and his eyes, looking up swiftly into the cabby's face, were a sudden star-studded cornflower blue and his lips curled as though he were about to break into a wide grin.

"*No*," he shouted, so that several people turned round to stare and the cab driver's heart plummeted, for he thought the young man was refusing to pay him and how was he to argue with a chap of his size?

"Sir . . . ?"

"Bugger it, I said *no*! I'll no' give in! I'll no' give in so bloody easily, not if it takes me for ever. She's mine and I'll no' win her if I'm away up in Glasgow. Wouldna you agree?"

His eyes, such an incredible blue now, blazed into the cab driver's and he fell back in alarm. Some answer seemed to be needed though, so he gulped and nodded his head.

"Right, yer right, sir," he gasped, ready to look round for a police constable, for the bugger must be off his head.

"So I am, so we'll get this lot back to Upper Duke Street," bending to seize and lift the trunk by himself as though it were no heavier than his Gladstone bag.

"Upper Duke Street, sir, but . . ."

"Aye, man, and then ye can take me to the ferry, for I'll need to be off across the water tae have a wee word with Mr Laird."

Mr Laird! The shipbuilder! Bloody hell, the fellow had lost

his wits and if he thought Albert Ross was going to share his cab with him again then he was sadly mistaken.

The half-guinea in the big chap's hand and which passed to his soon changed his mind.

It didn't seem to matter that it was raining – "cats and dogs", Cook said reprovingly – she knew that if she didn't get out, go somewhere, *anywhere*, she'd run mad about the house, screaming her pain and loss for everyone to hear. May had already indicated with a sly wink that she was dying to hear all about it, whatever it was, presumably imagining that Poppy was up to what she and Johnny had got up to in the barn before they were married.

"I'm going for a walk," she had to tell them in the kitchen, even if they did look at her as if she'd lost her mind, because if she didn't tell them, within five minutes someone would want her for something and if she wasn't found there'd be a hue and cry which would not only reach Richard's ears, but every pair of ears on the farm. Richard had already reduced her to private tears, tears she knew were very near the surface this morning, calling her "a stupid, clumsy bitch" when she spilled some water on his nightshirt. His empty grey eyes had leaped to life as he set about the only pleasure he had in his sour, arid life: the cruel baiting of the woman he loved to distraction. The woman who stayed with him, or so he told himself, for no other reason than pity and who he now hated in equal part. He loved her and hated her and he had nothing else to punish her with – though God only knew why he should feel the need to punish her, since this was not her fault – but his tongue and so, whenever he had a chance he whipped her with it.

"And for God's sake take . . . that woeful look off your face. What in hell's name have you to be woeful about? tell me that. At least you can get out of this bloody room."

"Richard, you've only to say and the men will carry you downstairs. We could make up a bed on the couch in the study."

"I don't want to lie on the couch in the study."

"I could read to you or play the piano if you like."

"Dear God, am I never to be allowed to forget . . . my mother raised you from a . . . a skivvy and taught you to play. Quite the lady."

"I won't play then, but you could look out of the window and watch what's happening in the yard and . . ."

"In this rain? What will be happening in this weather or hadn't you noticed the rain? Are you blind as well as half-witted?"

"Tell me then. You have only to tell me what you want."

"I want to . . . to . . . get out of this sodding bed, or, failing that have you in it with me where I would . . ."

Here he began to describe to her in graphic detail what he would do to her if he had the use of that part of his body he would do it to her *with*! He had been tormenting her in this way for several months now, his voice falling to a low and nasty pitch which no one but Poppy, even if they stood outside the door, could hear. For the most part she ignored it, moving calmly about the room, tidying this and that, but today, the act she had imagined sharing so many times with Conn, lovely, loving, pure in its desire, was too much for her in this filthy form and she ran hastily from the room followed by his mocking laughter. She stood on the landing, shaking and doing her best to pull herself together, for anyone could come upstairs, scrubbing at her face with her sleeve and knuckling her eyes like a beaten child.

So, "I'm going for a walk," she told them.

"In this?" Aggie gasped, looking out of the streaming windows to the yard where a few bedraggled hens pecked and strutted.

"I . . . I need to see Elly," she lied desperately.

"She'll be up in a bit, lass," Cook said kindly, for though no one knew what Master Richard oppressed his lovely wife with, Cook had seen what it did to her.

"Yes, I know, but a walk would do me good. I've . . . I've a headache and it will help to clear it. And I wanted to have word with Jinny about . . ."

About what? Blabbing to a perfect stranger the state of affairs at Long Reach Farm which Jinny must have done to Conn, for Nelly wouldn't dare say a word to anyone, apart from customers, she didn't know. But then Poppy could hardly reprimand Jinny for innocently telling the truth, could she? Everyone in the district knew. Oh, dear sweet Lord, give me strength to bear this burden, for I'm sadly bowed down with it now. It was at least bearable before Conn came back into my life, before I felt his love surrounding me, his lips on mine, his hand, the strong warmth of his arms and body . . . and as she plodded up the track, the rain drenching through the hood of her cloak, it astounded her that what she had longed to happen between her and Conn bore no resemblance to the words Richard spewed out in his madness. Richard dirtied the act of love, coating it with filth in his damaged mind, and though she had experienced it with no man, she knew quite positively that with Conn, that between all men and women who truly loved, it would be clean and beautiful. Richard seemed to be getting worse, almost depraved as his incapacity chained him year after year to his bed with no hope of release. To suffer women to change him and wash him as though he were an infant, to tend to the bedsores which, if neglected, bloomed on his thin body, was enough to drive any man to a state of bitterness that would eventually destroy his mind. He was even weaker now since he flatly refused to allow the exercises she and Elly performed on his body for his lungs and limbs and heart which the doctor had advised. But in all this corrosive hatred and railing against the life the fates had chosen for him, Poppy knew that his need of her, his distorted love for her, was the one thing he had to hold on to in his disordered mind.

She stood by the gate at the top of the lane and stared through the slanting rain towards the spinney where, only a few short hours ago, she had known precious moments of rapture in Conn's arms. She could still smell the sharp aroma of the lemon-scented soap he used and feel the fabric of his shirt beneath her hand. She had longed, for the past ten months, ever since he had come back into her life, to run her hands through his thick, springing hair which was like a lit torch, imagining it would be hot to her touch, but she had not done so last night and she wanted to weep because now she never would.

It was totally silent in the spinney and she was surprised because normally the air would be filled with the woodnote of the birds which nested there. Today not a bird sang, as though her own desperate unhappiness had transmitted itself to the place where last she had been with Conn.

The small pond at the bottom of the slope suddenly became noisy with some commotion caused by the ducks which swam on it. She turned and watched as one flapped its wings, standing on its webbed feet on the surface of the water, screeching its indignation to another. The rain stopped with an abruptness that surprised her. The sun broke through the scurrying clouds and water dripped rhythmically off the gate into the sodden ground. A dog barked, a door banged somewhere and when he stepped in front of her, his footsteps deadened by the waterlogged ground, swaggering in that arrogant way he had, she found she no longer feared him.

"Good morning, my dear Poppy, or should I call you 'my blessing'? I'm afraid I haven't the Gaelic, which I suppose he was using, your lover, I mean, so that's the best I can do."

He grinned and waited for her to speak but she merely sighed and turned away from him, leaning her back against the gate. It was an exasperated sigh, one which a mother would use with a tiresome child. It signified her total indifference and weariness with his silly games and he frowned, since he would have liked to see her afraid, or at least apprehensive.

"What, no denial? No protestation of innocence? No appealing to my better nature to keep your shameful secret to myself? Do you not understand?" he asked her silkily, bending his head to peer into her averted face, "I saw you last night in the arms of some big chap who seemed to be very keen to get his hands up your skirts. Not that he was having much luck, I noticed, since you did not appear to fancy having a—"

"That's enough." She whirled to face him, her eyes icing over, neither grey nor blue but almost transparent in her outrage.

He smiled then, satisfied, fingering his cravat, which seemed tight about his neck. She noticed with the part of her mind not shuddering away from him that he was putting on weight, that his neck had thickened and that what had once been a young man's masculine bulk was turning to fat. It was five years since that day, his twenty-first birthday, when he had accosted her as she delivered produce to the kitchen at Coopers Edge and now, at twenty-six, the life he had led in between was showing in the thickening of his figure and the blurring of his handsome features. He had been harassing her all these years, building up this picture in her mind of a man to be feared, to be avoided, and yet in all that time that's all he had done, threatened her. He had kept her fastened to her own kitchen, in dread of meeting him alone, and now, here he was, the demon who had preyed on her peace of mind, and she was frightened of him no longer, for she had so much more to fear in her life than him.

He saw it in her eyes and his own became suffused with blood red rage.

"Walk up to the spinney," he snarled, catching her wrist in his strong hand, "and I'll have some of what the big chap wanted. You'll oblige me or I'll shout it to the world that the saintly Mrs Goodall, who has nursed her crippled husband for three long years without complaint, has a lover. While her husband was fastened to his bed she's giving it away to any Tom, Dick or Harry who fancies it. Go on, walk up there and I'll follow. I'll just fetch my horse. He's tethered to the wall down the lane and we don't want to advertise my presence, do we?"

"Dear God, will you never give up, you bastard?" she shrieked, throwing off his hand. "Go home to your wife. Make love to her if that's what you're short of and leave me alone."

"Aah, there's a problem there." He smiled in what he evidently thought was an impish manner. "My wife is expecting our third child, a son, I hope and pray, and no longer cares to accommodate me. Not that I go without, you understand."

"You're a foul-mouthed swine, Dominic Cooper. For any man to speak of his wife as you do is . . . is . . ."

"Never mind my wife, my pet, or your husband, or that big chap who seemed intent on taking what Richard cannot manage. It's a real tease to a fellow, d'you know, to realise that I have here a married woman who is, one presumes, a virgin. Talk about titillation . . ."

She turned then, walking away from him in swift and furious strides, her wet skirts swishing about her legs but in no way impeding her. She didn't care if he came after her. In her present mood of total despair at that moment she didn't care who knew about Dominic Cooper. If she screamed every man within a mile would come running and if Tom went off his head, even ran amok at the sight of the man who had crippled his elder son, well, she found she didn't care. If Johnny was upset, calling her a liar to accuse a gentleman of such wickedness, or her pa was inclined to throttle Dominic Cooper and hang for it, she found she couldn't care about that either. In fact, when she looked back over the years she had let this man menace her, she wondered why. It had seemed to be important then, to keep it to herself as though it shamed her, his lust, and she supposed it did.

But now, with Conn gone, with her ruined life stretching out before her with nothing in it the Goodall men cared to help her with to make it more bearable, it all seemed a waste of time. Her pain was so great, nothing they or this man could say or do to her mattered an iota. Perhaps this feeling would vanish. Perhaps one day she would find something to . . . to gladden her heart again but now she didn't really care what happened to her, or the Goodalls. Last night she had made the biggest sacrifice of her life. In fact she had sacrificed her life for them, for Richard, for the farm and all those who lived beneath its roof and worked its broad acres. She was well aware that Johnny, should she desert the farm, was not yet capable of taking up the reins she held in her strong hands. That May was not mistress here, despite being wife to the man who would one day be its master. Her own heart was breaking. No, it was broken, shattered and in agony at what had been done to it, and it had been her choice to have it so, so she must deal with it. But just for now she needed peace, a great empty space in which nothing rippled against her, wounding her already badly damaged self.

"Come here, you little bitch," the man at her back hissed and when he put his hand on her arm, gripping it with iron fingers, she began to scream. She whirled about and screamed directly into his blanched face, then into his ear as he turned his head away so that he recoiled as though she had plunged a red hot wire into it.

"You slut . . . you foul, dirty skivvy," he shrieked, but already he was swerving away to run in the direction of his horse, ungainly as he slipped in puddles and deep, rutted mud. He fell, just beyond the gate, going on his back. Struggling to his feet he turned for a moment and Poppy, who had, for a delicious moment, wanted to laugh, saw the bitter enmity in his face and the laughter died in her throat. His expression said that once again she had got the better of him, made him look a fool, treated him as though he were a fool, but she'd not do it again. What had started as a whim, a simple ache in his loins that he had fancied she could ease if he could get her alone, had become a vendetta and she'd best be careful.

He had galloped off at breakneck speed when the first of the men got to her. Tommy it was. He'd been in the next field but one, inspecting the uncut hay, deciding whether the rain of yesterday had done much damage, for it would be ready for harvesting soon. He was red-faced and panting as he ran down the sloping field and from Primrose Bank Elly, with others trailing behind her, was struggling up the muddy bank. Her pa, white-faced, for he had recognised her voice, Tom and Johnny, Evan, Jacko and Ernie, Evan ready to have a heart attack, he promised, and who was it who'd frightened her? Fair give him the willies, it had, and even the women from the house were straggling up from the yard. Their faces were white and crumpled with concern, terrified for her, every last one wanting to pat her, soothe her, put a loving arm about her, begging her to tell them what had terrorised her, for the field was empty and peaceful.

She began to weep then, falling into Elly's motherly arms, unable to speak as they crowded round her. Tom said he'd kill anyone who harmed her and Johnny was to run and fetch his shotgun, by God. She was surrounded by the very people she had, minutes since, longed to discard as albatrosses round her neck, for was it not they who kept her and Conn apart? They were the people whom she had, for a few hours, hated, resented, wished to the furthest corners of the earth so that she might be free to be with Conn.

"Come, lass, take my arm," Tom said lovingly. "There's nought to fear here," not knowing what she had been screaming about and not unduly concerned as long as she was unharmed.

"I'll run on an' put kettle on," from Marigold.

"See, don't cry, child," Cook soothed.

"Come on, chuck, theer's . . . nowt worth cryin' over." May had almost said "there's no man worth crying over" but she managed to restrain herself in time.

"Eeh, lovey, tha's soaked. Come away in," Aggie beseeched her.

They loved her. They cherished her. Despite what Richard

said to her, she was valued and any threat to her had them up in arms, rushing fiercely to defend her for the very simple reason that they loved her.

Conn . . . Conn . . . her broken heart silently called out as they led her tenderly back to where she belonged.

26

The letter came the next day. Though she had never seen his handwriting she knew it was from him and for a miraculous moment her broken heart was mended, threatening to burst with joy, then it began to beat a rapid tattoo of fear. She had never, in all the years she had lived at Long Reach, received a letter and when the postman handed it in, as curious as the servants about who should be writing to Poppy Goodall, she was surrounded by them, jostling and arguing, all surmising on who it could be from, begging her to open it at once and put them out of their misery.

She was stupefied, her brain struggling to find some logical explanation that would satisfy them without the need to tell them who it was from, which would, of course, be impossible. Though she was inclined to hold the letter tenderly to her heart since his hand had penned it, she was also filled with fury that he should so carelessly jeopardise her world again after all she had said to him on the matter. She had believed she had convinced him as she tore madly down the field two nights ago, her eyes blinded with tears. Made him understand that they could never be together and now, barely thirty-six hours later, she held a letter in her hand from him.

"It's probably from Mr Hilton," grabbing the first name to come to her mind. Her voice sounded false and breathless even to her. "He . . . I suppose he wants . . . well, to see me about something."

There! Already, before she had opened it and read what was inside, unconsciously her enchanted mind had prepared, not only a rational explanation of who had sent the letter but a reason to go to town and meet him should that be what it contained. Oh, dear God, forgive her. She was torn between exultancy and anger, between a lilting joy and deep despair, aware that they were all watching her in some surprise and curiosity, particularly May.

"Well, this isn't getting the work done standing about here, is it?" she said crisply, as sense began to filter back into her stunned mind. "The team's up in the hayfield and has been since six and they'll need something nourishing inside them at noon. Marigold, have you brought the beer up from the cellar? Well, you'd best go and get it. You and Clara can take it up there; oh, and some lemonade as well for the women and children. They'll want something for their 'ten o'clocks' and it's nearly that now. Those pies I made will do for their noon-piece."

With a catalogue of tasks to be performed, the routine of their day mapped out for them, though after all these years they didn't really need telling, they began to drift away, disappointed that she had not opened her letter, still inclined to look back at her in puzzlement as though they were not quite convinced about Mr Hilton, whom they knew to be the bank manager, but were not quite sure why. They had not got any sense out of her about what had happened to her yesterday when her screams had lifted the hairs on the back of their necks and fetched them out of the kitchen and into the yard like a pack of hounds, scattering the hens like leaves in a wind. There was something strange about their little mistress. All big eyes, she was, in a face that was ... well, you could only call it haunted, her normally honey-coloured skin a pasty white, even her hair dragged back in a most unbecoming way as though she had not the slightest interest in her appearance.

Now she was scurrying off like a woman caught in a whirlwind, saying she had some papers to see to and would be in the study for an hour or so if anybody wanted her.

"Shall I send cheese and pickles with the new bread, lass?" Cook called after her and was surprised to have flung back at her the response that she must do as she pleased, which was all very well and good but so unlike their Poppy who had a great concern for everything, in the kitchen and out, they looked at one another in amazement.

Her fingers shook so violently she could barely break the wax seal which, she noticed, even in her urgency, was in the shape of a leaping stag.

"Dear Mrs Goodall," it said, "I would be glad of a moment of your time if you could spare it. Perhaps at two thirty, if that is convenient." It was signed "A. Scot, St James & Co".

She knew, of course, as he had known she would, exactly what he was telling her, but should anyone but herself have got hold of it, it would mean absolutely nothing to them. It was businesslike, certainly not a love epistle and, even if she were to leave it open on the desk, would rouse no suspicions, particularly among these simple folk, most of whom could not read.

She wouldn't go, naturally, she told her frantically beating heart. What the blazes did he mean by sending her this, asking her to meet him again when she had made it quite clear – she would wear her new bonnet and gown of barley coloured *poult de soie* – when she had made it quite clear he must go back to Scotland and – had she time to wash her hair? – he must forget her as she would do her best to forget him. St James's, that was the cemetery, of course. How clever. And A Scot! She had meant it all when she said it and she was determined to let him see, simply by not going that . . . She would need to remind Marigold about the fruit for the jams, and should she ask Jem to get the gig out, for the lane was still muddy and she didn't want to dirty her new cream boots?

She deliberately took her time tidying her desk, lining up paper and pens in neat, symmetrical rows, then, doing her best to calm her jangling nerves, tucked the note inside her bodice next to her heart, smiling at her own delightful foolishness. She stood up and smoothed her apron, then her hair, putting her hands to her flushed cheeks, then walked through to the kitchen to tell Marigold to get out the jars, for she meant to start the jam-making. "We'll do the damsons after dinner," she would say, but what actually came out of her mouth was no surprise to her, though it was to the others.

"I'm to go to town this afternoon, Cook," she said calmly. "That letter was from John Evans, the ironmongers in Paradise Street. I showed some interest a few months ago in an improved wringing and mangling machine and it's now on show in his shop." She was amazed at her own ingenuity and talent for deception. "It will make a big difference to us all with so many beds to be changed and laundered each week so I'm to go and see it. No, I shall go alone, Elly," she told her stepmother as Elly made a move towards the back door with the intention, or so it seemed, of dashing off to Primrose Bank to change into her "going-to-town" outfit.

Elly came to a full stop. Her jaw dropped and her eyebrows rose and though the others were not aware, as she was, of

Poppy's fear in the past of going anywhere alone, they all turned from what they were doing and stared from Elly to Poppy and back again as though again something strange had caught their attention.

"What's the matter?" Poppy exclaimed sharply. "Don't you want your working day to be made easier? Do you wish to continue to use that old mangle in the laundry which Mr Goodall's *grandmother* had as new?"

"No, lass . . . no." Elly put a soothing hand on Poppy's arm, for she, of all of them, with perhaps one exception, knew that this was not about mangles or changing beds or laundry or indeed anything to do with any of those who lived on Long Reach Farm. And if Poppy, whose cheeks since the letter had come matched her name, did not calm down, hide that flicker of excitement that pulsed through her, they would all have their heads together in speculation.

"We'd be right glad of a new mangle, wouldn't we?" Elly asked them all brightly. "Me back were in two day before yesterd'y turnin' that damned 'andle. No, chuck, you put yer bonnet on an' get ter town. Me an' Marigold'll see ter't damsons, won't we, lamb?" turning to smile at her simple, sweet-faced second stepdaughter.

"But yer usually go wi' 'er, Elly," Marigold said innocently and they all nodded in agreement.

"Norr always. 'Sides, Poppy'll be there an' back before I've got me changed."

They turned away satisfied, all except May who laid Master Tom in one of the two cradles in the corner of the kitchen and lifted Master Jack out of the other, clamping his rosy mouth on to her nipple. She smirked, trying to catch Poppy's eye but Poppy turned and left the room, doing her best not to break into a run.

Richard was vituperative on the subject of her going to

town a second time in one week, since it was only on Friday that she had been to the bank. His eyes blazed from the pillow as she changed from her plain grey cotton to the lovely gown she had had made for her by the aged Miss Yeoland, or at least Miss Yeoland's clever seamstresses, at the beginning of the summer. What the devil did she mean by getting all tarted up just to go to the ironmongers, Richard snarled and if she thought he believed a tale like that she was off her head. Where was she really going and who with? he demanded and if she had not been safely cocooned in the shell of joy that had slowly and unshakeably come upon her in the past hour, she might have wondered at the sharp intuition – for the very first time – which had him hit on the truth. The irony of it was not lost on her but neither did it stop her.

It was Elly who had persuaded her to buy the new gown for, let's face it, Elly said mischievously, it was well known that Mrs Goodall had left Poppy a bob or two and it wasn't as if she couldn't afford it. Elly had thought a new outfit might lift the spirits of her young stepdaughter. Good God, the girl was barely twenty-one and all she did was look after a crippled husband and his family. She went nowhere, saw nobody but them and the servants, did nothing that could be described as fun and it was well known a new bonnet worked wonders for a woman's morale.

The fabric of the gown, a rich twilled silk, though it was the pale colour of barley, was shot, as she moved, with pale gold and lemon. The bow which held the bustle at her back was of gold-coloured velvet. It was the fashion to have the bustle jutting out like a shelf on which, some wag had remarked, a good-sized tea tray could be carried. Poppy's was not like this, being modest in its fullness. The front of the gown was simple, cut close in a princess line from her throat to her ankle, fitting to her figure. The sleeves were long and tight, edged with a narrow frill that matched the one at the neck and hem. Her bonnet of straw was small, and small-brimmed, set back off her face with a wide velvet ribbon of gold tied beneath her chin. On the crown was a froth of tiny primroses made from the same material as her gown, since Poppy found the fashion for decorating bonnets and outfits with dead animals, real or imitation, to be quite gruesome. She had been horrified when Miss Yeoland told her that these days some ladies were decorating their bonnets with birds' nests complete with eggs, beetles, cockchafers, centipedes, lizards, scorpions, rats, mice, snakes, spiders and even fleas!

He was sitting on the same bench they had sat on in March and he rose to his feet at once as she approached. Then it had been sunny but cold; now, as though to make up for the dreary downpour of yesterday, it was sunny again but this time it was warm.

It is doubtful either of them noticed. If rain had sliced them with slivers of ice, if a snowstorm had raged about them, if the elements had chucked at them every atom its force could muster they would have stood exactly as they were doing now in the shining truth and acceptance at last of the love they had for one another. They had parted cruelly less than forty-eight hours ago, Poppy ice-cold in her determination to cut him from her life, to cleave, as they said, to her lawfully wedded husband, to be loyal and faithful, devoting herself to the family that had taken her in and been hers for ten long years. So what was she doing here? She didn't know really. She didn't even know why he had written or what he was going to say to her. What had changed since the night before last when he had told her he was off to Glasgow the next day? Why hadn't he gone? All day yesterday she had grieved for him as though he were dead as he travelled further and further away from her, believing he had gone for ever. She had prayed, why she didn't know since she had little faith in anyone, apart from herself, getting her out of any fix, that her suffering would ease, and it had not. Until the letter came. Until the letter had taken away the agony of losing him, since he was here and, because of that letter, so was she.

He knew. He saw the change in her and the glory in his eyes was so great, such a deep blue glory of love and incredulous joy, she felt tears start in her own eyes.

"*Mo annsachd*, dinna weep, ye're here."

"Yes, I'm here, Conn."

They did not touch or even move closer to one another, standing wordlessly now, each searching the other's face, finding what they sought and sighing with the fullness of it.

"I didna bargain for this," he said quietly, knowing she would understand. All the bitterness, the hurt, the anger had gone, sharpness made smooth as though their love and acceptance of its limits had softened, warmed, melted the ice which she at least had done her best to encase her heart in. He had imagined, if she came at all, that he would have to convince her, use all his powers of persuasion to keep her, or some part of her and now she was smiling at him with love in her tear-dewed eyes and he felt the cruel grip loosen about his heart.

"Why did ye come?" he went on.

"I don't know. My soul was . . . so lonely without yours. I don't know," she said again. "It just seemed right and I accepted it."

"Even without knowing what I was to say to ye?"

"Yes, it didn't seem to matter. I was afraid, not just of

us, but of everything." She looked back for a fraction of a
second into the malignant face of Dominic Cooper.

He saw it, he who was attuned to her every mood, to
every change of expression, every inflection of her voice;
he saw it and he frowned.

"What is it?" He took a step towards her and on the path
several passers-by stared curiously at the strange couple by
the bench.

"Nothing."

"Yes, there was something." His mouth became a grim
line, for let anyone hurt her and they would have Conn
MacConnell to answer to.

"No, really. But please, won't you tell me why . . . ?"

His face cleared, his momentary unease gone.

"Come and sit on the bench, *a muirninn*." His sweet
smile lit his face. "*A nighean mo ghaoil. Thug mi gaol d'ar
righribh dhuit.* My beloved girl, I love you most truly. Will
I no' teach ye the Gaelic so that you'll understand?"

"Yes, please," smiling through more tears.

He took her hand then, placing her reverently on the
bench, sat beside her. He unbuttoned the cuff of her glove,
slowly drawing it off, and bending his head, placed his lips
on the inside of her wrist. At once a spark of warmth flared in
the pit of her stomach and her breasts tingled. He looked up
at her and his eyes were deep and eloquent with need and
hers answered, their desire for one another a driving force
that would not long be denied. Again he bent his head, this
time placing his lips to the palm of her hand and her other
hand rose to his tumbled hair and smoothed it back behind
his ears as she had always longed to do. They could have
gone on, speaking the first soft, tentative words of sensuous
love, murmuring, telling each other all the wondrous things
lovers exchange, especially as they had thought it all to

be lost. Poppy's cheeks blazed bright flags of rose in her honey-tinted face as he kissed her bare fingers, astonished and enchanted by the feeling which it awoke in her. She wanted the hard, masculine feel of his body against hers as it had been two nights ago. She wanted his hands on her, his big, blunt-fingered hands, his lips, hot and moist and all the rest of the unknown but rapturous things men and women did to one another in the act of love. She could see the fine reddish-gold fuzz on the backs of his hands and on his wrists, the quick rise and fall of his chest and the rapid pulse in his neck. He was a large man, powerful, his body come from some ancestor warrior who had been honed in battle hundreds of years ago and she wanted to lean on him, to share his warmth and strength, his gentleness and sweetness. She loved him so much, wanted him so much, her heart knocked frantically and her mouth dried up so that she had the greatest difficulty in speaking.

"What's happened? Why haven't you returned to Glasgow?" she managed to say.

Still holding her hand, he turned to stare out at the beautifully landscaped park in which the cemetery was set, then, his mouth wide and soft with tenderness, he smiled, turning back to her.

"I couldna go. It was as simple as that. It was as though there was a thread fastened from my heart to yours, a thread which wouldna break but neither would it stretch from here tae Glasgow. I'd got as far as the station, bags an' all, and . . . I couldna go. The thread wouldna let me. I couldna leave ye, ye see, and travel hundreds o'miles to where there was no chance of ever seeing ye again, so I turned round and came back. I dinna even know what we're to do, lassie, ye being married an' all, but just now it doesna concern me. I was dying, and couldna live unless I was near ye. Ye're my heart and soul and all I want is you." He raised his russet eyebrows ruefully. "God alone knows what my grandfather will say when he hears that I'm no' to come home just now but" – he shrugged – "it canna be helped. Mr Laird'll give me work, he said, when I saw him yesterday, so we'll let the future take care of itself for a while, *mo annsachd*."

"Oh, Conn . . ."

"Dinna fash yersel', lassie*.*" Suddenly he strained his strong neck, looking up into the sky. "Jesus, I love ye, my lassie. I canna tell ye what it means tae me to see ye . . . to have ye here beside me when I thought to lose ye." He looked down at their clasped hands, his face suddenly haggard.

She put a finger to his chin and turned him to look at her.

"I'm here, Conn."

"Aye, I know lassie, but what does it mean? Why are ye here? I'd no hope ye'd come after what ye said the other night, ye ken. I though it to be the end but now ye seem to be saying . . ." He peered into her lowered face. "What are ye saying, *mo annsachd*? What does it mean . . . this afternoon, here?"

She raised her head to look into his face. "It means I love you, Conn." He gripped her hands so tightly she winced. "I . . . accept it. I don't know where it's to go, or if it's to go anywhere but I just can't turn away from it. It's too strong for me. It's a marvel to me, this gift of love. Can I throw it away as if it had no value? No, Conn, I can't, so . . ."

"Ye'll . . . meet me?"

She felt her love and gratitude swell that he asked for no more than that.

"When I can."

There was a deep and eloquent silence as their eyes spoke the question and answered it. Who questioned who and who answered did not matter, it was there between them, as of course she had known it would be. Perhaps not so soon but it did not matter. She was ready.

"Now?" he asked her softly.

She nodded her head, shy, for he was her first. He was enchanted with it.

They stood up and, placing her hand in the crook of his arm, walked without haste towards the incline which led out of the cemetery to the corner of St James Road and Upper Duke Street. They did not speak again until they reached the three-storeyed terraced house in which Conn had rooms. It was well kept, the paintwork and brasswork and windows gleaming, the step donkey-stoned to within an inch of its life.

"Here," he said huskily, fitting his key in the lock and pushing open the door to let her go ahead of him.

"Upstairs . . . to the left," following her up the steep and narrow staircase to the first-floor landing. Another key in another freshly painted door and they were in a sitting-room which had a small balcony looking out on to the street. The room was obsessively tidy as though the occupant no longer lived there and she remembered thinking vaguely that he would have packed everything for his trip to Glasgow.

Another door stood open, a communicating door leading to a room in which Poppy could see a double bed, neatly made and several articles of clothing thrown on to a chair. The furniture was solid and shining and she could smell the furniture polish and the lemon-scented soap she associated with Conn. She was surprised to see a splash of red and pale orange in a vase, then was delighted for they were mixed poppies. It seemed right.

"*Mo annsachd* . . ." He did not want to frighten her by being too precipitate but it was very evident that the sooner he could get her into his arms and his bed, the better he would like it.

"Ye know I love ye?" His voice was husky with longing. "That I'll always take care of ye, whatever comes . . ."

"Yes, I know." She moved towards him, stepping into the arms he held out to her and for several minutes they just held one another, her head pressed to his chest, his cheek on her bonnet.

"Bloody thing," he said, with a smile in his voice, bending to untie the ribbons, his big hands inclined to tremble but gentle. He tossed the bonnet on to the table. He was not a man experienced with women since he was only twenty-two and had lived for many years in the home of a God-fearing Presbyterian Scot, but his joy, his love, his sensitivity, which told him this must be right for her, helped him to understand and employ the gentleness that would lead to physical love.

He undressed her, not with haste, nor indeed any sense of urgency but with a loving attention not only to the beauty of her body which he slowly revealed, but to her shyness, her lack of knowledge of this act they were to share. She was a virgin, and he himself was not far from that state and his hands and his startling blue eyes were reverent. They worshipped her and when at last they were both naked there was such delight in them, in Poppy as well as Conn, he knew she was as eager as he to explore this wonder that had come so unexpectedly upon them. No fear then, no false modesty, just an unashamed wonder which overwhelmed them. They stood facing one another, each absorbed with smooth satin skin, soft firm flesh, hard muscle, rosy peaks, sweet curve of breast and thigh, the musky scent of need.

"I love ye, my lassie," he murmured, then put his mouth to the hollow of her collar bone and his hand reached to cup the firm lift of her breast, feeling the nipple rise to his touch and the answering tremble from her body to his. He had in his eyes the wondering quality of a child who has been given a gift of immense worth and cannot quite believe it. His other hand smoothed her shoulder, her neck, her cheek, as exquisitely tender as only a man can be whose love is as endless and depthless as the deepest ocean. Her own hands were like butterflies, not knowing where to alight, longing to touch this beautiful man in some part of his body but ignorant of where to start. Her hair fell about her, the soft brown tones in it lit with gold where the sunshine streaming through the front window touched it and he pushed it back, lacing his fingers through it then cupping her face with his big, gentle hands.

"Ye're beautiful, *mo annsachd*," he told her, his face showing signs of his great emotion, almost an agony, then his hands slid down to her waist, drawing her against him. She felt the hard thrust of his penis against her belly. She had seen such a thing many times, of course, but the soft, flaccid, vulnerable mass between Richard's thighs bore no resemblance to the proud lift Conn bore.

"I . . . canna wait," he murmured. "I should wait, but I canna . . . forgive me." He lifted her into his arms and carried her into the bedroom. With a rough urgency, which in her inexperience she did not recognise as *his* inexperience, he placed her on the bed, parted her legs and thrust himself inside her. His voice rose jubilantly, a great hosanna in words she did not understand, his face joyous, his thrusts enthusiastic. His back arched, his head was thrown back, his eyes were tight shut as he shuddered to a climax, then he fell on her as though he had been clubbed. There had been no finesse in his lovemaking, no real tenderness but Poppy felt no resentment. She, who knew nothing of the art of making love, knew this man loved her. He had not the polish, the accomplishments of the experienced lover, but that pleased her for she did not want the ease which spoke of practice. Though he had not satisfied the aching need which seethed still in her own loins, it did not matter. Not at this moment of their first joining. They would learn together.

"Oh, God, I'm sorry," he said hoarsely. "I didna mean to hurt ye, and . . . I was too quick for ye. I wanted the first time to be . . ."

"This is still the first time, *mo annsachd*," she told him, smiling at his delight at her clumsy Gaelic, "and now, if you please, we will start again from . . . yes . . . just there . . . and . . . slowly . . . Oh, dear heaven . . ."

He was careful the second time, aware that she must be sore, for there was blood on her thighs but she urged him on, demanding his caresses, moving his hand to her breast, to her belly, to the mound of crisp brown hair at the base of it, to the warm, secret place where no man had been before him, moaning deep in her throat and when, his body quivering with need, for he was a young man with a young man's stamina and need, he entered her again, she arched her back, tightening her buttocks, clutching at his, driving him deeper into her until they exploded together with such noise, later she was to confide to him that she was sure next door must have heard them.

"*Mo annsachd*," he murmured, as he lay on her breast, "I dinna care if they're standing with their ears to the wall and if they were to come knocking I couldna get up to answer the door, not if they had the whole of the Liverpool police force with them."

They drowsed then, hands inclined to smooth and caress and touch.

"Ye're a clever wee woman tae learn so quick, or was it my expertise that did it?" She could feel his smile against her breast.

"We were both . . . quick learners."

"I didna mean that, ye cheeky young madam, I meant the Gaelic. Say it again."

"*Mo annsachd.*"

"Mmm, just a wee bit more emphasis on the last syllable."

"Oh, go to the devil, Conn MacConnell. This is not the time for a lesson in the Gaelic. I want . . ."

"What! Not again?" he asked with pretended incredulity.

"Does it say anywhere that more than twice is forbidden?"

"I canna vouch for it, lassie, but to hell with it if it does."

He slept afterwards, his long legs tangled in the bed linen which they had thrust to the bottom of the bed and Poppy sat up, her legs crossed, studying his large frame in the dim light which came from the sitting-room. He lay on his stomach, his face turned towards her, his neat ear and the blunt angle of his jaw all she could see. The bright red flame of his hair was repeated in the tiny hairs that ran down his spine, brushing his thighs and buttocks with a soft, red-gold fuzz. Very gently she reached out and touched his cheek and in his sleep he smiled. She traced the faint scars on his back with her finger and her mind stretched away to that night years ago when they had begun to love one another. Her love for him, the truth and purity of it, the enduring quality of it which she had known as a child and now as a woman, was fastened, like that thread Conn had spoken of, with a grip that could never be cut loose. Now it had become a physical thing, the physical love she had of his body and she agonised on how she was ever to part from him. On how they were to do this again. On how she could weave him into her busy and intricate life and if she could, would it be enough for him who was as free as a bird. She came to the bank once a week, but obviously this would not be enough for him, nor, now that she had experienced this physical love, would it be for her. So she must make other excuses, think up other reasons to get to town, alone, so that they could . . . *Oh, dear Lord* . . .

She leaped from the bed with such violence Conn woke and did the same, looking round him as though expecting a horde of hairy, kilted Highlanders to be threatening him.

"What the devil . . ."

"Oh, Lord . . . Oh, Lord," Poppy was crying over and over again as she struggled into her petticoat, her bare, rose-tipped breasts jiggling enticingly in Conn's direction.

His eyes narrowed speculatively and he began to smile but she put up a peremptory hand to stop him.

"None of that, Conn MacConnell. Have you seen the time?"

"The time?"

"Yes, for God's sake, the time, and I've forgotten all about the bloody mangle."

27

And so it went on through the warm, drowsy days of summer, the mild, russet-tinted days of early autumn and only Elly guessed at it and May knew of it, though neither spoke to Poppy or each other about it. It was as though the dream-like drifting she moved in, the slow, languorous tread she adopted must not be disturbed, even May, who was as basic as Mother Earth herself, standing back from it with some awe.

The haymaking was almost finished. In the farming manual Poppy had pondered over after Richard's accident, it had spoken of the importance of grassland management. Some of the fields at Long Reach had been grazed by the cattle which kept the taller, stronger grasses down, encouraging dwarf grass and clover to flourish, which in turn nourished the soil. In other fields grasses had been allowed to grow freely and it was these which were cut for hay.

The servants were astounded that during this hectic time, when every pair of hands was needed with the hay that would provide winter feed for the cattle, their little mistress should find so many errands that all of a sudden needed doing in town. All of them, no matter what their normal daily duties might be, helped out in some way during haymaking.

Men, women and children worked from dawn to dusk, the children making bands to bind the cut hay, leading the horses or carrying down the food and drink that Cook, who was the only one to be exempt, prepared for the workers. Scythes flashed in the sunshine, the men walking in a steady row across the field. Extra men, Irish labourers who were always on the lookout for work, were hired. It was hard, hot work. The women wore large cotton sunbonnets to protect their faces but the men were exposed to the full glare of the sun and their already weathered faces became like seamed leather as the weeks progressed. A simple meal was part of their wages. Bread, bacon, cheese, pickles, pies, cold tea, beer or lemonade, which were devoured while they took a brief and well-earned rest in the shade of the trees that edged the field. Old Tom Goodall was proud when his daughter-in-law brought his sturdy grandsons down to see him and show them off to the admiring men and women and he was probably the only one on the farm who did not wonder why Poppy Goodall, who usually worked alongside them at this, the busiest part of the farming year, should be so often missing.

The wringing and mangling machine had duly been delivered, though it had been remarked upon by them all that day that it had taken Poppy a great deal of time to look the thing over. Just before two Jem had brought the gig round to the door and driven her down to Old Swan and the hands on the kitchen clock had stood at just gone six when she bustled in. She'd enjoyed herself, that much was obvious, a vivid colour to her cheeks and eyes and a spring in her step which they hadn't seen for many a long day. She was brisk, a strange almost hectic briskness at which Cook had raised surprised eyebrows, but still it was better than the sad lethargy she had shown for so long. She hadn't been able to decide, she told them, between the new, improved wringing and mangling machine, and the washing, wringing and mangling machine combined where the pressure on the rollers was obtained, or so Mr Evans had told her, by self-adjusting levers that required no effort on the part of the user.

"Well, I never," Aggie said, since she didn't understood what Poppy was talking about, sitting down at the table with a great sigh, easing her boots off her aching feet, not at all concerned with what anybody thought, since she had been up and down to that dratted field a dozen times today and she was exhausted.

Richard had been asleep, the dose the doctor had left him, which had been administered by Elly when Poppy failed to return within the hour, keeping him fast under so that when he did wake Poppy was seated quietly by the fire in the plain skirt and blouse she wore every day. Thank God for Elly, she had thought to herself as she changed. For a moment, as she stood in her thin shift she had looked down at her body which still glowed, at the peaks of her nipples which hardened the moment her thoughts turned to Conn and what they had done this afternoon, then she ran her hands over her breasts and belly where Conn's had been less than two hours ago, amazed at her own lack of shame.

She had turned away from the bed as though to hide what was in her eyes and face, even though she knew Richard was sound asleep. She meant to pull out the truckle bed later since she knew that, no matter how he ranted at her, she could not sleep beside him, at least tonight. Not after this afternoon!

Their parting had been harrowing to them both, especially Conn, who wanted to keep her here, in his bed, in his arms as he was surely entitled to now, his expression seemed to say, though he did not voice it. She had come to him virgin. Now she was his woman, he could not help but add possessively, and though he knew that yesterday he would have been content with what he had today, now he had it he wanted more. She was his, he told her jealously, trying to hold her back from the life that separated them, then had become quiet, sad, so that her heart ached for him. He had insisted on taking her to the very door of the ironmonger, wanting to come in with her, ready to scowl when she said no. She was *his*, his lady, and he, as a gentleman, was meant to protect her, he told her in his new-found, young man's love for her and when she came out of the shop after hurriedly ordering the wringing and mangling machine, he had walked with her to the tram stop, handing her up the steps of the tram as though she were made of fine bone china, his face pale, for they did not know when they would meet again. He had managed to get the day off today to arrange his affairs, he had told the man in charge, but it would be the last, apart perhaps for an hour here or there when he visited men who did business with Lairds. She could not leave the farm during the evening when he was free, which left that odd hour when he could manage it, or Sunday, and what excuse could Poppy Goodall have for coming to town on a Sunday?

"I'm going to see an exhibition tomorrow at the Walker Art Gallery," she said boldly the following Saturday and had the twist of tension inside her not been so tight she might have laughed out loud at their expressions as they all turned their faces towards her.

"Yer wha'?" May asked, then, understanding suddenly, added, "An' why not?"

Before she could collect her wits May had been about to say she'd come with her, for there was nothing she'd like more than to go and see an exhibition, whatever that was, for it would give her a chance to wear her new bonnet. The bonnet, the crown of which rose abruptly in a tall, flowerpot shape, was the very latest fashion. The brim narrowed at the front forming a point over the face and because of this was called a Gable hat. At the peak of the gable was a mass of artificial pink roses, the whole thing the most beautiful article of clothing May had ever owned. To go and show it off would be splendid. Her lads would be safe in Elly's or Dilys's care for a couple of hours. Besides, her Johnny had taken to playing cricket again in the local team and there was a match tomorrow, so it would have been grand to accompany Poppy but of course, Poppy didn't want company, at least not that of her sister-in-law!

"An' what's wrong wi' that?" May added defiantly, and at once all the faces turned back to her as though to ask what the dickens she was talking about, and anyway, what was it to do with her? Only Tom, calmly tucking into his bacon, eggs, mushroom and fried bread, seemed unaware that anything untoward had been said. After each forkful was lifted to his mouth, while he chewed it his eyes turned fondly to the two cradles in the corner where his noisy grandsons were doing their determined best to sit up. They were all he cared about now, them and the work he did on the farm, instructions on what he should be about passed on to him by Evan or Tommy, or even his own son, who was beginning to shape at last. He was a supremely contented man, forgetting for days on end his other son who lay transfixed to his bed upstairs. He lived only to see his grandsons grow and thrive and not only them but the others who were to follow, for May was already pregnant again. She'd only "missed" once but it didn't take her long to spread the news to every last man and woman on the farm, she was that proud of herself.

Sunday was, of course, the day on which they relaxed. Those who wanted to went to church, wandering down the field to St Anne's where Eliza was buried, where both Poppy and May were married, and the twins christened.

When Poppy, dressed in her elegant gown and bonnet, shouted through the back door to Jem to bring round the gig, though she was the wife of the son of the house, and their mistress, there were some resentful glances exchanged.

"I don't know what yer pullin' a face for, Clara Bamber," May exclaimed tartly the moment the gig pulled away. "Yer'd best remember 'oo's in charge 'ere 'cos it's not you. If Poppy fancies a day out it's none o' thy business, far as I can see."

"I'm not sayin' it is." Clara did her best to curb her tongue, but it was hard when she remembered that only a year ago this young woman who was rebuking her had been Clara's subordinate and had obeyed *her* orders. "I'm only sayin' when we're so pulled out wi' work wi't haymakin' she's suddenly took it into 'er 'ead ter go ter town. An' on a Sunday an' all. It's not like 'er, is it?" turning to the others who nodded their heads in agreement. "An' 'e's shoutin' 'is 'ead off over summat. We 'eard 'im when we was upstairs makin' master's bed, didn't we, Aggie? 'E's not best pleased she's off again, I can tell yer."

"Look, if she wants ter go ter Blackpool fer't weekend it's nowt ter do wi' you, nor me. Bloody 'ell, she's bin at everybody's beck an' call fer years now, allus 'ere purrin things right what go wrong an' I fer one say good luck to 'er."

It had taken all May's self-control, which was not much at the best of times, not to question Poppy on the identity of the man she was obviously going to meet but she'd held her tongue, for there was something . . . well, almost *otherworldly* about her sister-in-law and May felt reluctant to break the spell, her own restraint astonishing her. It wasn't just a passing fancy, May could see that and so, though she wondered on who could have put that look in Poppy's eyes, she never asked. The big, red-haired lad, that was evident, but who was he and how had Poppy come to meet him?

The servants exchanged looks of confoundment at May's last remark, for when did May Jebson, as some still called her, stick up for anyone, least of all Poppy who once she'd resented so bitterly? Of course, it was Poppy who had saved May's bacon, so to speak, when May was in a fix, so they supposed it was only natural that she should be grateful. Still, it was a mystery and no mistake.

Their second meeting was even more ecstatic than the first. They made love slowly, languorously, spending an age over the renewed wonder of each other's body. She made him lie on his stomach while she ran her mouth down the length of his beautifully proportioned and sculptured back. Her lips lingered at the scars he still bore from his flogging on the *Lahore*, a tracery of faintly raised weals over which she was ready to weep, remembering. She gently bit his rounded buttocks, then turned him over to admire, with her eyes and her hands, his broad chest, smiling as her enquiring fingers roused his nipples. She smoothed her hands across his flat, lean belly, the length of his muscled legs, the delicate structure of his long, narrow feet then back up to the proud lift and thrust of his penis and the thick bush of crisp red hair from which it sprouted. It was warm, hard, smooth and while he groaned in exquisite agony, she took it in her hand, amazed at this power she had over him. When he climaxed, arching his back and straining his head into the pillow, she kissed him tenderly as though he were wounded.

Later, when he had recovered, she knelt above him, straddling him, unashamed of her nakedness, no longer shy, her rosy peaked breasts flaunting their beauty to his lips with pride as he smoothed her, studied her, moved her drifting limbs this way and that to suit some need in him. He entered her, sighing, dreaming, both of them, their fulfillment rich and satisfying. He could not be said to have taken her for they took each other and gave themselves with rich generosity, again and again, and when it was time to part, knowing she could not make this excuse again, they were devastated. They stood in one another's arms, her face pressed to his chest, his head bent until his forehead rested on her shoulder.

"I canna manage this, *mo annsachd*," he told her brokenly. They were desolate and lost, for their lives were so irrevocably linked now they simply could not bear to be parted.

"Even my hair hurts," she moaned, doing her best to lighten the moment but she could not bring a smile to his pale lips. He looked like a man in deeper shock and she was painfully aware that his suffering was deeper than hers. She felt she couldn't leave him, not without some small light to comfort the darkness of the days they were to spend apart.

"Can you ride, my darling?" she asked him suddenly as the idea came to her.

He pulled away in surprise, looking down into her strained face which, this time, did not have the hectic flush of their first lovemaking.

"Aye, not to enter the Grand National, ye ken, but enough. Why, lassie?"

"Have you the money to hire a horse? Because if you haven't, then I have."

He managed a small lift to the corners of his mouth.

"Och, that's the way of it, is it? A wee heiress and no telling me in case I should be after her money. But, yes, I could afford to hire a nag of sorts. Why?" he asked again.

"If you should ride up to Long Reach it would take you no more than twenty minutes . . . that is if you want to . . ." somewhat breathlessly.

"Want to! *Want to!* Oh, Jesus . . ." He clutched her to him so fiercely she gasped.

"I could get up to the spinney when they've gone to bed."

"But, your husband?" he asked delicately. "Would he no' . . .?"

"He has a draught." She seemed remote for a moment and her voice was flat and detached.

"I see. Then . . . ?"

"Remember the stable . . . all those years ago?" Her voice was muffled in his shirt front but he heard her.

"Aye, *mo annsachd*, I remember the stable."

"When winter comes . . ."

He understood and he sighed, content for the moment.

He came every night, sometimes when it was pouring with rain, sometimes when it began to grow cold as autumn drew near, for he could not stay away though she couldn't always get out to him.

And so they whispered and loved their perilous way through the days and nights, meeting when they could in Conn's rooms, in the spinney or, more often, in the dark loft above the stable where she had mended his injured back and where now they made love in total darkness and silence. She had managed to smuggle out several blankets and they would make a cocoon, a shelter, a bed for their passion and for now it was enough. It was all they had so it was enough, both of them living for the precious moments when, at great risk, they could be together. He did not bring up the subject of her leaving Richard and coming to live with him but she knew he would. For the moment he was satisfied with what they had, since it was better than nothing but it would not last. His grandfather had been most displeased that he had decided to stay on at Laird's "for a while", he had written and Conn's fear was that the old gentleman, who needed his grandson in his own shipyard, might write to Mr Laird and insist he send him home.

They were to have a dance at Long Reach Farm when the harvest was in. Evan and Tommy said they had never had such a crop, surpassing everything in their experience and they had both worked on a farm since they were toddlers. There was the sugar beet which was stored in neat mountains reaching to the very rafters of the small barn. The root crops, potatoes, mangels, turnips and suedes, the latter two cropping for the second time that year, since the humid conditions of the north and west encouraged their rapid growth, were lifted and stored in long, broad clamps, well covered with straw to protect them from the frost until they went to market. Barley, oats and wheat had been planted in the spring and the harvest, like the rest of the crop, was good and, Evan said privately to Dilys, for who else could he discuss it with, that the Goodalls must have "houses in the bank" and it was all down to that lass Richard had married. A splendid dairy farm this had been for years but now that it was a mixed farm, using the fields in strict rotation to allow them to rest, it must be worth a bob or two! The good sound grain had turned golden in the sun, a sight any farmer would give his right arm for, he declared. It had been cut and carted in the most beautiful weather he had ever encountered and that alone was good reason for a celebration.

It was many a year, Evan and Dilys couldn't remember the last one, since they'd had a harvest dance and right out of the blue the little mistress had suggested it, saying it was the right year to revive the old custom, what with the yield being so good. A harvest supper and if Cook could make some suggestions regarding food and drink, which must be lavish, for the labourers and their families, she'd be much obliged, she said.

She was, despite the drawn look which sometimes lurked about her eyes, cheerful and bright and who could blame her, they all said, the success she'd made of this place. Master Johnny was coming on a treat, making a fair stab at becoming a decent farmer. May was doing her best in the house, which was all anyone could do, and what with those handsome lads of hers and another on the way, they were fair set to having the best time of their lives. If it wasn't for the poor lad up in his bed, whom most of them had never seen since his wedding day and whom, to be honest, they all forgot for weeks on end, the Goodalls had good reason to be satisfied.

The big barn where the supper was to be held looked a treat, everybody agreed. Poppy, Aggie and Marigold had worked hard during the golden, mellow morning to decorate it as Poppy wanted it. Great boughs of fir and copper beech had been hung from nails along the walls, looped with yards and yards of plaited, brightly coloured horse braid in which massed wildflowers from the meadow had been twisted. Fieldmouse ear and campion, buttercup and clover and shepherd's-purse, white and red, yellow and soft pink. Everything movable in the barn had been pushed and stacked into a corner and Marigold had swept away the dust and chaff and debris of years, raising a positive storm of dust into the air with the stiff, long-handled broom she wielded with enthusiasm and energy. She was that excited, she told Cook, she didn't know whether she was on her head or her elbow and did Cook think she should wear her green or her blue?

A long trestle table Evan had dug up from somewhere was scrubbed and scrubbed by Poppy, who had lost none of her zeal for cleanliness, and across its top, forming a "T", another was placed, the whole covered by a couple of Eliza Goodall's second-best tablecloths. There were jars of flowers down the centre of each table, joined by trailing ivy. Lamps were hung on the walls every few feet, well out of the way of the high jinks that Poppy was well aware the lads would get up to when the dancing started and they had a few tankards of Farmer Goodall's ale inside them.

It all looked grand. The sun was lower in the sky now that September was half over, a sky like nothing they'd ever seen before, they told one another, shading from deep lavender to hazed layers of pink and coral and apricot, rosy pink and gold down to the horizon beyond the spinney, the last rays slipping in golden glory through the wide-open doors of the barn.

Cook did them proud. There was a vast sirloin of beef, roasted to brown perfection on the outside, a delicate pink on the inside when it was sliced. There was a huge ham and a loin of pork, two enormous beefsteak puddings, for, as Cook said, the one thing they were not short of was beef, just as though they went short of everything else! There were mashed and roast potatoes and pickled onions, great slabs of their own cheese, fresh crusty bread, and, for a treat since they were not usually served on the farm, dishes of fragile butter shells which Nelly and Jinny had laboured over all day in the dairy. As though this were not enough to satisfy the most voracious appetite, there were a dozen blackberry and apple tarts with cream.

They came in hesitantly, overwhelmed by the unusual beauty of the barn which most had never seen except as a storage place for farm implements, and by the groaning table on which was piled food they could not have imagined and had certainly never eaten. They were labourers, carters, men who tended the pigs and cows, mended wheels and ploughs and dry-stone walls, drained ditches and cleared the land. They lived, those who were permanent, in Primrose Bank or in cramped cottages rented from Tom Goodall. They brought their wives and children, washed, tidied and excited and began at once to jostle for a place at the sumptuous feast. Poppy, May and some of the servants were at the top table, with Tom and Johnny, and beside them Dilys and Evan and when Tommy, his hair plastered like a skin of black satin to his head, crept in, leading the plump little widow he had been courting for the last six months, the place exploded with approving cheers and clapping. They were placed next to Evan and Dilys, both overcome by it all but pleased as punch just the same.

Reuben, minus Elly who had volunteered to do the first shift minding the babies and Richard, including Poppy's husband in the same category as the twins, with Jinny and Nelly and the rest of the farm servants sat just below the top table and with them were Poppy's two brothers, teachers now at the Mechanics Institute in Liverpool. Each had a young lady on his arm. Poppy had time to wonder what her mam would have made of these two serious lads of hers who had done so well in life but then, if Mam had lived they would not have turned out as they had done. Poor Mam!

They all fell to, earnestly engaging themselves in the serious task of filling their bellies with the best for once, prepared to enjoy an evening of plenty which would not come round again for twelve months, if then. The old mistress had been kind but she'd been a lady, come from the upper classes and had not the understanding of the little lass who had once been one of them and therefore knew at first hand their daily hardships. She had suffered as they did in her early years and now, after she'd done so well for them all, and for the Goodalls, she was stuck with the poor sod who, or so Reuben told them, who'd had it from his Elly, had flatly refused to be lifted downstairs to join in, as far as he could, the festivities. He was not going to be gawked at, nor pitied, by a bunch of louts, he'd apparently shrieked at his wife, though it seemed Reuben's Elly was of the opinion that Richard Goodall pitied himself. It seemed he was turning nasty as the years passed and could you blame him with a beautiful woman like Poppy in his bed and him able to do bugger all about it.

And by God, she was beautiful. There was something dazzling about her, a sort of glow which was strange when you considered the arid wilderness of the life she led. She was a woman meant for love, the men thought privately, born to it, built for it and it was a bloody shame to see it all go to waste.

Master Johnny stood up and made a speech in that easy, amiable way he had, making them laugh, thanking them for their hard work which had made this possible and if the thought crossed their minds that it had also put a few bob in his pocket, it did not last for long. It had been a good harvest, he said, and they were to drink up and enjoy themselves. They clapped and stamped and whistled and did as they were told, the good ale slipping down throat after throat with incredible ease.

The tables had been cleared and carted away and they

were dancing when young Master Johnny suddenly stood up and made his way to the door, holding out his hand and smiling in welcome to the big man who hovered there, wondering, as they pranced about in one another's arms in an energetic polka, who he was. A gent, that was evident, good-looking, but it was hard to tell who he was in the golden light from the lamps which cast shadows about the place.

They were thunderstruck as, recognising him at last, they watched the squire's lad calmly walk over to their little mistress, lift her limp hand to his lips and kiss it. Even the fiddler stopped playing, for there was not one person there who had not heard of Tom Goodall's hatred of this man who had crippled his son nor forgotten his threat to shoot the bugger if he came on his land again. Over four years ago that had been and it was true that Farmer Goodall was not the same man that he was then, but surely he was not so far gone he would not recognise his son's attacker.

"Good evening, Mrs Goodall," they heard Dominic Cooper say politely. "It was most kind of you to invite me." Though May was Johnny's wife and was seated beside Poppy he totally ignored her.

The young mistress stood up so abruptly the chair she was sitting on crashed to the floor. She snatched her hand away from the squire's lad, her face, they all saw it, set in lines of white horror. They could not hear what was said after that, for the fiddler, aware that he was not earning his fee, began to screech away on his fiddle again and though they all cocked their ears they heard nothing further.

"Tekk yer partners for Sir Roger de Coverley," the fiddler called out above the music and the fascinated guests had no option but to do as he said.

Poppy's mind was dazed with shock but it still had the clarity to realise that somehow, probably at the cricket matches that had been held during the summer months – and should she not have expected it? her agonised mind asked – Dominic and Johnny had become "chums" again. That was how Dominic had described their relationship years ago and now he was here once more with his chum and in his narrowed eyes as they looked into hers was the question, What are you to do about it? here under the public scrutiny of all the men and women who worked on the farm. I am invited here by the son of the owner, the man whose farm it will be one day and you, as a woman, have no say in the matter. His smile told her exactly what was behind it and that was that if he couldn't get to her by the back door, then his only alternative was the front and careless, unthinking Johnny Goodall had opened it for him.

Johnny had never been completely convinced that Dominic had felled Richard deliberately and in a foul rage. It was an accident, he had always said, even, as the years went by and the memory faded, a bit of horse-play gone wrong. He had missed their friendship, their rides out together, the fun they'd shared, the days spent hunting, shooting, and now that the farm was running so well and he might be considered to be a gentleman farmer he could see no reason in the world why they shouldn't do it again, which was why he'd invited Dominic tonight. He had, of course, taken no count of his strong-willed wife, whose own eyes glared dangerously at him, whose own mouth was not smiling, for May Goodall was certainly not afraid of this supercilious sod who had come to lure her husband away from his duties.

Tom Goodall stood up and Poppy's stony-eyed attention shifted from Dominic Cooper's smiling face to her father-in-law. The fiddle scraped away and the feet of two dozen partially inebriated dancers thumped enthusiastically on the floor of the barn, raising even more dust. It was noticed by the house servants who knew more than the farm workers about the disaster four years ago, that Evan and Tommy and Jacko had casually arranged themselves at Tom Goodall's back, ready, should he show signs of becoming deranged, to hold him steady, but it was not needed.

"Johnny, lad, introduce us to your friend," he said mildly. There was nothing in Tom Goodall's world now to upset and alarm him. He stayed on his farm, meeting no one but those he knew, wrapped up in the marvel of his two thriving grandchildren, protected by his son's wife whom he loved as a daughter, and his tranquil mind saw nothing untoward in the reappearance of the man who had crippled his son, since his tranquil mind did not recognise him.

"It's Dominic, Father. Dominic Cooper. We play cricket for the same team. The Grimshaw Arms team, d'you remember?"

"Aye, I do, lad. You were a right good batsman onceover. Even your mother, who was not interested in sport, liked to watch you play." He turned to Dominic. "My wife died some years ago and is sadly missed."

"Indeed, sir, I'm sure she is." Dominic bent his head sadly.

Tom brightened. "But I've two grandsons now. Tom and Jack and a pair of right rascals they are. See, May," turning to the rascals' mother whose demeanour boded ill for her husband. Indeed as he stood there grinning like a chimpanzee in her eyes was the warning that she was only waiting to get him alone and not for romantic purposes neither. She was his wife and to be ignored by this "fancy-dan", who was nowt a pound in her eyes, and her husband allowing it, made her see red. Cricket, she'd give him cricket, and anything else he might fancy that would take him out of her sight off this farm!

"Fetch them over, there's a good lass and let Mr Cooper have a look at them," Tom was saying. "Lively as imps they are, Mr Cooper. Sitting up and only just six months old, isn't that right, May?"

May did not answer.

"Really, sir, but perhaps . . . some other time? I'm sure they are tucked up in their beds at this moment."

"Oh, aye, you're right. Never mind. Come over in the morning and I'll show them to you."

"Thank you, sir. It would be a pleasure."

Johnny grinned in delight, not seeing the falseness of his chum's smile, the thin curl of contempt about his lips, the arrogant disdain which Dominic was holding within himself for the moment since it suited his purpose. Johnny did not recognise, or if he did chose to ignore, his wife's scowl but those who knew her in the kitchen had to smile, wishing they could be there when she got him alone.

Poppy stood like a statue, white-faced, her eyes deep pools of darkness, dithering, she knew that, on what she should do. How could she shout and smack his smiling face as she longed to do with her family and the servants all looking on? They had no idea what this man had tried to do to her in the past, only Elly, and she wasn't here, and even Elly didn't know who it was who had put the fear of God in her for all these years.

Dominic was watching her, his eyes glittering in the lamplight, his face dark and inscrutable, waiting, like a cat to see which way another will jump. She wanted to scream at him, like she had the last time. She wanted to run out of the barn away from his hated presence, to get away from his contamination, for surely he was mad. What was it in her that had him creeping about, making friends again with Johnny who he cared nothing about, coming here to an event which she knew full well was beneath his proud dignity? She gave him no encouragement. He knew she loathed him but some nasty thing inside him seemed to find a quiet satisfaction in it, making him want her all the more.

"Well," he murmured, glancing round and tapping his foot, "though these country dances are . . . er . . . charming, I'm afraid my dancing teacher did not include them in his curriculum. Now a waltz would be splendid. What say, Johnny, can that fiddler play a waltz, d'you think? If so I shall ask your lovely sister-in-law to take a turn with me."

"I'll ask . . ."

"Don't bother, Johnny, if you please. I do not care to waltz at the moment, Mr Cooper. I must go and check on my husband who, and I'm sure you will know the reason why, cannot be here with us tonight. Excuse me."

With her head high she walked out into the night. Like a young queen she was, they all thought, those who watched her go, but they might have been seriously alarmed had they seen the expressions which turned like dangerous eels in Dominic Cooper's eyes.

28

Conn MacConnell leaned his back against the broad trunk of the oak tree, his arms folded across his chest, and stared moodily down at the cluster of buildings that comprised Long Reach Farm. He had removed his jacket, since the evening was still and warm and though he was aware that his white shirt must be clearly visible in the gloom, he didn't seem to care. In fact, the mood he was in he wished someone would see him and then this whole bloody mess might be brought out into the open. It was not that he wanted deliberately to cause trouble in Poppy's life but then it appeared that was going to be the only way to get her to reconsider her absolute refusal to leave her family – and her crippled husband, the small, persistent and fair-minded voice in his head said – and come away with him. He felt so frustrated and helpless, not in any sort of control of his life, and so lonely. Three nights he had been up here and three nights she had not come and he wanted to smash his resentful fist into something, make a great commotion, shout his pain and jealousy and, quite simply, he couldn't.

He could hear the sound of the fiddle scraping away from the barn at the bottom of the big field, the crash of boots as the guests danced enthusiastically to its rhythm and the bursts of high laughter as the drink began to take hold of them. This was their night, the highlight of their year when they could eat and drink and be merry until the cock crowed and they were making the most of it.

He had not meant to come tonight. She had said three nights ago when he last saw her that she would try to get away but it might be difficult, for all eyes would be on her. Tonight was not like other nights when, saying she was tired or had accounts to do in the study and did not wish to be disturbed, she could throw on a dark cloak and slip up the track and into his arms for a moment.

"A moment is better than nothing, *mo annsachd*," he had told her ardently, for then she had been in his bed, her dear face looking up into his and the future, even tomorrow, did not seem to matter.

Now it did. On this dark night and the ones before when he was alone and craving for her, it did. When she might be dancing in another man's arms, it did, the thought slicing through him so that he was in real physical pain. No man should be asked to suffer what he suffered when she was not with him. It was like having an arm or a leg cut off without the mercy of an anaesthetic, the limb taken from him leaving him to bleed in agony and only when she was with him did he become whole again, unhurting again, and he wondered painfully how much longer he could bear it. His work suffered, he knew it did, since how was a man to concentrate when his mind was obsessed only with if he would see her today, if he would make love to her today, if he would ever get back to Glasgow, if he could persuade her to leave her husband, the farm, her family and come and be totally his.

These thoughts demoralised him. He was a man in love with another man's wife and he knew his feelings for Poppy were weakening his own beliefs in what was right and what was wrong. He knew himself to be an honourable man. He took pride in being so. He could look any man in the eye, he believed, without turning away in guilt or shame. He was honest, giving to everyone he knew truth and consistency and receiving trust in return, at least from most. He had been forced as a child to steal to feed his mother but he would starve himself before he took anything that did not belong to him and now, if he could, he would steal Poppy Goodall from her husband.

So, what was he telling himself? he wondered as he pushed his back away from the tree and walked out of the shelter of the spinney and into the open field. That he should give her up and go home? That after no more than a couple of months of deceit and lies, not on his part, but hers, since she insisted and he had agreed, he had had enough of it and was to tear her out of his heart and crawl back to Glasgow, wounded, perhaps dying of it? He it was who had refused to leave Liverpool. He it was who had said he would rather live like this than without her, and now, already, he was cringing away from the dread that this might go on for ever. He knew he was living, and was bitterly ashamed of it, in the hope that the cruelly weakened man who was Poppy's husband would die and free her, but what kind of man could wish for that and still call himself honourable?

There was a couple stumbling up the field towards him, their progress pushing aside the wildflowers and grasses and releasing their fragrance into the night. They were giggling mindlessly, fumbling with one another's clothing, the woman's breasts already tumbling from her unbuttoned bodice, white and somehow obscene in the moonlight. They were coming up here to do what he and Poppy did beneath the sheltering trees, he was only too well aware, and nausea rose to his throat. The thought diminished him, tarnished the bright truth and purity of what he and Poppy felt for one another and he wanted to sink to his knees, bend his head to the ground, cover it with his arms and weep, for her and for himself.

Instead he moved quietly back into the trees, picked up his jacket and began to make his way to the far side of the spinney where his horse was tethered. He would go back to his rooms and if she came up to the spinney tonight she would not know he had been here. He longed for her with a desperation that frightened him, wanting her to come and tell him she was deserting them all, that she loved only him, that they did not matter to her, but his dilemma was that if she did, if she was capable of doing such a thing, she would not be the woman he loved.

He was damned either way!

He led his horse across the field at the back of the spinney, heading towards the gate which opened on to the track leading down to Prescot Road. The gate opened silently, for Poppy, weeks ago and unbeknown to anyone, had oiled it so that when he and his animal crept through at night they would do so unheard.

He could still hear the music and the stamp of feet and just beneath the surface of it but from somewhere closer to him than the barn, which was across the field from the lane, the sound of a man and woman arguing. At least he thought they were arguing though there was a note in the woman's muffled voice which puzzled him. Their voices were not loud. It was probably another couple bent on rutting beneath the trees, he thought sadly, wondering why he should use such a terrible word to describe what, after all, he and Poppy did.

For a moment he had to stop as the nausea and grief

dragged at him again, tearing at his heart which, Jesus God, was already bleeding slowly to death, or so he imagined, though some practical part of him that still had reason in it told him that it could not possibly be so. He almost folded over with the pain of it, the despair and what he knew was the inevitability of what must happen soon. He loved her so . . . *mo annsachd, mo donn falt caileag, a gradhach* – dearest, greatly loved – *thug mi gaol d'ar righribh dhuit* – I love you most truly. She was his life, but his life was slowly draining out of him and he knew as he straightened up, his body like that of an old man at the end of its days, that it could not be borne much longer. He was preparing himself to say goodbye to his love, he accepted it, to Poppy Goodall, who was his love and his life, the sum and substance of his existence and it was destroying him. His need of her was still fighting though. It snarled inside him like a spitting cat, doing its best to overcome his self-respect, his honour, his obligation to his grandfather, which sounded trite but it was the truth. It had been a battle he had known that he was losing, little by little. His personal code of honesty and decency was being eroded by what he was doing to Richard Goodall who could not fight for what was his.

The sound of a human voice interrupted his deepening hopelessness. "Take your hands off me, you bastard," he heard a woman say from down by the barn, her voice hoarse with what seemed to be revulsion. Evidently whoever the man was his attentions were not welcome, his weary, dazed mind noted without interest.

"Oh, no, you don't, my fine lady. Not this time—"

The words the man spoke were bitten off as though a gag had been placed across his mouth. Perhaps the lips of the woman, Conn thought, but then she appeared to be objecting so why should she kiss him? Oh, dear God, don't do this to me, he moaned softly. Let me creep away to lick my wounds in peace. This woman is nothing to me . . . but then you are a hypocrite, he heard a voice in his head say clearly. You speak, to yourself only, of course, of honour and decency and doing the right thing while just across the field a woman might be fighting for her own honour and decency and you are ready to ignore it.

He sighed, looking about him, hoping to see an irate husband perhaps searching for a wandering wife, or a reveller who had come outside to relieve himself, someone who would hear the sounds of conflict and interfere with what was going on below him. He could hear it clearly now. Gasps and soft cries of muffled distress, then the sound of a blow and he knew he could not ignore it. Tying his horse to the gatepost he vaulted the rail and ran quickly and silently down the field.

The man had his back to him and was making a noise that sounded very much like those made by a dog holding down a bitch, a sort of snarling that made the hairs on the back of Conn's neck and on his arms stand on end.

"What the bloody hell d'ye think ye're doing?" he said quietly to the man's back, deriding himself, for was it not very obvious what the man was doing, or was about to do. The woman was pressed up against the barn wall with her face to it, held there by the man's forearm which was bent across her upper back. He had lifted her skirt, bunching it up about her waist and pulled down her drawers which were in a pool about her feet and her white buttocks gleamed in the shadow.

At the sound of Conn's voice the man jerked violently, half turning.

"Sod off," he snarled. "Can't you see we're busy."

"Well, you seem to be but I'm no' so sure about the wee lassie."

"Bugger off, there's a good chap."

"No, I'll no' bugger off until the young lady tells me she's enjoying this . . . this . . . as much as you. She seems curiously disinterested . . . in fact . . . Good God, man, she's barely conscious."

Horrified out of his own misery he took hold of the man's broad shoulders and despite his size and rage at being interrupted, dragged him away from the woman and, as he did so, her support gone, she slid bonelessly to the ground.

It was Poppy!

His sense of shock was so great her attacker had time to get a good hold of him, his arm about his throat, his fist smashing into Conn's face and head. For a second he was paralysed, wanting to turn and batter the man to bloody pulp and at the same time his need to get to his little love, to lift her defenceless body up into the shelter of his strong arms was overpowering and, at the same time, weakening him. He heard her moan but the man was choking him and his mind and his rage told him he must deal with him first.

His roar of white hot anger quietened every sound for miles around. Even Richard turned his head on his pillow towards Elly who had just come upstairs to replenish his fire. They stared at one another in bewilderment then Elly moved to the open window and, resting her hands on the sill, put her head out to see what was going on.

"What in hell's name was that?" Richard asked her. "It sounded like a bloody lion."

The animals in their pens and stables and out in the fields and woods stood still and silent, as animals will, even domesticated ones, at the scent or sound of danger.

Had the Zoological Gardens been closer there was no doubt the tigers in their cages would have answered the primitive call with one of their own.

Inside the barn, those who were still on their feet froze where they stood. Reuben started so fiercely he dropped his tankard, the good ale going all over his Sunday suit, and Herbert and Eustace stood up violently as though, the minute they knew what and where the danger was, they'd be off to conquer it, for hadn't they their ladies to protect. They'd both read about Sir Lancelot and Sir Ivanhoe, of course! The fiddle music dribbled away on a whine and Marigold, looking fetching in the blue she had decided to wear, clutched at Dilys in horror, her face losing all its colour, turning fearful eyes towards the door. Shouldn't they shut it at once, the terror in them asked, before the beast, for surely it was that, got in to them?

As creatures do, human and animal, the women huddled closer together, seeking the comfort of contact with their own kind.

"Oh, dear God," Aggie moaned, almost dragging Clara over and May began to run frantically towards the door, ready to brave what was out there to get to her sons.

Not one of them had noticed the disappearance of Mr Cooper, not even Johnny. Why should they? And if they had would not have questioned it. Men were drinking and as fast as the ale goes in it needs to come out again and where else were they to relieve themselves but at the side of the barn?

Master Johnny, his face a picture of astonishment, ran after his wife, neither the servants nor himself knowing why.

For an awful moment no one else moved or spoke and when the beast roared again the farm women began to clutch hysterically at the nearest male sleeve and Tom muttered that he was off for his shotgun.

"What was it?" Dilys asked Evan in a cracked voice and, as though she had broken the spell, Evan and Tommy, Jacko and Jem, safety in numbers, see, began to surge out of the barn and round to the back of it from where the most terrifying sounds were coming. They hung together for a moment, for God alone knew what might be out there, spectres of escaped animals from the Zoological Gardens entering their usually practical minds. As they drew nearer, thankfully they began to realise that the sounds were no more than those made by mortal man, two mortal men, not a creature from another world, a beast, or indeed nothing worse than two men locked in mortal combat.

The four men, joined by others now, circled the heaving mass which seemed joined together in some odd way until, with another roar, one half of the mass sent the other half sprawling and Evan caught a glimpse of what was lying on the ground against the barn wall.

"Cariad," he whispered silently and it was a measure of his distress that he used the endearment reserved only for his wife. He wanted to go to her, cradle her, but for the moment there was the question of preventing a serious crime being committed.

"Dilys," he roared instead, just as powerfully and just as madly as the one they had heard a moment ago, for Evan thought the world of Poppy Goodall. He didn't know who was fighting who or who had chucked their Poppy, bare bum showing for all to see, in the mire. Not yet, but one of them was getting the worst of it and if they didn't get the other off him there'd be murder done.

"Get your fucking hands off me," the big chap snarled as half a dozen pairs of hands dragged at him, reaching out to those who were on his back, throwing poor Jem several feet into the air and, as they remarked later, it was a good job it was grass Jem's head landed on or he'd have been a goner.

Hesitantly the women came, for they were still not convinced that some madman from the lunatic asylum was not among them. One of them, with great presence of mind, had snatched a lamp from the barn wall and even before they had crowded round the crumpled heap of clothing and bare flesh that was their little mistress, most began to weep with a woman's compassion for one of their own. She had been subjected, or so it seemed, to what every woman dreads, and their pity was immense.

Directed by Dilys, they formed a protective circle about her, rearranging her clothing decently, speaking in soft, soothing voices as they lifted her in tender arms. None had ever known a woman who had been raped. Perhaps she hadn't, please God, they were all begging voicelessly. Perhaps whoever it was who had come to her rescue, one of the men who had been fighting, presumably, had got there in time. Dear Lord, they prayed so as they took her away from the men who, though they would have given their life to save a woman from this, were male just the same.

More men, and there were plenty willing to help knock the bloody block off whoever was the perpetrator of this crime, were required to hold the big fellow, who was nearly out of his mind, wanting to follow the women who had Poppy.

"Poppy," he was roaring, to their amazement. "For God's sake, let me go to her. Is she all right? Please . . . please, let go of me, ye bastards. Poppy . . . Jesus God, I'll kill that bugger. That's what he was going tae do to her, bugger her, don't ye understand, *let go of me*," while the bastard in question lay like a limp, blood-soaked bit of rag, or a doll whose stuffing has been knocked out of it, which was about right, Evan was inclined to think. They could see who it was now, of course, but until they got him up, the two of them inside the barn and this lot sorted out they didn't know who to blame, did they? Best keep a firm hold on them both until Poppy was able to tell them the name of the scum who had done this to her.

"Please . . . please, let me go to her." The big chap was almost weeping as they dragged him, six of them needed to do it, into the barn. As Herbert and Reuben reached for a rope, ready to hang somebody by the look of them, the light from the lamp fell on his hair, a bright flame of red it was, and on his face, which was swollen and bleeding, was an expression of such suffering they all felt the need to look away as though they were spying on a man's private grief.

Mr Cooper was coming round and it was the opinion of the men who hung about that there was no need to tie him up. Great God, he didn't look as though he could knock the skin off a rice pudding and then, of course, it was not yet proved who was the attacker of the little mistress, and who the defender. The big chap was nearly having convulsions trying to get out of the ropes they had trussed about him, still imploring them to let him go to see how badly – God, it was pitiful to see him – how badly Poppy was hurt. He'd almost gone home, he told them, looking round the circle of fascinated faces, and if he had . . . Jesus – his face worked convulsively – it didn't bear thinking about. If they wouldn't let him go would one of them make enquiries, find out if they could if that bastard, glaring like a maniac at the slumped and bloody figure of the squire's son, had . . . had . . . God in heaven, he couldn't even bring himself to say the word, but let him swear this, he remarked with ice in his voice, if he found out that he had . . . had . . . well, let there be no mistake, he'd kill him with his bare hands and gladly swing for it. He'd be no good to Poppy then, he realised that, but at least that bastard would no longer be walking this earth. In his dementia he did not notice the shocked expressions which were becoming fixed on the men's faces as they began to realise the implications of what it was this big, distraught man was telling them.

Evan cleared his throat. "Slip over and see 'ow little mistress be, Jem, there's a good lad but don't make no fuss, see. Don't want to upset her, do we, more than's necessary that is."

"Thanks . . . Dear God, thanks," the big man mumbled and, bending his head, began to shake in what Evan recognised as shock.

All this time Mr Cooper had lain slumped quietly in the corner. They had sent for the constable, just to be on the safe side, and the doctor, for both men needed attention and Evan had thought it wise to let Captain Cooper know that his son was in a bit of trouble, if you could call it that. Silent he was, not badly hurt, they thought, for they had managed to prise the big chap off him in time and he had walked, somewhat unsteadily, into the barn. Perhaps they should have taken him into the farmhouse, him being gentry an' all, but it was beginning to dawn on them that it might have been *him* who had attacked their Poppy so they were keeping a watchful eye on him.

When he spoke through his torn mouth they all turned to look at him, startled.

"You'll pay for this, you scum," he mumbled, his eyes in his blood-soaked face alive with some dreadful thing. It was directed at the big, red-haired chap and was a look none of them would have cared to have directed at them. "She's nothing but a whore and every man knows a whore can't be raped. You've had her yourself. I've seen you up in the spinney and I only wanted a bit of what you had. Jesus, she must have been hot for it, living with that cripple all these years."

If they hadn't seen it with their own eyes, they were to say later, they wouldn't have believed it. Hell's bells, there was no one on the farm could tie a better knot than Tommy. Well, he had to, hadn't he, what with the bulls an' all.

With a murderous hiss, which was even more threatening than any sound he had made previously, the big chap tore off the ropes, breaking the skin on his wrists with the force of it, and with a movement like that of a panther attacking its prey he fell on Mr Cooper and began to knock the living daylights out of him. It was not the wild violence of uncontrolled anger but the systematic and cold murder of one man by another and if they didn't stop it Captain Cooper would certainly see his son's murderer hung.

They did the only thing they could in the circumstances. With a nod from Evan, Tommy picked up the shovel that had been carefully tidied against the wall before the dancing began and brought it down on the big, red-haired lad's head. He fell like a stone, dropping heavily among the untidy remains of the harvest dance, empty tankards skittering across the barn floor in all directions, chairs flying and bouncing off the wall, dust raising in a haze. Blood began to seep from somewhere under his hair.

"I'll have the bastard in gaol before the night's out," Mr Cooper snarled and aimed a cruel kick at the fallen man's ribs.

" 'Ere, we'll have none o' that, see," Evan said. "Do that again an' we'll tie you up an' all. There's no call ter kick lad when 'e's out for't count."

"Not even when he's been fornicating with the wife of your employer," Dominic Cooper sneered. "They've been pleasuring one another for—"

"That's enough if you please, sir. That sort o' talk—"

"What sort of talk? It's true. I've seen them with my own eyes and that poor bastard of a husband of hers—"

"That's enough!" thundered Evan. "Now we'll have no more talk until doctor gets 'ere ter see to . . . well, there'll be enough said later when . . ."

Not one of them noticed Tom Goodall move quietly but purposefully from the barn and walk towards the front door of the farmhouse.

29

The first thing she said was, "Where's Conn?"

They had placed her gently in the rocker by the fire. She seemed not to know where she was and could you blame her, poor thing, they were all thinking, after what she'd gone through. The clock on the wall said it was almost midnight and it was their custom to retire before ten, since their day started early, and they'd all be jiggered in the morning, but not one of them made a move to go to their beds. They were all as sorry as anyone could be at what had happened to the lass but they'd not miss this for all the tea in China. They would have been late, anyway, they murmured to one another, it being the harvest dance, an' all, but the sight of their little mistress huddled like some raggedy doll discarded and thrown down in the mud as though by a bad-tempered child had upset them beyond words, and as Aggie whispered to Clara she wouldn't get a wink of sleep until she knew whether Poppy was . . . well, Clara would know what she meant. Had he or hadn't he, whichever one it was? They stood about her in helpless pity, Marigold still weeping, Nelly and Jinny bewildered, May, her face set in grim lines, clutching a fretful baby under each arm.

It was Cook who got them going. She turned to the silent

group, her face stern, her lips thinned with some painful emotion that had her in its grip and they all leaped like horses raked with a spur. "Put that kettle on, Clara, and you, Aggie, run up to the mistress's bedroom and fetch her shawl. The warm one, and you'd best fetch Elly down an' all while you're at it. She'll be wondering what's up. Master Richard will be all right on his own for half an hour. Don't breathe a word to him about this, though, if he asks. Say it was a bull got loose, or something. Now, come on, the lot of you, take that daft look off your faces and do something useful."

Cook had been appalled when Dilys and Clara had practically carried in the almost senseless figure of Poppy Goodall. Dilys's whispered explanation had whitened her usual rosy face and stopped her old heart for a beat. Her usual neat and immaculate kitchen still bore signs of the hectic day's work she and her minions had put in and she had been about to set them to restoring it to the pristine condition she demanded. She couldn't go to bed, and neither could they, leaving even one teaspoon unwashed and not tidied away, but all this was forgotten as she got to her creaky old knees and took her young mistress's hands between hers. She began to chafe them, stroking the backs with her thumb as she spoke, her own voice ragged with dread, for what worse fate could there be for a woman than to be held down and violated by a brute of a man?

"Poppy, lass," she murmured, her wise old eyes, which had watched this lass grow from an ill-nourished and illiterate child to the accomplished, strong and lovely young woman she now was, soft with compassion. "Poppy, you're safe now. No one can harm you, see, we're all here," lifting a hand to indicate the women who, after a moment's furious activity had stopped to gather again about them in silent sympathy. Aggie had placed Poppy's shawl about her shoulders, tucking it in as tenderly as a mother seeing a child off to school on a bitterly cold day, and Marigold was hovering with a cup of tea in her hand, ready, when Poppy was, to place it in hers. There was a liberal splash of brandy in it, put there, surprisingly, and without any of them noticing, by Tom Goodall, who had taken a glass himself before retiring to the chair in the far corner of the kitchen where he was out of the way but he could hear what was said. He was his usual vague self, smiling and patting Poppy's shoulder with great affection as he passed her by, chucking his squirming grandsons under the chin with a gnarled but perfectly steady hand. He sat by the marble-topped table on which were piled dozens of plates waiting to be washed. Not only did they fail to notice the brandy that had gone into Poppy's cup of tea, they also failed to notice that though he looked as usual, genial, not quite of their world, his faded blue eyes were as sharp as once they had been. Though he appeared to be totally unaware of what had happened, what *was* happening, he was listening most carefully to what was being said. They would not have said it had they known.

"Won't you tell us what happened, lass?" Cook continued, then when Poppy failed to answer, indicated with a movement of her head to Elly who was hesitating at the door to come nearer. Elly and Poppy were close and Poppy might respond to her stepmother, come out of the white-faced trance that held her. She stared sightlessly at nothing, or so it seemed, unaware of those about her or of her familiar surroundings. She had a livid bruise on her left cheek and her left eye was swelling. There was mud and what looked and smelled like cow manure on her lovely silk dress. It was smeared all round the hem where it must have dragged in the grass as she herself was dragged round the corner of the barn. All down the front of the gown were stains and tracks of dirt as though she had been pressed up against something that was filthy. Her heavy hair which, when they had last seen her, had been gathered in a glossy knot at the crown of her head and fastened with the last of the cream roses to match her gown, was hanging round her dazed face and across her shoulders, falling in a tangled snarl down her back. There was a saying that kept repeating itself in Cook's head, "dragged through a hedge backwards", and that was exactly how Poppy Goodall looked. Dishevelled and misplaced and almost deranged and how could they bring her back to herself, Cook agonised, for there was no doubt in her mind that the longer she remained as she was the harder it would be to return her to her usual self.

Still she said nothing, deep, deep in shock and Cook sighed, beckoning to Elly to help her get her poor aching bones back on their feet and see if she could do any better with their little mistress. It had been a long, long day and Cook wanted nothing more than to get to her bed. To get this lot sorted out, the kitchen put to rights and the lot of them, including Poppy, hopefully back in her right mind, up the "dancers" to their beds, but of course, there was no question of that, not yet. Perhaps, when the doctor got here he'd be able to give Poppy something to soothe her mind, fetch her out of this stupor into which she had fallen but until then, happen Elly might reach her.

"You try, Elly, it's beyond me." She lowered herself stiffly into the chair opposite and rubbed her old knees. Elly took her place at Poppy's knee and framed in the doorway which led out into the yard Reuben and his sons hovered. With the big chap unconscious and Mr Cooper being watched carefully by half a dozen men lest he try some other dirty trick, or even begin again that foul-mouthed besmirching of their little mistress that they'd not put up with, the Appleton men had come across the yard to enquire anxiously after their Poppy, reluctant to interfere in what, at the moment, was women's business, but ready, should they be needed, to lend a hand in whatever way they could. If what had happened proved to be the worst then it would be God help one of those two chaps in the barn.

The police constable had arrived and was at this moment licking his pencil ready to take down the facts of what had happened here, but already it seemed to him it was not a matter for the law. Two chaps fighting, even if one of them was the son of the eminent Captain Adam Cooper, was something to be decided between themselves and as neither of them wished to make a complaint, at least Mr Cooper didn't, the other chap was still out cold, he was off, slightly annoyed to have been called out on such a wasted and damn-fool mission.

"Sweetheart, 'tis Elly. Will yer not 'ave a sip o' tea," for like most women she was of the opinion there was nothing more heartening at times of trouble than a good cup of tea. "See, let me 'old it for yer, an' then, if yer up to it yer can tell us what 'appened. Only if yer want to, that is. Doctor's comin' an' yer'll need yer face seein' to an' . . . well . . . 'appen . . ." She did not relish the idea of bringing up the question of what might turn out to be rape, not to this lass who was still a maid despite being married for so long. Who knew what damage that swine might have done to the most private part of her body? Perhaps the doctor might want to examine her. Dear sweet God, would there ever be an end to the trouble this family had suffered?

"Come on, lamb, try a sip for Elly, there's a good lass. I can hear the doctor's horse in the yard," as the sound of hooves crashed on the cobbles and Jem's voice could be heard, high and excited as the young are at any diversion.

"Theer's a chap injured in't barn, sir," they heard him say and as the words floated through the open door Poppy Goodall stiffened, lifted her head and turned it towards the sound. Her eyes sprang to life, a brilliant ice-grey, blazing with something the servants did not recognise. She tossed back her hair from her face which seemed, if it was possible, to have gone even whiter, pushing her hand through it in a sudden fever of alarm.

"Where's Conn?" she demanded harshly, as fierce as though they were keeping him from her, then, to everyone's amazement, she stood up. She looked about her, almost ready to snarl in defence of something, though God only knew what it was, her lip curling away from her teeth like that of a leopard about to spring. So vigorously did she get up Elly fell back against Cook's knees and Nelly and Jinny, who were the only two there who had heard the name before, exchanged frightened glances.

"Conn? Who's that, lass?" Elly gasped though it was likely that at that moment the pieces she had had in her possession for several months now fell into place and made a whole and understandable picture. May sat down, sighing as though she had the world's troubles on her shoulders, cuddling her babies to her protectively. It was coming, she could sense it, the storm, the whirlwind that was to blow apart the peaceful existence they all knew and had taken for granted for so long. What was to happen to them all when it was finally recognised that Poppy Goodall, the rock to which they all clung, let's face it, had taken a lover and, if her attitude was anything to go by, she didn't, at the moment, give a damn who knew it? Her next words attested to it.

"Dear sweet Christ, why didn't someone tell me? You let

me loll here like some . . . some gentrified lady who faints for no reason at all while Conn is lying injured somewhere and needs me."

She'd just suffered the worst experience known to a woman and she was speaking as though it were nothing. They couldn't believe it. She was unconcerned about herself, her only thought to get to the man who, it now seemed likely, had been the one to rescue her from the rapacious hands of Dominic Cooper. The faces of the women were all set in the exact same mould, horrified as understanding slowly seeped into their frozen minds, confusion, for could it really be true, what they thought they had just heard, and terror for what was to happen now. Her husband lay upstairs, her poor crippled husband and here she was running about like a woman demented in her effort to get to the man who was . . . what? What was he to her? They didn't know, not yet, but it seemed they were about to find out.

"Where is he? What's happened to him? Where've they taken him? The barn, did Jem say? Oh please, won't someone tell me what has happened? Is it Conn who's injured? I can remember nothing after that . . . that filthy bastard hit me."

Taking pity on her, Elly croaked, "They're in't barn, lass, both of 'em. Evan's there with the other men an' . . . well, they did say 'e were tied up so . . ."

"Tied up?"

They couldn't stop her, not even Reuben as she went by him. Her tangled hair flew back like a banner and her tortured face was like paper apart from the livid bruise which coloured one side of it. Her eyes were filled with some horror she seemed to see ahead of her and when her pa put his hand on her she brushed it impatiently aside.

"Not now, Pa . . . not now."

"But, lass, yer not fit ter . . ."

"Later, Pa, I must get to Conn. If that bastard's hurt him I swear I'll get Tom's shotgun and kill him where he stands. And if Conn's already done it then I'll swing with him for I'm as much to blame as he is."

They were like a tableau at the famous Madame Tussaud's up in London, each one frozen into a state of astounded paralysis, their expressions clearly saying that they could not keep up with the sequence of events that had overtaken them this night. Who was Conn? Was he the big fellow who had been fighting with Mr Cooper, but what was he to do with their little mistress? They could hardly bring themselves to believe that she . . . she and him . . . it was inconceivable and so, not even turning to look at one another in case they saw it in someone else's eyes they stared rigidly ahead of them waiting for they knew not what.

The doctor was crossing the yard coming towards her as she burst from the doorway. He had been told there was trouble up at Long Reach, the farm lad who'd come for him rattling on about Mrs Goodall being attacked and two men fighting, in such a ferment of excitement the good man could make neither head nor tail of it and now, here was little Mrs Goodall looking as though she'd willingly take on a whole army of attackers, whirling towards him, turning him about on his heel in the direction of the barn, darting ahead of him and dragging him along behind her.

"Mrs Goodall, please, I was told you'd been hurt," he managed to gasp as he did his best to pull his arm from her determined hand.

"Oh, I'm all right, doctor. A bruise here and there but I fear there may be an injured man in the barn. There was a fight . . ."

"So I heard but . . ."

When she saw the quiet figure of the man crumpled on

the floor and the blood that lay in a pool beneath his head she screamed out loud, the sound like that of an animal in agonising pain and every man in the barn winced, even the one in the corner who was being watched by several others. The sound echoed about the rafters looking for a way out and when it did raced across the yard to those in the kitchen and Dilys moaned, longing for this night to be over, longing for Poppy to be released from the suffering that seemed to hover over her, for you could hear it in her voice.

"Conn! No! no! no! Conn, darling . . . please, please, don't . . ." She seemed to leap in one bound across the wide barn, sinking to her knees beside the fallen man, putting a gentle hand to his bleached white face.

"Oh, Conn," she said broken-heartedly. "Conn, *mo annsachd*, what's been done to you? Conn . . ."

"It were me, lass." Tommy's voice was not only apologetic it was bewildered, for neither he, nor indeed any of them including the doctor, could believe what their eyes were seeing. They none of them knew the unconscious man on the floor but it seemed their little mistress did and in a way that had her in a spell of terror for his wellbeing.

"You see what I mean," a voice from the corner sneered. "She and this . . . clod have been lovers for months now. She's a whore, I told you so, and if that bugger on the floor doesn't die I'll see he spends the rest of his . . ."

Ignoring him, though it was very hard to do when he spoke such vile words about their mistress, Tommy squatted down beside Poppy, putting a gentle hand on her arm.

"I 'ad ter do it, lass. 'E were that violent. 'E went fer Mr Cooper."

"Can you blame him, you bloody idiot. The man was going to rape me. Conn was doing what any would have done, he was defending me. Oh, please, doctor . . ."

"Let me have a look at him, Mrs Goodall, if you please. Stand back and bring one of those lamps. I can't understand why he was not taken into the house." For whoever he was the man didn't deserve to be left lying on the floor of the dusty barn.

"Yes, that's what I'd like to know," Poppy shrieked, whirling on the men who stood about, her eyes so maddened they all flinched away from her. "Why didn't you fetch him inside? You can see he's badly injured. Oh, God, if he dies I swear I'll sack the lot of you. See, Evan, Tommy, lift him up."

"Just a moment, Mrs Goodall, let me have a look at him before he's moved."

"And what, may I ask, does it take to get a bit of attention over here. That sod is not the only one who has been hurt." The voice of Dominic Cooper was peevish, for was he not one of the landed, pedigreed class and had precedence, surely, over a mere farm labourer or whatever the man was.

They all turned for a moment to stare at him.

"You can go to hell, Dominic Cooper and may you rot there for ever," their mistress hissed. "You've done your best to get your filthy hands on me for years and I don't care who knows it now. Well, you succeeded tonight but believe me you'll not do it again, for I'll go to the law and have you restrained. Now get out of my sight or as God is my witness I'll kill you. And let me say that if anything happens to this man, this good man"– her voice broke painfully, and by the door where he stood in the shadows Tom Goodall bowed his head – "I'll come looking for you and personally castrate you . . . you . . ." She began to weep.

The doctor had gone after supervising the removal of the big, red-haired chap from the barn floor to the kitchen, saying that he was to be watched at all times and leaving instructions that he was under no circumstances to be moved, not even to relieve himself, looking sternly at Evan since it would be his job to attend to it. He had concussion and the blow to his head had needed a dozen stitches but he was young, strong and healthy and, with good nursing, he would quickly mend.

"He'll get that, doctor," Mrs Goodall told him firmly. "I'll see to it myself." A little colour had returned to her face.

"I'll call first thing in the morning and have a look at him but think on, he is not to be moved."

The truckle bed had been brought down and though his feet hung over the end of it he was tucked up tightly beneath the clean white sheets and blankets which helped to keep him from falling out, for the bed was very narrow. Not that he was doing much moving about even though he was conscious now, only his eyes as they followed the figure of Poppy Goodall about the room, waiting anxiously for her to reappear into his line of vision when she disappeared for a moment. The fire had been banked up and there was nothing anyone could do but still they hung about, fascinated and, they could not deny it, shocked, for it seemed what was being whispered was true. And if it was true it explained all those absences over the past few months, the days when she had taken off on her own and now it made sense, for here was the reason for it, lying before the kitchen fire.

The squire's son had gone, taken away by his distressed father who had been told in blunt terms what Master Dominic had tried to do to their little mistress, and Evan had remarked to no one in particular that they'd have no more trouble with that one. The kitchen seemed to be filled with them all, the men and women who had served this farm and this family for so long, for it had still not been revealed to them exactly what the swine *had* done to Poppy and when the big hand managed to escape its tight wrapping and a hoarse voice asked Poppy to come and sit beside him since he must know if . . . if . . . he must know what had taken place even if the truth crucified him, they all drifted into the shadows and waited, for they needed to know too.

"Oh, Conn . . . Conn," she whispered, and to their total astonishment, just as though she and the big chap were alone, she kissed him tenderly, right on the lips. She cupped his face with her hands, gazing down into his eyes with an expression none of them had ever seen before. He had a bandage wrapped neatly about his head and most of his hair was covered by it but on his forehead a strand or two fell into his eyes and she brushed them back, as gentle as a mother with her child. "I knew you'd come, Conn," she said to him, "even while he was . . . was pulling at my clothing, I knew you'd come." Elly turned her face to the wall for a moment and May, whose sons had fallen asleep in her arms, passed one to her husband and the four of them huddled together, for it was very obvious there were big changes coming to Long Reach Farm.

"I nearly . . . didna, *mo annsachd*. I was on my way home. Dear God, dear sweet Jesus . . . I couldna wait for ye. I was . . . hurting, ye see, wi'out ye."

"Yes, I know, beloved."

Beloved! What next? The men and women exchanged thunderstruck glances and Cook was seen to shake her head warningly, for it seemed a disgrace to her that Poppy Goodall should be speaking words of endearment to a complete stranger and with her husband no more than a few yards away.

"I was leaving, going through the gate, when I heard ye . . . and him . . ."

He began to shift on his bed as though he would like nothing better than to have another go at the man who had . . . who had . . . even now he hardly dared ask, but she seemed to know, leaning even more closely to him, her head beside his on the pillow.

"He didn't hurt me, Conn. You arrived there in time, just like Sir Galahad," trying to lighten the moment with a touch of humour but the big man didn't smile.

"Thank God," he said simply. Then, "Hold me, lassie, for I'm awfu' stricken."

"Darling, *mo annsachd*, I'm here. I'll not leave you. You're safe with me."

Safe with her! The size of him and her no bigger than two pennorth of copper!

It was at that moment that the pair of them suddenly realised that they were not alone, though, as Cook said, she didn't think they'd have cared if they had. Poppy raised her head and turned to look into the shadows where they hovered. She smiled, the expression on her face soft, not just for the big man but for them who were very dear to her. The women's eyes were out on stalks, all except Elly and May who had always known, but she could see it was too much for Cook. Cook was a God-fearing woman and though Poppy knew Cook was fond of her she did not care to have this . . . this whatever it was in her kitchen between a married woman and a man who was a complete stranger to them. Now that it seemed no harm had come to the lass, though it had been a dreadful experience, this was Cook's kitchen and this . . . this was just too much.

"Now then, Poppy Goodall," she began but the man in the bed spoke to her, his voice so soft and loving it stopped the words in her mouth.

"Whisht, woman, dinna scold her, for she's nae but a bairn really. Let her be."

"Let her be! Now see here, whoever you are . . ."

"Alick MacConnell, at your service, ma'am, and pleased to make your acquaintance though I could wish it had been in happier circumstances." His voice was weak and it was clear he was ready to slide away into sleep, but he smiled his lovely boyish smile and Poppy saw Cook's mouth twitch as though she would respond.

She spoke up before anything further could be said. "I think everyone should go to bed, don't you, Cook."

"I'll go to bed when I'm good and ready, miss, and what about those hands, young man. Your mam'd have a fit if she was to see them," for the doctor, in his concern for Conn's head, had not noticed the state of his bloody knuckles.

"My mother is dead, ma'am," he answered her softly and for some reason Poppy took his hand and held it just as though he were in pain over something. They all watched, fascinated and yet never doubting the look of absolute rightness between Poppy Goodall and the man who lay on the truckle bed.

"Well, I'm sorry about that, lad, but you'd best let me clean them for you. Only the Lord knows what you might have picked up from that filthy . . . beggar."

"That's kind o' ye, ma'am but could you do it when . . ." His eyes closed, the long russet eyelashes falling to his cheek, his breath deepening and they were all stunned when Poppy bent over him and kissed him again. She brought his other hand from beneath the covers in readiness for Cook's ministrations then turned and smiled at them all as though it were the most natural thing to do. They were all flabbergasted. The bare-faced cheek of it and yet, would you look at her, her face all shining with some light, candles in her eyes, an expression on her face just for him and just for them as though she could no longer hide it and must share it with them.

"An explanation's needed here miss," Cook was saying tartly as she poured hot water into a bowl and sent Jinny to fetch the medicine chest.

"Tomorrow, Cook. We're all tired."

"Aye, that's true. Now someone must sit up with this chap—" she began but Poppy interrupted her.

"I'll sit up with him, Cook."

"Nay," Cook was shocked and her expression said so.

"I'll sit up with him so when you've finished here you must go to your beds." That was an end to the matter and Cook, defeated, said nothing further as she gently bathed the injured man's hands.

It was almost an hour since Tom had gone up the stairs, nobody noticing his departure, for were they not all mesmerised by the events of the evening which held them fast to the kitchen.

He sat down on his son's bed and his old face was sad and yet filled with some light which was lovely to see. He leaned forward and kissed his son on the cheek and if Richard was surprised he did not show it. It was weeks since he had seen his father and then Tom had been vague, disorientated, as though he wasn't quite sure who Richard was. Now his eyes were clear and steady, his face calm and his hands were gentle as he brushed back the greying hair from his son's face.

"What's going on, Father?"

"Oh, you know, the usual stuff that happens when men are in drink."

"I . . . heard something roar."

"Aye, I expect it was the bull."

"I expect so."

His father smiled at him with a great and merciful love.

"How are you, lad?" he asked gently.

"As you see, Father, still here. I'm going nowhere."

"Would you like to, Richard?"

"Yes, Father, I would, but she won't let me. I've become . . . cruel to her. I love her, you see, but she won't let me go and I'm destroying her."

"I'll let you go, son, if you want to."

"Thank you, Father. I'd be glad if you'd . . . help me."

He drank the mixture his father held for him and went to sleep, his face soft and boyish, a sweet expression on his face that had been missing for a long time. His father held his limp hand for a moment, then went to sit in the rocking chair by the fire. His eyes had become vague again with that look of gentle acceptance which was familiar to them all and which had been there for the last four years, then his eyelids drooped and he slept.

When Elly, at Poppy's request, looked in on them later she smiled fondly, for it seemed father and son had fallen asleep in one another's company.